City of Beasts

BEASTS OF HEDGE END

I

A.N. SAGE

AWARD-WINNING AUTHOR

CONTENTS

CURSED ISLE
UPPERS
C
H
A
MIDDLES
E
LOWERS

HEDGE END

A. ALDRIDGE HOUSE
B. CITY HALL
C. COOKE MANOR
D. TOS LABORATORY
E. LIBRARY
F. MARKETS
G. CITY PARK
H. STONE MANSION

INDEX OF AFFECTED GEM PROPERTIES

1. **Amethyst:** Bends light to create illusions and invisibility.
2. **Ruby:** Generates and controls heat for fire.
3. **Emerald:** Promotes rapid wound healing.
4. **Sapphire:** Moves and shapes water and ice.
5. **Diamond:** Emits powerful magnetic field.
6. **Topaz:** Controls and generates electricity.
7. **Garnet:** Absorbs light to create darkness.
8. **Opal:** Influences dreams and sleep.
9. **Turquoise:** Creates and controls wind and weather.
10. **Amber:** Bonds materials together strongly.
11. **Peridot:** Speeds up plant growth.
12. **Moonstone:** Sees ultraviolet light and hidden details.
13. **Aquamarine:** Calms emotions and reduces stress.
14. **Onyx:** Controls the shadows.
15. **Jade:** Generates protective energy fields.

16. **Bloodstone:** Boosts physical stamina and endurance.
17. **Citrine:** Emits bright light for illumination.
18. **Lapis Lazuli:** Enhances memory and cognitive skills.
19. **Obsidian:** Breaks down organic materials, causes decay.
20. **Quartz:** Clears and enhances wavelengths.
21. **Malachite:** Creates and neutralizes toxins.
22. **Zircon:** Alters perception of time.
23. **Spinel:** Increases ability to lie.
24. **Beryl:** Increases ability to tell the truth.
25. **Tourmaline:** Stabilizes electromagnetic fields.
26. **Kunzite:** Enhances emotional connections, influences the heart.
27. **Alexandrite:** Temporarily changes the form of objects.
28. **Tanzanite:** Influences biological matter to motion.
29. **Ametrine:** Controls polarized light for special effects.
30. **Heliodor:** Ability to bend light to create illusion.
31. **Morganite:** Influences thoughts and behaviour.
32. **Sardonyx:** Influences target mobility briefly.
33. **Chrysoprase:** Slightly increases good luck.
34. **Sard:** Enhances or suppresses fire.
35. **Rhodolite:** Enhances vision and removes distortions.
36. **Kyanite:** Restores physical and mental balance.

CHAPTER ONE

Clara Aldridge was not afraid of the beasts. It would be unbecoming of a mayor's protégé to cower in fear, to show weakness, to allow the mere presence of a Cursbeast to define her personality. Instead, Clara focused on the parts of the beasts that used to be. The parts that trembled at the sound of a particularly loud thunderstorm. The parts that yearned for the familiarity of others like them. The parts that were still human.

It was these parts that allowed her to walk the streets of Hedge End with her shoulders set and her head high even under the weight of the horrid, heavy top hat a woman of her status was expected to wear. The hat, while wildly uncomfortable, was a necessary appendage her uncle would not budge on. In his eyes, it said, without the vulgarity of words, that Clara held a place among men in city council, that her voice weighed in matters of law and ledger as heavily as any male. To Clara, all it said was that her scalp itched by midday in the warmer months.

The beast's growl rumbled through the air, pulling Clara's

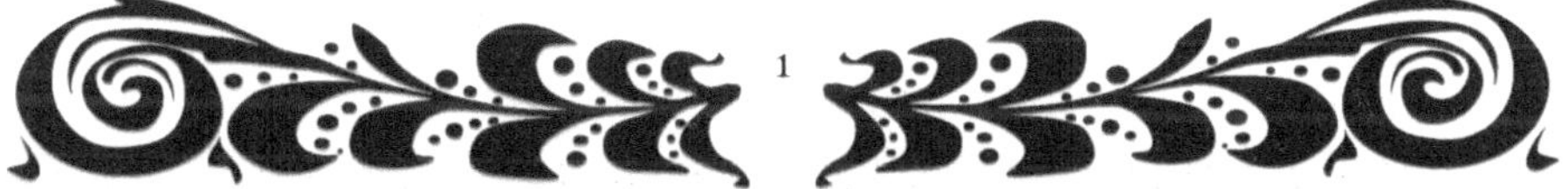

gaze to its horrific form. The sound hollowed her chest, and suddenly any place in society felt completely useless to her now. Because on any other day, Clara would not be terrified of a Cursbeast in the slightest. That is until she found herself cornered by one in her own damn garden of all places.

The monstrous creature seethed and hissed; its long snout wet as it sniffed out the air between them. Two rows of sharp teeth snapped once. Twice. Three times. Saliva foamed around the creature's jaw and dripped down the filthy, ragged fur that covered almost all its body. Its limbs, if you could even call them that, towered high above the ground, reminding Clara of the street performers she used to love as a child—the ones who dared to defy gravity with their stilts.

Clara took a shaky step, her shoulders crashing with a solid object. Behind her, the tall ivy-covered fence that hid Aldridge House away from the rest of the world stood unyielding. The fence was built all around the property before the first brick had even been laid. It circled the vast land, surrounding the house and the lush garden Clara stood in. Sprawled behind the ancient manor, the garden was a thing of beauty. Winding paths, barely visible under a blanket of moss, criss-crossed between beds of roses and thick, leafy bushes. An ancient oak stood in the center of the garden with a stagnant pond whose still waters reflected the afternoon sky beside it. All of it protected by the twisting wrought iron of the fence. A guardian keeping all those inside safe.

Clara cursed under her breath. It wasn't the outside world she needed protecting from now, was it?

The Cursbeast paused to inspect her better, its legs snapping unnaturally at the knees. The wrong way. The wrong everything, truly. Two white orbs stared Clara down with the intensity of a trained hunter. Waiting.

When she was a little girl, Clara's father and uncle allowed her to accompany them on hunting trips every so often. She recalled those days to be the happiest of her young, inexperienced life. To be alone in the wild forests surrounding the city and yet to feel utterly at peace. Clara not once thought about the other side of the hunts, never imagined the killings. Standing here, with her back pressed against the cold iron and her heart hammering away, she was beginning to doubt the memory. Clara had never pictured herself in place of the deer; had never been prey until this very moment.

Before her, the Cursbeast uncurled its spine. Its shoulders rolled and its joints snapped as it came to a stand at full height. Sharp, pointed spikes jutted from its back and Clara gasped when two leathery wings shot out from its body. The membrane stretching between the phalanges of the wings was torn, as though it had been caught in a shredder and only barely made it out. It didn't stop the things from blocking out the sun above. Much like everything else on the beast, the wings were enormous and dreadful. They cast dark, stretching shadows on the ground that reached toward Clara's trembling gardening boots in the same manner a drowning man reaches for land. With absolute resolve.

Clara's own resolve hardened.

There was little point fighting off a Cursbeast. The citizens of Hedge End had the notion ingrained in them from birth as a means of protection. The wretched things owned the streets and if you ever found yourself staring one down, your best bet was to say your goodbyes and pray for a quick ending. The creatures attacked at the smallest folly and, judging by how the one in front of Clara crept forward, she most definitely did something to spurn it. Sweat beaded on her forehead, cooled by the sudden drop in temperature around her. Terror tripped up her spine as her gray eyes darted left and right, searching for an escape.

There was none. Clara was in the section of the garden no one else dared to visit anymore, not since the untimely death of her parents. The little gazebo by the pond was her mother's favorite place and those who remained working for the family refused to step foot here for the memories the secluded area returned. It was the opposite for Clara. This was the only area of Aldridge House where she felt like herself and she made certain to come often. The colors of the roses made her head swirl. Ruby red. Amethyst purple. Citrine yellow. All of her mother's favorites. Clara's gaze flitted to the creature's flashing eyes. It snarled. Clara yelped.

And now she was to die here.

Slipping her fingers into the folds of her full, cotton skirt, Clara searched for a weapon to use. Her desperation flowed off her in buckets, drenching the silk of her corset with every strained attempt. The beast took another step, and the ground shook under its weight. Clara's fingers moved faster. How many times had her uncle told her not to leave the house without a weapon? Clara wished she hadn't been so stubborn. Why was she always arguing? Was it truly that difficult to let the maid slip a dagger into the hidden compartment in the lining of her dress as her uncle often insisted on?

Clara huffed out an exasperated breath. A dagger wasn't what she needed right now; what Clara wanted more than anything was a miracle. Or a gem. Preferably one of the stones that granted fire magic to its user or perhaps an amethyst that could aid with summoning a wind strong enough to blast at the dreadful creature before her. Uncle Oswin was dead set on never using the magic of the gems and she agreed with him for the most part, but surely, he would make an exception if it meant her life would be spared. The magic of the gems was the only thing that Clara could think would help her in this dire moment, no matter the consequences of wielding their magic served.

Clara huffed out a defeated breath. Her hand fell away from her dress. No dagger. No gem.

No way out.

All she had was the spade she brought with her to dig up the incessant shrubbery that overtook the flowers growing by the gazebo and beginning to snake their way over her late mother's shed. She doubted it would fare well against the monster before her. A vice closed over her throat and her lungs refused to expand. Tremors settled over her body; her skin covered in gooseflesh as the gravity of what was about to happen finally set in. Clara was going to die a horrible death right in her own home. *Was this what they thought of when it happened?* Clara pushed all thoughts of her parents aside. She was not going to go like them. It was not her time.

The Cursbeast disagreed. Its jaw unhinged, the skin around the foul thing's mouth tearing open as it stretched it wide. The smell of rotting flesh and sulfur filled Clara's nostrils, making her gag. Clara white-knuckled the metal spade and threw it at the beast with as much strength as she could muster. The handle cracked in half on impact with the creature's hard form, crashing to the ground in pieces.

Oh, no, Clara thought. *Now you've done it.*

She pressed a hand to her face right as the beast lunged. Clara cried out, but the sound was buried in her sweat-slicked palm, never making it past her lips. She shot her arm up to protect her face so fast it spun her sideways. Pointed yellow claws nicked the soft skin of her forearm. The force of it strong enough that Clara teetered backward, her skull slamming into the gate. Her vision spotted. Blood welled on the wound where the creature scratched her. Her screamed from the pain of the Cursbeast's vicious strike. In front of her, the creature's eyes dulled a shade before narrowing on her slight form. She wrapped her hand over the wound and slid down the gate until her bottom hit the cold, wet ground. Tears burned the rear of her lid. As she closed her eyes and waited for the final blow, they flowed down her cheeks freely.

The beast reared back for a second attack. It shook its vile head, its inhumane eyes vacant of any emotion. Snout skyward, the monstrous creature sniffed the air and puffed vapor through its wet nostrils. It cocked its head to the side, inspecting her slight form.

Clara took in a sharp, jagged breath and counted down.

Three.

Two.

One.

A loud bang rang out over her head. Behind her, the gate shook violently as three more shots fired. Clara's fingers dug into the soil beneath her. The deafening roar of the Cursbeast fed her with false bravery and she opened one eye, then the other. Before her, the creature was no longer wide-jawed and ravenous. Instead, its eyes narrowed as it searched the garden for a free path, much as Clara had done only moments ago. Black, oozing liquid poured from its shoulder where a fresh wound oozed rotten blood. The creature screeched and stomped its deformed paws into the earth. In seconds, it was airborne. The wings that made Clara nearly lose her lunch before flapped madly as the beast took to the sky and flew out of sight and away from the garden. A fourth shot pierced the air, this one a warning.

Clara's eyes rolled past the torn-up soil left in the wake of the Cursbeast, all the way to the smoking gold rifle and the man attached to it. Her shoulders slumped in relief.

"Nice day for a stroll around the garden," her uncle said, his expression solemn.

Clara took a stab at a smile but only grimaced. "Much nicer now."

In one expert move, Oswin Aldridge swung the weapon over his shoulder, letting it hang across his back and pull his entire frame into diligent obedience. For a man of average build and height, he carried himself with the air of someone twice as large, and it made all those in his presence cower before him. Of course, being the city's mayor certainly added to the powerful hold Oswin held over those he met. Even now Clara could see the ceremonial bronze star peeking out from the lapel of his long leather coat. Her uncle never left the house without it. She once asked him if he regretted the choice to accept a position that came saddled with too many responsibilities, and Oswin simply laughed.

There was not a thing in the world that scared Clara's uncle. She looked up at the distant sky. Not even a Cursbeast.

Uncle Oswin raked his rough fingers through wavy silver hair, a single thread of it falling over his hazel eyes. He pulled on the sleeves of his coat to draw them over his hands. "You left your rifle in the library," he said. "Again."

"I didn't realize I'd need it to tend to the roses," Clara replied. *Nor do I want to carry the damn thing around all day.* She cleared the distance between them in three quick steps, pulling up on her toes to plant a soft kiss on her uncle's cheek. "How in the gems did that thing get on the property?"

"They're getting bolder. You should get used to carrying," Oswin instructed.

Behind him, the gold details of the rifle reflected the daylight falling upon the garden, and Clara felt blinded by its incessant sparkle. It shone with gold inlays that caught the light, the polished wood glowing like glass. The carved pieces made the more suited to a collector's wall than the battlefield, yet she could not deny that the rifle did its job.

Her uncle was right, of course, as he often was about everything. The city was not safe with the beasts around, but surely her home was an exception. She couldn't believe she would need such fervent protection this early in the day when she wasn't even wearing the straps of her stockings yet. A gloom settled at the base of her stomach. Was no place safe anymore?

"Walk with me, dear girl," Oswin said, motioning for her to step forward.

Clara's legs buckled under the weight of her skirt and the flashing memory of the beast's cavernous mouth. She bristled, her uncle catching the motion in his ever-lingering stare. She steeled her spine. No doubt. No fear. No way but forward.

Brushing away the remnants of the garden from her clothing, Clara joined her uncle on the paved walkway leading past the pond, crushed leaves falling away behind her with each step. As they walked—her taking two steps to each of his one—Clara's heartbeat steadied. She found herself back in that familiar place that she loved so deeply; by Oswin's side where she belonged. It was as close to her father as she could get with Oswin's features closely resembling her dad's. The same stoic nose, the same intense glare. Even the slightly crooked shape of their brows was mirrored; it was uncanny.

Occasionally, Uncle Oswin paused to readjust the weapon on his back, the movement making his slight limp push forward. The only sign of age on her otherwise ageless hero.

The sun's rays hit Clara's cheeks, and her lips quirked at the warmth finally settling over her. She cast a side-glance at her uncle. "Perhaps we should—"

"No gems, Clara," Oswin scolded.

"But why? The guard is allowed to cast," she argued. "And you said it yourself. The beasts are getting more daring. We had never had one break inside before."

Oswin rubbed the bridge of his wide nose. "The guard are not my niece."

"But I—"

"No!" Oswin replied. His voice hitched and for a second, Clara saw a darkness fill his eyes that jarred her—she had never seen Oswin get upset, at least not with her. It was gone instantly. Softening his brow, her uncle studied her with so much care she couldn't stand it. "I promised your father I would raise you as my own should anything happen to him. I will not break that promise."

When Clara remained silent, Oswin's chin jutted toward a nearby bench and she followed him, sitting down and letting her legs drop open. An unladylike maneuver that she didn't care to correct.

Oswin settled in beside her with a groan. "You are quite like her, you know," he said. "Rowena. Your mother used to talk my ear off about gem magic every chance she got. It infuriated Wellan. But I reminded him that he married her for her mind as much as anything else."

"I didn't realize mother was a gem supporter."

"Not a supporter, per se," Oswin corrected. "She had her doubts like everyone else, but I like to believe she also saw the good that could come of them. Rowena respected the delicate power of the gem magic, even as an outsider to our city. If it wasn't for the side effects of their use—if we didn't turn to Cursbeasts—I am certain she would have found a way to use the gems for the sake of the city. It was how her heart was created." His eyes crinkled. "Constantly thinking of others above herself."

Clara peered at him through thick lashes. "You don't agree with her."

"Do you blame me?" Oswin asked. "Even if your parents didn't die the way they did... No matter. The gems are not to be trifled with. If you are to lead the citizens of our fine city, you must do so by example. We have enough trouble keeping the gems off the streets."

"And your guard?"

Oswin's posture stiffened. He tapped a finger to the tip of Clara's nose, his voice lowering. "The mayoral guard are the true patriots. To make the sacrifice they make every day is no easy task," he said. "It is a weight I carry on my shoulders that will unfortunately be yours to bear as well. If you choose it."

"Ha!" Clara guffawed. "I think we both know I've wanted your seat since I was five, old man."

An elbow jabbed Clara's side. "I believe this old man just saved your sorry young behind. Don't make me regret it."

Across the path, a bush rustled, leaves shuddering as whatever was hiding inside scurried forward. Clara's eyes narrowed while Oswin reached for the weapon he rested on the side of the bench. The leaves parted and Clara's throat filled with panic that she refused to let spill into her features. From inside the bush, a black paw emerged, its small talons digging into the earth as the creature attached to it pulled itself free.

A laugh bubbled out of Clara.

"Ah," Oswin said. "The true beast of Hedge End."

Now it was Clara's turn to nudge her uncle. She opened her arms, and the black cat leaped into her lap, immediately preceding to lick itself clean from whatever nonsense it picked up while wrestling with bushes. She rubbed the animal's soft fur, the purr of Socks' contentment echoing through the garden. In return, the cat stomped little white paws against the fabrics of her skirt. "He's probably hungry," Clara said.

"When is he not?"

Smirking, she picked up the cat and waited until her uncle stood up to walk back to the house. The afternoon heat burned her exposed shoulders, and she eagerly awaited the shadows of Aldridge House with each step. Uncle Oswin would be off into the city soon, no doubt, leaving Clara alone to roam the halls as she often did. Perhaps Elisea would let her help with dinner today.

In the distance, the bell tower sitting atop the house came into view, tall and solid. A beacon calling her home. The manor was truly beautiful this time of day. Ornate gables and turrets reached toward the sky, crowned with finials that gleamed in the golden light. Ivy climbed the walls, its tendrils weaving through the wrought-iron balconies that jutted out from the upper floors. On the lower level the narrow stained-glass windows cast colorful patterns across the winding brick pathways below.

Clara glanced over her shoulder once to make certain the garden was empty, then sat the cat down. Reaching toward her uncle, she snatched the rifle from him in one swell swoop, hiked up her skirt with her free hand, and took off running. Her thigh muscles strained as she raced to the house with all her might.

"Last one in cleans the stables!" she yelled.

At her rear, she could almost hear Oswin mutter, "No doubt. No fear. No way but forward."

Clara never stopped to check if he was behind her. Uncle Oswin would follow her until the end of eternity. It was what family did.

CHAPTER TWO

Aldridge House smelled of cloves and butter, so much so that Clara's stomach grumbled as she sat the book she read back on the library's shelf. *The Rise of Hedge End Art Trades.* A yawn pulled at her lips. No matter how much Clara wanted to impress her uncle, learning the bylaws of the city was a uniquely dreadful way to spend her evening. She would have preferred to be staring down the Cursbeast again if it meant never having to read another long-winded text.

Clara touched the bandage on her arm where the healer had tended to the beast's wound. The beauty of living in the uppers and being under the mayor's care was the exceptional medical aid she could receive at a moment's notice. Her skin would scar but surely a scar was better than losing her head to the creature. A shudder raked over her skin. It was too soon for such morbid jokes.

Shaking her long black tresses loose, she ran a finger over the list of tomes she was yet to get through. *The History of the*

Hedge End Council. Allocations of Budget and Coin. Street Names: A Complete Collection.

"You must be joking," Clara huffed out. She folded the paper and tossed it on the singular desk in the corner of the room. Around her, old decaying spines stacked atop the mahogany shelves of the library, reaching as far as the ceiling. Clara considered a second go at her uncle's list but thought better of it. "I'd die of sheer boredom before I even inherit the mayoral seat."

As if in answer to her prayers, a clamor sounded from the lower level, coming from the kitchen. Clara's gaze darted to the open door. "Elisea? Are you all right?"

When there was no answer, Clara grinned. "Better see what happened," she told the books. "I'll be back. Perhaps."

Clara's skirts floated behind her as she rushed out of the library and down the twisting stairs. The deep red carpet squished under her heavy footfalls. She skipped the last step, landing with a thud on the bottom landing. Above her head, the glass of the chandelier twinkled with light, hundreds of crystals swaying in the light breeze of a window left open. As Clara walked down the narrow corridor that took her to the kitchen, she tried not to look at the gilded frames hanging on the walls. Many of them depicted beautiful renditions of the predecessors of Aldridge House, but those were not the faces that haunted Clara. The images she couldn't bear to lock gazes with were the multiple paintings of her parents that Oswin refused to take down. Clara understood why, of course. The memory of her family, of his brother and sister-in-law, was too precious to erase.

And yet she hated this part of the house all the same.

Hurrying her steps, Clara skidded to a stop in front of an arched entryway, twisting on her heels to face inside. The smell of food cooking that beckoned her earlier was overwhelming now, and Clara found herself floating into the kitchen on a cloud of anticipation. She barely reached the wide island in the center of the room when Elisea emerged from the pantry.

The old woman rearranged the knot of her colorless bun, patted down her dark gray dress, and fixed Clara with a knowing glare. "The roast is not yet ready," she said. Then, pointing to a small, steaming bowl sitting on the edge of the counter beside the stove, added, "I warmed some soup for you."

Clara clapped her hands together. "You are a psychic, Elisea. How did you know I was starved?"

"You and that mangy cat are constantly looking for scraps," the housekeeper said. "One does not need to have psychic powers to know you'll show up well before dinner is ready."

"Where is Socks, anyway?"

Elisea reached for a knife off the block, using it to point to the pantry. "Enjoying his own bowl. Now eat up before it gets cold."

While Clara settled in at the island, the housekeeper finished chopping ingredients for tonight's dinner, expertly slicing and dicing as she did daily since she joined the family when Clara was a child. Despite her age, the woman moved faster than anyone else in the manor, which explained why everything in the house was just so. Elisea had an eye for detail, a trait Oswin valued greatly. It was why he doubled her wages after Clara's parents passed; begged her to stay on.

His decision made Clara laugh. She knew the truth as well as anyone. Elisea would have remained for free if he had asked her—she loved the Aldridges like they were family.

To Clara, that was exactly what Elisea was.

"Ah, before I forget," the housekeeper said. She reached into the pocket of her dress and pulled out an envelope, sliding it to Clara across the island. "Mr. Pollen left this for you. Said it was important."

Clara used the edge of a butter knife to slice open the seal and peered inside. She pulled out the letter Oswin's right-hand man drafted and read it quickly, her brow furrowing.

"Not good news I take it?" Elisea asked.

The creases in Clara's skin deepened. "Sergei says that Uncle will be gone until tomorrow evening," she replied. "Urgent council matters. The usual nonsense. I am expected to sit in at the annual budget meeting in his place in the morning." She sighed dramatically, tossing the letter aside. "Do I look feverish to you? I fear I might be coming down with the flu."

Elisea swatted the air between them with a tea towel.

"Truly, I do not feel well. I may even faint."

To add to the desired effect, Clara snatched the towel from the housekeeper and fanned herself with it, her gray eyes rolling backward. She stretched her fingers over the counter, sucking in a sharp breath, then another. A single eye open, she beamed as she looked at the woman grimacing before her. Clara dropped the towel. "Fine, I'll attend. I suppose I need to get used to the tedious events if I am to be mayor one day."

"And a marvelous mayor you will be," Elisea said. The woman nudged her pointed chin at the bowl in front of Clara. "But you won't live to see the day if you don't put some meat on your bones. Eat your soup. I have bread in the oven."

"What would I ever do without you?" Clara cooed.

"Starve."

Chuckling, Clara obeyed. The soup went down easily, as most things Elisea cooked did. Clara's taste buds exploded from the taste of sauteed onion and mushrooms. The warmth of the liquid sloshing down her throat made her body slump, a calmness spreading from her stomach all the way to her heart.

Bless your soul, Elisea. The woman was a miracle worker in the kitchen, as she was with all else

Nothing happened at the house that Elisea didn't know about. Her sharp eyes and quicker ears picked up every whisper in the halls; rumors and secrets alike passed through her like water through pipes. By the time anyone else noticed, Elisea already knew.

Clara's gaze darted to the abandoned letter on the table. "When did you find out he'd be gone?" she asked.

Elisea stopped chopping. "Last week. Eat."

Clara pulled her attention off the letter and kept on. There was no point fretting over the next day when this one had not yet ended. And she meant what she said, it was best to get into the habit of pretending to be interested in the politics of the city. Her uncle wasn't getting any younger and if she knew Oswin, he was waiting until she proved herself to kick start her training as his replacement. Hedge End needed a servant who could put themselves aside to do what was best for the citizens. It was how it had been since the days of the Stone King and Clara doubted it would change any time soon.

She could remember sitting on Oswin's lap when he told her the story of Hedge End's first king and the Trust War that saw him dead. Of the first Cursbeasts who tore their creator limb from limb and killed his entire bloodline. Hedge End had not crowned anyone since for fear of the beasts' savagery.

"It was only us and the monsters going forward," her uncle said.

Clara's eyes widened when she asked, "But why do we have mayors?"

An invisible string tugged at one side of Oswin's thin lips. "Because, my darling girl," he replied. "Someone must keep both sides in check."

Soon, that someone would be Clara. On days when she

didn't feel as strong as Oswin, she reminded herself of that story. Retold the history of the city in her head until her bones grew rigid, and her pulse flowed downriver in her veins. If it took a few sleep-inducing meetings to keep all of Hedge End safe, it was a sacrifice Clara was willing to make.

She glanced at Elisea over the bowl in front of her. And for now, there was soup.

Clara woke up with a start. Her head pounded and as her vision adjusted to the darkness of the surrounding night, she worked to make the incessant beating subside. Beyond the shutters of her bedroom window, the moon hung low in the sky, an eerie shade of red tinging its silver glow. It took Clara several seconds to rub the sleep out of her eyes. A few more to realize the pounding wasn't inside her foggy mind but coming from downstairs.

Someone was beating the damn door down.

Clara reached for the nightstand and lit a match to ignite a candle wick. Lifting it, she pointed the flame to the pocket watch resting on her journal, her eyes narrowing. *Who in the gems is visiting at this ungodly hour?*

Tossing her legs over the side of the bed, she hurried to dress, opting for a simple draped dress since it required little lacing. All the while, the pounding on the front door continued.

She bolted out of her room and down the stairs with the speed of a jungle cat.

"Elisea!" Clara yelled as she slid towards the front door of the manor. "Elisea, someone is here! Come quick!"

Hair lifted on her nape as she reached for the lock with

clammy hands. What if something happened to Oswin? When Clara opened the door wide and saw the three mayoral guards in full uniform on the doorstep, she flinched.

"Miss Aldridge," one guard, a young man no older than Clara's mid-twenties, said. "We're sorry to disturb you. Is everything well with you?"

Clara pressed a hand to her chest. Gathered her senses. "Me? Why?"

"We received notice of screaming coming from the mayor's house," the guard explained. Clara didn't fail to notice the two behind him peering over his shoulder to get a better look inside.

"Screaming? I have heard nothing of the—"

It was then that a blood curdling shout pierced the silence of the house. Clara's heart stopped. Her leg muscles tightened as she turned to face the dim interior of the manor, following the shrill, panicked voice all the way to the garden. A second scream tore through the night. Clara forced herself to move. Her feet pummeled the hardwood as she sped toward the sound, the guards on her heels. She heard them order her to stop, but she would do no such thing.

Body slicing the air, Clara ran past Oswin's study, ducking inside only long enough to grab a spare rifle off the wall. She continued to run with the weapon in hand, charging toward the rear of the house and into the night. Cold, frigid air slapped her face as she barreled past the doorway and into the garden. Around her, the trees and flowers seemed to whisper when she passed them, hushed secrets only they knew filling Clara's ears.

When Clara saw a familiar figure standing by the pond, she stopped stock still.

Her eyes rounded, mimicking the moon above. "Elisea?"

The housekeeper bristled but said nothing. It was then that

Clara noticed the red stains covering her freshly ironed dress. Elisea was drenched in blood.

"Elisea, what's happened?" Clara begged.

Behind her, the guards' boots stomped louder. Clara's breath came out short, her gaze rolling over the housekeeper to make certain she wasn't hurt. In her anguish, Clara had missed one vital detail. By the time her attention landed on the ground beside the housekeeper, it was too late. Too late to stop the guards from grabbing the woman she had loved most of her life. Too late to make sense of what she was seeing.

Laying on the damp earth of the garden was a man Clara had met only a handful of times and yet she would recognize him anywhere. A brutish build, fine gray hair, a thick mustache above his even thicker upper lip. Eyes the color of the sky. Except this time, Elisea's husband's eyes were glassy and vacant, and his hair was matted in the same blood that covered her housekeeper from head to toe. Thomas's blood.

"Elisea Hawke, you're under arrest for the murder of Thomas Hawke," she heard the young guard say as he fastened heavy metal cuffs around the woman's slender wrists. "May the gems grant you mercy."

Then, they marched the housekeeper out of the garden and out of sight. Leaving Clara trembling in her dress in the middle of the night with a rifle in hand and a corpse not ten feet away from her.

CHAPTER THREE

The third floor of city hall was laden with stuffy air and even stuffier conversation.

"The museum requires its funding doubled by next fall if it is to arrange for transfers overseas."

"You must be mad! If we double their funding, the galleries will knock the doors down, asking for the same. And you seem to forget the railway budget has ballooned since construction started in the lower streets."

"Not to mention the additional guards hired for the market arrests."

It had been over two hours of this, and Clara was tired enough of the tedium of budget debates that she was certain she was half asleep by now. Her eyes may have been open, but her brain was in a coma. Or at least retreated somewhere where she didn't have to think about coin allocation or visiting exhibits. It all seemed pointless. How could these people sit here and pore over financial obligations when a woman Clara worshipped awaited her death in a jail cell?

Clara had trouble reconciling it. The logical part of her

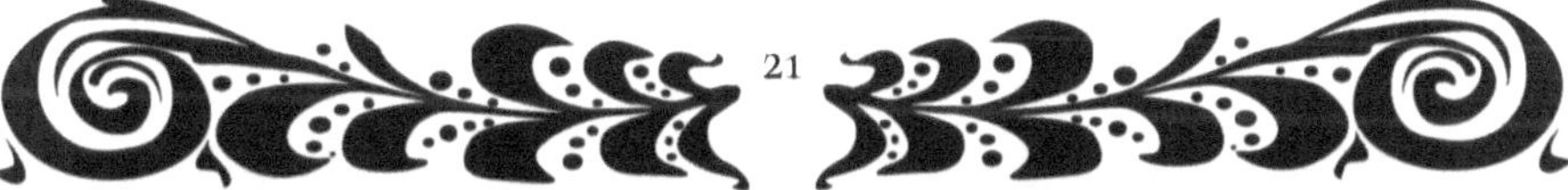

knew that the fine men and women who made up the Hedge End council did not know about the incident in her garden last night, and if they did, they stayed silent out of respect for her and her uncle. She knew that facts were facts—Elisea was caught red-handed, literally, and there was little to prove her innocence.

Then there was the doubt of which Clara had plenty. She had known the housekeeper for almost all her life and there wasn't an inch in her body that believed Elisea killed her husband. Why would she? She stuck by him and his brutish, sometimes abusive ways throughout their entire marriage. It would make little sense she would snap now, as the guards were so easily convinced of. Elisea Hawke didn't snap. Ever.

"What does the mayoral seat suggest?"

Clara's eyes blinked rapidly, the veil of her inner thoughts lifting. "Pardon?"

The man sitting across from her at the wide table grimaced. His fingers twirled the ends of a thick beard that reached all the way down to his chest. "The museum, Miss Aldridge. What is your opinion on the matter?"

"Oh, um..."

Clara winced.

"Perhaps we should wait for the mayor to return," a woman made entirely of angles said. "When we have the full attention of the seat to discuss such important matters."

A woman is wrongfully arrested and about to be subjected to torture! Clara wanted to scream. She didn't, of course. Instead, Clara straightened her spine and sat up taller. Her elbows knocked on the table as she leaned in to inspect the council. There were less than a dozen here today, half of the number that usually gathered for these budget meetings. Clara assumed the rest were either with her uncle on whatever urgent business pulled him away or refusing to allow her to dictate them. Despite her uncle's best efforts, there were many that believed Clara too young to take up the seat. It was precisely those fools she needed to impress. And she couldn't do it with her brain elsewhere.

Clara cleared her throat, looked around the table. "Give the museum their coin," she said. "If the galleries follow suit, we ask for their plans to allocate a bigger budget and tell them we will considerate it in the following quarter."

The woman who rudely interrupted her before opened her mouth, but Clara held up a finger to stop her.

"Remind me if I'm wrong, but as far as I recall, the railway project has been on pause for two seasons. No one seems to be missing a train they never wished for to cut across the city. We should be fine not to add more coin where it isn't needed. It's much better to give that funding to the guards." Her gaze burned. "After everything they sacrifice to serve us."

A few agreeable nods told Clara she was back on the right track. She found the attention of the men and women they belonged to and held it when she asked, "How many market arrests have been made last month?"

"Fourteen," a short, rat-shaped man replied.

Clara let out a low whistle. "That's almost double as the month prior."

"Illegal goods are finding their way into the hands of the lower streets," the man explained. "We don't know how, but they are. Only last week, our guards apprehended three citizens selling chips of amber in broad daylight."

"Affected amber?"

The man nodded.

"Huh," Clara mused. "No matter how many gems we take off the market, they seem to pop up, anyway." She tapped a finger on the gold ring on her pinkie, a family heirloom left to her by her mother. The shape of the rose etched into it scratched at Clara's soft skin and immediately bolstered her bravado. She fixed the room with a deathly glare. "And you wish to add a train making it easier to smuggle stones out of the city! Why not start handing out affected gems at town meetings and save the market sellers some time?"

There were a few throats cleared, followed by bodies shifting weight on plush velvet seats. The council didn't expect Clara to have such strong opinions. Heavens, they likely didn't think she had a thought in that head of hers. Little did they know that Oswin had been training her on how to deal with the spineless group since before she could read all her letters.

Elisea's blood-covered hands flashed before her. Clara pushed the thought away, about to continue to hand the council their due when the frosted glass doors to the room burst open. In the doorway stood a bulky, rectangular man with shoulders so wide Clara wondered how he could fit inside without shattering the wood frame.

Clara's lips edged into a smile.

"Mr. Pollen," the rat man said with a nod of a pointed chin.

Sergei Pollen rolled his tree-trunk sized shoulders backward. "Apologies for the interruption, ladies and gentlemen," he said, his eyes landing on Clara. "But I must have a word with Miss Aldridge. Alone."

A few rebuttals floated in the room, hushed by the sound of Clara's seat scraping across the hardwood as she rose to stand. She cast a quick glance over the group and fought to contain her smile as she ushered Sergei out of the room and closed the door behind them with a definitive click. Her chest expanded with a much-needed breath. Taking long strides, she followed her uncle's right-hand man down the dark, narrow corridors of the mayoral estate and into Oswin's office. When they neared it, Sergei reached into his vest pocket to produce a skeleton key, fitting it into the lock.

He held the door for Clara, and she slid by him briskly, floating toward the settee under the bay window instantly. Her gaze stretched past the room, past her uncle's desk and the wall-to-wall shelves of texts filling the vast office, and all the way outside. Beneath them, four stories down, Hedge End came alive. Citizens rushed down the streets, their shoulders bumping and their hands waving in courteous salutes. A few horse-drawn carriages stood outside, and Clara watched as the drivers shouted at each other over the sounds of the bustling city. Two boys fought over a gazette, a third one joining shortly.

From here, you would never know Hedge End was a nightmare in the waking.

It wasn't until Clara spotted a woman with horns jutting out under a mane of thick brown hair and teeth shaped like nails that she drew her gaze away. Another person affected by using too much of a gem's magic. The affected were scarce to see around the city, most choosing to relocate to the Cursed Isle as soon as the first signs of the beast emerged. Clara assumed it was because of the horrific ways in which the magic of the gems marked one's body that they left. Much easier to be with others in the same predicament while you slowly lost everything about you that made you human and turned into a monster. Of course, once one stopped casting gem magic, the change stopped as well; the fully formed beasts were nothing more than a testament to the greed of people. The more magic you cast, the less human you became until there was nothing left at all. Until you were a walking curse. If Clara was ever to fall under the pull of gem magic, she would surely leave as well.

Perhaps if the alchemist who created the gems originally considered their abysmal cost and left well-enough alone, their city would not be in its current predicament. As it was, power was always more enticing than doing the right thing when some people were concerned. Besides, wondering about things that didn't come to pass did not change Hedge End's situation one bit.

Clara studied the horned woman with care to try to understand her better. The woman appeared to be well off, like she lived in the upper numbered streets. Clara wondered why someone who was that fortunate might risk their humanity, the chance of turning into a Cursbeast, for a bit of magic. Then she recalled herself asking Oswin for a gem to keep on hand after the beast attack in the garden.

Clara's lips pressed into a thin line.

She peeled her focus from the window and locked eyes with Sergei instead. "Not that I'm not grateful," she said, smiling, "but why the sudden rush to speak to me? Is it about Uncle? Is everything all right?"

Sergei chuckled, the sound rocking through Clara. "Only you would be concerned about someone else after last night."

"Ah, you heard?"

"There has been talk," the impossibly tall man admitted. "A Cursbeast attack followed by a maid gone mad is no small news."

The blood in Clara's veins sizzled. She dug her nails into the cushions, her knuckles white with rage. "Elisea is no maid," she hissed out. "And she's innocent."

Before her, Sergei quirked one dark, bushy brow. The scar cutting across his cheek reddened, and his jaw set as he took a few calculated paces toward Oswin's desk, pretending to look over the loose papers scattered there. Out of the corner of his eye, he watched her. Sergei was always watching. It was part of his allure for Clara's uncle and a point of mystery for Clara. A man with the eye of a hawk and the mind of an alchemist was not someone who went unnoticed. For the most part, Clara admired Sergei's attention to details and his sharp mind. It took a lot of courage to build oneself up from nothing in a place like Hedge End, let alone land a prominent position at the mayor's side.

She did not appreciate Sergei turning his tricks on her, though.

Clara's throat tightened. "Don't tell me you believe the nonsense the guards were spewing," she said. "You know Elisea. She could never!"

"I also know Thomas, as does your uncle. If you recall, he was the one that stopped your father from bringing him on staff when they hired Elisea, " Sergei said. "The man was not good, not in the least. No one would blame her for acting in self defense."

Unfortunately, Clara did know the housekeeper's husband. She saw the broken skin Elisea sometimes tried to hide under face paint and carefully positioned sleeves. Everyone at Aldridge House knew that Thomas Hawke was a caricature of a man masquerading as a gentleman. Yet there was little Clara could do about it and not for the lack of trying. Whenever she brought it up with Elisea, she deflected the matter and told her to leave well enough alone—that she could handle her own husband. *Did you do just that, Elisea? Did you handle him?*

Clara frowned. She could not give purchase to the accusations the guards set forth, no matter what she saw last night in her garden. She knew Elisea too well to think she would have anything to do with what happened to her husband. Yet there was so much blood...

A worse thought pulled at the rear of Clara's mind. The justice system of Hedge End was fair to a point but Clara, much like most of the residents of the uppers, had little experience of it from the other side of the bars. Self-defense or not, unless Elisea could persuade the guards of her innocence, she was as good as gone. An accusation of murder was the highest of offences, second only to being caught red-handed selling affected gems. With the guards determination of Elise's guilt in her husband's death, there was a good chance she'd be swiftly sentenced and punished for the act. Death would be within weeks. If not sooner.

Her stomach lurched, and she had to swallow the pooling saliva in her mouth to keep the nausea at bay. "The woman had thirty years of marriage to exact her revenge," Clara said, her voice pitching. "If she wanted to kill her husband, she would have done it already. And she certainly wouldn't have done it in our garden."

At the desk, Sergei did not reply, but she could see his brown eyes narrow. He rubbed his neatly trimmed beard, unbuttoning the top two buttons of the crisp white shirt under his blue vest. That was one thing Clara admired about Sergei through and through; like her, he valued comfort above fashion. Reaching into his pocket, Sergei checked the time on a shiny pocket watch and placed it back inside. A new trinket, Clara noted. His gaze drifted past the desk to the framed attributes table of gems hanging on the opposite wall. Clara's eyes followed.

Amethysts to bend light and create illusion. Rubies to generate and control heat. Emeralds to promote rapid wound healing. Sapphires to move and shape water. Clara made it past the first few before turning away. She had studied the table ad nauseam when she was younger and could recite each of the thirty-six affected gems in her sleep. Why her uncle kept the table in his office, she had no idea. They had the same one pinned up on a wall back in the manor and the purpose there eluded her as well. Perhaps as a reminder of the curse placed upon the city. If one was constantly staring at the gems, one had less chance of wishing to use them.

Or maybe he simply enjoyed the visual. The colorful stones were awful pretty to look at.

"Your uncle wanted to see how you were holding up," Sergei suddenly said, pulling Clara from her daydreams. "There is a chance he might be delayed further, but he asked me to relay that if you need him, if you are distressed after what happened, he can cut his visit short."

"His visit to…"

Sergei's jaw ticked. "You know I can't tell you unless the mayor gives me clearance to do so," he said. "Excellent attempt, though."

"You two do realize that I am to be sitting right in that chair one day," Clara said. Her arm stretched to point to the long-backed throne of an office chair behind her uncle's desk. "I can be trusted to know where Oswin goes."

"That is not my call to make."

Clara sighed. Her legs stretched out, and she breathed heavily as she lifted one over the other beneath the weight of her full skirts. Checking to make sure the door was closed, she reached into her hair and pulled out the pins holding her top hat in place, removing the dreaded contraption from her head. With the heavy weight of the hat gone, Clara could think a little clearer.

Shadows crept under her eyes as she regarded Sergei. "What does my uncle plan to do about Elisea?"

"I beg your pardon?"

"Our housekeeper," she said in annoyance. "How is he planning to get her acquitted of the charges placed against her?"

The room filled with an unbearable silence.

Clara slapped her hands on her thighs. "Please tell me Oswin does not believe it!" She cried. "Elisea is family. He knows her as well as I do. I'm sure he has a plan for these ridiculous accusations as soon as he returns."

"If he does," Sergei said, "he has not shared it with me."

Clara's mouth slacked. She bent her neck forward, her posture slumping. Vision unfocused, she tried to concentrate on Sergei, but her reeling mind would not allow it. Was she the only one who knew the truth around here? If her uncle were here, she would make him see reason, but with him away at the most inopportune time, Clara was all alone. She looked at Sergei, then quickly turned away. The man's loyalty was to the mayor. She couldn't convince him to help her no matter what she tried. When it came to Sergei, even gem magic couldn't make the stoic creature leave his duties to her uncle. No, if Clara wanted to help Elisea, she would have to do it alone.

Her heart sank into her boots. How in the gems was she going to help her housekeeper before it was too late?

A wild thought tugged at the back of her mind.

Absolutely not, Clara thought. She couldn't, could she?

While she looked around the room and the stuffy decor of the mayoral office, Clara couldn't help but scoff. What good was it to be next in line for the prominent position if she couldn't save an innocent person from dying for a crime they didn't commit? Clara would not be able to perform the duties of mayor in the future if she didn't act morally today. After all, it was her uncle who told her that the citizens of Hedge End needed a leader who cared for them to take the seat. And Clara did care. So deeply it made her bones ache. She loved Elisea fiercely, and if that meant that she had to find out what happened to her deadbeat husband herself, so be it.

Except Clara had no intention of doing anything alone. There was someone she could turn to for help, a person with the specific skill set she needed at this very moment.

Someone she vowed never to speak to again.

CHAPTER FOUR

The blue glimmer of a sapphire made Willoughby's stomach turn. His head, heavy from being knocked about, lifted an inch, green eyes narrowing on the stone in the guard's hand. The man behind the gem sneered. He was going to enjoy this.

Fucking hell, Willoughby thought.

This was going to hurt.

The guard, six feet tall and getting larger somehow, rubbed a thumb over the gem. His eyes rolled to the back of his head as the magic in the stone came to life, filling the man commanding it with its power. Even in his decrepit state, Willoughby could see the magic take hold of the guard's body. His skin stretched over his massive neck, and his veins bulged as the blood within them thickened. The guard's fist shook as he squeezed the gem.

Willoughby wondered how much of his humanity the man had to sacrifice to doll out the punishment today.

He didn't have long to think about it before the basin set before him began to shake. A few feet away, the guard raised

his hand and the water in the basin shot up in the air. It flowed upward, forming the illusion of an upside-down waterfall. Willoughby would have been amazed if he didn't know what followed. With a flick of a sapphire-holding wrist, the guard directed the water at Willoughby. It turned at an unnatural angle, blasting into his mouth before he had a chance to close it. Willoughby's arms wrestled with the shackles locking him to the damp brick wall of the jail cell and his head smashed into the stone, his brain rattling inside his skull. Sputtering, Willoughby tried to turn from the flow of the water, but no matter which way he swung his head, it kept filling him. The taste of river water coated his tongue, and he gasped for air, the motion making things much worse.

Willoughby was drowning.

Panic surged through his body as he thrashed in the chains holding him down. He coughed, sending more of the water down his throat and into his burning lungs. His arms flailed wildly as the all-consuming agony that followed made him convulse. His muscles, once strong and lean, now felt leaden. Anchors dragging him under. With each failed breath, Willoughby's motions slowed like he was moving through quicksand. It was a losing battle. Willoughby's vision flickered into darkness, then back again. He felt the world begin to slip away.

A second later, the water was gone. Vanished into gas as though it never existed.

Willoughby's legs gave out from under him and his shoulders ached as he dropped down, his arms hoisted up by those damn chains.

"The coins," the guard said calmly. "Where are the coins you stole?"

A laugh sent Willoughby into a fit of coughing. When he

was done, he spat out the remnants of river water onto the floor at his feet. "You have the wrong guy."

"Somehow, I doubt that."

The guard placed the sapphire on the table in front of him and reached for the next gem in the lineup. A topaz. Willoughby cursed under his breath. He was soaked from head to toe; the electricity the gem would summon would cook him better than a turkey in a boiling pot. Though that was no doubt the exact effect the guard wished to employ. It wasn't the first time Willoughby had been subjected to gem torture. Getting caught came with the territory of being a thief, but it was the first time he feared what might happen.

Wet brown curls fell into his eyes. He tossed his hair to the side to see better, and the motion sent daggers of pain through his body. Willoughby bit down on his tongue and trained his eyes on the guard's shoulders, where two small spikes protruded through thick flesh. Wings growing.

He caught the man's gaze with his own and held it. "Is it worth it?" He asked. "Giving up your life to torture some poor prick who stole a few coins?"

The guard's ears perked. "You did steal them, then?"

Willoughby was about to deny his involvement in the crime when the door to the cell creaked open. Another guard stepped through the threshold, this one with a face that was nearly all beast. Large canines fell from his gaping mouth, and his ears had shifted high up on his head to the point of appearing to be glued in place. His hair fell in greasy strands over his cat-like eyes that followed Willoughby as he crossed the cell.

The guards exchanged quick words, which left Willoughby's torturer deflated. He looked down at the topaz in his hands, growling deep in his chest. Placing the stone on the table, he nudged his chin in Willoughby's direction and turned away as the second guard approached the wall. With a quick turn of a key, the shackles holding him dropped to the floor with a loud clang.

Willoughby instantly rubbed his bloodied wrists in relief.

"What's going on?" he asked.

The torturer kept his back turned, stayed silent.

"Your bail has been posted," the second guard said. "You're free to go."

Willoughby watched in disbelief as the guard bent a knee to unfasten the chains on his feet. Face gruff, the guard pocketed the keys, grabbed Willoughby by his filthy shirt sleeve and pushed him toward the open cell door. The smell coming off Willoughby from having spent four days getting tortured by these fine gentlemen made the guard scrunch his long nose and Willoughby took slight pleasure in seeing him wince. When they reached the bars, he cast a sidelong glance at his torturer.

"Can't say it's been a pleasure," he said with a smirk.

The guard scoffed. "I'll be seeing you again, thief. I have no doubt of that."

To say he was optimistic would be downplaying the truth. Willoughby had spent as much time behind bars as he had walking the streets. All par the course of his chosen career, but it was enough to make a person question their life from time to time. Today was one of those times, and as Willoughby walked down the familiar mold-infested corridors of the jailhouse, he reevaluated his entire existence. Not that the money of his market dealings wasn't good, only that it may not have been quite worth it.

The pain of two broken ribs ricocheted through his body with every step, a lingering reminder of the last few days. Definitely not worth it.

Willoughby's eyes caught on a newcomer in a cell and his

brow twisted questioningly. He had seen all sorts of people down here, but the likes of the woman shivering in the corner stood out amongst the rest. She didn't belong here. If he had to guess, she was from the middle streets. Maybe even as high as the fifties.

Bushy eyebrows arching, Willoughby jabbed a thumb in the direction of the woman's cell. "Hey, what's with—"

He was rudely interrupted by another shove that sent him stuttering toward the singular set of stairs leading out of the gem-forsaken hellhole. Willoughby shook out his sweaty curls and pointed his long nose up. Never show defeat. No down here. The air lightened as they climbed toward the top of the jailhouse as though its burdens were as relieved as every other living soul that managed to escape this place. It felt fresher, less constipated with the scent of death and human abandon. Not at all like the cells below. As he placed a shaky foot on the top landing, Willoughby paused to look at the guard leading him. "Who bailed me out?"

"You have friends in high places, it appears," the guard replied. "I'd never have guessed it."

Willoughby agreed. He racked his brain, but as far as he recalled, he didn't have any friends at all. The guard gave him a final shove out of a second doorway. Willoughby's eyes battled the blinding light of the outside world that streamed in through the vaulted windows on this level of the jailhouse. Around him, guards and criminals filled the vast space, each hurriedly busy with whatever task they were performing. Not the criminals, of course. They did the same thing Willoughby did each time he landed himself in a precarious situation— planned their escape.

The poor idiots had no idea what awaited them below.

With a shudder, Willoughby waited for the guard to duck behind the gated security desk in one corner of the lobby.

When he returned, he rammed a paper bag full of Willough-by's pathetic belongings into his chest, the gruff look from before intensifying.

"Better go thank her before you go off to rob someone else," he instructed.

"Her?"

Willoughby's neck twisted to follow the guard's extended finger. In a flash, his entire world shifted. There was one thing Willoughby Tanner hated more than getting caught, and it was standing right in front of him. His gaze rolled over the pristine dark waves cascading down the lace of the woman's dress. Heat clawed up his chest and he tamped it down, returning his attention to the loathsome creature. Her gray eyes danced over him with a glimmer that reminded him exactly why he couldn't stand her company. This could not be who bailed him out. Why in the gems would she care whether he lived or died? He hadn't spoken to the deplorable, opinionated, spoiled brat since... The muscle in Willoughby's neck feathered.

He turned to the guard, threw his wrists out, and let out an exasperated sigh. "No, thank you," he said. "Lock me up again. I'll take two more days of gem torture over Clara Aldridge any day of the week."

CHAPTER FIVE

Clara's cheeks warmed as she watched the thief attempt to avoid her. Red splotches marked her neck, her inner rage battling to stay contained. The idea that this man was to be her salvation was as preposterous as Willoughby's reaction. She never should have come here. Yet here she was, unmoving at the sight of a common thief who behaved as though she were the problem. Not that it should have surprised her in the least.

Willoughby was an unbearable pain in her behind. And a dramatic one at that.

After several more attempts of returning to the jail cell, the nuisance of a man finally gave up his shenanigans and turned to face her. Distaste covered his features like molasses, and Clara wished for nothing more than to wipe the incredulous look off his face. Unfortunately, that was not in the cards today. She needed information, and she needed it found out discreetly. As many awful things as Willoughby Tanner was, he was damn good at stealing. Something Clara couldn't afford to

do in her position. He was also the only of his profession she knew on a personal basis. Unfortunately.

Forcing herself to keep eye contact, she scratched the itch under her top hat discreetly, waiting for the thief to make his way over. He did so with little enthusiasm. If Clara was a betting a woman, she'd wager he enjoyed getting slammed about by gem magic more than having to thank her for his life.

Not that Willoughby was on death's toll. Whatever he stole was worth a punishment, but not one quite as severe. There were only two offenses that landed you on the row in Hedge End—selling affected gems and murder. The thief couldn't be so dumb as to perform either. Then again, neither was her housekeeper.

Clara's eyes wetted. She swiped at them, pushing all thoughts of Elisea out of her mind. There was no time now to get emotional, not with Willoughby inching closer to her. She couldn't let him affect her. Whatever grievances they held toward each other didn't weigh against what was at stake—a woman's life was on the line and Clara had to put their differences aside for the greater good. She hoped Willoughby could do the same once he heard her proposal.

The thief sauntered toward her with short, brisk steps. Willoughby's shoulders rolled and Clara tried not to glimpse at the solid muscle of his arms as he raked his fingers through the messy curls of his hair. He slid his arms into a long leather overcoat, buttoning it up high enough that his neck disappeared beneath the armor of his clothing. Green eyes locked on her form, making Clara shrink beneath the thief's intrusive gaze.

"You look like a politician," Willoughby said, disdain dripping off every word.

Clara smirked. "You smell like a sewer," she retorted. "Is there a thank you somewhere in that vocabulary, perhaps?"

The remark earned her a scowl, and a lame note of gratitude whispered under a quickly expelled breath. Clara looked skyward. She clutched to every bit of self-control she could grab as it fell through her fingers until she could force her face into a neutral expression. When she was certain she had her wits about her, Clara dared to glance at the thief again.

"I won't sugar coat this," she said. "I didn't post your bail out of the goodness of my heart."

Willoughby arched one finely shaped brow. "Implying you have a heart is a stretch, I'd say."

"Would you prefer to return to your very important appointment in the dungeons?" she bit out. "Or would you rather hear me out and be on your merry way? Spend the night in the comfort of a bed and not chained to a wall. Possibly endure a bath to wash that stench away."

Before her, Willoughby worked his chiseled jaw. His hands fisted and relaxed as he considered her words. Each motion seemed to bring him pain, and she wondered if it was her mere presence in his universe again or if the guards went a little too heavy in their punishments. This wasn't the first time she'd heard of Willoughby's visits to the jailhouse, not that she kept track of him, but it was the first time she'd seen the aftermath. Is this what all prisoners looked like? With faint scars across their cheeks and pain flowing off their bones so heavily Clara could feel it reverberate against her own skin. Did Elisea have the same appearance now?

Her stomach seized.

Willoughby folded his arms over his chest, the leather of his overcoat straining to contain him. "Tell me why."

"Walk with me," Clara said. She gestured to the street outside with a gloved hand. "I could use the fresh air."

"Is the poverty in the place too much for your delicate senses, princess?"

This time, Clara didn't hold back. She reached for the chain of her coin purse, twisting it around her palm to yank it tight. In one slick move—taught to her by Sergei years ago—she spun the purse over her head and behind Willoughby's. The coin-filled velvet pouch smashed into the rear of his hair, shoving him with its momentum. The thief lost his balance and teetered forward. His forehead slammed against the window in front of them, and Clara didn't hide her laughter when he hissed between clenched teeth.

Willoughby peeled himself off the glass, a red bruise growing on his skin. "Duly noted. Let's walk."

Cobblestone clicked under Clara's feet as they took to the street. Her ankles strained to stay steady, but every second step sent her sideways as the heels of her lace-up boots got trapped between the spaces of the uneven stones. She grimaced, keeping her eyes on the road and not on the obnoxious man walking beside her.

A carriage drove past them and quickly sped away. The jailhouse was located in the most southern part of the city, in the single digit streets and overlooking the river. To see a carriage here was rare and Clara assumed it was only someone from the higher numbers passing by. Her assumption proved correct when the carriage made a sharp turn toward the bridge leading to the park. It continued to race away until all Clara could see was the black dot marking the carriage and the horse that pulled it.

She briefly wondered who was inside.

"Out with it, Aldridge," Willoughby hissed out.

She clenched her jaw until her teeth ground together. Glancing both ways to avoid getting plowed down, Clara crossed the road and stood at the edge of the river. Her hand rested on the stone railing, head tilting to look at the streetlamps marking the tall posts that lined the barrier. The lights glimmered in a warm yellow glow, already on despite it being mid-afternoon. At their backs, dark, bricked buildings rose high in the sky. The roofs were sharp and jagged and reminded Clara of knifes pointing the wrong way in a block. There were too many windows that Clara couldn't count them all if she tried. Another reminder that they were far from the upper streets, where houses never spanned higher than three stories.

The city descended in layers. The uppers perched on the highest ridges, their streets cobbled clean and the air thick with the scent of wealth. Every home was secured by massive iron fences and gates covered in barbs, protection from the terrible monsters that stalked the city. It was here that most of the guard was positioned for regular patrols, scaring the Cursbeasts away by sheer manpower from those more fortunate. Below the uppers sprawled the middles where the majority of the buildings one might don as tourist-worthy stood stoic amongst city-paved walking paths and neatly lined gardens. The guard patrols were less frequent here and beast attacks came and went, though it was not as frequent of an issue. But here, in the lowers, it was a different story. The streets dipped into shadows, squeezed by narrow, leaning buildings that seemed to fold in on themselves. People lived on top of each other. Saving space and huddling together whether for warmth or safety, Clara did not know. Guards showed up only to catch illegal dealings or to patrol the few streets that caused enough havoc to spread into the higher numbered streets. Without their dedicated protection, the lowers were an open buffet for Cursbeasts and thieves alike.

Shouts and arguments filled the dank streets of the lowers, each voice battling for attention over the other. There was the distinct hum of a song being played and Clara followed it to a young woman strumming a viola on a street corner. An empty coin purse sat open at her feet, its interior shredded.

The laughter of children playing warmed Clara's chest. She never heard this many sounds in one place.

Aldridge House was located high in the city, spanning between north eighty-seventh and ninety-first streets. Not right at the tip, but close enough that Clara rarely had the need to venture further down. When you lived in the uppers, everything you longed for was right there for the taking. If not for the boredom of being on the more spread-out areas of Hedge End with few neighbors in between, Clara would have not minded her home all that much. Still, the thrilling sounds of life rarely entered the lush estates in the uppers, what with people keeping to themselves. Here in the lowers, it was all so—

Clara scowled at a missing person's leaflet tacked onto the lamppost next to her.

So very different here.

"Hello? Look alive, Aldridge—" Willoughby waved a rough hand in front of her face "—I don't have all day."

"I beg to differ," she said. "Unless you planned on another con later in the evening."

A rogue smile tugged at the thief's lips. "You never know. I just might."

Breathing in, Clara tried to stay on track. She was already exhausted by the man, and they hadn't even discussed her proposition. She rubbed her temples to dispel the headache that careened between them. "My housekeeper was arrested for the murder of her husband," she finally blurted out.

It took Willoughby long enough to reply that she began to wonder if he heard her. When he spoke, she wished he had stayed quiet.

"I see you finally made someone lose their hinges," the thief said.

Clara's grip tensed over the chain of her purse. "This is

serious," she snapped. "Elisea is innocent, and she's about to die for a crime she didn't commit. I can't—" she paused "—I will not allow it."

"Sorry to be the bearer of bad news, but you don't have much say. Last I heard, you're not yet mayor, and I doubt your uncle will let a killer roam the streets." He lamely motioned to the freakishly tall buildings surrounding them. "How else would he keep us in our place?"

"Keep the city safe from crime, you mean?" Clara asked. "I don't know what your issues are with my family, but I think we can both admit that this is the last place I want to be, and you are the last person I want to speak to."

Willoughby bowed theatrically, then popped up to stand. "Wonderful. I'm glad that's settled. I'll be on my way then."

Despite his statement, the thief didn't budge.

The two continued to stand side by side with the lively voices of the lower streets at their backs and the rush of the river beneath them. Clara's chin tilted up, her nose catching a whiff of a sour and foul scent. Though, considering his current state, it could have been Willoughby. Her eyes watered, and her stomach clenched as unease prickled along her skin.

"I need your help," she whispered.

"I'm sorry. What was that?"

Clara scowled. The cocky son of a gem heard her. She was certain of it. It wasn't enough that Clara had used her own coin to save him from the jailhouse, but now he was going to make her grovel. It was the most Willoughby move. The nitwit had been pulling power plays with her since they were kids running around the mayoral office pretending to hunt Cursbeasts. She truly should have known he would grow up to be doubly obnoxious. Sadly, Clara appeared to have been correct.

Fighting the urge to smack him with her purse again, she

bit the inside of her cheek. Hard. "I require someone with your specific set of skills," Clara ground out.

"And what skills would those be?"

Clara pretended not to see him wiggle his brows as he inclined his head toward her. She elbowed the absolute nuisance in the ribs. "This is serious," she scolded. "I need information, and I cannot get it myself."

"Hmm," Willoughby mused.

"Oh, come on! Are you really going to make me beg?"

A gust of wind split the air between them. Clara's gaze narrowed on the man next to her and for a moment, she thought she saw him smile. The brightness in his features vanished instantly, replaced by the thunderous gaze Clara was used to.

"Why can't you get it yourself?" Willoughby asked.

"Because it has to be discreet."

The thief's jaw set. "You mean illegal. Say what you need, Aldridge. Stop toeing around it."

"Ugh, fine. Thomas Hawke was not a good person," Clara said. "He was violent and cruel, and surely did deserve to die. But he didn't do so by his wife's hand, no matter what the guards say. I want you to see what you can find out about him. Get inside their residence and gather information. Anything and everything of note that can help me prove that Elisea is innocent."

When Willoughby didn't reply, she added, "I'm willing to pay you."

"While I would never say no to an easy job," Willoughby said, "if I'm caught, they will link this back to you. You know that, right?"

Clara nodded.

"And you're sure she didn't do it? Your housekeeper?"

"I'd bet my life on it," Clara said without a second to think on the matter. She turned her head, her eyes locking on the thief. "Are you in?"

Willoughby's lips parted, but his words were cut out by a loud whistle piercing the air. A second later, several more whistles tore through the lowers, each one triggering the next. Clara spun on her heels to face the street, searching for the commotion. Citizens ran amok before her, vanishing into darkened corners. She spotted two men whistle at each other before rushing away.

A warning.

A strong arm looped around her waist, and she was yanked sideways and pulled away from the railing. A yelp broke free of her as Willoughby dragged her, feet scrambling, toward a narrow side street. The heel of her left boot caught on a loose stone and her ankle twisted in the wrong direction. A sharp, agonizing pain ripped up her leg. Clara started to scream, but Willoughby's palm pressed against her mouth, muzzling her as he slammed her back into the wall.

The alley he pushed her into was so tight that she could feel Willoughby's breath against her cheek.

His finger shot upward, signaling for her to stay quiet. In a flash, Willoughby's lips were on her ear, the warmth of his breath tickling the soft skin there. Her lungs forgot how to work. Clara bristled, shivers coating her skin as Willoughby whispered into her ear. "Cursbeast. Big one."

Clara's gaze drifted outside the alley. The last thing she saw before Willoughby dragged them further into the darkness were gargantuan claws shimmering in the sunlight.

CHAPTER SIX

The first time Willoughby Tanner saw a Cursbeast he was three years old. Some people say that your memories do not become fully formed until much later in a young person's life, but to Willoughby, the day was as clear as what he had for breakfast yesterday.

It was summer. Willoughby could clearly recall the heat in the air that sat on his skin for hours and the wetness beneath his chin from the humidity rising off the river. In his young age, all Willoughby wanted was to jump into the glistening water, but his father often warned him away, shooing him off with tales of poisonous snakes and fairytale creatures that lurked below. It was obvious to him now that the stories were the best his father could do to steer an adventurous mind. No one swam in the vile river that flowed through Hedge End. The damn thing was used for one thing only: to further segregate their cursed city from the rest of the outside world.

But that wasn't a thing you told a child, was it?

You certainly didn't tell the child that his father's fear of the river was deeply rooted in his mother's drowning when

Willoughby barely yet walked. And you didn't tell that same child that any time his father so much as looked at water, a shiver tripped down his spine that twisted his mind into the darkest of places. No, instead, you told tales. Tales of women with fins and monstrous creatures with teeth sharper than any Cursbeast.

Those often did the trick.

Thus, when Willoughby stuck a sweaty toddler toe in the river and heard his father's panicked yells, he assumed it was because a river monster was coming for him. Little did he know, another beast lurked nearby, one beyond the sum of falsehoods and bedtime stories.

The creature was at least ten feet tall with a hunched back that made it resemble a massive hill upon which Willoughby could roll down easily. Its beady eyes sat too wide apart to make room for a nose that stretched in the wrong direction on its cavernous face. Below it, jagged, crooked teeth fought for real estate in an unnaturally large mouth. The beast's knuckles dragged low to the ground as it stalked West Third Street, its hips crashing into the buildings on either side. Willoughby was too small then to recognize the alarm whistles the citizens of the lowers developed as a means of warning so there was nothing to alert him to the presence of the beast nearby. Except the smell. There was a stink in the air that Willoughby would never forget. It smelled of sulfur, an unmistakable stench belonging to all Cursbeasts, but there was also something else. It wasn't until he was older that Willoughby understood what it was.

Rot. The beast stank of decay and death.

It was the same smell that clung to the hairs inside his nostrils as he pulled the impossible woman he was stuck with down the dark alleys of the city. Clara's sweat-slicked fingers entwined with his own and he had to keep his grip airtight, so she didn't slip away. Knowing Clara, she would want to run back to the riverside to see the beast better. There was once a time when he reveled in her curiosity. Then again, there was also a time when he trusted Clara Aldridge with his entire being.

His gaze darted to her briefly.

These days, Willoughby couldn't trust the mayor's niece as far as he could throw her and judging by the weight of her dress and the ridiculous hat she wore, he likely couldn't even lift her high enough to toss.

"Where are you taking me?" Clara demanded.

Willoughby yanked harder on her hand, not answering.

"I'm not going another step until you tell me," Clara said. She buried the heel of her boots in between two stones and bucked back like a horse tired of pulling a carriage. With an incredulous look, she added, "I'm dead serious, Will."

"Interesting choice of words. Dead is what we'll be if we stop moving. Or did you not notice the beast?"

Clara made no attempt to walk. The infuriating woman.

Her hip cocked to the side as she ripped her hand from Willoughby's vice grip—why was he still holding it?—to rest on her waist. The impossibly wide girth of her skirt made her resemble a teapot topper. Clara's nostrils flared with each heavy breath, and Willoughby didn't fail to notice that she had that weapon of a coin purse clutched extra tight again. He had no doubt she would beat him senseless if he didn't entertain her theatrics.

Rubbing the exhaustion from his eyes, he gazed down the length of the alley behind them. "We need to get further out," he said. "For once in your privileged, sheltered life will you listen to sound advice?"

"From you? The man who'd rather steal than get a proper position?" Clara spun around, her neck stretching to look in the direction they came from. "Did you hit your head while you ran, and I simply missed it?"

"For gem's sake... There is a literal Cursbeast on our tail, Aldridge!"

Clara scoffed. She actually scoffed. "It is by the river, *Tanner*," she rebutted. "The beast isn't going to follow two people through the city. It doesn't have a vendetta against us. It's a beast!"

"Oh, and you're some Cursbeast expert now, is that it?" Willoughby asked. "Has dear old uncle been teaching you the ways of the monsters in between etiquette lessons? You're unbelievable."

"What I am is rational. Unlike some people."

At this, Willoughby decided that he had heard enough. If the princess wished to die today, that was a choice she could make without him. He twisted from her and stomped down the alley, leaving her standing with a jaw agape behind him. With each retreating step, his heart raced faster in the tight confines of his ribcage. How was she this nonchalant? The citizens of Hedge End had long learned how to live in the presence of the beasts, but they still took precautions to run like hell when one showed up. No one could be this oblivious. And yet here was Clara Aldridge, without a care in the world and full of blind bravery once again. It was almost as if the years had done little to change her, though Willoughby knew that was a lie.

If Clara was still the girl he once considered a friend, he would not want to be as far away from her as possible.

The sound of heels clicking on cobblestone filled his ears. Willoughby groaned. He should have known by now there was no escaping the blasted woman. If you wished to avoid an Aldridge, your best bet was to leave the city. The family was everywhere. Perhaps there was a chance Willoughby could dettach from the woman haunting his nightmares for decades.

His eyes darted around the narrow space they occupied. The only place he could go was forward, and he was certain Clara would follow; once she sank her shiny teeth in, she didn't let go.

"I'll double my offer if you can guarantee to scope out the Hawkes residence tonight," Clara yelled at his stiff back.

Case in point. Teeth. Too many teeth.

Willoughby stopped in the middle of the alley. He could surely use the coin; there was no doubting that. It had been ages since he could afford a proper meal which didn't come from a five-finger discount. Longer since he slept somewhere warm. The trouble with his occupation was that he was constantly on the run. You couldn't very well perform half the activities Willoughby did and stay in one place or else he'd place a target on his back for the mayor's lackeys. That and clients had been scarce to come by lately, adding to Willoughby's ever threatening financial ruin. Besides which, spending coin collected in less than moral ways was dangerous. No, Willoughby had to be smart about where he spent his hard-earned coin. And it wasn't on lavish rooms and fancy dinners. Everything he made from his dealings at the markets went into a hiding spot only Willoughby knew about. A stash for a darker day.

"Have you lost your tongue between here and the river?" Clara demanded.

The day was beginning to look quite bleak right now.

Willoughby twirled in place to face her. "As wonderful as your offer sounds, I'm not interested."

"Triple the coin."

A hiss snuck out from Willoughby's tense jaw. He bit down on his tongue before he said something he might regret later. Clara was not making it easy for him one bit and he had the inkling that he could convince her to go even higher if he put his mind to it. That wasn't the problem. The main reason he didn't want to tie himself to the mayor's niece, even if it was for a good cause, was because of what was at stake were she to find out who he truly was.

Not a thief. Not really.

Someone much, much worse.

Willoughby felt along the hidden lining stitched into his coat pocket. His fingers grazed the jagged edges of the gems he was yet to move and his blood warmed. A ruby and a jade were hard to come by, and he had just the right buyer for both. It was the same poor sap that purchased the last gem chips from him. This was, after all, how gem dealing worked in the markets. It was always someone who knew someone, a secret agreement, a passing of hands under tables. No one could make more gems, so people resorted to chipping stones away until they were mere dust, multiplying the damn things in the best way they knew how. The Stone King had likely never imagined the lengths people would go to to reproduce magic— to get their hands on it. The citizens of Hedge End had dwindled the original sets of stones to mere shards in the years that passed until pieces hit the streets by the thousands. People like Willoughby made the trades easier for the common folk...and sometimes the more prominent figures of society. When it came to getting paid, Willoughby didn't discriminate. And this buyer had coin to spend and a reputation to uphold so Willoughby trusted him to keep his mouth shut about their arrangement.

Besides, if Willoughby worked quickly, he could be free of the damn stones and fill his stomach with wine that wasn't from the bottom of a barrel by the end of the day.

A slender foot tapped impatiently in front of him.

Willoughby's gaze traveled up Clara's leg, past the obnoxious layers of her skirt, and to her annoyed expression. Getting involved with her was messy. Even if he put their past aside, which he couldn't do for any amount of coin, there was the matter of who her uncle was. Who she was to become in the near future. People like Clara Aldridge put people like him behind bars. Worse, really. The punishment for illegal gem dealings was death by the same gems you peddled.

Absolutely no fucking way.

"Watch your language, please," Clara hissed out.

Willoughby's skin paled. Did he speak out loud? His heart raced in his chest as he tried to gather his senses. It hadn't been an hour and Clara already drove him mad. Wonderful.

He cleared his throat, readjusted the fit of his coat. "There are plenty of other thieves around," he told her. "Leave me be."

"No one I'd trust with this, I'm afraid," Clara said. "I am not willing to gamble with Elisea's life. Let's be clear. I don't enjoy you. You don't enjoy me. But I don't think you'd send an innocent woman to her death. At least, I hope not."

"Your housekeeper… Is she in her later years?" he asked, recalling the woman he saw in the jail cell earlier. "Gray hair, sunken cheeks? A back so straight it could plane a wall?"

Clara blinked at him rapidly, her thick, dark lashes caressing her skin. "Y-yes," she stuttered. "How did you know?"

"I saw her. And before you ask, she seemed fine. Shaken, but that's expected considering where she was."

"H-had they…"

Willoughby's legs buckled. The fear and emotion in Clara's voice, the raw pitch of it, was not what he expected from the cold and calculated woman he knew her to be. Had he misjudged her? And if he had, what did that make him if he refused to help someone save a person they loved? It was odd to imagine Clara caring for anyone but herself and yet…

He rubbed the bridge of his nose, flinching from the pain it caused to do so. The damn guards did a number on him this time. Willoughby's body grew laden as he faced Clara. In the hidden compartment, the gems rubbed together, and he forced himself to pull away from them, leaving the stones to rest until he was ready to take up the task of selling them. A sigh fell from his lips, and he took two steps backward to put some space between them. Clenching and unclenching his fists, Willoughby ground his teeth into pulp as he considered his options.

His shoulders slumped.

"Quadruple that coin, Aldridge," he said, "and you've got yourself a deal."

CHAPTER SEVEN

The thief was true to his words, a shocking revelation to admit if Clara was frank. She had the right of mind to give him half the coin for the job ahead of time and promised the rest when he returned from the Hawkes residence with information she could use to free Elisea. With her uncle gone, the night made for a perfect arrangement to meet. Though she would have preferred a swim in the river during high tide over speaking to Willoughby again, Clara had no choice but to bite down her frustration and slink out into the dark.

The house groaned under her hurried steps, and she willed the manor to stay silent, so she didn't wake the remaining staff residing with the family. The number of people that stayed within the manor's walls dwindled considerably after Clara's parents died—there was little use to keep a full-time staff for only two people and even Elisea chose to reside in her own home, spending the night occasionally when Oswin took his longer trips out of the city. Still, Clara did not wish to interrupt anyone this late in night save for the questions they might have in the morning. She doubted they could hear her with two floors separating them but stayed light on her toes regardless as she made her way down the winding staircase and toward the rear of the house. Her gaze brushed past a tall, ornate mirror. Clara flinched. Dressed entirely in black with her blouse buttoned up to her chin and her hair neatly tucked beneath a lace scarf, she didn't resemble herself at all. Clara couldn't recall the last occasion she wore her riding gear since her uncle insisted she take the carriage for all her outings. Tonight, a carriage would not do.

Clara could not afford to attract unwanted attention, and a horse bound carriage cutting across the city in the middle of the night would do exactly that. The Hawkes lived in the middle numbers, and, by Clara's calculations, it would take her well over an hour to walk to their agreed upon location. No, if Clara wished to meet with Willoughby, she had to be more discreet.

When she got ready, after her maid had left for the evening, she briefly considered going on foot. If she left before the sun set, she would make it in time. But Clara could not risk it. Having a light in the sky meant someone could spot her. That and in the possible case that a Cursbeast crossed her path, it would be easier to hide out in the dead of night. With those deterrents in mind, Clara opted for the most rational choice—a simple horse.

Well, not quite as simple, considering it took Clara nearly twenty minutes to mount herself onto the saddle and another fifteen minutes of fussing with the stirrups until she found a comfortable position. Or at least one she felt she could hold for the full journey to her destination. Judging by the weakness of her legs and the mare's clear dismay at her inaptitude, she allotted an added ten minutes should things go south.

Clara tightened the reins, then checked her pocket watch. Best to get a move on.

Guiding the majestic animal through the darker passages surrounding the manor, Clara turned over her shoulder to inspect the grounds before dashing through the front gates. She groaned when she realized she would need to dismount to close the damn gates. Pulling up on the reins; the mare came to a halt beneath her. This time, it was much easier to get back into position, and she mentally rewarded herself with a deep, relaxing breath as the animal galloped down the road and away from Aldridge House.

With more distance between her and the manor, Clara relaxed. Her muscles eased around the saddle, and she leaned forward, allowing the momentum of the ride to pierce her bones. Wind slapped Clara's cheeks. Loose tendrils of hair flowed behind her as the horse picked up speed. The cool of the evening made the hairs on her arms stand up straight despite the thick layer of her riding blouse.

An invisible thread pulled at the corners of her lips. It had been too long since Clara felt this free. She vowed to make it a point to ride more often after this nightmare with Elisea was over.

The mare bucked as they reached a fork in the road. Clara's body jerked, and she fought gravity to stay atop the animal. Her eyes watered. She blinked rapidly to clear her vision, concentrating on the location she was now in. The architecture in the area was a strange mix of the lowers and the uppers, enough that it gave Clara vertigo to look at the surrounding buildings. Some were tall and spanned several stories, their turrets limned by the light of the fat moon in the sky. Others sat nestled low to the ground and reminded her of Aldridge House, if the manor shrunk in size and lost its carved embell-ishments. What made Clara dizzy wasn't the appearance of the homes on the dark street she rode through, but how little sense it made. Alleys jutted out at random intervals and while some homes had well cared for yards, others appeared to be abandoned entirely. Moss overtook the gravel walkways that led to dilapidated porches, and there was a strange smell in the air that came and went in the passing wind.

Then there were the taller buildings that had lights glimmering on one floor, only to be followed by boarded-up windows on another.

The middles of Hedge End were a blemish on the eyes.

"Please tell me you didn't actually bring a horse."

Clara's breath hitched in her throat. She closed her eyes tight, opening them as she pulled the reins to spin around. The sound of the mare's heavy hooves echoed down the empty street and Clara noticed a few shadowy heads pop up inside lit up windows. Her teeth snapped shut as her gaze traveled down to the man standing on the opposite sidewalk.

"How else was I to travel to meet you?" Clara asked.

An exasperated sigh reached Clara's ears, followed by the shuffle of Willoughby's feet as he crossed the street toward her. His palm patted the horse's wide side, and it bucked its hind legs in approval. "I thought you didn't want to attract attention to yourself?"

"It was either this or walk," Clara answered. "And I doubted you'd wait for my arrival."

"On that you are correct, princess."

Her jaw tensed. "What did you find out?"

Without as much as a reply, Willoughby patted the horse again. The animal jerked under Clara. She white-knuckled the reins to keep from falling over the side. Her riding pants chafed from the friction of the saddle, and while she adored the freedom of a pair of trousers, she missed the breeze her skirts offered. Although all the work she was putting in to stay atop the horse while Willoughby led them to a side street may have had something to do with her discomfort.

She watched the thief maneuver the animal knowingly and with care, her eyes bulging. For someone who didn't grow up in a wealthy family, Willoughby certainly knew his way around a horse. She attempted to recall their childhood to see if perhaps she had underestimated the slippery man, but nothing came to mind. Willoughby was the son of a custodian, not a stable hand. Whatever stable skills Willoughby had developed; it was after his time at the mayoral office.

A sharp pain twisted Clara's heart. She hadn't thought about her childhood in ages; certainly not of Willoughby Tanner's part in it. Sometimes she wished his father never worked for the mayoral office and that she never met the insufferable dunce. But deep down, Clara knew that wishes were a luxury she couldn't afford. One couldn't change their past, no matter what they were willing to sacrifice to do so. Besides, Willoughby sure was fun before...

The horse came to an abrupt stop. Clara skidded forward on the saddle, her hands scrambling to hold on. Thighs straight and strong, she crushed herself to the animal, barely balancing. Her lips tingled at the memory fresh in her mind. The supply closet. The kiss. Willoughby's abrupt departure after.

Clara's blood ran cold.

She straightened her curved spine and brushed off invisible lint from her trousers before dismounting. Her riding boots hit the cobblestone with so much force, she kicked up loose stones at Willoughby's shiny boots. *Good,* she thought. *I hope the leather is scratched.*

A slight guilt tugged at Clara's chest; one she struggled to tamp down to no avail. She shouldn't be quite that awful. Willoughby was helping her, after all. For the right price, and yet, he was risking his neck to get her the information she required, and she was behaving like a proper brat. It was best to let the past lie and focus on the current predicament. Besides, she doubted Willoughby had an endless supply of loafers, no point ruining the man's only good pair of shoes.

Clara's gaze slid over the thief's body. Tonight, Willoughby was clad in black from head to toe. He had the same overcoat Clara saw him put on in the jailhouse, but beneath it was a silk button up that was dangerously unbuttoned. Clara averted her eyes from the glisten of his olive-toned skin. Her attention caught a gold chain with a simple silver ring dangling from it. As unceremoniously as she could manage, she worked to read the inscription burned into the metal, but it was too dark, and Clara's vision was too distracted by Willoughby's exposed skin.

"You'll have to pay me more if you wish to undress me with your eyes, Aldridge."

Clara's cheeks set aflame. She cleared her throat, suddenly full and bone dry, and stifled embarrassment as she looked everywhere but at Willoughby. A cold sweat pooled at the base of her back. She cursed the thick fabric of her riding jacket in her head.

"Lighten up, Aldridge," Willoughby said. "I'm only teasing."

Someone shouted down the street and Clara's knees knocked. *Get a hold of yourself.* Clara pictured Elisea's face in her mind until it was clear enough she could have sworn the woman was standing before her. She needed to keep her wits about her if she was to speak to Willoughby about what he discovered and make it back in time before the staff noticed her gone. Didn't Sergei mention dropping by in the morning to check on her? All the more reason to hurry the night along.

Clara unbuttoned the collar of her jacket, then closed it

again. "I have no time nor patience for comedy," she said defiantly. "Tell me everything you have, and we can both be on our way."

"Life's too short to have a personality," Willoughby said, smirking. "Got it. As for what I saw while I was snooping on your housekeeper, you might not like my answer."

"Why in the gems not?"

Willoughby winced. "Are you absolutely certain that you want to know? Because there's no hiding your head in the sand after this."

"Out with it, Will. Quit messing about."

The thief's nostrils flared. A vein throbbed in his forehead as if he was preparing for an attack. Clara had no idea what could have such a strong effect on a man that was otherwise unaffected. Whatever Willoughby uncovered in the house had him nervous. Her own nerves spiked.

"She isn't innocent," Willoughby finally announced.

The world spun around Clara, and she had to use the stirrups hanging off the mare's saddle to steady herself. What did he mean 'not innocent'? Elisea did not kill her husband. There was no world in which that was possible, but then why was he so convinced?

Clara wiggled her nose, pointing it at the moon. "What did you see?"

"At first, not much," Willoughby admitted. "I went through the house as you instructed, left nothing unturned. It appeared like any other home in this area."

He paused, likely wishing he used different words. There was no way he would know what the inside of a middles house looked like unless he'd broken into one before. Or was invited, which Clara doubted was the case. She motioned for him to continue.

"Anyway, I was about to leave, but I remembered what you

said about the housekeeper, that she was a calm and collected woman that wouldn't make a snap decision. Someone who plans."

Clara's forehead wrinkled. "What does that have to do with anything?"

"People who plan often keep journals. Lists, ideas. Especially women and especially those that wish their husband dead."

"For the last time, Elisea did not—"

Clara's words fell away as Willoughby produced a book from inside his coat. She inspected the worn leather diary in front of her with awe and fascination. Head tilting from side to side, she reached out, her hand slightly shaky. When Willoughby placed the diary in her grasp, the first thing she noticed was how soft it felt. Butter against her skin. The leather had been handled regularly and used often enough to wear the grain out. Whoever owned this diary, they wrote in it daily. The next thing Clara saw were the gold stamped initials in the front.

E.H.

"Elisea Hawke," she whispered.

Willoughby inclined his rugged chin. "Turn to the last page." When she did as he asked, his finger tapped a line in the entry. "Read that."

"If this continues, I will surely see one of us dead."

Clara gasped. Her eyes skimmed the rest of the entry before focusing on the date at the top of the page. "This was written the day Thomas was killed," she said.

"It seems your housekeeper made good on her promise."

Paying him no mind, Clara perused the rest. She read almost every word, her heart galloping in her chest on the parts that detailed Thomas's abuse of Elisea. She couldn't believe the woman had put up with it for as many years. The verbal abuse alone was enough to make Clara's skin crawl, but it appeared Thomas was quite the drunk and a violent one at that. For all intents and purposes, it was easy to see why someone in her position would want to erase the devil that caused her such pain. But Clara could not believe it.

She shook her head, wiping the words from her vision.

"This is not enough to prove a thing," she said. "What else did you find out?"

The blood left Willoughby's face. "Did you not see what she wrote? How can you possibly believe her innocent after that?"

"Because I know her," Clara replied. "It may be hard for you to understand, but some people stick by those they care for. No matter what happens. Especially when they know the truth."

"And you think the truth is the exact opposite of what the evidence points to?"

Clara scoffed. "I see no evidence here. Only the words of an abused, tired woman who deserved better from this life. If this is all you brought me, then I don't think you upheld your part of the bargain."

"I broke into the damn house!"

"But you did not give me anything to save my friend!"

Clara's jaw clenched. Heat flushed up her neck, and she ground her teeth to keep her rage from spilling. This was not what they agreed on. Willoughby must see it. She curled her upper lip. "Was there anything else in the house that might imply Thomas had enemies other than his wife?"

A strange emotion flashed across Willoughby's features. Though she couldn't quite place it, Clara knew a liar when she saw one having spent her life around politicians. The thief was hiding something.

"Spill it," she insisted.

"It's nothing of the sort you're imagining," Willoughby

said. He waved his hand, but that odd expression was still plastered on his face. "I found a ledger in Thomas's study."

Clara's stomach churned. "What type of ledger?"

"I'm not entirely sure. Sales, perhaps. It was written in shorthand and coded to avoid detection."

"Interesting. Why would Thomas go to such trouble to keep the information in the ledger secret?" A twinkle gleamed in her eyes. "Unless what he kept note of wasn't legal. Please tell me you took it."

Before she could even finish speaking, a thick paper pad dangled in front of her face. She tried to snatch it from Willoughby's hold, but the speedy bastard was too smooth. His arm jerked back, taking the ledger with him.

Clara huffed out a breath. "Fine. Tell me you can decipher what it says, at least."

"I can," Willoughby answered. "For a price."

There was a good chance Clara would end the man before the night was done. Reluctantly, she agreed to raising her original offer, but only if Willoughby promised not to keep anything from her again. She didn't know how much good a thief's word was worth, but it was the best she had to work with. Which was why when Willoughby reached out a hand, she took it, giving it a steady shake to seal the deal.

"If you're going to go down this route, you should speak to Thomas's employer." Willoughby raked his fingers through the wild curls of his hair. "A Mr. Cooke, I believe. One of your people. High in the uppers with more money than most can dream of. Thomas was his gardener."

Clara's body stopped moving. The sway she had before was gone, replaced by a stillness so heavy that she wasn't sure her heart was even beating anymore. It wasn't until she felt it rushing in her veins, heard the stream of it in her ears, that she realized she was still breathing.

Gaze locking on Willoughby, she blinked away her wayward thoughts. "Did you say Cooke?"

She didn't need to hear Willoughby agree to know her next move. The night had suddenly gotten lighter, the pressure between Clara's temples lessening. There was only one person who shared that surname in the uppers, and she happened to be Clara's very best friend.

CHAPTER EIGHT

When she was young, Clara played a game that she learned from her mother. The rules were quite simple, and if one knew how to read their opponents; it was easy enough to win. At the start of each visit to whatever nursery tea her parents arranged, Clara and the other children sat in a circle, their hands clasped together tightly. All you needed to do was say three things about yourself—one of which had to be a lie. Once you stated your facts, the others took turns guessing the untruths, and if you were found out, you lost. Every person had one turn; you had to make it count. Clara won every time. Never Have I Ever was by far her favorite way to pass the afternoons.

If she were to play the game now, she'd surely beat herself out of a turn. *Never have I ever brought a thief to afternoon tea.* Her brows creased as she drudged up the roundabout leading to the Cooke Manor. The house her best friend resided in with her husband was the exact opposite of Aldridge House. Where Clara's family home was dark and full of shadow, the Cookes lived in golden rays of sun. Everything Clara's eyes landed on

had a shimmer to it. Even the brick was whitewashed to remove the deep shades of red that covered the rest of Hedge End architecture. Clara recalled the first time she visited and the way her jaw dragged on the ground upon approaching. It wasn't that the house was an eyesore, simply that it didn't quite fit with the gloom that settled into the bones of their city.

Clara hiked up the lower edges of her navy skirt, a welcome change from last night's outfit, and marched ahead. Behind her, Willoughby continued to make obnoxious remarks about every detail of the home and its surroundings. If it wasn't the gilded gates, it was the bridge crossing the pond. If not the fountain in front of the manor, then it was the marble sculpture in its center. Everything carried some form of contempt for the thief and Clara was beginning to wonder if Willoughby was simply a properly miserable individual.

"Is that knocker made of pure gold?" he groaned.

Clara stifled the urge to smack his pompous head. There was no gemmed way that she would let Willoughby ruin her only chance of getting to the truth. Instead of replying, Clara wrapped her fingers around said knocker and banged it three times over.

The sound made Willoughby flinch.

She smiled, satisfied, and waited for someone to greet them. They did not have to wait long. Before Clara could lower her hand, the massive front door swung open fast enough to make them rear back. A short, stout man in a gray suit stood in the doorway, his thick mustache tickling the top of his hooked nose. The man's drooped eyelids rose as he took in Clara.

"Miss Aldridge," Persimmon, the butler of the house, remarked. "Welcome. We weren't expecting you today."

"Good day, Persimmon. It's a rather unexpected visit on my end as well. I hope Violet won't mind too terribly."

The butler's eyes softened as he opened the door wider and

stepping aside. "You are always welcome here," he said. His gaze flicked to Willoughby, a shadow crossing his beady eyes.

"This is an old family friend," Clara explained quickly.

"Of course. Right this way."

Persimmon led them through the entrance foyer of the manor and down a wide hallway, looping through the right side of the home. Much like in Aldridge House, framed portraits lined the pink wallpaper of the residence, though these images did not stir an ache within Clara she could not contain. She studied the faces as they passed, all holding a resemblance to her best friend's husband. The same tanned skin and dark hair. An unwavering air of arrogance in all their pale brown eyes. There were a few paintings of Violet's family as well, but those were far in between. Being orphaned was one thing Clara and her best friend had in common.

Violet's parents weren't departed, of course, but you wouldn't know it if you spoke with her. The energetic woman cut all ties with the horrid clan the second she married. "Good riddance," Violet said time and time again.

As they marched down the hallway, Clara could feel Willoughby's overwhelming presence against her back. His breaths were deep and heavy and hung low to the ground in a way that made her hurry her step. She wondered if he was thinking of his own family in that very instant—of the hole their absence left behind.

Another orphan.

Clara dared to steal a glance at the thief. He didn't appear to be out of sorts, though you never knew with Willoughby. He wore the mask he carefully crafted perfectly, and Clara knew that if he felt anything at all, she'd be the last to know it.

Finally, Persimmon stopped gliding across the polished floors and opened another door to a vast seating area. There were four settees arranged to face each other in the center of the room, a fireplace on one wall, a larger-than-life window on another, and a second gallery of family portraits to the left. The wallpaper in this room possessed no floral depictions. Violet opted for a bizarre pattern of feathers and twigs instead. A neutral selection, as she called it. Clara tried not to laugh at her friend's definition of the word. There was absolutely nothing neutral about Violet Cooke or her lavish house.

As Persimmon spun around and left them to wait for the madam of the home, a moan drew Clara's attention. She turned, the lace of her corseted dress itching her skin. When she saw Willoughby sprawled across a settee with his filthy boots kicked up on a glass side table, she nearly fainted.

"Collect yourself immediately," she scolded. "I will not be embarrassed by you."

Willoughby's one brow rose. He jerked his thumb to a bronze sculpture of a horse in water occupying the better half of the room's corner. "I don't think I'm the humiliation in the room."

"So help me, Will, if you as much as—"

The swinging of the door cut Clara off. A loud yelp sliced through the air and her mouth dried. She narrowed her eyes on Willoughby, motioning to his feet before turning around. Her best friend filled the double doors of the sitting room from edge to edge with the most extravagant gown Clara had ever seen. Layers of silk and chiffon in alternating shades of pink dusted the floor; a pair of sparkly gold heels peeking out from under them. The top of Violet's skirt was adorned with crystals, and Clara's eyes watered from the reflection they cast around the room. As per her usual style, Violet's breasts were pushed up high to the point of her chin nearly touching them. Her pale golden hair hung in waterfall waves down her back, and she trained two light brown eyes on Clara.

"Well, look at what the beasts dragged in," Violet said with a smirk. "What brings you by today? Gossip, I hope. It had been dreadfully tedious with Lawrence gone on business."

Clara tried not to dwell on the fact that her friend's husband was gone more than he was present. She wondered how much business a watchmaker could have to keep him away for such long periods of time. Her eyes flicked to the obnoxiously large painting of Lawrence hanging above the mantel. Lawrence Cooke looked the picture of wealth in the painting. He wore a blue silk blazer embroidered in gold that parted at the neckline to reveal a white-ruffled shirt. Above the ruffles, the slightest shade of a beard accentuated a jawline shark and hard as rock. Lawrence's hair was slicked into tight curls and parted down the center with what appeared to be a ruler judging by the straightness of the line. His wideset eyes seemed to watch Clara like he was in the room. She shuddered.

A disinterested groan dragged Clara's attention to the wreck of a man perching on the settee behind her. She bit her tongue, pointing to Willoughby. "That's Willoughby Tanner," she said. "A family friend."

"Oh, how wonderful! You brought a plaything."

"What in the—"

Clara stepped around Willoughby before he could finish speaking. Her shoulders slumped. In front of her, Violet wiggled her brows playfully, making inappropriate motions with her hands at Willoughby. This was going to be a long day. Not entertaining either of them, Clara briefly questioned her choice of company, then focused on why she was visiting her friend in the first place.

"I'm afraid we're not here on a social call. Something has happened. Something terrible."

Panic colored her friend's face in shades of gray. Her high cheekbones sharpened as she took in a breath, her gloved hand pressing to her lips. A gasp broke free between her fingers. "Is it Oswin?"

"No, thank the gems," Clara said. "Elisea's husband was killed, and they think she did it."

"To interject, they might be correct."

She shot daggers at Willoughby over her shoulder. The thief didn't seem to be affected by her death glare and simply said, "What? It's the truth."

"It certainly is not."

"I would have to agree," Violet said. She sidestepped Clara and sauntered toward Willoughby, her skirt trailing the shiny marble floor. "Elisea is an amazing woman. She basically raised Clara, and I doubt the mayor would allow someone capable of murder to be in such proximity to his only niece. Why do they think she's responsible?"

Arching his spine, Willoughby smirked at Clara. "Go ahead. Tell her."

"It's possible they found her next to Thomas's body," Clara said, cringing. "Covered in his blood. In my garden."

Violet made no sound. Her fingers wrapped over the fabric of her skirt, and she hiked it up higher, stomping away from them and toward the doors. Her heels clicked against the marble flooring and the sound made every hair on Clara's arms stand at attention. When she reached the door, Violet poked her head into the hallway, her gold-spun hair spilling over her shoulders.

"Persimmon!" she shouted. "We're going to need drinks stronger than tea!"

As she turned back to them, Willoughby nodded curtly. "I like her."

Clara's hands fisted at her side and her jaw worked itself out. There was no time for tea, or whatever else Violet had planned, and there certainly wasn't any time for niceties. She pulled out her pocket watch from her purse, glanced at it. Oswin could be back at any moment, and she didn't want him catching her hanging around Willoughby Tanner. After the thief's father was caught stealing from the city's funds, her uncle was clear that she was to cut all ties with the ruined family. Which was quite easy to do since Willoughby left her in the dust, regardless.

Out of the corner of her eye, she spotted him admiring a small gold trinket on the side table, wanting to steal it, no doubt. Like father, like son.

Clara stomped over and snatched the piece from the table, keeping eye contact with Willoughby as she held it tight. "Violet. I was hoping to ask for your help."

"Of course!" her friend exclaimed. "Anything you need. What can I do?"

"This will sound absurd, but I recently discovered that Elisea's husband was your gardener," Clara said. She kept her eyes locked on her friend, ignoring Willoughby entirely. "Can you think of anyone that might have wanted to harm him? I know it's a big ask and you likely have many people on staff, but I am desperate. Anything you can recall would be brilliant aid."

Her friend's smile dropped.

"I'm sorry, darling," Violet said. "But Lawrence let our previous gardener go months ago."

"He fired him?" Willoughby asked.

Violet nodded. She folded her arms over her chest, and it pushed up the large domes even more. Clara pretended not to see Willoughby's eyes flash to the bare skin of her friend's bosom. Her chest tightened as she asked, "Why was he let go?"

"You'd have to ask Lawrence that," Violet said. Then, under her breath, added, "If you can catch him at home."

"He didn't consult with you before doing it?" Willoughby asked.

Clara and Violet exchanged twin looks of amusement. If there was any question about Willoughby's position in the city, it was clear as day now that he did not belong in the upper streets. Things were different for people in the women's position. When you married for anything other than love, as Violet had without shame, you did not get a say in your husband's business dealings. Violet's lifestyle may not have been one Clara wished for, but the woman was perfectly fine with not having to worry about serious matters. Clara knew only a little of Violet's past, but from what her friend shared, she'd have given up a lot more than domestic power to be free of her family's clutches.

Lawrence Cooke provided her with a comfort Violet had wished for—a life which required little worry.

Dropping her eyes, Violet shook out her long hair, the tresses shiny under the rays of sunshine streaming through the window. "I am not my husband's keeper," she said. "And he isn't mine. Things are different for us here. A wife is not often privy to her husband's affairs, nor does she wish to be."

"And that suits you fine?" Willoughby asked.

"It suits me exactly."

Violet's neck lengthened as she turned to look toward the hallway again. She held up a finger, grinning toothily. "I'll go see what's holding up the drinks."

With her friend vanishing into the labyrinth of the Cooke estate, Clara walked to the window to look down at the garden below. They were well cared for; she assumed that Thomas was replaced briskly to fill the position he left. A nagging feeling scratched at the back of her mind that Clara couldn't put her finger on. Why did Lawrence fire Thomas? And why not tell Violet about it? No matter what her friend told them moments ago, she was certain her husband would share the reasons behind letting a staff member go. After all, they both occupied the manor, and Violet would be privy to what happened within these walls. If not for any other reason than to avoid startling her when a new person showed up for the job.

Behind her, Willoughby made off-hand comments about them wasting their time and Clara filed her questions away for later dissection. Eyes rounding, she rolled her shoulders, her gaze watching the flower beds outside. While Violet was right and wives behaved differently here in the uppers, the same could not be said for everyone else in Hedge End. If Thomas lost his position, Elisea knew about it.

"Do I want to know what you're plotting?" Willoughby asked.

The words inside Clara vanished. She knew that he could not help her with what she planned to do next no matter how she wished for the company of another soul. Clara had to go directly to the source, and she dreaded every second of it.

CHAPTER NINE

The lower levels of the jailhouse were exactly as Clara imagined. Wet, cold, and dreadful. She walked at a fast clip to keep up with the guard leading her down the stone steps, her entire body on alert. On either side of her, large impeding brick made it impossible for Clara to breathe. The walls seemed to be closing in on her with each step. It may have been her imagination, but Clara had the notion that the jail was designed to make one feel trapped, which was exactly what Clara felt she was now.

Ahead of her, the guard did not appear to be bothered, having been used to the place by now. They reached the lowest landing, and he took a sharp right toward an even more claustrophobic corridor. Here, the walls were slick with beading water that dripped from an invisible leak somewhere in the ceiling. The sound of it hitting the ground made Clara's skin crawl. Drip. Drip. Drip. A torturous soundtrack playing on repeat in the depths of her brain. Clara ran a fingertip along the wall, the droplets rolling down her palm. They were colder than ice against her sizzling skin.

They passed two empty cells, Clara's posture slumping in relief. She did not wish to see anything that might haunt her for the remainder of her life. Before coming here, Willoughby had warned her about what happens in the cells, the gem torture often used to punish criminals. Not that it was news to Clara, who had heard the stories from her uncle a long time ago. Still, it was one thing to know a thing and quite another to see it up close.

Now that she was down here, Clara wished for neither.

The guard turned on his heels in front of a narrow door that reminded Clara of the wine cellar at home. It was made of thick, impenetrable iron with only one slit at eye level to peer inside and three large latches holding it shut. She tried not to stare at the bones protruding from the guard's shoulders, two wings growing from too much magic use. It was strange to her to see the results of affected gems on the human body. No matter how many people walked the streets with beastly features, Clara held in a gasp like it was her first time seeing them. Which was what she did when the guard's teeth split to reveal a mouth blackened to the color of ink. His lips stretched, slits slicing across the flesh of his cheeks as his jaw opened wider than was humanly possible.

"Are you sure about this, Miss?" he asked.

Clara nodded. "Take me to her. I wish to say my goodbyes."

That was the story she came up with to get inside the cells without raising suspicions. The mayor's niece stepping foot in the jailhouse twice in one week was already strange enough. It would be doubly odd for someone to report seeing her in the jail cells. After all, she had no business to be here. She certainly had no business visiting a convicted murderer who was on death's toll. But to play on the guard's emotions and to tell him that she wanted nothing more than to express her sorrowful goodbyes to the woman she felt utterly betrayed by... Now that was a story he would agree with.

The guard's horrifying mouth closed into a tight, thin line. A massive improvement, as far as Clara was concerned. He reached for his belt, unlocking a ring of keys from it. One by one, the guard worked a key into the latches on the door and swung it open.

Pity coated his featured when he glanced at Clara over his shoulder. "It's the third cell on the left," he said. "Five minutes is all I can promise you. We don't usually allow death toll prisoners to have visitations."

"I understand," Clara said, slipping past him. "I'll be quick. Thank you."

With a little bow of appreciation, she turned her back to the guard and walked further into the darkness of the jail. On either side of her, barred doors lined the walls, each one gloomier than its predecessor. The first one Clara passed appeared to be empty, but a pained moan made her jump, startled. Reaching through the bars, a man hung his dilapidated arms and made crude remarks as Clara passed by. She noted the stench coming off him was quite like Willoughby's upon his release, a sure sign the prisoner had been here a while.

The space between Clara's brows wrinkled. She counted the doors, her heartbeat slowing when she reached the cell holding Elisea.

Rubbing the nape of her neck, Clara stepped up to the bars, her hands reaching for them in short, jerky movements. She wrapped her fingers over the cold metal. Nose brushing against the bars, Clara whispered, "Elisea? Are you there?"

What a daft question. Of course she was there. Where else would she have gone to?

Clara scolded herself mentally.

"Clara?" a hoarse voice drifted from inside the cell.

There was a flash of movement and a heavy sigh as Elisea inched closer to the door. The little light there was down here illuminated parts of her skin and bile clawed up Clara's throat at the sight of her friend. Tremors jolted her body, her legs weakening. This was not the Elisea she knew. The woman before her was at least ten pounds lighter and had the harried, wild appearance of someone who had been lost for years. Elisea's hair, usually in sleek updo's, hung around her ashen face in oily clumps. Her cheekbones were sharper than before and any flush to her skin was long gone.

Clara checked the woman for signs of injury and was relieved to find none. At least Elisea hadn't suffered at the hands of the guards' magic.

Her face pressed into the crack of the cell. "I'm glad to see you," Clara said. She blinked away the tears welling in her eyes, her breaths coming out in rasps. "I don't have much time, but I didn't want you to think I abandoned you."

"You would be wise to do so," Elisea said.

"Never. I know you're innocent and I will prove it." She looked over her shoulder and lowered her voice. "Elisea, please. Can you think of anyone who might want to hurt Thomas?"

The woman's lips drooped. "Leave it alone, sweet girl. Do not go to all this trouble on my account. The guards have made their mind up already. They will not let me go."

"They will!" Clara cried out. "I know they will. I only need to present a case they can't refute."

"And how do you plan to do that?" Elisea asked. "My Thomas may have been a brute, but he wasn't foolish. Whatever enemies he had; he took his secrets to the grave."

The room closed in on Clara. She fought through the racing pace of her pulse and the gnawing ache in her chest. At the first doorway, she heard the latches come undone as the guard readied to call her back. Clara needed to speed things up. Immediately.

She locked eyes with Elisea. "Why did you stay with him?" she asked, a quiver in her voice.

"Perhaps I was the foolish one," the housekeeper answered. "After a certain time, I didn't know anything else but Thomas. I'm sorry you had to find him in such a state. If I regret anything, it's that."

"Are you certain you don't know who wanted your husband dead? A name, a passing comment," Clara pressed. "A sound you may have thought was strange." She paused as she recalled the ledger. "Thomas kept a sales ledger written in code. Do you know anything about it?"

"How did you find it?"

Clara bit her bottom lip, saying, "I hired someone to look through your home. You can scold me for it when you're free. Now about the ledger."

Boots hit the ground not far from the cell, making Clara jump. She looked from Elisea to the dimly lit corridor. The guard would be here any moment. Clara was running out of time.

"Please, try to remember," she told the housekeeper.

"The markets," Elisea replied. "I don't know much, but Thomas had dealings in the markets. He didn't speak to me about them because I wouldn't approve and...well, my opinion held little value. But if sales are involved, I'd bet it would be there."

Clara was about to speak when the housekeeper added, "I must warn you, my girl. Whatever Thomas did, it was not legal."

"I gathered as much," Clara said. The steps echoing down the corridor became louder, closer. "I must go. Don't say a word to anyone until I come for you. I will come for you, Elisea. I promise."

Closing her hands over the housekeeper's, she gave them a light squeeze before twisting away and making the brisk walk down the corridor. On her way out, she passed the guard, thanking him quickly. Clara's boots stomped on the stairs as she bolted upward. Her lungs were paper thin, the shock of seeing Elisea crashing around her. The edge of a step caught her heel, and she fell forward. Her arms shot out to break her fall. She slammed them into the stone, nearly breaking her teeth on the hard surface. Clara worked to breathe. She scrambled to stand upright, shook off her rising panic, and kept going.

When she reached the top and pushed through the door leading out of the cells and to the main floor of the jailhouse, her eyes refused to focus. Vision spotting, she slammed into a hard surface with a yelp.

"Clara?"

She knew that voice. Clara rubbed her battered forehead from where it met her uncle's chest. She looked up at Oswin in surprise. "Uncle? What are you doing here?"

"I could ask you the same question. This is the last place I'd expect to run into my one and only niece."

The look of concern on Oswin's face did not escape Clara. She struggled to think of a lie that would convince him he had nothing to worry about but came up short. There was no real point in it anyhow. Even if she did find a way to slither out of the situation, the truth would return to haunt her somehow. The guard who let her into the cells could slip his tongue. Someone Oswin knows may have recognized her in the lobby. She could develop a sudden and urgent condition that made her speak the truth in her sleep outside of her own awareness. The possibilities were endless.

There was also the matter of Clara hating being deceitful with family. That reason took the cake above all others.

She tucked a curl under her top hat and peered up at Oswin. "I came to see Elisea."

"Clara…"

"Uncle…"

The two stared at each other like goats on a narrow bridge. Neither wanted to back away. Finally, Clara averted her gaze, breaking eye contact for a brief moment. She looked back, a warmth in her smile. "You must have known I'd come here," she said. "The woman basically raised me."

"I understand why you did it, my darling girl, but you cannot be here."

"What are you going to do to clear her name?"

Oswin fumbled with the gold buttons on his burgundy tailcoat. A tremble in his hand shook his fingers and he let go of the dreaded buttons, letting his sleeves fall. He rubbed his chin, the stubble of his beard making his fingertips vanish in a sea of gray. When Oswin didn't reply, the truth dawned on Clara.

Her teeth split. "You're not serious."

"I cannot help acquit a killer," Oswin snapped. "I am the mayor."

"But she is family!"

His eyes crinkled at the edges. "A man was found dead by her hand, Clara," her uncle warned. "There is nothing I can do. I must abide by the laws of this city, you know that. It is my duty, our duty, to lead the citizens by setting the right example."

"And what example will you set when you let an innocent woman die for a crime she didn't commit?"

Rough fingers wrapped around her wrist as Oswin led her away from prying eyes and into a corner of the jailhouse lobby unoccupied by guards. He ducked his head under the banister of a mahogany staircase, inclining closer to Clara, who huddled in the corner, fuming. Above them, the stairs creaked beneath the weight of guards passing. Clara's heartbeat matched the uneven sounds.

"Believe me when I tell you that it pains me to be in this terrible predicament," Oswin said, his voice hushed. "But my hands are tied. No matter what I believe, there is no evidence to prove Mrs. Hawke's innocence. I cannot intervene."

No evidence yet, Clara thought.

"You must promise me you will not return here," her uncle warned.

"But I—"

Those fingers clutched her arms once more. Tighter this time. "Promise me, Clara," he warned. "You are to occupy the mayoral seat soon. You cannot be seen with a convicted felon."

Clara winced. The reaction made her uncle retract his grip, take a step back. He looked at her, his red-rimmed eyes pleading. "Promise me."

"A-all right," Clara stuttered.

As her uncle patted her on the shoulder and extended his arm, Clara's mind reeled. She placed her hand in the crook of his elbow, her back rigid. Gaze downcast, Clara allowed him to escort her out, away from the jailhouse and into the cold clutches of the city where a carriage waited to take them home. The horses neighed, and the wheels bumped across the cobblestone road beneath them. Clara's attention stayed glued to the flashes of Hedge End outside the window. In all the commotion, she didn't even get to ask Oswin about what he was doing in the jailhouse.

It didn't matter, though, did it? There was a very important fact Clara gleamed from the encounter, and it had nothing to do with her uncle's itinerary.

If Clara was to save Elisea's life, she had to do it discreetly.

CHAPTER TEN

Willoughby watched the mayor's niece climb into the carriage, his chest heaving. The look on Clara's face was not that of a woman who received good news. If Willoughby was a betting man—which he was when the coin called for it—he would have guessed she didn't get much out of her interrogation.

Or conversation. Willoughby had to keep reminding himself that the housekeeper may not have been guilty of the crime. It was a far stretch, but he promised Clara he'd keep an open mind and her persistence on the matter made him question his original opinion.

Though, judging by Clara's forlorn expression, perhaps he was correct all along.

His hands fondled the leather strap on Thomas's ledger as he reclined against the wall of the bookshop across the street from the jailhouse. An overhead bell rang out, a customer exiting the shop with several hefty tomes tucked under his arm. Willoughby inspected the texts. *Echoes of the Past. From Settlement to Society. A Lesson in Magic.* His eyes rolled

skyward. Considering the price the man must have paid for those books you'd think he'd leave with information more interesting than the history of the Cursed Isle. Unless, of course, the man knew someone affected. Most of those touched by the gem's magic ended up on the dreaded isle north of the city one way or another. Either by choice or by force. Willoughby couldn't imagine living there with the affected.

A carriage rolled over a puddle in a dip in the road and splashed his trousers with mud and debris. Willoughby shook his fist at the departing wagon, his brow furrowed. Sometimes, the city made the Cursed Isle appear nearly favorable.

"Blasted hooligans," Willoughby muttered as he pushed away from the wall. He glanced to either side, skipping over the damn puddle that ruined his last pair of clean pants to cross the street. Passing by the main entrance to the jailhouse, he skirted around the building and down a side street that smelled of ale and urine. In the distance, a bronze sign hung over an arched wooden door, swaying in the breeze coming in from the river.

Willoughby paused. He reached into his coat pocket and pulled out his watch. "He best not be late," Willoughby said to no one in particular.

With a shove, he barreled through the door and into the greasy establishment. The interior of the Oily Spoon was only slightly more welcoming than the dirty street outside. The pub reeked of bodies and cheap drinks, both of which were the guts the place was built on. Above his head, a domed ceiling sat low to the ground and Willoughby had to duck several times to avoid the ill-placed lanterns that hung from its beams. Round tables with sticky tops filled the small space, a few of which were already occupied despite the early morning hour. He brushed past a billiard table with one leg shorter than the rest and made his way to the long bar at the furthest end of the room.

His blood ran cold at the sight of the uniformed guard sitting on a tall barstool.

With hesitation, Willoughby cleared the last few steps between them, slid onto the empty stool beside the guard, and dropped his elbows on the bar top. Tucked into his belt, the ledger pressed against his abdomen and made Willoughby slightly nauseous. He side glanced the angular built of the bones poking out of the guard's shoulders. Two Cursbeast shoulder joints ready to sprout wings. His skin crawled. In the hidden pocket of his coat, the gems he held weighed him down. Willoughby averted his thoughts from them, refusing to give the stones any purchase.

He tapped two fingers on the bar top to get the bartender's attention. Beside him, the guard bristled, pushing a nearly empty glass of whisky forward. As the bartender approached, Willoughby dropped three coins on the table and motioned for the guard's cup.

Then he twisted in the chair to face the man.

"What did she find out?" Willoughby asked.

The guard waited until the bartender filled his glass. He downed it in one go, the liquid sloshing down his throat like the flush of a toilet. If Willoughby wished for a drink before, he was clear of the need now. When he was certain the guard was finished, he tapped the table again. The glass was refilled, the whisky vanishing into the guard's gullet.

Without pause, the guard said, "I could lose my job talking to you."

Willoughby was grateful that the man, half man half beast now, kept his gaze on the bottle-lined shelves of the bar instead of on him. The deep slits running from the edges of his lips all the way to the middle of his cheeks creeped Willoughby out, and he knew that if he were to face him, he wouldn't be able to look anywhere but on the beastly deformities evident on his face. Following the guard's lead, he twisted in his seat and gaped straight ahead.

"Couldn't lose it from drinking before breakfast, then?"

The guard winced. Licked his lips with a tongue in the shade of the night sky. "I had to clear her out before she got anything substantial," he said. "The mayor made an unexpected appearance."

"Did she find out any information about the dead husband?"

"Not anything of note," the guard said. "The housekeeper stays firm that she didn't kill him, and your lady is falling for her lies."

Willoughby stretched his fingers wide, the callouses on his palm rubbing against the stone tabletop. "Not my lady," he corrected. "I promised Clara Aldridge my help, nothing more."

"How does the likes of you know a woman of her caliber, anyway?"

A tick pulled on Willoughby's left eye. "I don't recall paying you for a public roast. What did the housekeeper tell Clara about Thomas Hawke?"

"Not a whole lot, to be frank. They mostly wept, but there was no real information traded. At least not anything we didn't already know."

"Such as?"

The guard shifted his weight, his partial wings moving slowly with ear-piercing squeaks. Willoughby grimaced. His chest rose and fell with quick breaths. Then it was true that the guards were looking into Thomas's life after all. A part of him was relieved to know that the mayor's lackeys did not completely abuse the legal system, though he doubted they were putting in much effort to clear the wife's name. Their so-called talents were better used at torturing poor folk than on actual detective work.

He leaned across the bar, snatching a pickled pear slice from a nearby plate and popping it into his mouth. The bartender, a man with shiny blond hair and eyes pale and resembling glowing orbs, frowned but said nothing. Willoughby grabbed another slice while he was ahead.

"Beast got your tongue?" Willoughby asked, immediately regretting his choice of words.

The guard didn't seem to notice, saying, "The husband was running some shady sales in the markets. The housekeeper told your la—" he stopped himself "—Miss Aldridge as much. That was all they spoke of."

"What type of sales?"

"Not gems," the guard replied. "That's all we know."

Willoughby's palm brushed against the ledger hidden beneath the folds of his coat on instinct. He tried to swallow, but his throat was drier than the deserts of far-away lands he read about in travel books. The muscles of his hand quivered and twitched and he dropped it away from the ledger, letting his arm fall to the side like a limp appendage. Willoughby knew Clara too well not to be worried. If she had even a hunch that Thomas may have earned enemies at the markets, her next move would be to investigate further. The woman was relentless and one of these days, her curiosity would get the better of her. What was it they said about cats? Willoughby couldn't recall.

That wasn't what troubled him, though.

The problem wasn't what Clara could uncover about Thomas Hawke; it was what she could find out about him. It was in his best interests to keep the mayor's niece away from the markets, or to steer her in a direction that didn't lead back to him and his role in the gem sales the mayor was attempting to squash.

There was only one way he could do that.

Willoughby reached across the bar again, this time grabbing for a napkin. He pulled out a gold nibbled fountain pen, licked the tip, and jotted a quick note. Using the wax from a burning candle, he sealed the makeshift letter and slid it to the guard. "Deliver this to Miss Aldridge and consider our deal completed," he said. He tossed a pouch of coins which the man caught greedily. "If I find out you broke the seal, the chief will hear of every interaction we've shared."

With that, he stood up and walked out of the bar, his entire life hanging in the balance.

CHAPTER ELEVEN

The turrets of Aldridge House blocked out the midday sun with their obnoxious heights. Willoughby watched the front gates from the shadows of a weeping willow, his entire body on alert. The urge to flee had him sharpened to a fine blade. And yet Willoughby could not budge from his spot, not until Clara came out. If the blasted guard he paid off delivered the letter, that is.

An ancient pocket watch swung back and forth on Willoughby's finger, the only thing of his father's he had left. The reminder made his chest ache, but he wouldn't dare to rid himself of the watch's heavy burden. As far as Willoughby was concerned, he didn't deserve to lessen the guilt that ate away at him. Not ever.

He looked at the time as the watch swayed past him. The dreadful woman was late.

Right as he was ready to depart, the gates creaked. The sound echoed through the wide driveway of the mansion and made the leaves hiding Willoughby shiver. His gaze narrowed on Clara's burgundy dress, on the blunt curve at her rear as she

squeezed herself between the iron before closing it shut behind her. Suddenly, the leather of his pants felt impossibly tight. A second body appeared beside her, and he froze in his hiding place between the trees. A stocky man towered over Clara, his heavy footsteps shaking the ground beneath them as he stalked behind her. A thick, angry scar cut across one of his cheeks and reached all the way down to the man's glass-cut jaw. Willoughby recognized him instantly.

Sergei Pollen.

The man carried himself like a soldier: spine rigid, head unbowed, every movement measured. Even standing still, he seemed strung tightly. His mere presence unnerved Willoughby beyond words and yet Clara seemed unbothered by the irksome man.

"Are you certain you will be all right on your own?" Sergei asked. His voice echoed through the trees in a deep throttle.

"I will make do," Clara replied coyly. "If it makes you feel better, you can tell Uncle you never left my side. Lest he make you disappear for the offense of not watching my every move."

Sergei's brows lifted a fraction, though his scar made the gesture seem more menacing than amused. A low chuckle rumbled from his chest, but the sound was as sharp as the edge of a blade. "While I know you are teasing, I fear I don't enjoy the implication. If anyone has the mind to end me and can, it is your uncle."

"I'd like to see him try," Clara said. "I'm sure you can take on an old man. Now me on the other hand..."

She raised her fist playfully.

At Clara's teasing threat, Sergei lifted his hands up in mock surrender. The smile spread on his face. "Point received. Enjoy your walk, Miss Aldridge. Stay out of trouble."

And then, almost as an afterthought, he leaned closer to her ear. "If you can."

Clara rolled her eyes, dismissing him with a flick of her hand before stepping away. With that, the giant man finally stepped away from the gate and walked down the length of the driveway. Horse neighs drifted from the end of the path and the sound of carriage wheels turning reached Willoughby's ears. In front of him, Clara stood alert. Waiting. He pulled on the collar of his shirt, his fingers finding purchase on the ring dangling off the end of a silver chain. *Let's get this over with.*

Parting the low-hanging branches of the tree, he stepped out and into Clara's path. The woman gasped as he emerged; her gloved hand pressing to her lips to stifle the sound.

"You startled me," she said. "Why are you skulking?"

"It's not good for my image to be seen here. People might talk."

The mayor's niece let out a barking laugh. "Gems forbid someone might find you doing anything other than stealing."

"Well, the night is still young. I wouldn't write it off quite yet."

With a nod of her head, Clara reached into her purse, a lacey number with crystals sewn into its handle, and produced the napkin Willoughby sent. She waved it in front of his face, the act making the tall black hat she wore fall off kilter. With an expert shove, Clara pushed the hat back into place. There was a hint of a frown on her face, and Willoughby wondered if she hated the damn headpiece as much as he did.

The leaves rustled around them. Clara shot an ominous glance at the gates and the menacing trees lining the path they stood on. "Interesting choice of mail carrier," she said, gesturing to the napkin.

"Not a fan of the Oily Spoon, Aldridge? I favor the place. You never know who you will run into."

Clara tapped her foot impatiently. "Spare me the details of

how you convinced a poor guard to help your sorry behind. Now what was this about?"

"I have a lead on your cadaver," Willoughby said. His head dipped and his dark hair fell over his eyes, casting them in shadow. Willoughby flicked a strand out of the way to look at Clara through the thick of his brows. "The ledger is for sales, as we thought. Your ill-fated gentleman was dealing in the markets. Had quite the long list of clients, by the looks of it."

Clara's nose wrinkled. "That was what Elisea told me as well."

I know. Willoughby stifled a grin. "Look, Aldridge, I don't have to tell you this, but if Mr. Hawke was selling, there is a good bet he wasn't peddling beans and potatoes."

"I gathered as much myself. Why bother using coded ledgers if he was selling legal goods?" Clara agreed. "I truly believe it was gem related."

Willoughby winced. He was not making stellar work of veering her off track. The entire purpose of meeting with Clara was to convince her to steer clear of the markets. On the way here, Willoughby had practiced what he would say to play the ledger off as a sad man's attempt to move antiquities under the museum's nose, which, in his defense, could have been true since he never bothered to decipher the stupid thing. He didn't want Clara to even think of the word gem. A difficult task since that appeared to be the only thing on her mind.

The leather cords of his laced shirt stretched taut as he struggled to breathe. Was it hot in here? Impossible considering the season. Yet his lungs struggled to fill with air, and he felt more catastrophic than the time his father took him on a tour of the catacombs below the city. Willoughby's skin from chafed beneath the layers of his clothes. A bead of sweat rolled down his neck, and he watched Clara track it with precision.

She was not going to walk away from this. No way in the gemmed hell.

Dastardly woman. Willoughby cursed in his mind, plastered on a false smile. "Likely not gems, no," he replied.

"What could be bad enough to kill over, then?"

"Do you own profit shares in the assumptions business?" Willoughby asked. "We don't know if his market deals are the reason Thomas is dead."

Clara arched a perfect eyebrow. "We?"

"Yes, Aldridge. You dragged me into this, or have you forgotten already?" Willoughby tilted his head to look up. Above his head, the clouds drifted past at an increasing speed, the first sign of a storm brewing. The inside of Willoughby's chest was in much the same turmoil. He breathed in deeply. "I suppose there is only one thing to do now."

Before him, Clara's face brightened as hope fluttered across her features.

"What's that?" she asked.

Last night's dinner churned inside his belly. Willoughby had never been a religious man, but he prayed to whoever was listening that his next words would stop the stubborn creature from moving forward.

Willoughby's spine stayed rigid as a rod. "We must track his market sales. Infiltrate the dealings and speak to whatever crooks Thomas may have worked with."

He didn't know Clara Aldridge anymore, but he was willing to wager that the future mayor would not dare step foot in the underbelly of the city. Certainly not deep enough to speak to actual criminals. It was her job to clean the streets of them, not bribe the so-called scum of Hedge End for information.

Spinning around, Willoughby was about to leave Clara behind for good. He could taste his freedom in the thickness of air. Could see it right before him.

"I'll ready the carriage."

Willoughby sputtered. "Pardon me?"

Stepping by him, Clara motioned for the weeping willow as she made her way back to the gates. Her skirt dragged on the ground, black silk and navy lace peering out from underneath. She unlocked the gate, opening it wide enough to slip inside.

Clara glanced over her shoulder, disregarding his gaping mouth and dumbfounded stare. "Best get back to your tree for now," she said. "I'll bring the carriage out. Unless you have a faster way to get to the markets."

Silence filled the space between them. No matter how hard Willoughby tried, he really couldn't think of a faster way to reach his death than by horse.

The market buzzed with activity and voices carrying over each other like bees circling a ripe flower. Nestled in the heart of the lowers, the Hedge End marketplace was the busiest part of the city, coming second only to the jail cells. Stalls, overflowing with goods, lined the narrow lane that stretched for as far as the eye could see. Overhead, spanning between two tall buildings, a webbing of iron and glass hid the market from the sky. And from the flying beasts, though no one ever mentioned that part.

The vendors yelled as Willoughby and Clara passed them, each one attempting to attract a potential customer.

"Catch of the day!" a gangly woman with a beak like a bird's shouted.

"Maps! Maps! Maps!" a thick-thighed man screamed.

"Get your paints here!" a young boy no older than six called out.

Each beckoning was louder than the next and each more desperate. The clatter of clinking coin was few and far between, at least it was in the stalls selling legal wares.

The air was bloated with a mixture of scents, and Willoughby couldn't help but watch Clara sniff it as she walked. He could only imagine what she was thinking. The upper citizens never came to the markets. Why would they? All they needed was provided by their staff and he doubted Clara had ever stepped foot here before. It was surprising she hadn't turned to run yet, though.

A polished boot flew past them, followed by its pairing. Willoughby pushed Clara backward in time to avoid her getting struck as one vendor passed a trade to another. Willoughby smiled.

It was good to be home.

He led them past stalls he knew like the back of his hand. On the walls, posters for missing people fluttered in the light breeze, and Willoughby focused on anything but the gaunt faces in the images. Faces from the lowers he'd likely met before. He trained his attention on the street and getting through the chaotic mess of the market. Each time Clara stopped to inspect a piece of fruit or old tomes bound together in even older leather, he couldn't help his surprise. More shocking was when the mayor's niece pulled out a stack of coins to trade for a bronze brooch shaped to resemble a thorny rose. She thanked the vendor, a girl no older than twelve, and hid her find inside a pocket in her skirt.

When she caught Willoughby staring, she said, "I have a thing for roses." As though that explained why she was over-paying for an item she didn't really need.

Willoughby despised her niceness.

"This way," he grumbled. He pointed to a turn in the street, five stalls from them. "The guy we want sells over there."

"Friend of yours?"

Willoughby shrugged. "Sort of."

The statement was far from the truth. Soltan was as close to family as Willoughby had. There was even a time when his parents took young Willoughby in during the years that followed his father's untimely death. A death that marked the rest of his days and defined his entire adult personality. After the accident at the mayor's office, Willoughby had nowhere to turn, no one to ask for aid, and Soltan was more than happy to provide. The Dressers didn't have much, but whatever they had, they shared with Willoughby. It was a kindness he could never repay. The coin he sent from his less than honest trades was a start, but Willoughby would spend the rest of his meager life returning what he owed.

He grabbed a pinch of Clara's dress sleeve and pulled her behind him. They were only a few stalls away from the turn when a commotion made Willoughby pause. Neck straining, he craned to see over Clara's enormous hat. Not far from them, at the stall selling the rose brooches, two guards towered over the young girl. One was mostly human, but the second had a tail jutting out of her tailbone and two large incisors that pushed from her large gums as she snarled. Willoughby saw the flash of green beryl in the guard's hand and cursed. Beside him, Clara's eyes rounded.

"What are they doing?"

"Interrogating," Willoughby replied. "The beryl is to make her tell the truth."

Clara's fingers fisted at her side. "I know what the gem does. Why are they using it on her? She's only a child."

"Age does not make a difference here. If she's selling illegally, she receives the same punishment as the rest."

Tears streamed down the girl's face, carving paths through the dirt and grime on her cheeks. Her shoulders shook violently as she struggled to fight off the effects of the cursed stone. In front of her, the guard clutching the gem hissed out a command, the words dripping with hatred. The magic surged, and the guard's tail grew longer—payment for using the gem.

With a final, guttural shout, the guard's voice sliced through the air, and the girl collapsed into a heap on the table. She babbled incoherently, spilling whatever secrets the guards sought. The sight made Willoughby's stomach lurch, bile rolling into his throat as the second guard swept his arm across the girl's table. The brooches clattered to the ground, clinging against the cobblestone.

Thick, calloused fingers clamped over the girl's thin arm, yanking her toward the guard with such force that Willoughby feared her bones might snap. His heart raced.

She screamed for help, but every person in the market turned away. Refusing.

"We have to help her!" Clara yelled.

Willoughby pressed a hand to her lips and pulled her against him. With hurried steps, he dragged Clara into the side street. The mayor's niece kicked and thrashed, but Willoughby held firm. He could not risk them getting caught. Not when there wasn't anything they could do to help the child, anyway.

Sharp teeth penetrated his skin. Willoughby yelped, pulling his hand away from Clara's mouth. He shoved her away from him and into a singular chair next to a lonely table. His teeth clamped shut. "Did you just fucking bite me?"

"Let me go, you brute!" Clara yelled.

She made a move toward the main street, but Willoughby pushed her down. "You cannot help her. All you'll do by going out there is draw attention to yourself. Are you ready to explain what you're doing traipsing around with a thief, princess?"

"I don't care! We have to do something!"

Willoughby shook his head, his eyes stinging. He peered around the corner.

"They've already left. Let's go."

It took a moment for Clara to follow him as he stomped away from her and toward Soltan's stall. But follow, she did. He could hear her rage-filled steps behind her, muttering under her breath at his retreating back. Willoughby let her words fall off with ease. This wasn't the first unfair incident he witnessed in the markets. When Willoughby first began to run his trades, he used to get hauled into the jailhouse regularly on account of not having yet developed the skills to hide better. And if he recalled correctly, he wasn't much older than the girl the guards snatched up today.

Someone like Clara Aldridge could never understand. Staying put meant staying alive. Everyone in the markets knew that.

Willoughby's boots skidded to a stop. Behind him, Clara ran into his back, pushing them forward from her momentum. He brushed off his jacket lest he get her rich girl scent on his clothes and scratched his head, his gaze on the empty stall before him.

"I don't understand," he whispered.

Walking past Clara, he made his way to the adjoining stall and leaned over the small table. The man on the other side smiled a toothless smile. "Will! What brings you by?"

"Hey, Benjamin," Willoughby said. "Is Soltan off today?"

"You haven't heard?"

Willoughby quirked a brow at the man. "I've been otherwise preoccupied. What's happened?"

"Poor son of a beast vanished."

"What does that mean?"

Benjamin shrugged. The nest of hair tied at the top of his head bobbled from the motion. He leaned on the table, his pot-marked hands quaking. "Gone into thin air. His dad came by to clear out the stall, told me to keep an eye out. And yesterday, some guards poked around. Took his gems and made a stink over watching our corner more closely now."

The breath caught in Willoughby's throat.

"What gems?" he asked. "Soltan wouldn't be caught dead with stones."

"Well, they got them. An emerald and a heliodor, last I heard on the street." The seller eyed a couple wondering between the stalls and stood up tall. He motioned for Willoughby to step aside, frowning as he did. "I can let you know if he turns up."

Willoughby nodded. "Sure. Thank you."

Leaving the table, he stomped toward his friend's empty stall where Clara stood, her face a question mark in the making. "What was that about?" she asked.

"My contact is gone," Willoughby answered. He worked hard to contain the gnawing feeling at the back of his brain that told him something was terribly wrong. Instead, he focused on Clara. One problem at a time. Once the business with her housekeeper was over, he could find out more about what Soltan was doing messing with magic. For now, he needed to stay on track. He couldn't very well help anyone if he was caught dealing gems and sentenced to death.

Willoughby's eyes narrowed on her. "How do you feel about slumming it for a little while longer, princess?"

CHAPTER TWELVE

As the inner skeleton of the lowers unfolded around her, Clara questioned all her recent life choices. The buildings that seemed to grow out of the concrete were so tall, it gave her vertigo to walk between them. Each step was like being crushed by brick and glass. At her back, the sounds of a city refusing to rest clawed at the exposed flesh of her neck. Clara bristled. What was she doing here? Following a man she couldn't trust toward a place she'd never stepped foot in.

If her uncle were here, he would have scolded her for the inaptitude of her decision making. And for not bringing a weapon, but that was neither here nor there.

A shadow passed overhead. A few paces ahead, Willoughby stopped dead in his tracks, his hand waving for her to catch up. She rushed to reach him; her eyes skyward. Above them, high in the blackening sky, a pair of giant wings circled.

Shudders tripped down Clara's spine. "Are we near?"

"Almost," Willoughby said. "Soltan's family lives a few blocks from here. We should hurry."

To punctuate his point, the flying Cursbeast screeched. Its thunderous voice boomed from the sky and shook the surrounding buildings. *You don't say*, Clara thought, but stayed silent. She followed Willoughby, stopping only when he did to whistle an alert to anyone in the vicinity.

They cut across an abandoned park which reminded Clara of a place one might go to bury a body under the blanket of night. With only a handful of trees and benches that have long outlived their purpose, the place was a far cry from a fine location. On the opposite side of the park, a walkway tied two tall buildings together, its brick crumbling down to the unfinished railway tracks below. Clara hopped over the metal, her skirt catching on an exposed nail. She tugged at it hard enough to rip the silk. No matter. The faster she could get to their destination, the faster she could get out of here. Leaving the tracks in the dust, Clara made a note to remind the council to speak with the builders responsible for the trains. If they paused building due to fund allocation, as she assumed, they certainly should secure the site before someone impales themselves on the nails. Today it was Clara's dress, but tomorrow it could be a toe or an eye. Clara hated that the only reason she was even having the thought was because they were in the lower numbers. This would never occur where she lived.

Another point to raise with her uncle. The more time Clara spent with Willoughby, the more items she added to her mental itinerary of changes to put into motion when she took the mayoral seat. It was mildly exhausting but refreshing all the same. Clara had every notion to make a difference.

Her foot tripped over a discarded wine bottle, and she came an inch away from cracking her skull against the side of a building.

At this rate, Clara may not see the day that she was to become mayor.

"Get that child indoors, Adeline," a gruff voice said not far from her.

Clara glanced over her shoulder to see a woman wrestle a young boy into a grimy doorway. She pushed the child inside with enough force to send him barreling forward with a screech. Behind her, a burly man followed, checking the street as he walked.

"Did you hear the whistle? There's a beast around," he warned. "Get inside quickly and barricade the windows and doors. Now!"

An ache swelled in her chest for the family. How did people survive down here? Clara couldn't imagine it.

Ahead of her, Willoughby turned a sharp corner and disappeared from view. She struggled to keep up with the buffoon, her breath heaving under the pressure of her corset. For gem's sake, she truly needed to ask the girls not to use all their force tightening the damn things each morning. Hiking up her skirt, Clara bolted down the dimly lit street she saw the thief scurry to. The stench of sewage wafted in the air and when Clara pressed her hand to the brick of a wall, it came away sticky.

Her stomach lurched, but she forced herself to keep moving.

"Will?" she called into the abyss of the street. *Why is it empty here?*

A head of curly black hair popped out from inside a doorway. Clara jumped, yelping. "This way," Willoughby said.

She followed him through what appeared to be a side entrance and up a narrow set of stairs that seemed to have no end. Each time they reached a new level, Clara had to take a moment to breathe, hopeful that the rotten doors greeting them led to their final destination. Each level was nothing more than another disappointment.

"Do...they...live...on the roof?" Clara asked, heaving.

The thief paused, looked back at her over his shoulder, then kept climbing.

"Wonderful."

After what felt like a lifetime, he finally stopped their ascent. His hands reached into his trousers, and she heard a few jingles from his pocket, followed by a poisonous glare directed at her. Finally, Willoughby produced a tarnished skeleton key and fit it into the lock on the door. The lock creaked and moaned with each twist, but it gave way, nonetheless.

Blinding light shot out from the doorway, brightening the corridor they stood in. Clara wished the door had stayed closed. With the light spilling into the stairwell, it was easier to see the negligence covering every inch of the building. There was broken glass in the corners and the wood that made up the rickety steps they climbed was rotten to the core; it was a surprise they hadn't fallen through.

Clara's gaze landed on a rust-colored stain on the floor. "Is that blood?"

Willoughby shrugged. "No maid here to do the daily cleaning."

"That still doesn't explain why there's blood."

If he heard her, he paid her no mind. Willoughby pushed the heavyset door and walked into what Clara could only assume was to be yet another colossal mistake. She stepped in after him. The sound of dishes clanging filled her ears instantly. She tried to orient herself in the space, but it was nearly impossible. Not only did the bright light that emanated from the three windows on the far side of the room blind her, but the apartment they were in was a hazardous maze. Several veins of hallways opened before her, with more doors than Clara could count. To her left, a mess of stacked shoes and boots climbed up the torn, ragged wallpaper and when she turned, she was struck by her own reflection in the shattered mirror hanging on the opposite wall. Clara quickly realized she was in the entrance way of the apartment. The flesh of her arms covered in bumps as she considered what she might find within.

Seeing her absolute mortification at the state of the place, Willoughby rolled his eyes, tossed his boots off with more force than was necessary, and stalked past her down the hallway to the right.

It took Clara a few moments to unlace her boots, and she cursed herself for not choosing more reasonable footwear. The purpose was to conceal where she went, but surely there were better shoes she could have worn to do so. After a few more choice words and a lot of huffing and puffing, Clara was finally free of the contraptions and ready to take on whatever Willoughby had in store.

When she reached him, her jaw slacked.

Clara watched the thief carry a large boiling pot from a stove to a windowsill with split teeth. His back strained with muscle, his jacket and waistcoat discarded on a kitchen chair, leaving him exposed under the thin fabric of his shirt. Clara averted her gaze and concentrated on the rest of the kitchen. And the glowering woman in front of her.

"Who's this?" the woman asked, her arms folded tightly over her billowing chest.

Willoughby cast a side glance at Clara. "A stray. I know how you love those, Josephine."

The woman chuckled. She tossed a stained tea towel over her shoulder, the wetness of the fabric staining the light green collar of her dress. Without breaking eye contact with Clara, she twirled a wooden spoon in a second pot, this one nearly overflowing from the heat of the flames below.

"You hungry?" she asked.

Clara shook her head even though her stomach was growling and the concoction in the pot smelled divine. "No, thank you. My name is Clara."

"I know who you are," Josephine said. "I didn't crawl from under a rock." She pointed to the small, wobbly table in the corner of the kitchen. "Sit. Get the woman some tea, Willoughby. Where are your manners?"

If it was possible to fall in love with a complete stranger, Clara may have done so with Josephine. Anyone who could put the thief in his place with a simple word was a friend in her books. She watched in awe as Willoughby bowed his head and sheepishly picked up the teapot sitting idly on the counter. His neck muscles ticked. Filling two cups with hot tea, he placed them on mismatched saucers and carried them to the table, bringing them down with a clang in front of Clara.

Willoughby's shoulders hunched. "A drink, your majesty," he said with a sneer.

Faster than Clara could blink, Josephine slapped the wet tea towel on the thief's head. He muttered an apology under his breath and pulled out a chair to sit in. His gaze remained low.

Clara sipped on her tea, which, considering the circumstances, may have been the best leaves she'd ever drank.

"This is wonderful," she told Josephine. "And we are sorry to barge in on you."

The woman shook a beefy hand in the air between them. She nudged a thumb at Willoughby. "This one has been coming and going since he was a wee lad. I'm used to it." Then, she turned to the thief and added, "I take it you were locked up again?"

"I would have come sooner," Willoughby said solemnly. "Is it true what I heard about Soltan?"

Twisting around, Josephine faced the stove and busied

herself with the cooking pot. Her spine rounded as she stirred and for a second, Clara thought she saw her shoulders shake. The woman took up the spoon, tasting the broth, and nodded in satisfaction. "True enough," she answered. "My son is gone."

"What happened? When did you last see him?"

"Five days ago. He never came home after a shift at the markets."

Clara kneaded her hands in her lap. She tried not to compare the situation to her past, but it was impossible. Despite being a mere teen, she could, to this day, recall the agitation of waiting for her parents to return as they did each night, only for them not to show up. They continued not showing up for years to come. Clara could only imagine what Josephine was going through and the absolute war inside her when she thought about her son.

She was about to say it when the woman threw the spoon down on the counter and spun toward them. "He never used those gems," she said harshly. "I don't care what they say. My boy would never..."

A tear rolled down her cheek. Josephine swiped at it, sniffling. She turned again, this time not bothering with the pot. Her eyes stared at the empty, brown wall before her like it might offer answers no one had to give.

Across the table from her, Willoughby stiffened, deadpanning on Clara.

"I don't believe it either," he said.

"If he had gems," Josephine continued, oblivious to his words, "it was from that slithery man he got involved with."

There was a long pause during which Clara could swear time stopped. The air seemed to have been sucked from the room. A few feet from her, Josephine turned off the flame under the pot and covered it with a lid, oblivious to the surrounding strangeness. Somehow, Clara could sense that whatever she said next was going to change everything.

The thief sucked in a quick, sharp breath. "What man?"

"The one who promised my boy coin and riches. You know how these men are," Josephine explained. "They come around our streets thinking we'd be swayed by their big talk and hefty promises. I told Soltan not to believe a word out of his mustached mouth, but he didn't listen. Spent his last days hanging around that vulture, waiting for a handout. Never came. As I expected."

"What did the man want with him?" Willoughby asked.

She could see the concern creasing his brow, worry gathering for the tasks Soltan may have had to perform. But that wasn't what she was stuck on. The thing that drew most of Clara's attention was the description of the mysterious stranger. A mustache. Like the one Thomas Hawke took great pride in.

Clara harrumphed. "Do you remember his name?"

"Something about a bird," Josephine whispered.

"Hawke, perhaps?"

The woman's eyes twinkled, and she clapped her hands together. "That's it! Tell me you didn't get caught up in his schemes too? Nice girl like you shouldn't be running around with bad men." She glanced at Willoughby briefly, as though to imply he may be another to avoid. Clara didn't require the reminder.

"Anyhow, it wasn't what this horrid person wanted from Soltan that was the problem," Josephine said. "It was what he promised to provide."

"What did he have that your son wanted?" Clara asked.

The woman rubbed her wrinkled brow, a darkness crossing her features. "Spun tales about helping Soltan find his girl. She'd been missing for weeks, you see. This Hawke said he could use his connections to locate her." She shook her head, her auburn hair spilling out from under the dirty rag tied around it. "All lies."

"Soltan was courting someone?"

"You bet your gems he was!" Josephine yelped. "Even asked me for the ring his father gave me. But I told him, Genevieve Morning doesn't care for rings and jewels. She was a good egg, that girl. Smart head on her shoulders. A shame what happened."

A few things happened all at once then. The building shook violently, pots and pans clanging above the stovetop where they hang. The light that filled the apartment grew dim and a whooshing sound outside the windows made Clara's heart leap into her tight throat. She looked at Willoughby, who was already on his feet and running for the shutters, Josephine on his heels. Working in concert, they barricaded the glass only moments before the sound of massive wings passed by.

The Cursbeast they saw from the ground earlier.

Clara stifled a gasp. Watching her closely, Willoughby pressed a finger to his lips. She nodded.

The shaking continued for several minutes as the beast made its rounds over the building and through the street. Outside, a few yells broke the silence and Clara's stomach filled with dread as the screams were instantly snuffed out. She didn't want to think why. In her mind, Clara pictured people getting to safety despite the reality that likely took place.

Urgency thrummed through her as she worked to recall a memory hanging on the edge of her mind. She stayed unmoving as a broken clock. Clara kept rolling Genevieve's name on her tongue. The girl Soltan courted sounded familiar, but she couldn't quite place how she knew of her prior to this conversation. Clara didn't have any friends outside the four walls of Aldridge House, except for Violet. Their friendship had been stitched together in odd little moments; Violet pulling her into gossip she had no business knowing, dragging her along to fittings, or showing her how to sit with her legs angled just so. Clara had often visited Violet's family home, but it was never for too long a time as both women had other engagements to be dragged to—Clara on business outings with her uncle and Violet off to one ball or another. It was one visit that now relentlessly clung to Clara's mind. While Violet chattered on about the latest uppers scandal, Clara excused herself to slip away, ending up in the kitchen of all places. She accidentally knocked over a bowl of dusting sugar, sending white powder flying all over every surface. It was Violet's lovely cook that helped her clean any evidence of her clumsiness from the fabrics of her skirts.

She gaped at Willoughby, waiting for the shaking to end so she could let the realization dawning on her spill from her lips. Clara knew Soltan's lady friend; had met her even.

Genevieve Morning was Violet's cook.

CHAPTER THIRTEEN

Fire crackled in the fireplace, the embers hitting the stone floor with a deafening hiss. Clara's lips chapped from the heat in the sitting room, but she dared not move. Her back rigid, she remained glued to the confines of the chair she occupied, watching her uncle. In front of her, Oswin perused the latest issue of the Hedge End Gazette. His eyes darted right to left as he read each article. Occasionally, his gray brows would hike up high on his forehead, surprise registering on his face from whatever news appeared on the cream pages.

For all intents and purposes, Oswin did not appear any less agitated than he usually was. Even the wrinkles on his face seemed to have lessened. Whatever happened on the council trip relaxed him, which played well into Clara's hand. She needed him as pliable as possible this evening.

Oswin's brows danced again; his cheeks sucked in.

"Read anything of note?" Clara asked.

The bridge of a nose peered out over the edge of the gazette, followed by two narrowed eyes. "Our efforts in the

markets appear to be working. They're predicting a third less affected gems to end up in the hands of the lower street citizens by the winter." Oswin dropped the papers down, squishing them into his lap. "What time is your friend coming by?"

"Violet will be here shortly," Clara said. "I hope you don't mind that I invited her for dinner."

Or that I plan to use her as a decoy.

The plan was simple. After the trip to the lowers and the visit with Soltan's mother, Clara had no choice but to move full steam ahead. The days were counting down for Elisea. With death's toll never lasting beyond two weeks, a time agreed upon by the mayor and Chief of Guards as the acceptable span to allow for visits with the convicted prior to their end. That put her housekeeper ten days from execution. While Clara knew she would not allow the end to come to term, she was running out of ideas. Now, with the discovery of Genevieve's name and the connection between Thomas and two missing people, she finally felt she had a thread to pull. A plan lingered on the edges of Clara's mind, nearly there but still indistinguishable.

It was all connected. Clara simply did not know how.

There *was* a way she could find out, or at least get closer to the truth. Unfortunately, it involved spending more time with Willoughby than she was comfortable with and sneaking around under her uncle's nose. Since she couldn't remedy the first problem, Clara tackled the second head on.

The first step of her scheming was to question Violet about the missing cook. Once Clara decided to involve her friend, a new opportunity presented itself. She could avert Oswin's attention by providing him with a likely alibi while she was off gallivanting with the thief.

That was where Violet came into play. Her uncle wouldn't

bat a lash if he thought she was spending her days with someone he approved of. Besides, Clara didn't have many friends—none really unless one counted Willoughby, which she did not—so she assumed Oswin would be delighted to meet Violet. She should have introduced them sooner but her uncle was always terribly busy. Besides, when it came to matters of friendship, she wished to keep Violet to herself. Their visits were few and far between but an excellent break from reality. Clara knew her uncle too well to know that if he got whiff of Clara spending time with a woman of the uppers, his first act would be to push her into social gatherings to improve her status amongst the citizens. Clara got a headache simply thinking of the balls and parties she'd be forced to attend in the name of gained popularity.

The sound of metal on wood echoed down the hallway, jarring Clara from her thoughts and back to the room. She snickered. Time to put her plan into action. She hopped from the stuffy chair and threw her hand out to her uncle. "There she is! I hope you're ready for this."

"Should I be concerned?"

"Not at all," Clara said. She roped her hand through her uncle's arm and pulled him to the door. "But Violet can be a lot to handle. You've been warned."

Oswin tittered. "Duly noted. I'll have Sergei on standby in case Mrs. Cooke needs to be escorted off the premises."

"It wouldn't be the worst idea."

His laugh bounced off the walls as they walked toward the dining room where the staff had arranged three table settings. Hosting a dinner without Elisea giving orders from the kitchen was going to rattle Clara deeply, but she opted to keep her mind on the bright side of things; if all went well tonight, she'd be one step closer to having her life back to how it should be. Clara took small, quick steps with her uncle beside her. Nerves played an incomprehensible melody against her ribcage, and her corset tightened with every inch closer to the room. Next to her, Oswin was oblivious to her inner turmoil. *Perfect,* Clara thought. The plan was already working.

Rounding a corner, they walked through the dark wood of a doorframe and into the dining room. Heavy velvet drapes in the color of rich wine framed tall windows on the far end of the long space. The glass, stained to depict historical events of the Stone King and the creation of Hedge End, let slivers of light in that bounced off the deep plum wallpaper in random patterns. A mahogany table dominated the center of the room, surrounded by upholstered chairs with backs taller than some of the buildings in the lowers.

Above the table hung a chandelier that added to the surreal glow of the dining area and drew the eye up. Behind the table, a narrow hutch holding fine silverware and drinking glasses was nestled beside an old clock ticking time away.

The room smelled of beeswax polish and freshly picked roses from the garden that adorned the multitude of vases scattered throughout the place.

And yet none of it compared to Violet.

Dressed in a canary yellow dress that fell lower at her back, Clara's friend was a sight to behold. Her corset, a gold chain mail fabric that wrapped around her tightly, was fastened at the shoulders with intricate braided straps. With her hair up in dozens of braids, Violet stood nearly taller than the clock. She had even taken the time to weave crystals into the pale locks that reflected the light cast by the chandelier.

To put it bluntly, Violet Cooke was draped with opulence and clashed remarkably with the atmosphere in the room.

Clara's uncle coughed into his sleeve, his jaw refusing to shut.

"Mrs. Cooke," he said, approaching Violet with an extended palm. "You're looking lovely this evening."

Violet bowed playfully. She took Oswin's hand and allowed him to lead her to the hutch where several glasses filled with wine waited. Clara couldn't help but laugh inside. One second in Violet's striking presence and she was already forgotten.

This was going to work out pleasantly.

She walked around the table to snatch a wine glass. Before she could place it to her lips, a sharp pain stabbed at her ankle and Clara jumped, the wine sloshing in the glass. Some of it stained the hem of her dress, luckily in a similar shade, so it wasn't a complete disaster.

"Is everything all right?" Violet asked.

Clara rolled her eyes, pointing to the small space below the hutch where a furry paw was retreating into the shadows. "We have an uninvited guest."

"For gem's sake," Oswin hissed out. "How does that cat keep getting in here?"

Flinching, Clara reached into the small pocket of her dress and pulled out a dry toast square. She bent down, tossing the food under the hutch. A second later, the sound of sloppy chewing emerged from below as Socks devoured his treat. Clara looked at her uncle through batted lashes. "I may have let him in."

At this, both Violet and Oswin barked out hearty laughs and clinked their cups together. Giving the furry rascal a second toast square, Clara joined the others when they made their way to sit down. She chose her spot carefully, forcing Oswin to the head of the table so she could signal Violet should the occasion call for it. Not that Clara planned for anything to go awry. This was a simple dinner, nothing more.

With the chairs occupied, the serving staff, a brother and sister Oswin hired recently, brought out the first course.

Mouthwatering smells of herbs and spices wafted through the dining room and Clara had to abate her hungry belly to keep from inhaling the warm salad right off the plate. She noticed Violet wasn't holding back and was already stuffing her mouth with a third forkful.

Seeing Clara stare, she chewed, swallowed, and patted her stained lips with a napkin. "I am simply ravenous," she said. "Must be all that time at home alone. All I do is eat these days. I must include more exercise into my regimen."

"Lawrence has not yet returned?" Clara asked. When she saw her uncle's face scrunch up, she added, "Violet's husband travels for business often. He's a watchmaker."

A doubtful crease deepened on Oswin's forehead. Clara was relieved when he didn't press the odd situation and instead said, "A good meal is the answer to everything. Never apologize for enjoying one."

Glasses clinked again as they exchanged pleasantries before digging into the meal. The hour passed wondrously, with good humor and delicious food. By the time the last course arrived, Clara had to wipe the sweat from her brow with a napkin. She was relieved when Violet did the same despite having eaten a considerable amount less. Even her uncle slumped in his chair, the weight of the dinner dragging him down like an anchor.

A cart was wheeled into the dining room. Upon it, more drinks in varying sized glasses emerged and an array of sweets followed. Clara couldn't even look at the desserts but placed a raspberry scone on her plate for appearance's sake, regardless.

"We should have done this sooner," her uncle said. "You are a wonderful guest, Mrs. Cooke. And a great friend to my dear niece."

Violet's eyes glittered in response. "We found each other at the most opportune time," she replied. "It's a shame I have to share her with—"

A thud blasted from under the dining table. Clara's eyes grew several sizes as she fixed her friend with a stare that meant only one thing—silence. When Violet's eyebrows met in the center, Clara kicked her friend's leg again, this time lighter.

"Socks is running amok again," she said, chuckling uncomfortably.

"Right." Oswin nodded. "That ghoulish cat. You were saying, Mrs. Cooke?"

Finally getting the point, Violet waved her hand nonchalantly. "Violet is fine. We're all good friends here," she said, her voice chipper. "And I don't recall anymore. Tell me more about you, Oswin. Being mayor must be a marvel position."

"It has its privileges, I suppose."

Clara smiled. "And then some. But I have to say, Uncle, I do not envy you. That last budget meeting was an absolute bore!"

"I heard you handled yourself well. It is hard to get accustomed to, but once you do, you will do remarkably well. I'm sure of it."

"And maybe you can finally get those blasted gems off the streets," Violet added.

Oswin rustled at her words. He rested his elbows on the table and leaned far enough in that his necktie dipped into the jam on his plate. If her uncle noticed the mess, he did not make a move to correct himself. "I'm glad you see it our way," he told Violet. "The gems have been nothing but trouble since the day they were first forged."

"If only you had an alchemist that could help destroy them," Violet said. "It *was* alchemy that created the affected gems, was it not?"

"So it was." Oswin nodded. "The Stone King's royal

alchemist to be exact. But alas, the knowledge to correct the gems or destroy them was lost when the king died."

Clara sucked in her cheeks. "Don't you mean got himself killed by the beasts his gems created?"

Silence rolled through the dining room; Clara had hit the nail on the head. Everyone knew the story of the Stone King and the creation of the gems. The same gems, shards of the originals, that now circulated in their cursed city and ruined the lives of all those foolish enough to use them. It was the Stone King, the man who named Hedge End, that forged the first ones. Well, his trusted alchemist, that was. Back then, everyone wanted what the gems had to offer. Thirty-six massive stones with thirty-six specific magical attributes, each one made to defy logic and reason in its own way. The Stone King bade the alchemist to forge three sets, one for himself, one for his royal guards, and one for his oldest heir.

Clara always hated the part that came next.

The citizens found out about the gems and rebelled against the Stone King, who, in turn, forced his guards to use magic to keep the revolution at bay. What began as scattered riots quickly turned into full-scale battles, with barricades rising overnight and the clash of weapons echoing through the alleys. The Stone King's guards scorched districts to ash in an effort to root out dissent, while the rebels armed themselves with stolen gem shards and improvised weapons. Families were driven from their homes, trade collapsed when the King closed all access to Hedge End, and famine tightened its grip on the citizens. The city was left divided, at war with itself. The Trust War lasted for months.on the citizens. The city was left divided, at war with itself. The Trust War lasted for months.

It all appeared to be settling until the truth of the stones came to light. Magic was not free, never had been, but the magic of the gems was pricier than most—a sliver of the user's humanity. It consumed a person from the inside out, turning them into Cursbeasts. By that point, though, it was too late.

Horrified, the Stone King killed the alchemist and burned his notes to make certain no one could create more of the ghastly stones. He tried everything he could to destroy the affected gems, but nothing worked. With much devastation, the Stone King divided the gems amongst his trusted court and herded the Cursbeasts, his own guards, to a piece of floating land far from the city's walls. The Cursed Isle.

This was where the story usually got muddled. Word of mouth was not the best resource for the truth and though there were many texts that documented the history of Hedge End, few agreed on what happened. The way Clara learned it was that the Cursbeasts returned to kill the Stone King and every heir to his name. When a new king was crowned, they came back again for another kill. Such was the vicious cycle until the city decided to do away with kings and focus on more refined politics instead. Somewhere along the lines, gems made their way into the city and into the hands of regular citizens. This was the part that Clara always found fascinating—that people still wanted to use magic despite the consequences, so much so that they went out of their way to steal and bargain for tiny slivers of affected stones.

"Don't you think?"

Clara shook her head, and the thoughts died away inside of her. She looked around the table, trying to gauge who has spoken. "I'm sorry. I got lost for a moment there."

"I do that often," Violet agreed. "I was asking if you thought we should instill higher punishments for those caught using magic?"

Clara's stomach turned. "Higher than death, you mean?"

"Well, of course not! I don't mean the scoundrels selling the damn things under the mayor's nose." Next to her, Oswin shifted in the chair awkwardly. Violet didn't appear to notice and said, "I'm speaking of magic use in general. Make it illegal and call it a day."

"What of the guards?" Clara asked.

Oswin nodded. "She's correct. It is an unfortunate situation, but affected gems are the guards' best defense against crime."

"Then think of a better defense!" Violet exclaimed. She caught herself rapidly. Clearing her throat, she squeezed the napkin in her hands, then let it fall limp on the plate. "But what do I know? Don't pay me any mind. These are the words of a woman who had too much wine, I'm afraid."

"No need to apologize, Mrs...." Oswin caught himself. "Violet. Nothing is off limits to discuss between friends. Speaking of mayoral obligations—" he turned to Clara "—I was hoping you might accompany me to a few more meetings this week. Get your feet wet."

Clara didn't hesitate when she shook her head negatively. An invisible string pulled at her lips, and she smiled at her uncle with all the warmth of a midday sun. "Actually, I'm afraid I cannot. Violet and I had already made plans for most of the week."

At the table across Clara, Violet's eyes flared a little, but her face remained neutral. She kept quiet, probably afraid of being accosted by a boot under the table again. No matter what her reasoning, Clara knew she would have to explain her extracurricular activities to her friend sooner or later. That was fine by her. It was easier to come clean to Violet about what she was doing than her uncle.

Clara caught up with Violet later that evening in the foyer before she stepped out, the soft rustle of skirts and faint perfume announcing her friend's presence before she slid close beside her. Violet draped her coat over her shoulders, buttoning the collar with practiced ease, tilting her head as though they were sharing a secret already.

"So," Violet began, eyes glittering like polished glass, "you're using me as your excuse now? I should be flattered, though I do wonder what sort of scandal I'm covering for. An illicit affair? Secret lessons in dancing? Or"—her voice dropped conspiratorially—"are you finally sneaking off to meet someone you shouldn't? A Certain gruff gentleman with a chest of steel, perhaps?"

Clara laughed softly, though her chest tightened. "If only it were that romantic. You know my uncle—he wants me at his side for every dreary meeting. And while I do love a good speech about road repairs or tariffs,"—she rolled her eyes—"I needed a reason to step back for a few days. You were the perfect choice."

Violet gasped, feigning offense, though the corner of her lips quirked. "Because I'm so charming and reliable? Or because I never say no to a bit of trouble?"

Clara smirked.

"Both. And because I trust you to play along when he inevitably asks what we were doing."

"Oh, I'll do better than play along." Violet leaned forward, lowering her voice. "By tomorrow, half the ladies in the uppers will be whispering that we've been shopping for new gowns. The truth won't stand a chance against me."

Clara's smile softened. "You're brilliant, Violet."

"Nonsense. You're the only one in this dreary city who's worth a damn for company. If you need cover, I'll give it. Just promise me that you're not walking into anything dangerous."

Clara swallowed, heart hammering, and forced her expression to stay calm. "I'll be fine, Violet."

Violet studied her a moment longer, then sighed theatrically and leaned back.

"All right. But if you are sneaking off to meet a lover, I expect all the details. Names, locations, wardrobe choic-es...everything."

Clara laughed, but deep down, the secrets she was keeping from her friend weighed heavily on her. Violet had no idea what she was actually covering for. She would have to come clean soon enough, just not yet.

Heart drumming, Clara pushed her shoulder blades back, her restless fingers tapping away at her sides .

Tomorrow, she would start.

CHAPTER FOURTEEN

All it took to convince Violet to keep Clara's secret was the promise of juicy gossip from her exploits in the lowers. It was a bargain Clara was willing to make. Mostly because it offered her the opportunity to get the weight of guilt off her chest and, more importantly, someone who knew where she was in case she got in trouble. Violet even went as far as to offer her aid with the search; help Clara agreed to quickly since her friend uncovered secrets faster than a truffle pig.

The plan, in this case, was highly questionable at best.

Clara's fingers fidgeted with the hem of her bodice. She cast sidelong glances in the direction of the building Willoughby entered nearly an hour ago, her body inclined backward and away from the horrid establishment. If she thought the apartments Soltan lived in were dreary, this place was a bottomless pit of despair. Shattered glass adorned almost every window in the tall structure. The brick that held up the walls crumbled upon a mere glance, and there was the distinct stench of urine and vomit wafting in the air. The buildings surrounding this one were in no better shape. A few had people sleeping right there on the street in front of them, something Clara hadn't seen before today. They huddled under shredded blankets, their skin sallow and their teeth yellowing.

Unease filled Clara to the brim.

The door, or, in this case, wood beams roughly cobbled together to create one, swung open and Willoughby stepped into the light. His leather pants strained over the muscle of his pumping legs as he jogged across the street to meet Clara. In his hands, the missing flyers they gathered earlier in the day fluttered in the wind. Clara's eyes narrowed to slits as she watched him approach. She tried to gauge the expression on his face, but it was of no use. Willoughby was harder to read than the council members.

She scoffed. And he called *her* a politician.

"Well?" she asked when he was in front of her.

The thief ripped out a single flyer from the pile, folded it in half and tucked it into the inner pocket of his leather coat. "The husband says he remembers her speaking with a guy fitting Thomas's description."

"That's the fourth missing person that had a connection to him."

Willoughby shook the remaining flyers. "How much do you want to bet we'll find the same with these?"

"I don't understand what Elisea's husband was doing with all of these people," Clara said. "He promised Soltan that he could help find Genevieve. What about the rest? How could one man have the answers to everyone's problems?"

"He doesn't have to have them. He only needs to offer them."

The knot in Clara's throat doubled in size. She lifted her chin, looking down her nose at Willoughby. "You think he entrapped them somehow? For what means?"

Willoughby shrugged. "That I do not know. But nothing about this is good. I can tell you that much. There have been more and more of these flyers on the walls of the lowers lately. If Thomas had anything to do with them, I'd wager we'll be seeing less in the future."

"It doesn't help us figure out who killed him," Clara said. She narrowed her eyes at the thief. "Unless you're still unsure about Elisea's involvement for some bizarre reason."

"I'm never sure," Willoughby replied. "But I believe the missing citizens are your answer."

Clara glared at him. "How do you figure?"

"Find the missing and you find whoever is holding them. Thomas's partner, perhaps."

Head tilting to the side, Clara considered his solution. It was questionable at best, but she had to admit, Willoughby had a point. If it was true and Thomas was responsible for all the vanishings around the city, he couldn't have done it alone. It stood to reason that a partner would be involved. Clara blinked slowly. Why would a partner double cross him? More than that, what did they want with the citizens from the lowers?

"Oh, another thing," Willoughby said. "The husband mentioned some sort of society. Might be worth looking into it."

"What type of society?" Clara asked. She couldn't imagine someone like Thomas Hawke belonging to a gentleman's club, not when she knew the wages a gardener took home. "Did the husband get a name?"

Willoughby didn't answer. The stomping of boots reached Clara's ears at the same time as Willoughby rounded his fingers over her bicep. She glanced over her shoulder and down the street, her heart sinking into her boots; flat heeled today to avoid the hassle she went through previously. Though little good her shoes would do her now.

Clara's skin paled.

Marching down the street toward them were at least a dozen guards. Their eyes scanned the windows of the surrounding buildings, looking for anyone that might be breaking the law. She watched as one guard kicked a sleeping citizen on the sidewalk, barking out an order for the gentleman to get moving. The elderly man gathered his things into a filthy sack and scurried away, his palm rubbing the spot the guard's boot connected with. Acid filled Clara's mouth. This was not how the guards were meant to behave. Either the chief was letting them run amuck or he was too preoccupied to see what his roster was up to. Or perhaps, Clara considered grimly, this was not negligence at all but permission. After all, terror was an effective leash; what better way to keep citizens in line than through fear carved into their daily lives? No matter what the reason was, it disgusted her.

One more thing to take care of when she finally held the reins of the city.

The sound of stomping boots neared closer and closer. Panic surged within Clara when she realized they were standing directly in the guards' path. They haven't seen them yet, but it was only moments before the inevitable. She couldn't be found out. If the guards saw her here, her uncle would surely know soon after.

"Will, we need to—"

Clara's soul left her body as the thief pressed himself against her and maneuvered them from the main street into a dank alley. Her back flattened against the rough surface of a wall, breath coming out short. Willoughby's eyes rolled down her body.

He cursed. "That fucking dress is going to get us caught. No one wears that down here, Aldridge. You reek of the uppers."

"Well, I am not removing it, if that's what you're suggesting."

Muttering, he scanned the alley, his gaze landing on a discarded knit blanket on the ground. Willoughby took long strides to reach it, snatching it off the floor and rushing back to Clara. Spurned to action, he wrapped the dirty, smelly thing around her waist, letting the blanket drape down the length of her skirt. He left her side briefly to peer out of the alley.

By the time he returned, the stomps of the boots were that much closer.

Willoughby's eyes flitted to Clara's hat.

"No," she said.

He didn't listen. Without a second breath, he tore the top hat from her head, a few strands of hair ripping out with it. The pins that held it in place scattered to the ground and clanged against the cobblestone. Tears pricked at Clara's eyes. Not for the loss of the hat which Willoughby tossed into the murky depths of the alley, but for the pain left behind in her sore skull. In truth, Clara was glad to be rid of the damn thing.

What she wasn't glad for was what came next.

Using all his force, Willoughby pressed his body against hers until there was not an inch of air left between them. Their eyes met when he said, "Neither of us is going to like this."

Then he raked his fingers into the back of her cascading locks, pulled hard enough to tip her chin back, and pressed his lips to her neck. Clara's limp arms tightened. Her hands moistened and her skin crawled with goosebumps. The hair on the rear of her neck stood on edge. She parted her lips slightly, enough to only let out a shivering breath.

A few paces from the alley, the guards marched forward.

Willoughby's lips wetted against her skin as he lowered his

position to right above her collarbone. Heat clawed up Clara's thighs, and she worked every muscle in her body to contain her intrepid thoughts. Clara counted to ten. Twenty. Thirty.

She lost track.

The guards were close, such that Clara could hear their voices clear as day. Though it was a miracle she could hear anything at all over the sound of her heart pounding between her ears. Her eyelashes fluttered. She parted her eyes slightly to see the street.

A breath caught on her lips.

The guards marched right past their hiding place without as much as a second glance. One guard's attention drifted toward the dark corner they stood in, but after an amused chuckle he looked away and kept on. They were gone shortly after, the street empty.

Cold sweat licked at Clara's brow as Willoughby peeled himself off her and backed away. The edges of his lips twitched slightly, but he stayed silent. Clara was grateful to have a reprieve from his otherwise sharp remarks.

Noting her stunned expression, Willoughby bit his bottom lip and crooked a brow. "Are you all right, Aldridge?"

Clara managed a curt nod. Staying in the shadows, she waited until Willoughby checked the street to make certain they were clear to leave. He took some time to return, but Clara was pleased with the minutes she had to herself. They gave her an opportunity to collect her wayward thoughts and pull herself back together. She ripped off the blanket and picked up the top hat off the ground, giving it a good dusting. She did everything she could to keep her mind busy because if she was honest with herself, truly honest, Clara would realize that she was not all right at all.

CHAPTER FIFTEEN

"Are you certain you want to go in there alone?" Willoughby asked.

Gazing at the dark structure before her, Clara rolled her shoulders and tucked strands of unruly hair behind her ears. She looked at the thief. "It is only a library, Will," she said. "The society the missing woman's husband mentioned is our only lead at the moment. This place has a list of every functioning club in Hedge End, along with member statuses."

"Well, it looks ominous."

"There are better ways to admit you don't read," Clara teased. "Besides, I have no choice but to go in alone, don't I? Unless you have a registration card for the establishment I don't know about."

The thief scoffed but stayed silent. He stepped aside, bowing theatrically to let Clara pass by. In the sky, storm clouds gathered, brooding and charcoal. Clara concentrated on the wrought-iron gates holding the entrance to the library captive, on the curling spikes above. She hurried up the stone

path, her unsteady gait muffled by the sound of Willoughby shouting at her retreating back.

"I do know how to read, Aldridge!"

She shook her head, her eyes rolling. She reached the grand oak door, pushing it open with a groan to reveal the dimly lit interior of the building. In the foyer, the smell of polished wood and old leather mingled with burning candle wax and old tomes. Clara's boot squeaked on the shiny floor as she walked briskly past the reception desk and into the belly of the library. Around her, towering mahogany shelves lined the walls, each holding hundreds of leather-bound volumes. The room was bathed in the light from a singular chandelier above a row of long tables in its center, the walls punctuated by gas lanterns burning brightly.

Clara grazed the etched gold sign on the shelf nearest her with a long finger. She checked the section indicated in the text —not the one she needed. It took Clara the better half of the hour to orient herself in the space. She had never felt more scholarly in her entire life. The library at Aldridge House paled in comparison to the grandeur of this place and for a moment, Clara regretted being homeschooled and avoiding the university in the middles. It would have been nice to spend her days lost between these shelves.

Whispers drifted toward her from a row of shelves nearby and Clara froze in her tracks, overhearing her uncle's name mentioned. She rose on her tip toes to follow the voices, stopping around the bend from one tall shelf.

"Aldridge needs to find a better system to control the damn things if you ask me," a woman said sternly.

A low chuckle from her partner came in return. "What system would that be?" the man asked. "No one has been able to control the beasts in centuries. You think one man can change the trajectory of the city? The Aldridges are not gods,

Meribel. What can the mayor do that others have not been able to do before him?”

“Build shelters in the lower streets? Send his guards to fight off the beasts instead of hauling citizens into jailcells?” the woman suggested. “Not hide out in his mansion in the uppers, that’s for certain.”

“You give him too much credit. Oswin Aldridge is doing the best he can with the hand he was given. There is no hiding from the beasts, Meribel. Have you seen the missing posters? Those creatures are on a rampage. Best we can all do is keep an ear out for alerts and pray for a dark corner.”

Clara sucked in a breath and took a step backward. Her shoulder collided with the shelf and several books toppled over. She gasped, throwing her arms out to catch them. She was able to save one thick leather tome, but the rest tumbled out of her reach and crashed to the floor. She bent down, struggling to collect them before the people she overheard spotted her spying on them. The citizens had every right to their opinion on how her uncle handled city business, of course. Still, they didn’t need to know that the mayor’s niece could hear their grievances. That and she didn’t like the sour taste their words left in her mouth. Not one bit.

“Do you require assistance, Miss?”

Clara returned the book she studied, twirling around to face an elderly man wearing a monocle and tailcoat. The stack of books balanced in his hands wavered. He tucked the tomes back into place expertly, his focus never leaving Clara.

“Oh!” Clara said, surprised. “I was only looking.”

“If you decide on a topic of interest, come to see me in the front,” the man said. He extended a hand, gloved in white, for Clara to take. “Thelonius Casterly. I’m the keeper of words in this dusty old place.”

Relief flowed through Clara. She was getting a bit lost in

the vastness of the library and while she didn't wish to show her hand to a stranger, help from a librarian could have her on her way much sooner. Surely, Willoughby was crawling out of his skin by now.

She smiled warmly at the old man. "Now that you mention it, could you point me in the direction of the society lists?"

"Pre or post Trust Wars?" the man asked.

"Um, post I suppose," Clara said. Then, changing her mind, added, "Actually, both."

Thelonius met her with a questioning glare. He raised his arm, pointing to the left. "Very well. The modern societies are on the third shelf," he said. His arm switched directions. "Anything more ancient is in the history section. Through those double doors and up the stairs. You can't miss it."

Thanking the man, Clara looked in both directions, attempting to make a choice. In the end, she decided to tackle the older records first and work her way forward. It was a trick her uncle taught her when she was young and had trouble recalling current events. "Always look to the past," Oswin would say. "History never fails to repeat itself."

With his voice booming in her ears, Clara waltzed through the doors and climbed the narrow steps that led to the second story of the library. The air was stuffier on this level, the ceilings lower and the light less bright. The same shelves that filled the main floor stacked along the walls, but there were fewer of them, with only a singular desk tucked in a dark corner to the right. Clara was relieved to find the desk empty and the level quiet. It appeared she was the only one interested in history today.

Well, she and the cat-sized rat scurrying under the desk.

Clara shivered at the sight of the ghastly creature and gave it a wide berth as she made her way to the stacks. She read out each inscription, searching for the club listings. When she found it, her mood deflated. The book of historical societies couldn't have been longer than a short story collection. Clara expected a thick, heavy text that carried with it the weight of the years it documented. Instead, she held a book that was no better than her diary. A tiny scrap of leather with some parchment inside.

The disappointment continued when she splayed the book open. It turned out Hedge End was not keen on exclusive social clubs, or at least it hadn't been prior to the modern day. Clara found a few promising mentions of a group formed after the death of the second king to take the crown, and the last before the crown system was dismantled, but it wasn't much to go with. With only five kings to take the crown, the history recorded was slim at best. All she had was a name—The Order of the Stones.

As ominous as the name sounded, the order appeared to be nothing more than a group of men that hypothesized on the future use of the gems. After more digging, Clara found that any mention of the society stopped two decades after the dismantlement of the monarchy, likely because the club also ceased to exist. It came as no surprise to her considering how protected the gems that remained in circulation were. No one could smuggle a gem outside of Hedge End, nor would they wish to. There was a reason their city had miles of barren land around it. People tended to run away from places haunted by Cursbeasts.

Clara read a few more passages before shutting the book with a loud thud.

"What a waste of time," she told the rat. The brazen creature wiggled its whiskers at her before continuing to chew on whatever it had dragged to its hiding spot.

Clara snickered. "I suppose I'll leave you to it."

She made a quick way to the second section the librarian pointed her to; the one housing the more modern societies. Though heftier, the books she perused were no more useful. Most were as pompous as the area of study they covered with nothing but stuffy language to describe pretentious clubs. If Clara wanted to learn about the people in the uppers, she would have simply asked her uncle for names to avoid.

The joke stuck in her mind. Clara piled up the texts she had gathered into a tall stack and left the table to return to the shelves. Her eyes scanned the spine, landing on the specific tome she needed.

"Hedge End Families of Note," Clara read out loud.

Perhaps she'd get lucky and find Thomas's name inside. She highly doubted it but at this point, she had wasted plenty of time. What were a few more minutes?

Sliding the book onto the table, she aimlessly flipped through the pages. The paper was smooth against her skin, the parchment buttery. Clara checked the names on each page, scanning through them in the alphabetical order they were listed in.

"Hawke, Hawke, Hawke," she whispered, willing the family name to pop up.

It didn't.

Before giving up entirely, Clara decided to read what the dumb book had to say about her own kin. The Aldridges had been in Hedge End for generations, ever since her father and uncle's ancestors came in by boat from one of the eastern regions that no longer existed. The turmoil of war over land never ceased to amaze Clara. One day, a township was there and the next it was gone. Vanished.

Her thoughts traveled to the missing people. Clara dragged

herself back to reality, flipping the paper to get to the front of the book. As she worked, a name stuck out amongst the rest.

Eyes focusing on the words, Clara took in a slow breath, spreading the book wide before her. "Cooke. Interesting."

Though Clara had never taken the time to get to know her friend's husband, she had to admit that Lawrence was an odd character. She knew he couldn't have made his fortunes from watchmaking; all the land the family owned, and the lavish manor Violet lived in must have been inherited from older generational wealth. Clara looked at the text again. She could ask Violet about him, but since the information was staring her right in the face, it made sense to take advantage. Maybe she would even find gossip to tell her friend over tea later.

As predicted, Lawrence's history was drowned in wealth. The Cookes were not only financially well off but also very well connected. According to their family tree, the name went as far back as the creation of Hedge End itself.

Clara let out a low whistle under her breath, continuing to read.

When she got to the section on notable clubs and associations, she slowed her pacing. It took her a few moments to get through the list, one name in particular catching her attention.

"T.O.S.," Clara read out. Her spine tingled. It couldn't be. She studied the abbreviation, recalling the society it corresponded with. "The Order of the Stones."

The Cookes were somehow entangled in the strange club. How bizarre. Continuing to read, Clara nearly choked on her own saliva when she reached a passage near the end of the page. Her eyes rounded, growing wider than saucers. Finger tapping under words she couldn't quite comprehend. Another name, one that shouldn't be listed here but was.

The air left Clara's lungs in a whoosh. She closed the book

and ran through the library, heading for the doors. On her way out, she stopped by Thelonius's tall desk at the front of the library. The desk was piled with books, and she could barely make out the man behind the colossal mess. Thelonius stretched his neck to look at her from beyond a stack of ancient tomes. "Find everything you required, Miss?"

"And more," Clara admitted. She grabbed the gold fountain pen from the tabletop and a piece of loose paper and scribbled down the name of the society. "I must be going but if you should happen to have the time, could I bother you to search your collection for this society name? It is rather urgent."

Thelonius took the paper from her with a short bow. "Of course, Miss. How should I contact you with my findings?"

"You can have them sent to my house to the attention of Clara Aldridge. The address is written down."

"Aldridge...as in the mayor?"

Clara smiled faintly. "One and the same. I am Oswin's niece." She started to leave, then stopped to look at the librarian. "And if you can be discreet, I would deeply appreciate it."

After a polite nod from the librarian, Clara thanked him for his kindness and hurried out of the building. The storm that gathered outside was stronger now, and the wind pushed against her as she battled her way past the iron gates. Willoughby was exactly where she left him. His gaze landed on her instantly.

"Got anything?"

Clara struggled to catch her breath. "We have to go see Violet," she said. "Her husband is part of some society that's been around for ages."

"What does that have to do with your cadaver?"

"Because the Cookes formed the society in the first place," she replied.

The tilted head and arched brows told Clara the thief did

not understand. Yanked by the collar, she dragged him to the street, not bothering to slow down. When she climbed into the carriage, pulling Willoughby behind her, she finally uttered, "They didn't form it alone. Apparently, another family was involved in its creation, one that was cast out later down the line."

"Let me guess," Willoughby said. "The Hawkes."

Clara nodded in agreement. Beneath them, the road swerved and Clara held onto the handles above the small window to keep from falling. Willoughby failed to do the same and was sent flying across the seat of the carriage, his shoulder slamming into the door. He groaned, righting himself only to slide in the opposite direction when the carriage took a turn.

On any other occasion, Clara would have laughed. Not today. She kept her expression serious throughout the ride. When Willoughby cursed, she didn't say a word. When he hit his head on the low, velvet covered ceiling, she averted her gaze.

There was nothing that could distract her from her racing thoughts. Not even the racing carriage she sat in.

Finally, when the driver brought them to a full stop in front of Cooke Manor, Clara sucked in a sharp breath and stepped out. She turned to look at Willoughby inside the car. "Stay here. I need to do this alone. She might not know anything, and I don't want to bombard her."

"You could also be pulling at strings," Willoughby said.

"That too."

Clara stomped up the driveway, past the fountain and the sculpture of a man wrestling a nasty Cursbeast, and to the front door. She gave it a good knock, her patience thinning faster than Uncle Oswin's hair. Luckily, Persimmon must have been nearby because it took him almost no time to let her in. After trying several times to persuade her to return at another time, he opened the door and asked Clara to wait in the sitting room.

"I'm terribly sorry," Clara said. "This simply cannot wait."

"I will check if the madam can be made available."

She better be, Clara thought. Allowing the butler to lead her down a vast hallway into a broad, bright room, Clara settled in a chair to wait. Her foot tapped maniacally with each minute passing. A scowl formed on Clara's face, and she pursed her lips as she folded and unfolded her hands in her lap. Groaning, Clara stood up, then sat down again. Her eyes tracked the movement of the seconds hand on the gold clock in the center of the room. Outside the large bay window, a horse neighed. She was on her feet again. "For gems' sake, what is taking so long?"

She would die of old age if she was to wait here any longer. Leaving the chair, Clara skipped to the door and poked her nose outside. The hallway was dreadfully empty and devoid of life. Had Persimmon forgotten she was here? She couldn't imagine him doing so, but perhaps he got distracted or pulled away on another urgent matter. Clara looked at the clock again. Best to go find him and see.

Staying light on her feet, Clara walked down the hallway in the direction of the foyer. As she neared it, voices rose from the entrance that made her halt. Her body iced over. The tones were hushed and whispered, though she couldn't mistake them if she tried. The woman's voice was obvious—she would recognize Violet's bright notes anywhere. It was the second voice, the man, that she couldn't come to terms with.

Moving silently, she slinked down the hallway and peered around the edge of the wall. Clara's mouth fell open. Her hand flew to her lips, touching them lightly. The boots she wore were suddenly pounds heavier, as though they wished to root her into the marble floor. Clara watched Sergei Pollen brush her friend's cheek tenderly as he leaned into her. His palm rested on the wall behind Violet's head and his body pressed against hers. It appeared to be swallowing her whole. Clara shut her eyes tight.

When she opened them, Sergei's lips were on Violet's and her entire world imploded.

CHAPTER SIXTEEN

The door to the carriage burst open with a loud screech, the hot air rushing out of the unbearable compartment. Willoughby inhaled the cold mist seeping in from outside as Clara climbed into the carriage. Her ashen face overshadowed the stormy sky behind her, cheeks sunken from whatever occurred in the manor. The mayor's niece hoisted up the bulging rear of her skirt and melted into the cushiony seat. With an aggravated groan, she reached into the nest of hair atop her head, ripping out the pins holding her two-story-high top hat in place. Then she threw the hat on the seat beside her, fuming.

"All went well, I take it," Willoughby said.

The amused grin on his face dropped when Clara picked up the hat and whipped it at his forehead. The damn thing sliced through the air like a battle ax, knocking Willoughby's head backward hard enough to cause whiplash. He rubbed the red line the brim left on his skin.

"Do you want to share what occurred and am I only here for target practice?"

"I don't want to speak of it."

Willoughby waited until she cooled down. His gaze averted to the window. Not speaking was not a part of Clara Aldridge's personality and if he remembered her as distinctly as he thought he did, it wouldn't be long before she broke the silence stretching between. Instead of pressing her for information, he concentrated on the overexerted opulence of the Cooke Manor.

The place was an absolute blight. Perhaps Willoughby had become too accustomed to the dark streets of the lowers, but if he had to describe the manor at the end of the driveway, he'd call it a playground for someone of little taste.

Every surface was polished pristinely and sparkled despite the lack of sun and the veil of rain clouds above them. Even the fountain appeared to be freshly cleaned. Can one polish a fountain? The idea seemed ridiculous to Willoughby, but he wouldn't put it past the Cookes to hold a fountain sweeper on staff. The statue in the fountain's center dragged at Willoughby's attention. He inspected the curvature of the marble and the way the details were captured down to the horns on the Cursbeast being taken down by a guard. *An interesting choice for a sculpture,* Willoughby thought. Especially for one that greets every guest.

He was still studying the gaudy thing when Clara cleared her throat angrily.

Peeling his focus away from the manor, he turned to face her. "Shall we try this again?" Willoughby asked. "Welcome back, Aldridge. What seems to be on your mind?"

"I...she..." Clara huffed out an exasperated breath. Her palms slapped her thighs, the hem of her dress bunching up. "I simply can't believe it."

"I'm not sure I follow."

Clara's gray eyes narrowed to slits. "I saw Violet and Sergei in a compromising scenario."

That was the last thing Willoughby expected to hear. On the way over, Clara had been dead set on finding out more about The Order of the Stones, a society he was not yet convinced still existed. He could see the determination the clue left behind on her face, clear as day. While he was stuck waiting in the carriage, Willoughby replayed all the possibilities in his head and how he would handle them. If Clara was to return with news that no such society operated today, he would bid her a good day and leave. If she discovered the opposite, he'd remind her that he had no connection to the upper echelon of Hedge End society. Then bid her a good day and leave. If she...

The cycle ended the same.

This, however, was nowhere on his list of possible outcomes. Could he have misheard? Maybe Clara meant a different Sergei. There wasn't a world in which Willoughby could imagine the mayor's right hand to have an affair with a married woman. Weren't there rules about such things?

Surely in Clara's circles, one would at least lose his job over it. Especially when Violet's husband held such high regard in the uppers. And in Hedge End history, if Clara's research was correct.

"Could you be mistaken?" he asked.

Clara's head shook, black curls bouncing around her shoulders. She heaved, her collarbone sharpening with each breath. "Absolutely not," she replied. "Trust me, I checked. It was him all right."

Willoughby swallowed a laugh at her shocked expression. "Tell me they didn't see you watching them."

"Of course not! I waited until Sergei left and ran as fast as I could," she explained. "Violet is going to be confused when she doesn't find me waiting for her. But what was I meant to do? I couldn't look her in the eyes after what I saw."

"People have affairs, Aldridge. It's not uncommon."

The color drained from Clara's cheeks. She ground her teeth together, her jaw working itself out as she considered her response. "Don't you think I know that?" she asked.

"Then why are you having such an adverse reaction? Why did you flee like you witnessed a murder?"

"Because it's Sergei and Violet!" Clara shrieked. Her cheeks puffed out until she resembled a well-fed hamster. "My best friend and my...I don't know what Sergei is. That's beside the point. I can't know of this, Will. What am I going to do? I can't tell Uncle without risking Sergei's position, and I definitely can't speak of it to Violet." She rubbed her temples furiously. "Oh, gems! This is going to kill me!"

Clara's hand wrapped into tight little fists on her lap. Her knuckles were whiter than fresh fallen snow and she had a crazed look in her eyes that Willoughby had only seen on poor sods locked up in the cells he frequented. Gaze darting from one window to the next, she looked like she was about to bolt, though Willoughby had no idea where she could go. It was either the carriage or the manor she escaped, and he very much doubted she wished to return to the Cooke residence.

Keeping his tone neutral, he said, "It may be best if we put some distance between us and the house. In case your friend sees us idling."

The words seemed to snap Clara out of her daze. She shook her head, her eyes sharpening. "Right. Yes, you're right. I need to clear my head with a good long walk in the garden. It often does the trick."

Sticking her hand out of the window, she gave the side of the carriage three knocks, a signal for the driver to move along. The horse neighed, its hooves hitting the cobblestone driveway. Wind blasted against the sides of the carriage as they took to the road, Cooke Manor growing smaller and smaller in the background. The wheeled contraption bounced with every rock and pebble, and Willoughby's stomach tightened and turned in return. At least this time he managed to hold on and avoided knocking about for the duration of the ride. He had no clue why people in the uppers chose to subject themselves to the torture of carriage rides. Willoughby preferred to walk. It was an easier way to get around the city unsuspected.

Sitting across from him, Clara didn't seem to mind in the slightest. She may as well have been tightened to the plum-colored cushions with a rope for how little she moved.

Their eyes met. Willoughby coughed into his sleeve, fighting the urge to look away. Something about Clara's concentrated glare unnerved him and he didn't have it in him to dig around his psyche to figure out why. Willoughby wiped invisible dirt from his pant leg, glancing vaguely past Clara's right shoulder. He reached into his shirt and dragged out the chain he never removed. Dangling the ring in front of him, he said, "This was my mother's wedding band. My father gave it to me after she drowned as a reminder of her, but when I look at it, I only think of one thing."

"What's that?"

His eyes flashed to her. "That my parents had a marvelous marriage; a meeting of the mind and soul that tied them together by some sheer luck." He deadpanned on the mayor's niece, letting the ring drop into the confinement of his shirt. "Not everyone has the same luck, Aldridge. Whatever your friend was doing with Sergei, she must have had good reason to do it. It is not up to us to judge the choices of others. And if she is as good a friend as you say, you'd be kind to keep her secret."

"It is all gem related," Clara suddenly blurted out.

The bottom of the carriage dropped out from under Willoughby. His legs tense to the point of actually hurting.

What was with the stubborn woman and the gems? Sweat beaded on his brow. He attempted to appear relaxed, but it was likely more akin to constipation.

Willoughby crossed one leg over the other, letting his knee flop open to the side. "How do you figure?" he asked.

"Isn't it obvious?" Clara questioned. "We have a man selling illegal goods at the markets who also happens to be from a family cast out of a society that specialized in gems. What else could it be?"

"Literally anything else," Willoughby said. The acid in his chest burned a hole in his jacket. "Besides, how does your theory explain the missing people?"

Clara's lips turned down. "When I was a little girl, I used to hate mathematics."

"Have you been drinking?"

"Hush and listen," Clara scolded. "No matter what the teachers tried, I simply could not wrap my head around numbers. I hated them. Not because they were difficult, which they were, but because I couldn't comprehend how there could be that many solutions that led to the same answer. It didn't align with real life, you understand?"

Willoughby nodded, motioning for her to continue even though he hadn't the smallest of inklings where she was going with this.

"I had all about given up," Clara went on, "until my uncle sat me down to get to the root of the problem. Once he heard what I had to say, he laughed. Not at me, you see, but at how I saw the world. He told me that I was correct to be confused, that it was bizarre to have a multitude of converging paths. Then he said to think of mathematics the same way I would of pulling apart a knot in one of my embroidery quilts. A subject I had shockingly mastered in my young age."

A smile tugged at Willoughby's grimace. "Smart man."

"Brilliant, indeed," the mayor's niece agreed. "Uncle Oswin asked me what I do when I encounter such a knot to which I replied that I simply pull on the loosest string and see what it uncovers."

Willoughby's eyes crinkled at the edges.

"It made a lot of sense to me after that day. Any time I was met with a math problem I couldn't figure out I found the loose string and pulled until I had the solution." Clara smiled warmly. "It was a crude way to solve equations, but it got me out of a rut. More importantly, I have passed on the analogy to all the problems life threw my way."

Resting his head on the seat back, Willoughby looked at the mayor's niece carefully. "And how does it relate to the missing people?"

"The missing people may be a thread, but they are not loose enough to grasp yet. Illegal gem sales, on the other hand, are sticking right out and tickling our fingers. That is the one we pull."

"You have a theory, Aldridge. Care to share."

Clara frowned. "I wouldn't call it a theory. A hunch, perhaps." She twirled a loose curl around her index finger. "The connection between The Order of the Stones and Thomas's family is not a coincidence. There is something there, something we are not seeing. The only thing I know is that we have nothing to tie Thomas to the missing people, but his name is directly tied to the gems. It isn't much, I know. And yet I feel this is the way forward."

The blood froze in Willoughby's veins. His head, heavy and stiff, felt like a stone anchor upon his shoulders. There would be no diverting her off his tracks now. Clara was convinced that following the gem sales would lead her to Thomas Hawkes's killer and once she went down that road, pulled on that thread, she would wind up at his door. His illegal, punishable by death door.

He had no choice.

Willoughby had to come clean about his dealings at the markets and pray that all the help he'd provided the woman thus far would pay off. Maybe Clara would find some way to keep his secret to herself, considering their past.

He blenched. Their past would surely be the reason she gave him up in the first place.

Steadying his galloping heart, he clenched and unclenched his hands, meeting Clara's eyes once more. "Listen, Aldridge, I—"

The carriage skidded to the side with such force that Willoughby's head met the glass, cracking the window. In her seat, Clara screamed as the retched vessel turned over and the wheels gave way beneath them. The horse carrying them neighed loudly. A second later, Willoughby heard the snap of reigns tearing and hooves retreating at a fast pace.

"What happened?" Clara asked, rubbing her bruised arm. She lay on the side of the carriage, same as Willoughby, her gaze darting between him and the window above them. "Frederick?"

The driver didn't reply. It wasn't until Willoughby saw a dark red liquid oozing down the window that he realized what happened. He gulped. "Eyes on me, Aldridge," he said to Clara. She shouldn't see this.

"What *was* that?"

Willoughby's started to speak but before he could answer, a dreary sight caught his attention in the window above. An eye gargantuan enough to make his skin crawl. He looked at Clara, noticing her focus on the same thing he was watching outside. The walls of the carriage shook, crushing under the weight of the creature climbing onto the side of the carriage. A massive set of black claws tore through into the inside of the carriage, another set blasted at the window. Glass rained down on them in beautiful rainbow glitter.

In front of him, Clara pressed a hand to her lips moments before the Cursbeast snarled, tearing the door of the carriage right off its hinges.

They were going to die.

CHAPTER SEVENTEEN

This was not happening. This was not happening. This was not...

Clara's head was about to explode from the sound of metal bending and fabric shredding to pieces. How in the gems did they end up here? Her crazed eyes searched for a way out but with the carriage on its side and the Cursbeast directly above them, there was nowhere to go. They were properly trapped.

It seemed Willoughby had the same idea in mind. He turned to use his hands to rip away the fabric lining of the carriage, fingers moving swiftly as he checked every inch of the core for a possible solution. Clara's insides turned to liquid. She knew there was nowhere to go but up if they wished to escape, but up was currently unavailable.

Her gaze rolled over the destroyed carriage and toward the beast. This one was unlike the others she had the misfortune of seeing, nor was it like anything she'd heard described by those who had encountered the blasted things and survived to tell the tale. There were few beastly physical traits on the creature

and if Clara had to retell the story, she would describe the monster currently trying to kill them as a giant skeleton. It was as though the human that it once was had rotted away and returned with a vengeance, and a good three feet of height added.

The beast raised its clawed hand high, the abnormally long fingers cracking. The length of the digits made a shiver trip down Clara's spine. She stifled a gasp.

In a flash, the Cursbeast slammed its hand through the window and went straight for Clara. Muscular, leather-clad arms wrapped over her midsection as Willoughby pulled her away moments before the beast reached her throat. He spun her around, twisting them until she lay directly atop him. The space between their bodies vanished when the beast punched into the wall of the carriage and another section bent inward.

"He'll crush us to death if we don't move," Willoughby said.

Clara looked up at the beast. "He?"

"It, he. Why does it matter? We need to go!"

"Where?"

The carriage shook fiercely as the beast wrangled with the thin layer of metal that protected them from its hungry grasp. Clara caught a glimpse of its rotting, gray skull, a few strands of oily locks sticking to the flesh hanging off the bone. She gagged into her hand. The smell was getting worse with them stuck inside. It wafted from the shattered window and drenched Clara in a combination of rot and sulfur. Her stomach turned in wild circles.

Sniffing the air, the beast snapped it's disgusting teeth then rapped its spindly fingers on the glass hanging onto to the frame. Shards rained upon Clara and Willoughby. She shielded her eyes, turning away from the vile creature and nestling into Willoughby's chest.

"Hang on tight, Aldridge," Willoughby said.

"Why?"

The carriage shook again, tilting and rolling over. Willoughby landed on top of Clara, knocking her breath out. She sputtered a moment before the carriage rolled a second time.

Breathing into her ear, Willoughby rasped, "On my say, jump."

"Jump where? What are you talking about?"

Another roll had Clara's body slamming around like a rag doll being shaken.

"Now!" Willoughby yelled.

She tried to focus her blurry vision. "What?"

"For the love of... Go!"

With incredible strength, Willoughby hoisted her off him and tossed her through the broken window. Glass tore at the exposed skin of her arms, blood welling on the wounds upon contact. Clara hissed through her teeth. Her body hit the ground, and she screamed when her ankle twisted beneath her.

A loud thud jerked her gaze to the left, where Willoughby landed in a crouch. "Are you hurt?"

She felt around her boot, testing the ankle quickly. "I don't think so. You?"

Willoughby didn't reply even though she could see blood covering fresh wounds on him as well. He grabbed her hand, motioning for the dense copse of trees not far from them.

"Can you run?"

Clara looked behind them where the Cursbeast was destroying the carriage like Socks destroyed fried liver. It would not be long before it realized they weren't inside. "Do I have a choice?" Clara asked. "Let's hope it takes a while to—"

A searing pain slashed across her shoulder and pushed her

forward and into Willoughby's arms. Her face paled. Shoulder throbbing, she touched the skin, and her hand pulled away bloody. At her back, a guttural screech filled the wooded road they stood on. Clara shook as she took hold of Willoughby's arms for balance and turned around. Towering over them, the beast screeched again, its yellow eyes glowing. The nails on its right hand dripped with blood, Clara's blood. It uncurled its hooked spine and stood taller, then let out several more shouts.

The world seemed to narrow into the beast's shadow. Her breath caught, chest straining as if the air had vanished from her lungs. Heartbeats thundered in her ears. Her hands trembled violently while her legs rooted into the earth against her will. The edges of Clara's vision dimmed, and for a single moment, she could do nothing but stare.

"Fuck," Willoughby cursed under his breath.

Clara followed the trajectory of his gaze to the trees beyond the Cursbeast. Two more sets of glowing yellow eyes flanked the beast, shadowy, skeletal forms inching closer from the woods.

"Are there more of them?" Clara asked.

Willoughby hissed out a breath through clenched teeth. "Appears to be. Listen, Aldridge, I'm going to have to do something here or we're both dead. If this goes wrong, you run like hell, you hear me? Don't stop for anything."

There was no time to ask him what he meant. Pushing her behind him, Willoughby reached into his coat, his hands vibrating. Clara glanced over his shoulder as he pulled out his fist. Her heart dropped into her boots.

With one slick move, Willoughby tossed a ruby and caught it in his right hand, his eyes narrowed on the approaching beasts. He snarled, his jaw tensing until she could hear his teeth grinding. A muscle bulged in the side of his neck.

"Die already!" Willoughby shouted.

The magic of the stone coursed through his blood and Clara's skin grew hot from simply watching. Or was that heat coming from Willoughby? His body sizzled under the leather of his clothes and Clara had to teeter backward before she burned along with him. Willoughby's shoulders rolled, and he shoved his palm out toward the beasts. Where he pointed, a blazing fire roared. It formed a wall between them and the Cursbeasts, one that spiked higher toward the sky, blackening it with smoke.

Willoughby screamed and pushed the fire further. Into the beasts. The two that joined scrambled back, their bony legs creaking as they worked to escape the blazing inferno Willoughby threw at them. Sparks caught bone and in seconds, the beasts were aflame. Their pained shrieks filled the air, making Clara's eardrums burst.

She pressed her palms to her ears, tears forcing her vision in and out of focus.

The wall of fire grew, but it wasn't enough. Only one Cursbeast remained, the others reduced to ashes in mere moments, but it was the biggest of the three. And the angriest now that his sidekicks were taken. The beast howled and bucked its legs, an animalistic move for its somewhat human frame. The glowing orbs in its skull were trained on Willoughby and Clara knew in her heart that it was coming for the kill. Dirt kicked back from its skeletal feet as the beast crashed through the fire wall and ran for Willoughby.

The thief pushed Clara away from him. Her boots caught on a root as she stumbled from the road and into the trees. Clara tumbled, skirts flying over her head. She fought the layers of silk tooth and nail, finally emerging as she righted herself to balance on her knees. Her eyes widened in horror.

Mere feet from her, Willoughby stood unarmed while the

Cursbeast closed in on him. His gaze was unwavering and though she couldn't make out his entire face, Clara could see his lips moving. What was he saying? She tried to figure it out, but lip reading had not been a skill she ever sought to learn since everyone around her had no trouble hearing.

She leaned in closer. Her knuckles dug into the earth, mud slopping up to her elbows.

Is he counting?

The more she watched, the more she realized that it was precisely what Willoughby was doing. He was counting the beast's steps. Why?

Clara didn't understand. Instead, she counted with him. Four. Willoughby reached into his coat again. Three. He pulled out a second gem, a jade. *He isn't,* Clara thought. Two. One.

The beast shoved off the ground and leaped into the air. It lunged for Willoughby, its long fingers reaching, reaching, reaching. The beast didn't account for what would happen next, but Clara already knew. The jade. The moment the beast crashed into Willoughby; a protective shield of energy erupted around him. It combined with the speed of the beast's lunge, causing an outward hit like no other. The Cursbeast lurched backward, the attack sending it flying through the trees. Skeletal limbs flailed as the thing collided with tree after tree, knocking them down from its impact. When it finally stopped, Clara could barely see it. All she could spot from where she sat was a shadowy broken shape crashing to the ground, limp.

Clara's eyes darted to Willoughby.

"Will!"

She rushed to his side. Half crawling, half running until she reached the place where he lay crumbled on the earth. Hastily, she turned him over and bent down, her ear close to his lips. "Come on, you fool! Breathe!"

A groan fell from Willoughby's dry, cracked lips.

Clara checked him for broken bones or any other ailments, but he appeared to be fine. Winded, but more or less together. Her vision regained its focus. Raising a hand, she slapped him on the arm. The motion sent pain crashing through her shoulder and she cried out, the adrenaline of the moment wearing off. The beast sliced her up real good. She may even require stitches.

"Ow!" Willoughby moaned. "What was that for?"

Clara scowled. "Quite the show you put on. Where did you get the gems?"

A silence stretched between them, its length covering all of Hedge End. Rising on his elbows, Willoughby bit his bottom lip and looked at her. His unruly curls fell into his eyes. He brushed them aside, his head cocking. "Here and there," the thief said.

"Oh, for gems' sake!" Clara said, annoyed. "I know you're pawning them off on anyone willing to pay, Will. Enough with the charades."

Willoughby's self-assured smirk faltered.

"It's what you were going to tell me in the carriage before the beast attacked, wasn't it?"

His cheeks puffed out. "You already knew?"

"Of course I knew," Clara said. "I'm not an idiot. I knew the second you tried to veer me off track. And you just confirmed it."

It was all very obvious now that Clara thought about it. She had an inkling that Willoughby's arrests weren't for nothing and while he never got caught for dealing in affected gems, case in point of him being alive right now, a person did not get thrown in the cells that often without reason. Willoughby's reason was getting caught for lesser crimes to stop anyone from checking on what he was actually doing.

If she wasn't so insulted that he thought he could hide it from her, she'd have been impressed.

"Are you going to turn me into your uncle?"

Clara's eyes bulged. She rose to stand, brushing off the dirt from her dress. A dark stain marked the part where her knees hit the ground, which she doubted she would ever get out. Looking down at Willoughby, she said, "Do you truly believe I would send you to die?"

"But I am one of the people responsible for gems staying on the streets. I'm what you stand against. I am quite literally the main thing you're going to fight when you take over for Oswin."

"I am not my uncle," Clara bit out. "Do not assume to know what I will do when it is my turn to help this city."

She turned to inspect the absolute mess on the road. A carriage that resembled a busted tin can of peaches, two Curs-beasts in ashes, another dead in the distance. Not to mention the scorch marks from the fire wall Willoughby erected.

This was not going to go over well.

"Can you walk?" Clara asked.

"Yes."

She nodded slowly. "Good. You need to leave."

"But what about—"

Clara shot a hand up to stop him. She pointed to the destruction left in the wake of their attack. "I cannot explain this away if you are here, Will," she said. "Give me the gems and go. It's the only way I can save your life."

"You don't have to take care of me, Aldridge," Willoughby said.

Ungrateful little... Clara stopped herself. There was no use spiraling now. Surely, people had heard the commotion from miles away. The guards could be here any second and if she was to spin a tall tale, she needed to be alone. Her gaze flitted to Frederick's gutted body, then to her wounded shoulder. "If you weren't here, I'd be dead," she said. "A life for a life. Now go, please."

The thief stayed unbearably still for too long, and Clara wondered if he was purposefully trying to drive her out of her mind. Slowly, he put the gems on the ground beside him before standing up. As Willoughby departed, Clara dragged in a shuddering breath. Her hand pressed to her abdomen as she tried to steady a heart that was running for its life.

"Hey, Aldridge!" Willoughby yelled out from between the trees. "Use the gems if you have to. The beasts are getting stronger, hunting in packs. Don't be caught off guard out here."

She gave him a thumbs up. Willoughby had nothing to worry over. Clara bent down, wrapping her fingers around the gems tightly. She would never be caught off guard again.

CHAPTER EIGHTEEN

The ceiling of Clara's room was somehow lower today. She couldn't pinpoint when it happened, but sometime in the night, it dropped by several inches. In fact, now that Clara was looking at the room more, everything appeared to be much tighter. It was as if the architecture of Aldridge House had changed overnight, becoming as claustrophobic as Clara's skin felt this morning.

Her head sunk deeper into the mounts of pillows on either side of her, the fabric threatening to suck the air right out of the room. Clara groaned. She closed her eyes. When she opened them, the draping canopy above her four-poster mahogany bed seemed to brush against her forehead.

"This is impossible!"

Swinging her legs over the edge of the bed, Clara elbowed the pillows out of the way and climbed from the suffocating containment of her bed. She tossed the unfinished needlework she worked on with a loud huff, the threads coming up in a jumbled mess on the tapestry. The room spun around her as

she hopped down to the floor, a vertigo settling in the crevices of her brain. Skirt billowing, Clara paced the length of her bedroom, stomped past the wardrobe, looked at herself in the ornate mirror above the dressing table, then paced the same number of steps back. When she reached the plush mattress, she spun on her heels and dropped into the cocoon of the bedding. Her eyes closed. Opened again a second later. The cycle repeated.

She must have made the walk between her bed and the far wall of her lengthy bedroom a dozen times, hoping with each rotation that it would clarify the chaos in her mind.

It didn't.

No matter how many steps she took, she couldn't for the life of her understand it. How could Violet not mention her husband's family history in Hedge End? Her friend was nothing if not forthcoming with information; there were no secrets between them. And yet she never heard a peep about the Order of the Stones or about Lawrence Cooke's involvement with them. It made little sense to Clara that a past that fascinating might go unspoken of. Unless Violet didn't know. Clara found that to be even more unlikely. Her friend was an upper society encyclopedia; she would never marry a man whose life she hadn't unearthed prior.

It simply didn't add up.

For a brief moment in her wild pacing Clara considered asking her uncle about the society but she instantly changed her mind. Mentioning the Order of the Stones would surely spurn questions about how she received the information that would in turn lead Oswin down a rabbit hole of her recent activities, none of which she thought he'd approve of.

Then there was the matter of Willoughby and the incident in the carriage. She had to use her entire imaginative bank to get out of that mess. When her uncle arrived to collect her after someone reported a broken carriage and an Aldridge on the road, she spun a tale of such grandeur she even believed it herself. According to Clara, Frederick, her driver, was a city hero. He died for the noble cause of protecting Clara with his life from a pack of beasts that appeared out of nowhere. If it wasn't for Frederick—and his gems—she may never have survived.

It was a convenient way to get out of an inconvenient situation. Though Clara hated lying to her uncle despite the alternative being admitting to everything she had done under his nose with a person she'd sworn not to associate with. She hated even more that she had to tarnish Frederick's name as a gem-user and seeing the disgust in her uncle's face when he considered that a member of his staff used illegal stones was enough to make bile swirl in her stomach. Yet she had to settle it down and smile through her lies.

There were many things for Clara to contend with these days it seemed. Each time she closed her eyes, her mind replayed the incident on the isolated road in great detail. The way the Cursbeasts attacked, the way they seemingly worked together. That there were three with the same abnormal features at all was surprising. Most beasts shared abnormalities in their development once a person was too far gone to be considered human but surely not so much that they could have been related. Clara was yet to see a beast mirroring another in appearance, not that she had met them all, of course. Still, it was peculiar.

The wind trilled outside the open bedroom window as Clara repeated her pacing. She blew out a slow, exasperated breath.

"Willoughby would have a theory, I bet," she said to her reflection.

It was a true enough statement. The thief was the most

arrogant, most opinionated person Clara had ever encountered. And yet his opinions did tend to be close to Clara's in the past few days, specifically when it came to finding out more about Thomas's sordid past. If only Willoughby didn't spend days hiding his wrongful ways from her, perhaps she wouldn't have lost precious time in their search to uncover the truth.

A knock on the door startled Clara. She stopped in her tracks, fixing her wayward curls and brushing down the wrinkles in her forest green skirt before walking to the bedroom door. She shimmied in her corset, the boning looser today for a change.

As Clara swung the door open to reveal a young maid holding a tea tray, she smiled. "Hi Sara," she said to the girl.

"Mister Aldridge requested I bring you an afternoon tea," the maid said meekly.

"Uncle is worried I'd lost my marbles, isn't he?"

The girl's eyes jumped to the wooden floor and her shoulders hiked up so high they caressed her earlobes. She swallowed several times, like she was attempting to dislodge a chicken bone from her throat. "Not at all," she said. "We served lunch last hour, and he was afraid you'd be starved. And you received mail from a Mrs. Violet Cooke."

A letter from Violet? What could her friend possibly have to say that she couldn't arrive in person to do so? Clara's gaze darted to the tall clock in the corner of her room. More importantly, how had she missed lunchtime? She could have sworn only an hour had gone by since she came in after breakfast, but perhaps she had lost more time than she realized. It was happening quite often these days.

"Thank you, Sara. That's very kind of both of you. But I think I've simply lost track of time."

The girl took a step inside and slid the tray onto the wood side table near the door. She gave Clara a tight-lipped smile and rushed out to complete more tasks in Elisea's absence. With the maid gone, Clara felt the pressure of the room encroaching on her back once more, her thoughts returning to the obscure society. On paper, the Order of the Stones was a thing of legends. A club that nearly all mention of had been erased was a mystery Clara couldn't help but be drawn to. Why would a society remain secret all these years? There was nothing demure about Violet's husband. Though Clara had only met the man in passing, she could tell he was the type of individual to boast of his riches.

Then why stay silent about the society?

Fingers pushing aside the food tray, she reached for the sealed pink envelope on the tray and ripped the paper with the edge of her nail.

Just as she started to read the letter, a second knock startled her.

She frowned. Sara had only just left. Perhaps the girl had forgotten something? Clara smoothed the skirt of her dress and called, "Enter."

The door creaked open, but instead of the maid's slim frame, Sergei's broad shoulders filled the doorway. Her breath hitched, and she straightened at once, her fingers tightening on the paper in her hand.

"I came to see that you had all you needed," Sergei said, his deep voice rolling through the room. He closed the door behind him slowly, as though to keep their conversation private. The gesture put Clara on immediate guard. Her and Sergei were never close, mostly because of his steel-like demeanor, but she'd known the man for most of her life and so she knew that if Sergei needed a private word, something was amiss.

"Your uncle worries when you spend long hours alone."

So that was it. For a moment Clara thought he would come clean about his illicit affair... Not that she even knew how to discuss such manners with the man. Or Violet. This was an epic disaster.

"I—yes, thank you," Clara said quickly, too quickly, her words tripping over themselves. "Sara has already brought me food."

His scar tugged faintly as he smiled. "Good. Still, I thought to check for myself. We have known each other for many years, Clara. Your uncle trusted me then to watch out for you, and he trusts me now."

His presence pressed against the memory she had tried and failed to shake: Sergei's mouth against Violet's, Violet's hand tangled in his coat, the closeness of two people who had no right to be together.

Clara lowered her gaze to the floorboards, heat prickling uncomfortably at the back of her neck. "You needn't concern yourself with me," she murmured, her tone stiffer than she intended.

Sergei stepped farther into the room, his boots shaking the floor beneath them. His wide body filled the space, shadow spilling across the floor from the overhead chandelier light until it brushed the edge of her skirt. "Concern is a habit, I fear," he said lightly.

Clara forced her lips into a polite curve, though her pulse thrummed against her throat. She wished desperately that he would leave, that she could unfold Violet's letter and focus on something other than this ridiculous web of lies she was caught in the middle of.

At last, Sergei inclined his head. "Well, if you're certain you're all right."

With that, he turned on his heel, opened the door wide and stepped into the hallway. His footsteps echoed for what seemed like ages, though that could have been Clara's own heart. It was difficult to tell at the moment.

Only when clicked the latch closed behind him did Clara release the breath she'd been holding, the paper trembling faintly in her hands. Her eyes followed the cursive flow of ink, and her pulse galloped with each of Violet's written words.

"My darling Clara,

I feel I must confess. Your trysts with the delicious Willoughby Tanner inspired me to action. As I find myself rather lonesome these days, I decided to fill the time in helping you on your quest for knowledge. I am certain you are well aware of my eagerness to learn. You may call it gossip, if you wish, we both know I do not shy away from it.

But that is not why I am writing.

In my search, I have discovered something that is much too horrible to keep hidden. I'm afraid I cannot say more in this letter on the off chance your servants are as nosy as mine and should happen to read these words. Meet me tonight after sundown at Forlorn Park. I will wait for you by the largest oak tree near the fountain.

With undying friendship and care,

Violet."

This was why the secrecy was needed. Violet had discovered pertinent information and wished to share it with Clara in person, but it appeared that her friend was taking the sleuthing too close to heart. It looked that Violet had donned herself a detective, going as far as to arrange a meeting for after the sun set in the park in the middles. How inventive.

Clara looked around the room and at the cooling tea on the tray. If she stayed here a moment longer, she would be lost to theories and follies again, she knew it. Clara could not afford that. She tossed back the tea in the cup, wincing as the taste of over-steeped leaved hit the rear of her throat. Grabbing a cloak from a nearby chair, she wrapped it over her shoulders, the black velvet tickling the floorboards as she swept out of the room. The park would have to wait because Clara simply couldn't. She needed to know what Violet uncovered, and she needed to know it immediately.

"Miss Aldridge?" Sara yelled out from the top of the stairs.

Clara twirled to face the girl. "Let Uncle know I've stepped out to see Violet. I'll be back shortly."

"Mister Aldridge left a while ago," the girl exclaimed. "But if he should return before you, I will certainly pass on the message."

Clara's brow furrowed. Uncle Oswin was off on mayoral duties more and more these days. She should make a point of asking him about his work. Recently, Clara barely spent any time with her uncle, and she missed their chats by the fireside deeply. She made a mental note to carve out an hour for him later in the evening before shutting the front door behind her and summoning a carriage.

The sound of hooves on cobblestone drifted toward her shortly after, and a new driver greeted her from the riding seat. Clara climbed inside; the door slamming shut to lock the sunlight away. As the carriage rolled out of the driveway, she stared through the fluttering curtains aimlessly, her eyes refusing to focus.

"Let's see what Violet found," she whispered to herself.

The carriage came to a halt sooner than Clara expected and when she peered outside, she was surprised to see they had arrived at the Cooke residence. Or outside the property. For some reason, the driver had not parked them in the round-about entrance as they usually would, and Clara chalked it up to his newness at the position.

She poked her head out of the window, her body arching awkwardly. "Is everything all right?" Clara yelled out.

"We are barred from entering," the driver replied.

"Barred? What do you mean, barred?"

The driver's arm extended to point at the gates of the

manor. Following his finger, Clara gaped at the two mayoral guards positioned on either side. Her mouth drooped. Pushing the carriage door wide open, she hopped down the narrow steps and stormed toward the guards. Her boot heels stomped against the stone driveway, and her curls floated around her face as she marched on. She tried to see into the property, but the guards' chests were too wide and blocked out too much of the view.

When she approached the men, she smiled politely.

The guard's serious expressions did not waver.

"What is the meaning of this?" Clara asked.

When she received no answer, she rose on the toes of her boots to see over the guard's shoulder. The man moved briskly to shield the view. The pearlescent scales covering his skin shimmered in the sunlight and he growled deep in his throat, a sound more animal than human. "There is no entrance permitted," he bit out. "Mayoral orders."

"Surely my uncle would allow me to pass," Clara rebutted.

"I'm afraid not, Miss Aldridge," the second guard said. Clara appreciated his politeness compared to the man beside him, who looked like he wanted to chuck her out by the back of the neck. "The mayor strictly said no one was to get inside. He gave me the order himself."

"Uncle Oswin is here? Why?" Clara's intrigue piqued as the lump in her throat doubled in size. She attempted another peek beyond the gates with little success. "Actually, that's quite well. He can clear all this up; we only have to ask him. His orders couldn't possibly include me."

"Unfortunately, they do."

Frowning, Clara considered her options. She could turn around and return home to await Oswin's arrival and question him about what was happening at Cooke Manor. She could wait in the carriage and bombard her uncle as soon as he exited the premises. Or she could use her knowledge of her friend's home to her advantage.

Without as much as a second thought, Clara chose the last one.

She thanked the guards for their service and spun away from the gate to march in the opposite direction. For anyone watching, Clara appeared to be leaving as the guards rudely instructed her to do, but that was not the plan. Not by a long shot. Clara's gaze rolled over the length of the gate sectioning off the land of the Cooke estate, her eyes searching for a specific section Violet had told her about months ago. It was a project she'd been putting off for some time until she could convince Lawrence to replace the entire iron gate for a more modern version. Violet even went as far as widening the opening between the bars with a mallet to prove a point.

As Clara darted past the guard's field of view, she was glad that her friend's husband rarely entertained her dramatic flairs.

The trees lining the property were denser in this section, making it impossible to see the break in the fence unless one was specifically looking for it. Which Clara was, of course. She ran her fingers along the iron, shifting them from one bar to the next. A second later and her hand broke through the foliage and plunged into thin air. Clara beamed. Widening her stance, she pushed aside the branches to reveal two broken fence bars that were pulled apart wide enough for someone to pass. Sort of. Clara had to suck in a breath and punch the ruffles of her skirt through the opening in order to make it to the other side, but she managed to do so with minimal damage to her outfit and only a few strands of hair torn off.

Standing on plush, bright green grass, Clara inspected the area. She was far enough away from the main entrance that the guards wouldn't see her sneak by, and if they did, she had plenty of time to get to the front doors of the manor before they caught up with her. All Clara had to do was find Uncle Oswin to get clearance—ridiculous!—then she could spend the afternoon grilling Violet about the secret society her husband's family founded.

She checked the surrounding area and made a beeline for the front door. Tall oaks hid her from the vastness of the driveway, and she was able to clear a large portion of the distance in under two minutes. Ahead of her, the grand fountain came into view. Clara paused. There were guards everywhere. She tried to make out what the commotion was about, but she was too far away to see clearly. The guards circled in front of the manor, none of them looking her way. There was a flash of movement directly behind her, but when Clara turned her head over her shoulder, she saw nothing but trees. Focusing on the front of the manor, she took off in a run.

Clara's heart raced as she caught sight of a familiar tweed coat. Uncle Oswin stood stoic, with his back turned to her, his body angled toward the fountain and the bronze of his ceremonial star sparkling every so often.

Without skipping a beat, Clara tore toward him. Her boots pummeled the grass with such force that she sank with each step. The wind trilled as she closed the distance between her and the mayor. Somewhere not far from her, a guard shouted for her to stop, but Clara did no such thing. She ran faster. Breath coming out in short bursts, Clara skidded to a stop beside her uncle, her body vibrating. She placed a hand on Oswin's shoulder and cleared her throat to get his attention.

The mayor turned, his face ashen and gray.

"Clara. You shouldn't be here."

It was then that the scene finally made sense. Clara's head shook from side to side, her ears ringing. The voices around her were suddenly deafening and each step, each breath, felt like it was ripping her into pieces. Her chin trembled. Next to her, Oswin attempted to pull her away from the fountain, but she shook him off. Her grimy hands pressed to her ears, hot tears welling behind her blurry eyes.

Clara's lips parted and a primal scream tore from her very core.

She blinked rapidly, trying to erase the violent image before her. Sinking to the ground, Clara clung to the sides of the fountain, her knuckles white. Water beaded on her skin in icy drips.

"No," Clara begged. "Please. No."

Her pleading fell on deaf ears. A thick cloak was placed on her shoulders, and she heard her uncle order for her carriage to be brought in. Clara wanted to stand, to flee, but her body was numb. She couldn't even tremble, even though all she wanted to do was vibrate until her bones disintegrated into dust. Gravel crunched at her back as the wheels of the carriage neared her. With the last of her strength, Clara pulled herself high enough to peer over the edge of the fountain.

The blood-stained water inside did little to mask the gold fabric of an expensive gown. Long tresses that once had been blond were now stained a dirty red as they floated in the soft waves. Clara blinked away the tears streaming down her cheeks. She rose a little higher, her throat filling with bile at the sight of her friend's battered face. She could barely recognize Violet. Her skin was shredded beyond recognition. Large, gaping wounds covered almost every inch of her body and her eyes... Clara's knees weakened, the queasiness threatening to drop her where she stood.

Both of Violet's eyes have been plucked right out of her skull.

"Clara, darling, it's time to leave," her uncle said softly.

Clara shook her head. "Who did this?"

"Not who, my dear."

The world spun around her as she put his words together. Her friend was killed by a Cursbeast. Clara closed her eyes, her lids shutting tight against the brutality inside the fountain. No place was safe anymore. Not even the uppers.

CHAPTER NINETEEN

Sweat licked the rear of Willoughby's neck as he crouched behind a bench in the Aldridge House Garden. It took him the better part of the afternoon to sneak his way onto the property undetected, and now that he was here; he was unsure of his next move. He was equally uncertain of his reason for arriving in the first place.

If he was a cleverer man, he would have left Clara alone for good. Unfortunately, Willoughby had a knack for making rash decisions, ones that often landed him in a jail cell. His gaze rolled over the pristine grounds. A part of him would have preferred a cell to being here now. And yet Willoughby could not make his legs start working. He simply could not get up to walk away, not after what he witnessed at the Cooke estate earlier.

For once, Willoughby was glad he didn't listen to the little voice inside that told him to make rational decisions. Keeping an eye on Clara Aldridge had proven to be the correct choice after all. Who knew that the mayor's niece was exceptionally

good at sneaking in where she wasn't wanted? Not Willoughby. His first instinct, the idiot one, told him to follow Clara after the carriage attack—simply to see if she gave him up for the gems, nothing else, surely. When he spotted her rushing away with a determined expression and the gait of a woman who was onto something, he couldn't help but follow her carriage all the way to the Cooke residence where things went terribly, inexplicably wrong.

His heart jolted thinking about Clara shoving her extensively large skirt through the break in the fence. Was it pride or curiosity? Willoughby couldn't pinpoint the feeling, but whatever it was, he was surprised to see a piece of the ferocious girl he met years ago come into the light. He was certain Clara had lost that part of herself when she chose to follow her uncle's footsteps. Not that it surprised Willoughby in the slightest; the Aldridges were the type of uppers family that never strayed far from fame. Even when it meant they had to backstab those loyal to them to do so.

Rage rolled through Willoughby. He tamped it down before his mind was overcome with memories of Oswin Aldridge's betrayal of his father. There was so much in his life that Willoughby wished to be able to alter but not pushing his father harder to find another way out was at the top of the list. He did try, in the end. Tried to convince the prideful man to leave the city, to go somewhere where the two of them could start anew. If he only listened, then maybe...Willoughby shook out his curls. His father was dead and there was no bringing him back.

The trees whispered around him as he pressed his shoulders into the wooden planks of the bench. How long had it been since he snuck into the garden of Aldridge House? Hours, perhaps? Willoughby's legs tingled from being stuck in the same position.

He stretched one out, then the other, his head turning to peer through the slats of the bench. "Where are you?"

If what she said before was true, she should have been doing her rounds in the garden already. After what happened to her friend, there was no world in which Clara wasn't going out of her mind right about now. Then where was she?

All he wanted was to see her to make sure she was all right. It was the least he could do after she saved his ass by not reporting him to her uncle. But it wasn't the only reason, not by a long shot. Willoughby cursed himself out. Life was much simpler before Clara Aldridge had stomped her way back into his orbit.

The sound of a door creaking open froze him in place. His chest swelled with a breath held and his stomach tensed under the thin fabric of his shirt. Willoughby twisted into a pretzel, his eyes unblinking. The rear facing door of the house burst open, and a figure stepped into the light. From this vantage point, Willoughby didn't need to strain to recognize Clara, despite her appearance being more casual than he was used to. Gone were the skirts and corsets and lace; in their place, she wore a simple shift dress that reached past her ankles in the color of the evening sky with a purple border lining the bottom hem. Clara's hair was loose and without the top hat she often pinned to her locks, it flowed in the wind behind her as she walked. Her steps were sure. She reminded Willoughby of an untamed mare, wild and free and powerful.

Clara's shoulders shook violently as she sped away from the house and deeper into the garden. A knot formed in his throat when Willoughby realized she was crying.

Waiting until she was well past his hiding place and further down the path, he checked for clearance, then bolted after her. She moved so fast that he had to jog to keep up. His gaze jumped around the garden. Where was she going? The further into the greenery they walked, the less of Clara's shape he could make out. Around him, the garden grew wilder and less constricted, branches jutting out at odd angles and threatening to take an eye out if he didn't pay close attention. The smell of stagnant water reached his nostrils. Willoughby's nose pointed upward to sniff out where it came from. The toe of his boot hit a misplaced stone on the path, and he bit his tongue, his eyes watering from the sharp pain.

Suddenly, something pressed into his back. Hard and pointy. *Shit. Guards.*

"Have you lost your mind entirely?"

His spine curled inward at the sound of Clara's voice. He turned, slowly registering the object she threatened him with. Willoughby tipped his chin in the direction of the knitting needles. "Planning to turn me into a scarf, Aldridge?"

"What are you doing here?" Clara hissed out. "If my uncle catches you, he won't hesitate to shoot you on the spot."

"Brilliant for me, then, that it is only you and the needles." When Clara didn't speak, he added, "I wanted to see how you were."

The needles lowered a mere inch. "Has the news of Lawrence Cooke's wife's death not reached the lowers yet? My friend was mauled by a beast in her own damn house, Will. How do you think I am?"

Her voice wavered, the pitch of it too high and shaky. Streaks cleared paths down her cheeks from tears shed and Willoughby noticed her hair, though finally free of pins, was knotted throughout. Above all, though, it was Clara's cloudy eyes that gave him the most pause. The woman was as undone as he had ever seen her.

A spark of realization parted the storm within her. Clara pointed the sharp ends of her needles at Willoughby's chest.

"How did you know to come?" Her nose wrinkled. "It was you at the Cooke Manor, wasn't it?"

He nodded.

"I knew someone was watching! Why are you following me?"

"I, uh…" Willoughby rubbed the back of his neck, his thoughts wavering. He collected himself. "I wanted to thank you. For not saying anything about the gems." He paused again. "And to make sure you were all right."

She scoffed. "Would you be?"

"No," Willoughby admitted. "But I don't have many friends. And the one I do keep is, well, you were there. I'm sorry you had to see that today."

"I'm sorry, too," Clara whispered. "About Soltan. We'll find him."

It wasn't possible, not truly, but Willoughby appreciated the remark, regardless. That was one thing someone living in the uppers could never understand about life and the finality of it. In Clara's mind, searching for Soltan was as simple as breathing. A project for her to take on, a way to help. But Willoughby knew better. Once someone from the lowers vanished, they stayed gone.

His throat closed up briefly. Somehow until this very moment, Willoughby had failed to realize that he never mourned Soltan. Not properly. Not like his father.

"This was their favorite place," Clara suddenly said, pulling him away from his thoughts. "My parents. They used to spend every afternoon here. Laughing, talking, sometimes dancing."

Looking around, Willoughby tried to imagine the Aldridges standing in the same place he stood but it had been too long that he couldn't register their faces in his mind. He remembered Clara's mother had the same distinct nose as her, though that was all he could bring up.

His lips pressed together tightly. "Do you think of them often?"

"Every day," she admitted. "As I'm sure you do of your family."

And there it was. The rage. The hatred. The unbelievable need to hurt every Aldridge in his path. Willoughby's hands fisted at his sides; his teeth clenched tight; his jaw grated. He wanted to scream. No, he wanted much, much more. His eyes flashed to Clara briefly, and her lack of understanding made his blood boil. How dare she speak of his parents in such a nonchalant manner? As though it wasn't her uncle that started the downfall that would claim his father's life. The muscle in Willoughby's neck twitched.

He took a slow, steadying breath. "Right. Well, I was only passing through to check you haven't done anything foolish. Glad to see you're not a hysterical mess, Aldridge."

"Not anymore," Clara said. She turned, her pale eyes locking in on him with a force that made him buckle back a step. "Why are there more of them? The beasts, why are there more now?"

Willoughby shrugged.

"Tell me you've noticed it too," the mayor's niece pressed. "On the streets, here in the uppers. Then there was the matter of the carriage attack. They were smart, Will. Working together. Stalking us."

"What are you implying?"

Her fingers twirled the knitting needles around. Raising them up, she used one hand to roll her hair into a high bun and the other to secure the sharp sticks into the locks, holding them in place. A few stray waves fell to frame her heart-shaped face. Willoughby battled the urge to tuck them behind her ears.

Clara straightened her shoulders, her chest moving up and

down in the loose dress. "The beasts are changing," she said. "Evolving. Don't you want to know why?"

"I suppose it is odd."

"Odd? It's unheard of! In the history of Hedge End there have not been many in the uppers. And what of the affected?"

Willoughby's brows hiked up on his forehead. "What of them?"

"Where are they?"

That was an excellent question; one that even Willoughby didn't have an answer to. When he thought of it, Clara had a point. There had been less and less affected on the streets of their cursed city in the last year. It used to be that you couldn't cross the street without pumping into a horn or getting knocked over by a wayward tail. Willoughby rarely crossed paths with anyone he sold gems to, dealing mainly with in-between men, but even then, it was easy to say that the city used to be much fuller of those who used magic than it was now. These days you'd be lucky to spot anyone affected by gem magic outside of the mayoral guard.

It was...bizarre.

An idea clawed at the crevices of Willoughby's dusty brain. The corners of his lips twitched. "You know, Aldridge," he said. "I had never visited the Cursed Isle this time of year."

"Have you visited it in another season?"

He frowned. "I was trying to be inspiring."

"You were failing. Now what is this nonsense about the isle?"

"Where do you reckon the affected go if they do not stay in the city?" Willoughby asked. Clara's face brightened, her lashes batting as she thought over what he said. When he knew he had her hooked, he added, "You want to know why there are less of them and more beasts? Go to the source."

Her smile turned down. "You're not suggesting we travel to

the isle? Who's to say we won't get killed the second we step foot on the sand? We don't know what happens to the affected once they leave the city."

"They don't get to keep their gems," Willoughby said. "Once they leave Hedge End, they stop using magic. Their transformation stops. There are no beasts on the isle, if that's your worry. Besides, it's a good opportunity to find out how the affected are getting their hands on magic gems and if Thomas and his partner had anything to do with it."

"Aren't you partially responsible for that?"

Willoughby bristled. "Have you seen how many beasts there are lately?" he asked, scoffing. "Believe me, Aldridge, if I was running an operation of that size, I wouldn't be this poor. Someone else is supplying the citizens their gems and there's a good chance it's our guy."

When stayed silent, he asked, "So, what do you say? Fancy a boat ride?"

He could see the wheels turning in her clever head. *Come on. You know you want to.*

Willoughby didn't know why, but the thought of following through on this called to him like a mermaiden calling to a sailor. He had always wanted to see the isle with his own two eyes. Why not do it now? And why not drag little miss perfect along with him? Seeing Clara squirm outside the comfort zone of her pristine life was a bonus as far as Willoughby was concerned.

Next to him, the mayor's niece chewed on her bottom lip furiously. "Even if I did agree, which I am not, we don't have a way to get there. Unless you've stolen a boat lately, that is."

Willoughby chuckled. His gaze drifted past Clara toward the impenetrable gate guarding Aldridge House. Past the iron and stone and into the distance of the uppers. Clara could mock him all she wanted, but she wouldn't be laughing soon because Willoughby didn't have a boat—he had something even better. And it was going to wipe the self-satisfied smirk off her face once she saw it.

The fists he held tightly unclenched. He couldn't wait.

CHAPTER TWENTY

Sea kelp rocked against the wooden beams of the docks from the force of unruly waves and moving ships. The air reeked of algae and fish, a combination that turned Clara's stomach. They were on land, but she was already seasick. The port and Clara were not great friends.

Her eyes narrowed as the sun dipped closer to the horizon line, the blinding rays piercing her sight line like sharp sticks. She shielded them with the palm of her hand and glared at the commotion in front of her. Men and women hauled cargo boxes from one ship to the next, their backs straining and their loose-fitting clothes drenched from the splashing water around them. This place was chaotic on a good day, the port being the only way for Hedge End to secure the goods the city couldn't produce within its walls, but today it appeared to be an absolute mess. A large box slipped from the hands of the man carrying it and crashed to the floor. The planks forming it cracked, and metal tins poured out of the opening, rolling down the docks and slamming into unsuspecting boots. Several voices shouted at once. The man responsible for the commotion ducked out of sight instantly, leaving the others unloading the boat to deal with the mishap.

More foul language rose from the docks as those working the ships continued their tasks. Clara's nose turned up. She rearranged the top hat on her head and flashed a steely look at Willoughby. "Why do I get the feeling this will not go as smoothly as you described?"

"Trust me, Aldridge. You're in for a real treat." When Clara pursed her lips at him, he added, "You wanted a ship, I got you a ship."

Clara didn't bother to correct that it was his idea they make a day trip to the isle. The more she thought about it, the more ridiculous it sounded. As though they were off to frolic in the sand for an afternoon and have a proper picnic; not at all like they were heading into the lair of the beast, quite literally.

She peeled her gaze off Willoughby to take in the port in all its utterly miserable glory. The morning mist lifted, revealing the harbor in gritty detail. Ships of varying sizes lined the docks, their tall masts cutting through the sky like skeletal fingers that reminded Clara of the Cursbeasts that attacked them only a few days ago. Beneath the dock, the water was a murky green, churning against the sides of the ships in near whitecaps. Overhead, the light of day revealed the port's age. Buildings weathered and worn from the brutality of the sea; their brick facades streaked with soot and grime.

Clara took a tentative step forward, her boots sliding on wood slick with moisture.

Even in daylight, shadows clung to the corners of the narrow alleys that wound between the warehouses. Clara resisted the urge to cling to Willoughby's arm sleeve. Focusing on the docked ships, she concentrated instead on making out the vessel that would soon take them to their morbid destination.

"Where is this ship of yours, anyway?"

The thief strained his neck, rising on his toes to see past the masses of boats crowding the port. He stretched his arm and motioned for one, saying, "There he is."

Surely, he was mistaken. Clara's eyes wondered over the ship in question, saliva pooling under her swelling tongue. There were no silken sails on the gargantuan floating structure, and unlike the rest of the ships docked before them, this one had to be at least triple the size of a normal vessel. There were small oval windows punching the metal sides of the hull. Clara counted three floors below deck with another platform raised above that secured the captain's room. A chain wider than a driveway hung from the side of the ship, an anchor lowering into the misty waters. Clara blinked. The entire thing was built for war, not daily trades.

An inscription on the side of the ship gave Clara pause. "Does that say 'Stone'?" She asked. "As in Stone Voyages?"

"One and the same."

She started to ask how in the gems Willoughby secured transport upon Hedge End's largest trade charter when a thick hand clasped the thief's shoulder. The fingers took purchase, deepening their grasp. Clara's gaze trailed up the arm attached to it and to a vaguely familiar face. The man holding Willoughby was in his mid-twenties with blonde hair so bouncy it puffed up on his head like a dollop of cream. He wore a white ruffled shirt with a tall collar under a green velvet blazer that had a thousand brass buttons sewn into its front. On his pinkie, a gold ring held a shining sapphire that complemented the man's blue eyes.

His bushy brows wiggled in her direction, a chiseled jaw jutting outward. "Answer me honestly, miss," he said. "Are you being held against your will?"

"For gems' sake, Godrey!" Willoughby remarked. He

slapped the stranger's hand from his shoulder, turning to face him. "Stop scaring the woman. It's bad enough she has to hitch a ride on your monstrous boat."

"The Stone Kelpie is a beauty, and you know it," the man rebutted. He took a theatrical bow and extended a smooth-skinned palm to Clara. "Godrey Stone, miss. A pleasure to make your acquaintance."

Clara took his hand hesitantly, yanking it back when Godrey pressed a kiss to her glove. Beside her, Willoughby laughed under his breath. "Believe me, brother, this one is not easy to impress."

In a flash, the toe of Clara's boot met with Willoughby's ankle. He yelped. His left knee buckled. He used Godrey to catch his balance before he crashed down to the grimy dock.

Clara grinned.

"This one is ready to depart," she told the imbeciles. "The faster we get to the isle, the faster I can be free of your company."

"Him or me?" Godrey asked.

Clara raked her gaze over the two. "I am not yet certain, Mr. Stone. Shall we?"

"I like my chances, Miss Aldridge."

With a flash of her teeth, Clara pushed away from the dock and marched toward the cargo ship. Her skirt billowed behind her, and she heard the steps of the men hasten to keep up with her. The smell of fish and salt grew denser as she neared the water, but Clara barely noticed. Her attention zeroed in on the ship and the wide bridge that jutted out from its belly, the entrance into the darkness within. Clara placed an assured foot onto the plank. It wobbled under her weight slightly, her stomach pitching from the movement.

She steadied herself mentally. *Here goes nothing.*

The sea was angry today, as it often was when it sensed people nearby. White, foaming waves crashed against the hull of the ship, rocking it with such force it made the masts shudder. Clara tightened her grip on the railing of the small balcony she stood on. Her back was turned to the captain's cabin; eyes trained on the distant nothingness around her. It must have been midday by now, but the sun was yet to appear. Clara rocked her head backward to gaze above at the cloudy sky— even the sun was having trouble surviving out here.

A door slammed behind her and Clara jumped, her fingers rolling further around the metal.

"Godrey says we're getting close," Willoughby said, coming to stand beside her.

The thief's shoulder bumped against hers as the ship drifted over the water beneath them. They made a slow turn to the right and Clara fought to stop herself from sliding into Willoughby's body, which appeared to be extra on edge. His skin was the color of rotten peaches, a sure sign of the seasickness he battled.

Clara frowned. She hadn't realized the sea didn't agree with Willoughby until this very moment. At least her illness subsided after a few minutes on the water, which was not what she could say for her traveling companion. Why would he suggest they make the trip if he knew he'd be ill the entire time? The ship swayed again, and his Adam's apple bobbed.

"Godrey is an interesting character," Clara said, attempting to divert the thief's attention from the turmoil in his body. "How long have you known him?"

A slight blush crept up Willoughby's neck. He cleared his

throat, his fist shaking when he pressed it to his lips. "We go back a long time. Godrey comes off intense, but he's a good man deep down," Willoughby said. "Loyal to a fault."

"Truly?" Clara asked. She found it hard to believe the two were friends; they didn't exactly spend time in the same circles.

"Yes, truly. What? Did you think I wouldn't be able to befriend someone in the uppers outside of yourself?"

Clara smirked. "Who's saying you befriended me?" she countered. "And that is not what I meant. Although the Stones are not any upper family; they're renowned beyond Hedge End."

"Because of Godrey's father's trades," Willoughby agreed. "Before you ask, it's an entirely mutually beneficial friendship."

"How did you meet?"

Another cough raked Willoughby's body. He brushed it off, collecting himself before saying, "I robbed his house. He caught me. Been friends ever since."

Clara's brow creased. "He didn't turn you in?"

"As I said," Willoughby reminded her, "a good man. Besides, I think Godrey enjoys living through me when he can. His father runs a tight ship, in so many words. It can become stifling being an heir to such a pronounced fortune. Godrey only wants what we all do."

"And what's that?"

A darkness passed over Willoughby's features. His shoulder blades drew closer together; his jaw worked itself out. "To be free, Aldridge. To be profoundly and dreadfully free."

Two large waves slammed into the side of the Stone Kelpie in succession, forcing it to dip on one side. Willoughby's arm shot out, and he reached for Clara instantly. She didn't fight him off. When the ship leveled out, he slowly removed his hand, one finger at a time, his eyes never leaving the horizon line.

The spot he touched was a few degrees hotter than the rest of Clara's body. Wind slapped her cheeks, reddening them. At least, that was what Clara told herself was happening. She side-glanced at Willoughby. "I've been meaning to ask how you are holding up? After what happened on the road, I mean."

Willoughby finally looked at her. "Are you asking me if I've been affected yet?"

"I may be. You did a number on those Cursbeasts. A lot of magic use in a single go."

Willoughby touched a hand to his shoulders, then moved it to his forehead, after which he patted his behind. His lips curved. "No wings, no horns, no tail," he announced. "I think I'll live."

"It's not a joking matter, Will. The effects could be dormant, there is much uncertainty around gem magic. I wished you thought of that before—"

"Before I let those things kill you?" he asked. "I think not, Aldridge. I'd make the same decision time and time again. No one dies on my watch."

For some strange reason, Clara knew there was more to that statement than pride. The way the veins in Willoughby's arms pulsed as he held onto the railing, the way he didn't budge even when the wind knocked them about again. Clara was certain—someone died on his watch before, someone he cared for.

She placed her hand on his arm gently. "Will."

The thief turned to face her. He blinked rapidly, the sheen of unshed tears glistening over the threads of green. He parted his lips and breathed out softly. The breath he expelled brushed against Clara's skin, warming it. Beneath the surface of the ship, the sea moved violently, and this time when the pull of it dragged her toward Willoughby, she didn't fight it. Her chest pressed against his, her hand continued clutching his arm. Willoughby's eyes rounded in surprise. Hers narrowed to a point where all she could see were the freckles above the bridge of his nose. The space between them hummed with electricity and, for an instant, Clara could feel Willoughby's skin on hers even though they were both fully clothed.

His arm snaked around her waist as it did in the alley, but there were no guards leading his movement now.

Mouth dry as desert sand, Clara sucked in a slow, agonizing breath.

"Oh, my."

She dropped her hand from the thief's arm, letting it fall limp at her side. Her cheeks flushed, and the redness crept up until it painted her entire face with the color of her blood rushing. In front of her, Willoughby's lips tightened into a thin line. He took a step back to put distance between them and in unison, they turned to face the third person on the deck.

"Perfect timing, as usual, Godrey," Willoughby said.

"You'll recover, old friend," Godrey replied, smirking. He let the door to the captain's cabin slam shut behind him. "I thought you wouldn't want to miss this."

It took a moment for Clara to gain her bearings, but when she did, her head was clear and her embarrassment that had choked her vanished. She swallowed down several hot lumps and glared at Godrey. "What do you mean?"

Godrey pointed past her shoulder to a tiny piece of land surrounded by massive boulders that jutted out from the sea—like greedy hands cradling a treasure.

"We have arrived at the Cursed Isle."

CHAPTER TWENTY-ONE

Cliffs blocked out the sun as the ship floated down the passage leading to the Cursed Isle dock. The singular entrance was so narrow that the rocks on either side appeared to be mere inches from the metal hull of the Stone Kelpie. Clara knew it was only an illusion combined with fear, but she cringed every time a boulder came too close for comfort. The metal rasped as the captain of the ship—not Godrey, thank the gems—maneuvered the massive vessel forward expertly.

Clara glanced at the tradesman's son standing at the bow. His hair floated around his glowing face and his eyes sparkled gleefully with each inch cleared of the water. Godrey was enjoying this a little too much.

"How often does the Stone Kelpie dock on the isle?" she asked Willoughby.

The thief's stern expression faltered. "I'm willing to wager today would be the first," he replied. "I think we've made Godrey's week to offer the chance at adventure. His position at his father's company revolves mostly around paperwork."

As if waiting for his chance to speak, Godrey clasped a palm around a rope swinging off the foremast and used it for balance as he twirled to face them. "Can you believe this place?" he shouted over the sound of clashing waves. "The isle of beasts itself!"

"Keep your voice down!" Willoughby warned. "We don't want to draw attention to our arrival."

Godrey's thick blond brows wagged. "Afraid you'll run into someone you owe money to?"

"Best hold on tight to that rope!" Willoughby shouted back. "Wouldn't want you falling overboard."

Shaking her head, Clara ignored the bickering fools and concentrated on the path ahead. The jagged rocks loomed like closed gates; the stone etched with timeworn scars. As the vessel glided forward, mournful groans escaped from its decks below. Even the vessel knew the viciousness of the space it occupied.

A heavy mist curled around the cliffs, covering the passage. The air was thick with the scent of brine and decay.

In the distance, the mist began to part, revealing glimpses of the isle. Its harsh silhouette was barely visible, but Clara could make out a dusting of white sand and a rickety old dock that didn't appear to frequent many visitors. She assumed the only boats that came out this way were the ones that dropped off the affected and occasional supplies; one-way ferries hurrying to depart. The ship's progress slowed, and Clara strained her eyes to see the approach.

The passage seemed to tighten as if to swallow the ship whole, the cliffs pressing closer with each passing moment. A loud scraping sound echoed from the hull. Clara's reached for the metal railing around the starboard but before she could grasp it, Willoughby held out his arm for her to take. She clutched the fabric of his shirt carefully, her skin flushing from the memory of what almost happened on the deck.

Clara gritted her teeth as the ship came to a slow, dreadful stop beside the dock.

Walking briskly toward them, Godrey clapped Willoughby's back hard enough to send him barreling forward. The thief's arm slipped from under her hand, and she hated that she missed the secure weight of it. With a flick of his head, Godrey pushed his sheep-like hair from his eyes, smiling.

"Twenty minutes to explore," he said. "If father dearest knew I made the crew stop here between runs, he'll have my head."

Willoughby chortled like a wild goose. "We wouldn't want that."

"Don't be silly," Godrey said. "It's a rather fine head. Don't you agree, Miss Aldridge?"

"It's certainly bulky," Clara retorted. She was beginning to see why Willoughby and Godrey got along well; the two were frustratingly alike in their self-assurance. Pushing past both, she strode toward the stairs leading to the lower decks and the exit. "Let's not dilly dally, boys. We aren't here to sightsee."

Laughter boasted at her retreating back, the scoundrels having a jolly good time at her expense. Clara paid them no mind. She was here for one thing and one thing only—to find out why so many of the affected left the city and to question those willing to speak to her about how they purchased the gems that got them into their current predicament. Willoughby guaranteed that his illegal sales were not on a massive scale; it stood to reason someone else was running the markets and putting magic gems into the hands of the citizens. Clara was intent on finding out if that someone was Thomas and his mysterious partner. Perhaps even to get a name for the man.

For once in her life, she grudgingly agreed with the thief. The missing citizens were the answer, and Clara was adamant that affected gems were part of the equation. She had to see the isle for herself. What was it her uncle continually told her? Never leave a stone unturned when searching for the truth.

Well, this was it. Clara's rubble.

Boots on the planks of the drawbridge, she shielded her eyes from the sunlight and walked with hurried steps toward the dock. The ship's anchor plunged into the black waters and the splash from its descent gave her pause. She looked around at the barren landscape before her. On each end, the foreboding cliffs that welcomed their arrival stretched around the land, blocking it off from the rest of the worlds. It made Clara wonder if this was why the affected chose the setting for their final home; to have some separation from humanity that no longer accepted them. The more she studied it the more she understood the Stone King's choice to round up the beasts on the same shore. It was more prison than isle, truly.

Clara's steps echoed down the dock. She hopped down from the low platform and landed securely on the sand below. Her boots crunched on the coarse shoreline, and she stopped in her tracks, confused. The air here was heavy, almost suffocating. Blackened trees with gnarled branches rose in the distance. Clara perked her ears, listening for any sign of life.

The silence on the isle was oppressive.

Mist coiled around Clara's skirts, and she kicked at it, walking further down the beach and away from the water. A shuffle of feet drifted toward her as the men joined in the exploration. They rushed to reach her side, Willoughby sliding in beside her quickly.

The thief glanced at Clara, then at Godrey. "Strange. Where is everyone?"

"Further inland?" Godrey suggested. "From what I recall,

the village is close to the center of the isle. Should be right past that copse of trees."

Behind them, the bustle of the ship's crew preparing for a departure filled the air. Clara was glad for the loud, boisterous voices that carried through the isle. It made the place less ominous and empty. A whistle grasped at her attention. She twirled around to see a muscular woman run to keep up with them, two lanterns swaying in her hands. The woman stopped, her breath coming out in clouds amongst the fog.

"Here, sir," she said, handing the lanterns to Godrey. "In case you need to light your way."

Godrey reached for one lantern and let Willoughby take hold of the second. He dipped his chin. "Thank you, Marguerite. We won't keep you waiting. I know my father wouldn't approve of it."

The woman dismissed him with a slight wave. "The crew is yours, sir," she said. "We will not depart until you're on board." Her eyes glossed over the others. "Nor your friends."

There was a spark in her eyes as she spoke, and it reminded Clara of another woman whose loyalty she treasured. She used to see the same unwavering trust in Elisea. A pinch of sadness tugged at her heart, the memory of why she was on this gem damned isle simmering under the surface of her skin. The past several days flashed before her. Never in a million years would Clara imagine standing on the cold shores of the Cursed Isle in search of answers and yet...

She walked toward Willoughby briskly, her hand yanking the lantern from his grasp before he had a chance to argue. The thief stepped aside to let her stomp past him without a word. Perhaps he wished to avoid her after the incident on the ship, or perhaps he realized that she needed to do this without any help. Clara had not come this far to follow. She had ventured into the markets, survived two beast attacks, and, regretfully, lied to her uncle for days on end. No foreign land could make her cower.

"Lead the way, Aldridge," Willoughby said softly.

Clara suppressed an uninvited smile. Her feet sank into the sand as she walked, and it took all of her might to glide across the shore and into the rugged ground closer to the trees. Grains of sand poured from her skirts, but she cared not for the inconvenience. There would be plenty of time to put herself back together later. She held her hand up, raising the lantern higher to illuminate her path. It seemed Marguerite was correct to bring them. The old, towering oaks obscured any light streaming in from above.

They marched in a line. Clara at the lead, Willoughby behind her, and Godrey taking the rear with the second lantern. There were no paths to follow, and they had to rely on their own inner compass to navigate the overgrown forest. Every step made Clara's skin ripple with gooseflesh. It wasn't the deep, penetrating dark that made her weary, nor the fact that they couldn't see the ship at all now. It was the silence of the place.

The isle was quieter than a silo.

After ten minutes of walking aimlessly, the trees parted, and Clara saw a glimpse of light piercing through the trunks. She slowed her pace, turning over her shoulder to look at the men. "We're getting close."

"Shouldn't we hear voices?" Willoughby asked.

"He's right," Godrey agreed. "This is eerie."

Lips thinning, Clara marched on. The lantern swayed in front of her, deep shadows growing under foot with each pass of the light. Her belly tightened. Using her free hand to brush aside low-hanging branches, Clara pushed her body into the open space on the other side of the trees. Cold, stale air filled her nostrils and the sudden change in temperature made shivers trip down her spine. She lowered the lantern; pointless now with the sun illuminating the small houses before them.

The village was not as large as Clara imagined. There weren't nearly as many structures, less than a quarter of the homes in the mids if she had to guess. Each house was only one story high, which was a byproduct of necessity, Clara assumed. Since the homes in the affected village had to be built by hand with minimal supplies transferred by ships, it stood to reason that people opted for more quaint abodes than one would find in the city. The large clearing was surrounded in part by trees and cliffs, making it a cozy setting in an otherwise gloomy place. Mulch covered the ground, and Clara noticed several makeshift paths where people had laid down cobblestone from one house to the next.

She stepped onto a path, following it into the depths of the village.

"Where are they?" Willoughby asked.

Godrey shrugged, urging for them to keep moving, which Clara did without question. They passed several empty homes with doors locked and windows shuttered, and unease spread through Clara at the sight of them. Staying true to the original path proved difficult, and they soon found themselves making sharp turns to zigzag between closed off structures. Finally, the path straightened out, and they emerged in what Clara assumed was the village square. There was a large fountain in the center that had no water running through it. Several of the buildings in the square boasted hand-painted signs, each one pointing to a different business selling wares and food and spirits.

Clara stopped next to a fruit stand full of rotten apples. She ran a finger over the wood, dust speckling her skin when she pulled it up.

Her gaze met Willoughby's fermented expression. "This can't be."

"Hello?" Godrey yelled. He spun in a circle in the middle of the square, his arms outstretched and the ruffles of his shirt billowing in the wind. "Anyone here?"

He was answered by only more silence.

"Don't bother," Willoughby said. "No one is home."

"Where would they have gone?"

Clara didn't hear Willoughby's reply. Her eyes snatched on a shop a few doors down from where they stood. A crate sat in the window and even from here, Clara could make out a familiar shape etched into its side. A symbol she had seen too many times to note. She bolted, running toward it. Her steps faltered, the toe of her boot catching on the loose, haphazard stones under her feet. Clara regained her balance and kept running. Pushing the door open, she burst into the dusty, old space and moved toward the narrow window she saw from outside, to the wooden crate sitting atop a low bench. Clara bent at the knees to inspect the carving on the wood. Her heart rate sped up, the breath she held falling free from her lips.

Unease filled her gut as she ran her finger over the rose emblem. The same one that was etched into the ring on her delicate pinkie.

A second later, Willoughby skidded to a stop next to her. "What is it, Aldridge?"

Clara shook her head in disbelief. She pointed to the crate, motioning for Willoughby to lift the lid. The thief responded without question. His eyes flared, and the curve of his spine deepened as he peered inside. Clara stood on liquid legs. Her focus narrowed on the contents of the crate before turning to Willoughby.

Clara wanted to speak, but her mouth was stitched shut. At her side, Willoughby was equally baffled. They stood, their shoulders brushing against each other for support or comfort. Clara did not know. All she knew was that something terrible happened on the isle and for once, she was right. Gems were at the center of it all. She knew this because the crate beneath the window was full to the brim with them.

The stones glittered like a kaleidoscope: deep sapphires the size of a child's clenched fist, shards of ruby no larger than a fingernail, pale green slivers sharp as glass. Some glowed faintly, as though fire lived inside them, while others lay dark and heavy, swallowing the light. Clara's breath caught. If a single gem could grant power, what devastation could be wrought with an entire crate?

A shiver rushed up her spine. What in the gems happened on the Cursed Isle?

CHAPTER TWENTY-TWO

"Why were there gems on the isle?"

"How did they get there?"

"What do you mean, you know the symbol on the crate? From where?"

Clara's head spun as Willoughby fired off question after question. She sat on the singular chair in the captain's quarters below deck—one possibly made of knives and broken glass—and tried to follow the thief with her eyes as he paced the tight cabin. Dark, polished wood lined the walls of the small space, and it reflected his shadow as he walked back and forth. Taking a short break, Willoughby paused to lean against the heavy, ornate desk dominating the room, his buttocks resting on tattered maps. Behind him, a lantern swayed as the ship turned, the light from it limning him in a halo of yellow.

He sighed. "What does it all mean?"

Clara shrugged, unsure of how to answer. She hadn't the slightest clue of what the rose on the crate symbolized, nor why it was on the isle and filled with affected gems. None of the other buildings on the isle stored gems and Clara assumed

this shop was the main place for those who lived here to get their hands on magic. She counted almost twenty gems total; all different stones that now sat on the floor of the Stone Kelpie until Clara could figure out how to handle them. Her vision flickered. The Cursed Isle was gem-free. That was its entire purpose. Everything about their discovery was defying logic, and it made Clara's brain swell in her skull.

Head tilting sideways, she studied the bed tucked against the far wall of the room. Heavy embroidered blankets in deep shades of gold lay crumpled upon it. Above the headrest, a tarnished silver cutlass hung from thick chains secured to the ceiling. It also swayed with the ship, though the effect was much more terrifying than that of the lantern. Mostly because the blade appeared to be sharp enough to decapitate, should it fall from its harness.

Clara swallowed hard and motioned for Willoughby to step out of the weapon's trajectory. She lifted her hand, slipping her mother's ring off her finger and placing it on the small table beside the chair.

"I have had this ring since I was a baby," she said. She pushed it closer to the edge, then back to center. "It was my mother's and her mother's before her. I loved the silly trinket; the rose called to me. I could never quite explain it."

One brow crooked, Willoughby took two paces forward and leaned over. His fingers grazed Clara's as he took the ring from her to see the rose etching for himself. When he moved away, there was a strange cold spot in the air between them, the space where their closeness was mere moments ago evaporated. Willoughby did not seem to notice. He studied the rose in detail before asking, "What makes you think it's the same symbol?"

"Do you see the small font carved above the vine on the left?" she asked, waiting until Willoughby ran a finger across the metal. "I put a magnifying glass to it when I was ten. It says, 'Through the briar truth shall bloom.' The words were easier to see on the crate; you couldn't miss it if you knew what you were searching for."

"Do they mean anything?"

Clara shrugged. "Not to me," she admitted. "I always assumed it was nothing more than jewelry passed down through generations. No real meaning, simply a pretty ring. But now..."

"You think it could be more."

She nodded, agreeing. It would be foolish to believe this to be a coincidence, not when you put the pieces together. "I don't know what I believe anymore, Will. There's a pull in my gut that's telling me to keep digging, but I'm afraid of what I might uncover if I do."

"It's your call, Aldridge," Willoughby said. "But if you're looking for unwarranted advice, I'd say get the shovels out. You have five days left until your friend's sentencing. Every detail counts now."

"Sentencing? Don't you mean execution?"

Clara's breath felt hollow. No one sentenced murder suspects in Hedge End. The term was only used to cover the bitter taste of what actually happened to those who committed the act. A death, swift and brutal. The guards were too busy patrolling the streets, and the city did not have the manpower for trials and juries, not the way they were able to perform them in other parts of the world. Hedge End was its own orbit. One in which murder was punished by the same degree of brutality. The guard decided on the punishment and a single judge signed off on the decree. For the most part, the system worked. The citizens remained diligent, and it wasn't often you heard of someone dying by foul means. Yet when they did... Clara sighed. Five days until Elisea would pay the price the city set for her.

The ship's movement slowed, and the waves stopped their relentless attack on the hull. A horn rang out above their heads, followed by the sound of feet shuffling across the deck. There were too many voices to count now. They had returned to Hedge End.

Clara rubbed the exasperation from her eyes with the fleshy parts of her palms. She watched Willoughby as he moved about the cabin, her gaze lingering a touch too long. The same incessant need to find the truth crept to the surface again, though this time it hit closer to home. The answers Clara sought were centered around her own past—her mother's. She had devoured every text she could find about their family history; studied the beautifully illustrated Aldridge bloodline trees displayed in the library ad nauseam, but she had never seen another rose.

There was one place she never thought to look. But she couldn't, could she?

Her attention dropped to Willoughby's hands. If she were to dare to explore that part of the house, she would require the thief's help again. After all, what was a thief if not a master at opening locks?

Clara's mind settled on a plan, one she would surely regret later, and her memory clung to the words Willoughby uttered before. He was correct. It was time to get the shovels out.

"You are out of your mind if you think I'm staying here, Aldridge!"

Willoughby struggled to push his way out of the wardrobe

she shoved him into with little success. Around his head, her dresses billowed and swallowed him almost entirely in their laces and silks. Willoughby's mouth opened for a second attempt at argument, and she took the opportunity to cram a folded napkin into it, making him gag.

"It is only temporary," she said. "Once Uncle goes to sleep, I'll bring you out."

His eyes widened as she shut the door behind him. She heard him spit out the napkin and yell her name, but the dresses muffled the sound of his screams enough that he didn't alert the entire house to his presence in her bedroom. Stifling a laugh, Clara turned the key to the wardrobe, locking the thief inside. This earned her several curses and a pounding of a fist on the carved mahogany doors.

She pressed her ear to the wardrobe, listening. When Willoughby stopped complaining, she leaned down until her lips were level with the keyhole and said, "No more than an hour. I promise."

Moving briskly, Clara shoved away from the wardrobe, locked the bedroom door behind her, and made the short way downstairs, where her uncle awaited her arrival for dinner. As soon as she walked in, Clara regretted it. The room was suffocating despite the windows being wide open and the fresh air pouring in heavy bursts. Uncle Oswin sat at the head of the table, his face buried in the most recent issue of the gazette, his eyes scouring the news. A delectable array of meats and roasted vegetables spread out in swirling patterns before him. Clara's stomach growled instantly.

"I'm glad to see your appetite improving," Oswin said. He lowered the paper, watching Clara as she skulked into the room. "I was worried you'd be all bones soon."

She bit her bottom lip while sliding into the chair opposite Oswin. Her eyes stayed downward, the betrayal of the smuggled in man hiding in her wardrobe scratching its talons against her ribcage. At least Godrey offered to surrender the gems to help keep Clara's name out of the terrible discovery. One less thing to worry over. Clara's clammy fingers drew circles across her lap fast enough to leave her dress wet and wrinkled. It took all of her might to muster a smile. Hopefully, her uncle would chalk it up to her processing of Violet's death and not the lies she spun around him like embroidery threads.

"I couldn't resist myself," she said meekly. "It smelled delicious all the way on the second floor."

Oswin gestured aimlessly over the food on the table. "The cook has outdone himself tonight. You absolutely must try the beef stew, it is tantalizing. Even the hellcat agreed."

Clara's brows rose in surprise. "You fed Socks?"

"Of course," Oswin replied. "I couldn't very well have him starve, could I? Figured you'd tear me to pieces if I did."

Clara flinched at his choice of words, but let it go. She reached over two platters to stab a fork into the stew, fishing out a big chunk of beef to place on her plate. The way she saw it was, the bigger the piece, the longer she'd need to chew it and the longer she could stay silent and avoid blabbering the truth to Oswin. It was an excellent plan if Clara dared say so herself.

"So, what has my favorite niece been up to?"

Her fork dropped with a clang, the beef rolling on the silver plate and sliding into a mountain of mashed potatoes. *Abort the plan!* Clara gulped audibly as she forced herself to look at her uncle. "Mostly reading," she lied.

"Hmm. Anything of note?"

"I attempted another go at your list."

The corners of Oswin's eyes crinkled. He stared at her until Clara became one with the chair upholstery. A bead of sweat rolled behind her ear and into the collar of her dress. She bit down on her tongue, waiting.

A second later, Oswin's tense jaw relaxed. "My darling girl," he said mournfully. "Why would you subject yourself to homework at a time such as this? I don't expect you to study after you've lost a friend."

Clara stabbed at the escaped piece of meat with a fork. Her teeth ground together as she concentrated on the task at hand and not the intense eye contact her uncle held across the table. The blasted beef eluded her every attempt. A sliver of light flashed over her extended hand and her attention snapped to the sparkle reflecting off the metal of her mother's ring. She grimaced.

Looking up at Oswin from under thick lashes, she retracted her hand and placed it in her lap. "Did mom ever mention anything about roses?" she asked suddenly.

"The ones in the garden?"

Clara took note of the creasing in his brow and the glaze upon his eyes. If her uncle knew anything about her ring, he didn't show it. He appeared absolutely baffled by her question. Putting the poor man at ease, she forced a smile and reached for her wine glass, sipping it. "Never mind. Let's eat, I'm famished!"

"I'll never say no to a good meal," Uncle Oswin agreed. He raised his glass in salute. "To many more years in your fine company, my dear girl. I pray that we will have all the time in the world, though perhaps you'll be too busy when you take the mayoral seat to waste the evenings with your old uncle."

"I'll always have time for you," Clara replied.

Oswin smiled warmly. "You are my pride and joy, Clara Aldridge. The future of this city. You'll make a fine mayor, I'm certain of it. The burden is heavy but you, my dear, are strong."

As the evening stretched on, Clara was surprised by the

lightness of the meal and the pleasure she took in her uncle's company. She took the time to listen to him explain all the meetings he attended for the council and laughed when he imitated some of the stuffier members. To her absolute horror, she found herself agreeing to join Oswin on his week-long city audit at the end of the month, despite never enjoying the event before. But things have changed now. What happened to Violet gave Clara a new understanding of the meaning of time. Specifically, how little of it one had. The man sitting in front of her would not be alive forever, not if age had anything to say about it, and she intended to make the most of the years they had left. Even if that meant being bored to tears while Oswin dragged her around the city.

By the time dinner finished, Clara was too full to fit in her dress and had laughed so hard her eyes watered.

She dropped her napkin next to her empty plate with a sigh. "That was brilliant. Thank you for putting up with my absences. I hadn't realized how much I missed our meals together."

"I will be here," Oswin said warmly. "Whatever you need. Nothing stands in the way of family."

Before Clara could respond, the doors at the end of the dining room opened, and Sergei stepped inside. His expression was still as a lake, with the same dark depths hidden beneath a glassy surface. Clara's breath caught. She had expected to see him again, but not so soon, and certainly not here, intruding on an evening that was already wrought with anxiety. Her eyes darted briefly to the door for fear of seeing Willoughby there, somehow escaped from her room and making things worse as he often did.

Sergei cleared his throat, the sound dragging Clara's wayward mind back to the dining room. "Urgent business has come to my attention."

Oswin waved his hand with a dry chuckle. "Sergei, must you always come armored with business talk? Sit down or at least have a glass of wine. Whatever it is can wait until morning."

For a moment Sergei hesitated, then his gaze landed on Clara. "That's all right. I'm sure it can wait. I will leave a note in your study if you wish to go over the details later." His Adam's apple bobbed. "Enjoy the rest of your dinner, Oswin. Clara."

Clara studied him closely, searching for the smallest crack in his mask. Images of Violet's blood flashed before her, her violent death still raw in Clara's chest. Did Sergei mourn her? If it did, his face revealed nothing. His eyes betrayed no grief, no guilt, no anything. For the most part, Clara understood Sergei's position in her uncle's employ and the need to keep himself together, but she would have thought that Violet's death may have triggered him somehow. Made him less of a soldier and more...well, human. More of the man she knew he was under the layers of stone.

The silence stretched, and Clara's skin prickled. Sergei was impossible to read, as always.

"Suit yourself," Oswin said at last. "Stop by the kitchen on the way out, the cook will give you a nice meal to take home."

"Will do. See you both tomorrow." Sergei nodded, then strode from the room. His presence lingering for moments after he left.

Clara's fingers tightened on the stem of her glass.

Finishing the last dregs of her wine, Clara stood from the table, walked to her uncle and threw her arms around him. The smell of cigar smoke and old paper filled her nostrils, and she inhaled it greedily, trying to memorize every detail of the evening. After placing a soft kiss on Oswin's cheek, she ruffled his hair and let him know she was ready to turn in for the night.

Relief flowed through her when he agreed.

Clara bid him one final farewell and slipped out of the dining room to make her way back upstairs. As she climbed the long staircase, the vice she felt on her heart before tightened, making it nearly impossible to breathe. Oswin was a kind and generous man—practically a father to her. He had never once given her reason to doubt him. So why did it feel like he was hiding something now?

Surely, she was seeing this wrong. He would never purposefully keep her past from her. If he knew anything about the rose, or why her mother had the ring, he would have told her. Wouldn't he? The thought of him withholding the truth made her stomach churn.

Her mind was made up. This had to be a mistake, and she would not allow herself to believe otherwise. That settled it. She would march into her room and tell Willoughby to leave. There was no world in which her uncle would deceive her, nor one where she could deceive him.

Clara's fingers fumbled with the key to unlock the door, and she pushed her way inside, her skin tingling. The second she entered the bedroom, she froze. Things were terribly wrong. The wardrobe stood wide open, several of her dresses lying abandoned on the floor in piles of silk and wool. She glanced at the window, but it appeared to be in the same condition she left it in, locked. Besides, Willoughby would have to scale the side of the house down two floors to escape her room and she doubted even he was skilled enough to do so.

She looked around the empty bedroom.

Where was he?

Her eyes traced the wet, slippery footsteps leading from her bed to the bathroom. *He wouldn't.* Clara didn't have a chance to follow the trail when the bathroom door swung open, and Willoughby emerged from inside. He was soaking wet, his hair hanging in tight tendrils around his face and past his ears. Droplets of water dripped down his neck and all the way to his exposed chest. Clara's cheeks flushed. She folded her arms over her middle and pretended not to notice the heat rising within her.

The thief mussed his hair with a clean towel, his gaze seeing Clara for the first time. "Oh. How was dinner?"

Clara's jaw gaped.

"You were gone a while. I took the chance to freshen up," Willoughby said. "Hope that's not a problem."

Clara scoffed incredulously. "It is very much a problem!" She paused to look at the thief, her gaping wider. "Is that my dressing gown?"

The soft violet silk lay open around the thief's muscular chest, the belt barely cinched at his waist. Willoughby rocked back to lean against the doorframe and when he lifted one leg to cross over the other, Clara forced her eyes to the ceiling to avoid mistakenly seeing more of him than she bargained for.

Willoughby let out a teasing chuckle. "You can stop blushing, Aldridge. I have my pants on."

"I will need to burn that robe regardless," Clara said. Her gaze remained skyward.

"When you are finished memorizing the ceiling tiles, you might want to take a look at what I found."

That was enough to jolt Clara back into the room. Her head swiveled sharply to the bed, where several stacks of papers lay flattened on the plum-colored duvet. With Willoughby parading around her bedroom nearly in his birthday suit, she hadn't noticed them when she walked in. From here, she could see the same insignia marking the tops of the papers—the rose.

She tilted her head to the side. "You broke into Uncle's safe? Without me?"

"As aforementioned, you were gone for quite some time," Willoughby said, as if that explained anything. "And those weren't in the safe."

"Oh?"

"Did you know your uncle has a secret compartment built into his desk?"

Clara shook her head. She had been in Oswin's study more times than she could count. The safe was tucked behind a painting of her parents, that she knew for certain. Uncle Oswin showed her the safe enough times for her to remember where it was. But he never mentioned a secret compartment. Unless of course—

Her face paled. "That wasn't his study," she said. "At least, not until after he took over the home. My father built the room to his precise specifications."

"Is it safe to assume the desk was his as well?"

Clara pressed her fingers to her throat, feeling for a pulse. She nodded. "A gift from my mother."

"Interesting."

Walking to the bed, Willoughby nudged the papers toward Clara, and she took a few steps forward, lowering to kneel. Her trembling hands reached for the stack, and she swallowed the bile that collected under her tongue as she grasped the greasy edges. Her index finger ran over the rose stamped on the top of one page. "What are these?"

"Nothing I can decipher," Willoughby answered. "Some have lists of dates on them, but the rest, they look to be random numbers. Can you make sense of it?"

The second Clara's gaze reached the end of the page, she knew exactly what she was looking at. Her eyes narrowed, a steel ball dropping in her gut. "They're land tax agreements," she explained. "Why would my family have this?"

"More importantly, what land are they for?"

Clara flipped through the pages, trying to find the answer. There was nothing here. No address, no mention of a home, not even coordinates. The quick calculation she made told her the land in question was worth a fortune, double, if not triple, the cost of Aldridge House. Was there another property her family owned that she knew nothing of?

She glanced up at Willoughby. "You found all these hidden away in the desk?"

When he nodded, her shoulders slumped.

"I don't think my uncle knows anything about it," Clara said. "He added my name to the house ownership the second I came of age. He'd have done the same with whatever this was, but he hadn't. Which means..."

"That your parents had a secret lair somewhere in the city."

It was a truly ridiculous insinuation and yet the more Clara studied the pages laid flat before her, the more she had to agree. She twisted the ring on her pinkie in circles. What were her parents involved in? She didn't like the scenarios her brain cooked up in her head. Uncle Oswin and her father were as close as anyone. For a secret this large to be between them was unheard of.

Clara's pulse stopped for a brief moment.

What else did her parents hide in the dark crevices of the house?

"You have to spend the night," she muttered.

Across the bed, Willoughby's entire body grew more rigid than an oak tree. "Pardon me?"

"My uncle leaves for work at sunrise," she explained. "It would be much easier to have you stay here so we can search the remainder of the property than for me to sneak you in and out. I can think of tasks outside the house for the indoor staff, but we cannot risk the gardeners and stable hand seeing you. You will need to sleep here."

The thief turned in a wide circle. He cleared the pages off the bed and removed her robe from his wide shoulders. The heat in Clara's chest intensified as she realized what he was doing. Before she could object, Willoughby hopped into her bed, crossing his arms behind his head as he reclined on the mountain of cushions behind him. His long legs stretched out before him. His smirk pulled to match their length.

"Not there," Clara said sternly.

Willoughby's jaw set. "If you wish for me to help you search tomorrow, you will treat me as a guest. I do not sleep on floors, Aldridge," he said. "I am not a beast."

"You sure are behaving beastly."

"Must be the gems I used," the thief retorted.

In one fell swoop, he chucked off his trousers, revealing more leg than Clara had seen on a man before, and that included the time she accidentally walked in on Sergei stitching up his own wound in the stables. Willoughby's legs were not quite as thick, but for some reason, Clara found it impossible to look away. That is until the thief kicked back the duvet and climbed into the soft caress of her bed linens.

Caroline's eyes widened in disbelief. "What do you think you're doing?"

"Sleeping," Willoughby said, smirking. "We're stuck here until morning. I suggest you do the same."

Clara muttered under her breath, folding her arms. A yawn dragged at her mouth, and she refused to meet Willoughby's gaze when she settled in next to him, tucking two pillows between them, marking a barrier not to be crossed. Chest rising and falling, she trained her gaze on the tiled ceiling, her body rigid and tight.

It was going to be a very long night.

CHAPTER TWENTY-THREE

Willoughby could not recall the last time he had a less restful sleep. One would think that lying on a mattress made of the finest materials encased in sheets that cost more than he made in a year would provide a shuteye like no other. One would be mistaken. Perhaps he could have closed his eyes and drifted off had it not been for the woman lying next to him.

And Clara Aldridge was not exactly a sound sleeper.

When she wasn't tossing and turning in the throes of whatever caused her anguish late at night, she was having nonsensical conversations with herself in a voice that was teetering on the line of inhuman. At some point, Willoughby could have sworn he actually heard the woman growl. Clara turned away from him before he could confirm, but for the remainder of his days he would never forget that guttural sound. It was as though she was truly possessed.

The moon shone into the room through slatted shutters, casting deep, angular shadows across the bed and Clara. Her eyes fluttered as her dreams took over, and Willoughby

couldn't help but wonder what she saw in that wild mind of hers.

He rubbed the bridge of his nose until it hurt. Perhaps he could ask her in the morning if he were to survive the night.

His eyes raked over the small table near the canopied bed. Nearly a dozen texts on Hedge End and the surrounding regions piled one atop the other, each dog-eared and marked with scraps of paper. It seemed Clara was putting in a lot of work into studying their city and he wondered how much of it was for future mayoral duties and how much stemmed from her fervent need for knowledge. At the top of the book stack sat an abandoned tapestry. Willoughby's chest warmed at the thought of Clara's creased brow as she worked on the colorful piece.

A soft murmur beside him made his thighs tense.

The impenetrable wall of cushions Clara had built between them had shifted in the night and when she twisted, kicking high at whatever opponent she battled, her leg dropped on top of Willoughby's, pinning him in place. He stopped breathing. The warmth of her skin penetrated through him. Beads of sweat gathered on Willoughby's forehead, and he bit down on his tongue hard enough to draw blood.

Think of anything but that leg, he warned himself. *Think of Cursbeasts. Think of searching the house come morning.*

In the end, Willoughby settled on picturing the mayor in female britches and Clara's top hat. The image worked, and he clung to it for hours as the leg that straddled him rode higher and higher, nearing too close to his nether regions. He had to bite down on the corner of his pillow to stay still.

Beside him, oblivious to the torture she inflicted, Clara moaned.

"For the love of..."

Willoughby cursed under his breath and looked at her. She

was so peaceful. With her calculating eyes closed, Clara was nothing like the woman he knew now. Not at all a politician. If anything, she resembled the girl he chased through the mayoral estate when his father worked for Oswin Aldridge. This couldn't be the same person who abandoned him when he needed her most; couldn't be the heartless creature that watched her uncle fire his father for a theft he didn't commit and simply let him walk out the door. Let him walk toward his doomed destiny.

"Will?"

He startled. His body jerked, and the movement knocked Clara's leg off his thigh hard enough that she almost fell from the side of the bed. Heat colored her cheeks. She scooted away from him, putting more distance between them than there had been all night. Her eyes, groggy with sleep, focused on his lips. "If you're hungry, we have better options that my cushions."

Spitting out the fabric, he gaped at her as she rearranged the pillow wall.

"You snore," Willoughby said.

Clara slapped his chest playfully, then retracted her hand instantly when she realized he wasn't wearing a shirt. "I do not!" she exclaimed. "Why are you up in the middle of the night?"

"I already explained." He looked at the brightening window, the shutters lighting up in a golden ray. "The sun is coming up. What time does your uncle usually depart?"

"It depends on the work to be done," Clara replied. "Though recently he'd been gone all hours of the day and night."

Willoughby's brows drew upward. "Hmm. Did he mention why?"

"I haven't had much time to spend with him. On account of our activities. But I wager it may have something to do with the beasts." She paused to look at him, eyes slanted. "Or the excess of gems on the markets."

The bed dipped under her weight as Clara pushed off to peel herself from the mattress. She threw the covers off her, the plush velvet smacking Willoughby in the face. He scowled. His gaze caught a glimpse of Clara's exposed ankle, and the scowl deepened. Tossing his legs over the bed, he turned his back to her and proceeded to get dressed, if only to busy himself with anything other than thinking of the previous night. The rivets of his boot got caught on the rip in his sock and he had to hop around the room, bouncing off walls, to slip it into place. When he finally secured the dreadful shoe, he brushed his hair back, avoiding the taunting grin on Clara's face.

The mayor's niece ran a wide-toothed comb through the long wavy tresses that fell in a waterfall over her shoulders, then pinned half the mass into a loose knot at the rear of her head. Willoughby waited until she donned the stupid hat she often wore, pleasantly surprised when she didn't bother with a headdress of any kind.

His jaw parted slightly.

"What?" Clara hissed when she caught him spying on her.

"You're oddly casual this morning."

Clara scoffed, brushing down the layers of her loose-fitting dress. "I am at home. You don't possibly expect me to keep up appearances for you here."

The hardwood floors vibrated under his feet. Willoughby stopped moving as footsteps echoed down the hall outside Clara's bedroom. The stomping got louder and louder, closer. It seemed that the entire house was responding to the attack of heavy feet.

Oswin Aldridge was awake.

The corners of Willoughby's lips twitched. He looked at Clara, mouthing, "Is it safe?"

He was answered with a raised finger. Not yet.

A few minutes later, the front door slammed shut, and the shutters quivered at Willoughby's back, like the house finally let go of the breath it was holding. He expelled the air from his lungs. There were few things Willoughby feared in this life, but getting caught by the mayor in his niece's bedroom was high up on the list. Possibly higher even than being arrested for gem dealing. He had no doubt the punishment for both would be the same.

His legs were rubbery from standing still, so when Clara finally motioned for the door, he leaped for it. Before he could reach for the handle, she grabbed him by the collar and yanked him backward, the fabric of his shirt tugging at his neck, making him cough.

He faced the woman, disdain darkening his expression. "What now?"

"I need to handle the staff," Clara said. "Stay here."

"I will not—"

Clara pushed him away with her palm. His clumsy feet caught the edge of a rug as he stumbled away from her; the mayor's niece was surprisingly strong for her size. She deadpanned on him, her glare burning. "Do you wish to revisit my wardrobe again?"

Shaking his head negatively, he put his hands up in surrender.

"Good. I'll return shortly."

This time, Clara stayed true to her word and was back before Willoughby had a chance to properly inspect her quarters. He was about to rummage through a set of drawers beneath the window when the door creaked open, and she burst into the room.

Her focus landed on his hands, frozen in midair. "You will

not find what we're looking for in my undergarments," she said sternly.

His arms, suddenly weighing more than Godrey's ship, dropped as boulders.

"Let's go," Clara ordered. "I sent everyone away on remedial tasks, but I cannot guarantee how long they'll be gone."

They moved through the house as swift as Cursbeasts. Upon quick review, Willoughby suggested they leave the first level of the home to last as it was the most visited and thus least likely to hold anything of value. Clara vetoed the search of the top level altogether since she doubted her parents hid their deepest, darkest secrets in the staff quarters. That left them with the cellar—a dingy, wet containment area designated to holding preserves and wine—and the second level which housed the family bedrooms. It took Willoughby several tries to convince Clara to subject her own room to a search, but unfortunately, even after she succumbed, they found nothing there.

The same was said for Oswin's room, the library, and each of the three bathrooms on this level.

He was about to give up hope when he noticed another door at the end of the long, narrow hallway. One Clara was remiss to mention. He took a step toward it.

"Not there," Clara whispered at his back.

Willoughby turned to watch her, his skin cooling at the sight of her ashen face. Clara's back was rigid as a rod and her body tilted back like she was physically recoiling from the odd room at the end of the hall. Her fingers twitched; hands unable to stop moving.

"That was their room."

Right. Of course. He should have known from the moment he saw the door and the position of it in conjunction with the rest of the house. He had seen the cloaked windows when he was waiting for Clara down in the garden. The room had the largest set of windows, taking up a large portion of the south-facing wall. A room that enormous would surely have been reserved for the heads of the family. Clara's parents.

The small space between Willoughby's heart and his ribcage tightened. He sucked in a sharp breath and let it out between clenched teeth. Slowly, he placed a hand on Clara's shoulder, giving it a jolt of a squeeze.

"I can go alone if you prefer.," he suggested. "It's the only room left, and it's worth checking."

Clara's features twisted in pain.

"Or," he went on, "we forget it. We searched the rest of the house and didn't find a thing. It may be the secret compartment was a fluke."

The woman's brows scrunched in deep concentration as she entertained his words. She shimmied her shoulders, his hand falling away. "No, you're right. It is foolish not to see for ourselves. I highly doubt the desk my mother had custom made for my father had a compartment not commissioned by her. It is too far of a stretch."

"Are you certain?"

"For now," Clara whispered.

There was little sense in continuing to stand in one place or else she'd change her mind, so Willoughby did the only reasonable thing he could think of: he marched toward the door. Behind him, he heard Clara sigh before following. He cleared the distance in several long strides and wrapped his fingers over the handle, jostling it to make certain it wasn't locked. The handle gave way smoothly, as though it had been anticipating a visit long overdue.

As Willoughby stepped into the room, his breath hitched. Dust motes swirled in the thin beam of sunlight that penetrated through the grimy windows. The once-grand chamber, now aged in neglect, was the most depressing sight he had witnessed in all of Aldridge House. The furniture sat draped in white sheets and loomed around the gloomy space like apparitions. In the center, an oak four-poster bed stood high and mighty, its canopy tattered. Willoughby wondered if the cat had gotten a hold of the red fabric somewhere through the years. Even the mirror in the vanity was cracked like someone had punched it in anger.

Willoughby breathed in the thick, musty air, coughing. His gaze traveled to the walls, where a massive portrait of two people hung in a gilded frame. The paint was faded and chipping. In the corner of the room a wardrobe double the size of the one in Clara's bedroom stood slightly ajar and Willoughby spied several old-fashioned gowns peeking out from within.

Adrenaline carved up his spine.

He cleared his parched throat. "I can start here," he said. "Do you want to handle the bath?"

Willoughby knew there was little chance of there being a secret compartment built into the Aldridge's bathroom, but it was the only place he could think of where Clara wouldn't be suffocated by the memory of her parents. Here, in this room with the faint smell of rotting roses in the air, she would fall apart. And Clara needed to be useful. He knew that much about her at least.

He waited until she was out of sight to get to work.

There was one thing Willoughby was an expert in, and he didn't need any help from Clara to do it right. As part of his less than honorable profession, he had become quite accustomed to searching rooms. It was laughable what people considered to be fine hiding places for their most cherished belongings. Some crammed their jewels and gold into tight spaces between loose bricks, others chose the more inventive route and pried open hardwood flooring. There were even those that sewed pockets on the underside of their mattresses in a sad attempt to stave off people like him. It never worked. Willoughby always found the goods.

This time, though, the task proved to be more difficult. He didn't tell Clara this, but finding the secret compartment in the desk happened entirely by accident. In reality, Willoughby stubbed his toe on the leg of the desk and when he bent down to rub at the painful spot, he happened to glean a protruding edge. A few pushes and pulls and the compartment slid out, revealing the paperwork he later brought to Clara. It wasn't exactly a mastermind production.

As he stood in the center of the Aldridge's bedroom, their sanctuary, he struggled to find anything that didn't belong. He touched every crevice, tested each frame on the wall, even went as far as sliding under the dusty bed to check beneath it. Nothing.

Irritation clawed at him in new and unbearable ways.

Willoughby frowned. If he was an Aldridge, where would he hide his secrets? His gaze rolled over the room. Taking in the details, he walked to the wall on his left and ran his palm over the rose-patterned wallpaper, then he repeated the motion for the other three walls.

Not a glitch in the pattern. Blast.

"Anything?" Clara yelled out from the bathroom.

His frown deepened. "Nothing yet."

As he looked in the direction of the bath, his eye struck gold. Willoughby turned his head to the side. Jogging to the doorframe that led to the bath, he pressed his index finger to the brass strike plate in the wood. His head swiveled back, then returned to the plate.

"What is it?" Clara asked, suddenly appearing beside him.

He pointed to the doorframe. "It's a strike plate."

"And?"

Motioning to the opening between the two rooms, Willoughby said, "There is no door, only curtains. Why have a strike plate if there is no lock?"

A Cheshire smile spread across his face. He ran his finger delicately along the plate, searching for the inconsistency in the material. When he felt an edge, he pushed his index finger inward. A handle popped out of the plate and made him jump. It was the same brass material as the plate but had a hole large enough to fit a finger punched through it. Willoughby fitted his thumb into the hole and pulled.

As he expected, a compartment slid out of the doorframe, easy as butter sliding across warm toast. He turned the narrow brass box around, positioning it to lay flat before him.

"A security box?" Clara asked. "In the door?"

"In the wall, actually. Your parents were clever."

Clara did not look convinced. Her eyes kept darting around the room as though she was hoping to find more hiding spaces, more secrets that her parents kept from her in the time they were alive. It was unfortunate to admit, but Willoughby understood it all too well. He knew first-hand what it meant to lose a parent only to later find out that there was an entire world they kept from you. The betrayal was suffocating. Even if Clara's parents didn't take their own life like his father did, it didn't mean that what she was about to discover didn't sting; that it didn't rip a hole in her chest all the way through to the other side.

It wasn't until Willoughby opened the thin latch on the box that Clara stopped fidgeting. Her eyes narrowed to a singular focus—finding out what was inside.

"Here goes nothing," Willoughby said as he flipped the lid open.

The contents of the safety box were, in no better terms, disappointing. Either the Aldridges cleared out all the important bits from the damn thing or there was nothing of substance to discover in the first place. He saw the effect of the single sheet of parchment laying in the box had on Clara instantly.

Her eye twitched. "That's it?"

Reaching in, she snatched the parchment and held it up to the light, studying it intently. She turned the paper around over and over as she attempted to figure out what it portrayed. To the untrained eye, the yellowing paper covered in blue lines and dashes was a tangled web of useless information. A piece of modern art no one would pay good coin to obtain. Fortunately, as proven earlier, Willoughby saw things differently.

Clara puffed out her cheeks. "I don't understand. What is it?"

A wayward curl fell from her hair, covering her eyes. Unable to stop himself, and to his utter admonishment, Willoughby reached over to tuck it behind her ear. Her eyes rounded. Before she could verbally tear him into pieces, Willoughby lowered his arm and pointed to the blueprints clutched in her grip. "Aren't you the lucky one, Aldridge?" he asked. "I happen to know exactly what you're holding."

CHAPTER TWENTY-FOUR

It surprised Clara to find herself beneath the city surrounded by the remnants of the dead with only a thief for company. Her head turned left and right, up and down. Around her, those buried under Hedge End gobbled her up in their deadly maws.

Why did her parents hide the blueprints for this horrid place in their room? Clara didn't wish to find out and yet she felt herself pulled here from the second Willoughby revealed their presence. Another strange occurrence she didn't understand. It appeared there were plenty of those as of late.

The air was cold as she descended, dampness creeping into her very bones. Each step she took seemed to echo endlessly in the void that stretched far ahead. Walking a few steps further, Willoughby took the lead, lantern in hand. He led them down the twisting passageways and toward the labyrinth that sprawled under the city. Clara hadn't realized this place even existed. She vaguely recalled hearing her uncle mention the catacombs when she was younger, but she paid it no mind. Why should she have? She had no plans of ever visiting the dead. Besides the fact that they had been closed off for decades due to lack of funds for maintenance, the catacombs, back when they were still operational, were reserved for citizens of the lowers and middles to allow for burial of those who otherwise could not afford the rising price of burial plots. As far as Clara knew, no one in her family ended their days down here.

Large archways adorned in delicate patterns rose above her head; vaults lined the tunnels of the catacombs like rib cages. The walls were cut from pale limestone, stacked in places with rows of bones that formed uneven patterns in the stone. Skulls were set into the stone like markers, their hollow eyes staring from between layers of rock. Every few steps, Clara would stumble upon a decaying bone or a piece of a skull protruding from the walls, and shuddered, pretending it was only make-believe and not the treacherous reality that set her on this journey.

Willoughby's footsteps were measured and hard as he stomped his boots on the uneven ground. His breath came out in frosty puffs that formed around him like steam rising from a chimney. In the dim light of his lantern, ghastly shadows climbed the walls of the catacombs; the deeper they ventured and the narrower the passages became, the shadows seemed to reach for Clara's very soul.

Despite the dire circumstances, Clara's resolve was unshaken as they dug further into the dank space. Somewhere was the answer to her questions, or at least one of them, and perhaps the most crucial.

She squeezed the parchment and sped her step to keep up with the thief. "What are we looking for, exactly?" she asked.

Willoughby didn't stop walking, though he managed to slow down a touch, which Clara appreciated greatly. Her feet had begun to swell inside the tight confinement of her lace-up boots, and she was yet to see a place to rest on their trek through the clutches of hell.

Raising the lantern to shed more light down the passage, the thief shrugged, marching onward. "As on every other blind excursion we'd been on this past week, Aldridge, I haven't the slightest clue."

"And the plan is to, what? Walk the entirety of the catacombs and hope for the best?" she asked. When Willoughby didn't answer, she rolled her eyes and added, "How did you know it was the catacombs in the blueprints?"

A vein feathered in Willoughby's neck. He bit his bottom lip, turning it into a puffy red pillow under his teeth. Casting Clara a sidelong glance, the thief said, "My father took me here once when I was a kid."

"For work? I thought he was a custodian?" Clara's eyes narrowed on a set of bones piled on the ground. "Were his services needed here?"

"My father was many things," the thief said. Was she wrong, or did she sense a tone of resentment in his words? Clara shook the paranoia off, letting Willoughby continue speaking. "Before he worked for the mayoral office, before my mother died, he held a prominent position as a historical site inspector for the city. The catacombs were one location he cherished."

Clara's eyes blazed. "Because of all the bones?"

"Because of the lives this place remembers in its walls," Willoughby replied sternly. "Never mind. I wouldn't expect you to understand. I'm certain you forget all about people once they're gone, same as your precious uncle."

"What is that supposed to mean?"

The thief's lips tightened into a line. Glowering, he kept his gaze on the long passage before them and refused to meet her eyes. His strides lengthened to put more distance between them.

Clara reached for him, wrapping her palm over the pulsing veins of his arm to spin him around to face her. "I'm serious, Will. What are you talking about?"

"Don't tell me you don't recall," the thief bit out. "My father and what happened at the mayoral office? What your uncle did."

"My uncle caught your father stealing and he let him go," Clara said. Her voice pitched as the offense of Willoughby's hatred for her uncle settled into the depths of her gut. How dare he? "I don't know what you mean, but that is all that happened."

Willoughby's head lowered as he tucked his chin into his chest and took a slow, deep breath. "My father never stole a single coin from the city. He was no thief." His gaze flicked to her, the fire in it making her pulse stumble in her veins. "His son may have become one, but my father was a kind and decent man. After your uncle threw him out on the street for a crime he didn't commit, his entire life shattered. He was alone with a child in a city that didn't look well enough upon men labeled as common criminals. He couldn't get another position, no matter what he tried. Thus, he turned to the markets, selling every bit of our belongings until we had nothing left. He never stopped taking care of me, not until it was too late, and he couldn't handle it anymore."

His eye wetted and Willoughby swiped at them angrily.

"The life your uncle forced him into marked the rest of his days. My father took his life because he could not see a way out. I should have been there for him, sure, and I should have prevented his death, that is on me. It will haunt me forever. But you—" he paused to look at her, his gaze jabbing daggers into

Clara's heart "—you never even bothered to send your condolences. Some friend, huh?"

"Will, I didn't know."

His jaw ticked. "Like gems you didn't. Your uncle tells you everything."

"Not this. I don't know what happened, but I do know that Uncle Oswin truly believed your father was guilty; he would not have let him go otherwise," she explained. "As for what occurred after... I did reach out, Will. I wrote to you, but I never heard back."

Clara's mind reeled as she recalled the countless letters she sent him in the aftermath of what happened between their families. Despite her uncle's warnings to stay away, Clara couldn't abandon her oldest friend, not when he needed her. Not even after he shattered her heart that day in the closet. But she didn't receive a reply, not a singular letter. She assumed Willoughby was done with her for good, happy to be rid of the presence of the girl he wished to have nothing to do with.

But what if that wasn't the case? What if he simply never received her letters?

Her body stopped moving. *Uncle Oswin,* she thought. *You didn't.* Except no matter how much she tried to argue it, Clara felt that he may have. Her uncle would go to the ends of the world to protect her and if he thought Willoughby's father was a man he couldn't trust, he would prevent her from associating with anyone in his orbit. He would shield her from all undue pain.

Her spine curved and her shoulders drooped. "Will, I—"

The light from the lantern shifted position while Clara was thinking and she hadn't realized it, but Willoughby was no longer glaring in her direction. In fact, he wasn't watching her at all. She followed the thief's eyes to a large opening in the catacombs' tunnels. Taking a few steps, she pulled Willoughby along as she made her way to get a better view. The lantern in Willoughby's hands shook slightly as they approached.

Clara squared her shoulders, the pupils of her eyes adjusting to the brightness of the room they entered. Massive iron doors stood wide open on either side and light flickered from within, one that wasn't coming from Willoughby's lonely lantern. The room was as wide as it was long and just as tall, with the same vaulted archways forming the carcass of the ceiling. In the center, a heavy wood table took up the majority of the room with iron shackles built into its four corners. On one side of the room, a series of surgical instruments hung on the walls, the metal gleaming in the light. Beneath them, wide shelves held strange machines and beakers full of even stranger liquids.

The inside of Clara's body churned. *What in the gems was this place?*

CHAPTER TWENTY-FIVE

Though Willoughby wished he could spin on his heels and march out of the strange room they stumbled on, he had to say that, admittedly; the place held his attention. In all his twenty-six years of life, he had never encountered anything quite as bizarre. Between the twisting instruments, the machines buzzing at a constant speed of worker bees, and the distinct stench of iron in the air, the room was a puzzle.

No, that was not correct. It wasn't any mere room, was it? A laboratory. Willoughby was absolutely certain of it. The question remained—what was it for?

He walked into the room and noted each passing detail as he moved. His fingers grazed the side of the thick wood table, skin briefly touching the metal of the shackles. Willoughby's hand recoiled. Whatever the contraption was designed for, he was sure he did not want to be in such close proximity to it. The hairs in his nostrils tickled as specs of dust swirled around him. To his right, he spotted a wooden crate similar to the one they had seen on the Cursed Isle, his eyes trailing along the carving of the rose on its side. Willoughby tore his gaze from the crate to find Clara glaring at it in disbelief.

"Why would my parents know anything about this place?"

An infuriating shiver ran down the length of his body. Surrounded by the oddities of the laboratory, Willoughby had almost forgotten the woman he had arrived with. His vision tunneled as he faced Clara, who remained by the entrance, refusing to step foot inside. From here, she appeared innocent and lost, not at all like the liar she was. *Letters!* Ridiculous. If she had written him after his father's death, Willoughby would have devoured her words, desperate as he was not to feel abandoned at that young an age. The loss of his only remaining family member rocked Willoughby's world so deeply that he thought he wouldn't make it through a day after his father died. Somehow, he moved forward though. One day after the next. One excruciating minute after another. All without the help of the girl he considered a friend; one he once worshipped like she was the sun that rose each morning. *Letters! What a lie.*

And yet Clara was adamant she sent them. Perhaps they were lost in the post. Willoughby rolled his eyes at his own stupidity. If Clara did, in fact, reach out to him, the only way for her mail not to arrive was if someone intercepted it. Someone like the city's fine and respected mayor, who considered his father to be a thieving pariah. He looked at the room, then at the old blueprints clutched tightly in Clara's twitching hands. It was possible her parents were involved, too. It stood to reason that if Oswin had his mind set on the matter that his brother would bear a similar mindset.

Willoughby's teeth gritted against each other. The entire Aldridge family could rot for all he cared.

The color of Clara's skin paled drastically as she took in the laboratory, and he instantly regretted his rash admonition.

While he very much doubted that Clara wished to keep him in her life, he couldn't fault her for being afraid now. The place they stood in was terrible, monstrous even, and knowing that her parents may have had a hand in it must have turned her world upside down. If only they were alive so he could question the pair and get this over with sooner.

His shoulder blades stretched toward one another. "Your parents," he said. "They died of a Cursbeast attack, did they not?"

Clara nodded in agreement. "Yes. A year after your father —" she stopped to swallow, her gaze flicking around the room "—after he passed away. What does that have to do with where we are or why they were hiding the blueprints? What are you on about?"

"I don't know yet. Maybe nothing."

In truth, Willoughby hadn't the slightest clue why he asked but it seemed important at the time, though he couldn't say why. He was about to keep his interrogation of the mayor's niece going when he noticed she was no longer glaring at him as she was before. Clara's attention settled somewhere past his shoulder and on a set of crates stacked high in the corner of the room. She nudged her pointed nose in their direction. "What's that?"

Before Willoughby could follow, Clara crossed the room to stand in front of the crates. Her brows furrowed. Willoughby worked hard to understand why this specific item caught her eye and not any of the other gruesome things in the room. Why not the beakers that appeared to have black poison inside them? Or that horrifying metal stick with the sharp spiral tip hanging on the wall? Why these crates?

When Clara pulled the top wooden box down and sat it on the floor at her feet, he couldn't fight his curiosity any longer.

Willoughby crouched beside her, his stomach sinking as

Clara reached into the crate and pulled out a woolen cap similar to the ones some of the sellers wore at the markets. She held it up into the light, twirling the cap on the tips of her fingers. A small tag fell away from the article. Clara reached for it, but Willoughby was faster. He grabbed the tag, yanking at the thread that bound it to read the inscription written on the thick paper.

"What is it?" Clara asked.

The pit in his gut widened with dread and uncertainty. "A date," he replied. "September of last year. The letters R and the number 2 follow it."

"There's more," Clara said, digging inside the crate.

She shifted her hand and pulled it out so fast, Willoughby thought a demon bit her fingers. Clara opened her fist to reveal a small brooch in the shape of a rose. This one also had a tag. Grimacing, Clara said, "This is the same brooch as the girl we saw arrested last week sold." She picked up the jewelry and brought it close to her face. "And look, the date on it is marked to only a few days ago."

"Letters?"

"A. Number 4." Her gaze met his. "What do you think it means?"

The words would not leave his throat. They sat there, growing in mass like a tumor, choking him as he struggled to make sense of what he was seeing. His legs shook violently and every bone in his body suddenly liquified. Willoughby brushed aside Clara's arm and dug into the crate. His fingers touched a soft, raggedy fabric, and he pulled it out of the box with the utmost care. Around him, the laboratory stilled, the air settling into the crevices of the stone walls.

Willoughby rubbed the rear of his sweat-slicked neck, looked at the scarf in his lap. "This was Soltan's."

"Your missing friend?" Clara asked. "Are you sure?"

"I gave it to him for his last birthday."

She opened her mouth, then closed it again. Her arm outstretched and she placed her index finger beneath the hanging tag on the scarf, lifting it high enough to read. "Dated two weeks ago," Clara said. "Letter H, number 3. Letter E, number 2. I don't understand any of it."

"Neither do I," Willoughby admitted. "Hand me that fountain pen."

Clara turned over her shoulder to see where he pointed. Rushing, she ran to one of the shelves, giving the instruments on the wall a wide berth as she passed, and grabbed the pen sitting idly next to a set of tattered old books. As she handed it to him, Willoughby searched his coat, producing Thomas Hawke's sales ledger.

Clara's one brow rose. "You carry it with you?"

"Of course," Willoughby said. He wrote down the items in the crate, a total of twelve articles, and the information on their corresponding tags. Finished, he turned to the other crates. "Let's empty them out. Quickly."

They worked in unison to pull away several crates and lay the items in them on the ground for Willoughby to document their findings. Each tag resembled one another in structure. A date followed by a letter and number combination. The way the codes were displayed seemed oddly familiar to Willoughby, but he couldn't place the reason behind it. Whatever it was, it would come to him. Hopefully.

Willoughby was noting the inscription for a set of gloves when the passages of the catacombs filled with voices. His eyes flashed to Clara, and she nodded, briskly gathering the items and throwing them back into the crate. Willoughby helped collect the remaining pieces, and they grunted as they stacked the crates back to how they found them. The voices got louder, closer. Willoughby wiped his brow before clutching Clara by the cuff of her sleeve and pulling her to the exit behind him. If they were quick enough, they might be able to snake a path away from the laboratory and get past whoever was coming without being seen. They may not have found anything incriminating in the dodgy place, but Willoughby knew that he did not wish to meet whoever was taking a stroll in the land of the dead.

His feet moved faster to get away. Suddenly, his arm was jerked back and his shoulder yelled in agony as he was pulled in the opposite direction.

"Hey!" he hissed out. Rubbing his shoulder, he turned to see what in the gems Clara was up to, catching her reaching for a bottle of black liquid on a shelf. "What are you doing? We have to go?"

The absolute menace didn't even register his alarmed tone. Willoughby watched as Clara swirled the liquid inside, her expression that of a child seeing a rainbow for the first time. The slight wrinkles between her eyes drew together; she wiggled her nose as she used her thumb to pop the cork from the vial. Not a second later and the damn woman was shoving her entire face into the opening to study the contents.

Willoughby bit back the foul language sitting at the tip of his tongue. He grabbed Clara's shoulders with both hands and spun her around to face him. She had been lingering too long, her gaze flicking from the etched symbols on the glass vials to the rows of tarnished instruments glinting dully in the lamp-light, as if the secrets her parents kept from her might make sense if she just looked hard enough.

As he spun her, her palm—resting on the edge of the shelf—swiped across the wood and she yelped as one of the instruments tore into her flesh. Blood welled on the pillowy part of her palm.

"What in the gems, Will?" she yelled. "Was that necessary?"

She held her hand up to show him the fresh cut on it.

"Are you out of your mind? We need to leave before we're found out!"

Somehow, he got her to listen. Clara winced as she used her injured hand to slip the cork back into the vial's neck. Blood dripped down her hand and oozed into the glass before Clara closed it for good. For a second, Willoughby could swear he saw the pitch-black liquid inside swirl around the red droplet.

He shook his head. This was not the time to hallucinate. He slapped his cheeks hard. "Time to go."

Jabbing Clara's shoulders, he pushed her toward the open doorway and into the depths of the catacombs. The voices they heard before were nearly upon them, and Willoughby almost lost his footing from how fast he ushered them around the bend and out of sight. If he recalled correctly, there was another way out of the retched place, one less formidable but also less well known. Around the corner from them, the voices were close enough to make out a few words. Willoughby heard a gruff man ask about a package and another softer-spoken gentleman reply with a noncommittal 'yes.' Skirting the sharp turn of the passageway, Willoughby stretched his neck to see the men approaching, but all he could make out was a set of colorless hair and large gold glasses. He gave Clara one last shove before snuffing out the lantern and throwing them into complete darkness.

They walked silently for what felt like hours. By the time Willoughby gauged a safe distance from the laboratory, they were almost halfway to the surface. The route they were on was considerably longer. Willoughby's skin crawled with stress.

"What was that back there?" he gritted out. "You almost got us caught over a stupid bottle."

"Did you read the label?"

He huffed out a frustrated breath.

"It was Cursbeast blood," Clara whispered. "That place, whoever built it, they're experimenting with beast blood. And my parents knew."

The rest of her words didn't reach him and as they marched onward. While Clara hypothesized about the meaning of the laboratory, Willoughby could only think of one thing. Why the fuck was his missing friend's scarf left in a Cursbeast experimentation nightmare room?

CHAPTER TWENTY-SIX

A heady and thick aroma of roses swirled around Clara in the damp, shadowed air of the garden. She snipped a dying bud, placing it in the small pile at her feet. The hauntingly sweet scent of the flowers made her head spin. She lowered the shears and rubbed the sore spot where the metal had pierced her skin yesterday, peeling back the bandage to inspect it. Red, inflamed flesh stared back at her. If she didn't rest her hand, the cut would surely leave a mark.

Clara sighed, recalling the absurdity of the place. Though perhaps the word she searched for to describe the laboratory was atrocious. Devilish. An abomination upon the city.

There was no shortage of phrases Clara could summon for the horrible place.

Her uninjured hand grazed the petals of a fresh flower. She leaned into the briar, knees digging deep into the earth beneath her, to inhale the scent of the rose. Her head spun faster. "What business did you have there?" she asked.

Clara's heart ached at the solidness of the surrounding air.

It wasn't that she expected a reply from her deceased parents, but sitting here in their favorite spot on the property filled her with even more uncertainty. She refused to believe that her family had anything to do with a place experimenting on Cursbeasts. Her mother, much to her uncle's dismay, was a gem supporter. According to Oswin, she believed with all her might that the citizens had the right to choose their own fate, beast or not. Father, on the other hand, well, she knew nothing of his beliefs; he had not discussed such matters with a child. In that regard, her father and uncle were quite alike.

A thought dragged Clara from family matters. How did whoever run the awful laboratory even get their hands on a Cursbeast? The blood she found in the vial had to have come from somewhere. How in the gems did someone get close enough to a beast to draw it?

The idea rattled Clara to her very core. Flashes of the attacks she harrowingly avoided danced before her. The beasts were powerful, stronger than any man, stronger than even the guards who had been affected. To draw blood from a creature that vicious would be suicide. The image of Violet's broken body in the fountain left Clara breathless. She loosened the collar of her dress to help get more air into her lungs. Her vision flooded with red. If Clara had the power of the laboratory keeper, she wouldn't have used it to experiment on the beasts.

She would annihilate each and every one of them. For Violet. For her parents.

"Miss Aldridge?"

The softness of the voice at her back made the dark thoughts Clara had vanish instantly. Her cheeks flushed, shame dragging its hungry claws up and down her throat. She had no right to avenge anyone. Not when she couldn't even save Elisea, her living and breathing friend. Memories of the housekeeper reading to her when Clara was a small girl flashed before her. She swiped at the wetness clouding her eyesight with the fleshy part of her palm. The lilac perfume Elisea wore was suddenly filling her nostrils and she gagged, the memory of her friend dragging her into the darkness of despair. She shook it out, but it lingered in the back of her mind like a parasite.

Clara pulled away from the rose briar and stood tall. She brushed away the dirt on her skirt, starting as the rough fabric scratched at her fresh wound. Forcing a false smile, she turned to face the woman who called out to her. It was one of the maids, the one training young Sara now. Clara struggled to recall her name, her mind flicking between letters without grasping anything concrete.

"Yes?" she asked. "Is everything all right?"

The woman approached Clara with a curtsey, holding out a thick envelope addressed to her. Clara's brows met in the middle of her forehead. "What is this?"

"It came in this morning," the woman said. "A man named Thelonius Casterly dropped it off. He mentioned it was urgent and not to let any eyes but yours shed sight of it."

The librarian! Clara was so giddy she had to stop herself from skipping up and down. Her pulse sped up as she snatched the letter from the maid and thanked her quickly before turning to the briar. She waited until she heard the woman's footsteps retreat, then tore into the envelope in the same dastardly manner that Socks tore into steamed fish. Her eyes skimmed the handwritten pages. The penmanship was remarkable, a thing Clara expected from the librarian, and it was a pleasure to read notes from someone interested in research. From the looks of it, Thelonius devoted a good amount of time searching for information on The Order of the

Stones; there were entries sited from at least a dozen books, if not double that.

Clara's heart raced as she flipped the pages. "You marvelous, brilliant man!"

Glee controlled her every movement. She ran a finger over the entries, reading them in a hushed tone to the flowers surrounding her. "Founded by two families... Believed that gem magic was to be Hedge End's answer to geographical domination... Consisted of upper society members... Invite only..."

There was too much to remember, but Clara tried her best to commit the entries to memory. This moment was too significant to forget. She wished she could inhale the words right off the pages. One entry made Clara slow down.

"While the society was formed almost immediately following the death of the Stone King and his heirs, their commitment to understanding the beasts did not come into effect until the last century," Clara read aloud. Her blood ran cold as she moved to the next entry, a personal note from Thelonius himself. Clara blanched and read on. "Dear Miss Aldridge. While this information is not directly connected to the society you asked after, I found mention of the Cooke family petitioning for land rights over the city's catacombs roughly ninety-six years ago. There is no record of their success. I'm afraid this is all I could gather on the order. I hope it is satisfactory and to your liking."

Oh, this was much more than satisfactory. Clara's eyes bulged, and she reread the entry to confirm it wasn't incorrect. If this was true, then there was every chance that the Cookes were the ones who built that laboratory. The Order of the Stones could be responsible for what they found in the catacombs; they might be the ones collecting beast blood. But why? And what did Violet's husband have to do with it all?

There was only one thing to do now.

Clara rolled her shoulders, tucked the pages into her corset, and faced the house. "I have to tell Will."

Her boots kicked back dirt as she raced from the rose bushes and toward the rear entrance of her home. Opening the wide doors with a grunt, she lamely shook away the ground from her feet before taking off in a sprint through the house. As she passed the downstairs study, a throat clearing made her halt in her tracks.

"Off somewhere important?" her uncle asked.

Clara stopped in her tracks. Backing up slowly, she came to stand in the doorway and smiled meekly at the mayor. "I needed some fresh air. I won't be long."

"Were you not in the garden just now?"

"Um, yes. I meant fresh air and a walk to clear my head," Clara lied. "The weather seems to be warming up. I'd hate to waste such a lovely day indoors. Are you not in the office today?"

Her uncle started to speak but stopped to clear away a bothersome cough. He pulled down his shirt sleeves and checked his gold pocket watch, frowning. "Not for a few more hours." He looked her up and down. "But don't let me keep you. At least one of us should get to enjoy their freedom."

Chuckling, Clara wiggled her fingers to wave and sped away down the hallway. She turned past the dining room, skidding to make the sharp right that led to the front doors. On either side of her, the portraits of her parents sucked the air from the corridor, and she pumped her legs faster to put distance between her and their faces. One day, after she unspun the knots in the secretive tapestry of her parent's life, she would return here to meet her dead family eye to eye. One day when she knew why it was they hid so many things from her; when she didn't arrive with questions asked of unhearing ears.

The heavyset doors loomed before her. Clara snatched her wool coat from the entryway closet and draped it over her shoulder, not wasting a moment more to put the stuffy thing on. She would have plenty of time to get herself and her restless heart settled on the carriage ride. Glancing at the clock in the entryway, she gauged Willoughby would be in one of his most frequented establishments—a pub in the lowers if she recalled the thief's words correctly.

Clara swung open the door, looked behind her, then stepped outside. Her boot crunched on another shoe and her body collided with a muscular chest. She twisted her neck to face whoever she ran over, her eyes rounding. "Will? What are you doing here?"

The thief, looking bewildered, shook out the boot that Clara crushed with her heel. He started to reply, but Clara couldn't wait. She had to tell him what she found out.

"The Order of the Stones built the laboratory," she hissed out at the same time as Willoughby said, "I know what the letters mean!"

Clara reared back, her brow scrunching. "What?"

"The letters on the tags," Willoughby repeated. "I know what they are. What do you mean, the Order built it?"

A loud, chesty cough made the hairs on Clara's arms rise. She glanced over her shoulder in the direction of the sitting room, relief flooding her body when she didn't see her uncle emerge from within. Pushing Willoughby away from the house, she shut the doors, curled her fingers around the collar of his jacket, and pulled him behind her. "Not here. My uncle is home." She pointed to the garden. "Follow me. I know a place we can speak in private."

They walked with hushed steps around the perimeter of

the house and in the direction of the lush trees filling the rear side of the property. Every few moments, Clara scanned the area for the staff or her uncle, taking careful measures not to be caught. Her bones shuddered in the sudden chill of the afternoon. Draping the coat over her shoulders, she blew hot air on her hands and kept on. They were near the pond now, almost to the shed. No one used the structure but her, since it was close to the exact location of her parents' murder.

Clara's heart stopped. It was the first time she thought of their death as what it was, a murder. Not a death at all, not to the Cursbeast who dealt the fatal blows on their broken bodies. Since the beasts almost never attacked in the uppers—choosing instead the prowl where there were less guards on patrol and homes weren't sectioned off behind tall, barbed fences—there were no warning whistles here in the garden. Her parents didn't even see the dreadful thing coming let alone have the chance to defend themselves properly. Her father's rifle was found still clutched in his hand. He never had the time to pull the trigger before being torn to shreds. Clara bit the inside of her cheek. Between the recent attacks, the killing of her parents, and the laboratory, there were more ties to the cursed creatures than Clara liked.

They reached the narrow iron door of the small shed without being spotted; the small victory was enough to calm Clara's wild thoughts. She turned over a tall vase on the stoop, shaking out the key held within.

"A lot of security for a garden shed," Willoughby noted.

She glowered. "It was my mother's painting studio. She valued the privacy for her work."

Willoughby cast his eyes to the ground and rubbed the rear of his neck. His spine appeared to be turning to water as they stepped into the dark, dusty shed. He harrumphed, doing so again when Clara closed the door and shut the only source of light in the place out. She left the thief to walk to the small oval window on the opposite side of the tight space. With a sharp tug, she split open the curtains and allowed for the sunshine streaming in from the garden to illuminate the shed. Her breath hitched with emotion.

Clara rolled her gaze over the tubes of paint, to the stack of canvases against one wall, past the short stump of a stool in the corner, and all the way to the easel before it. To the unfinished painting sat upon it. It was a view of the garden from the pond; her mother's favorite place to sit in.

This was too much.

Clara clenched her eyes shut, refusing to allow the anguish in her mind to take over. Her fisted hands shook at her side, and the acid in her stomach lurched up into her throat. She tightened her teeth together. Her heart was a hollow chamber and no matter what Clara did, she could not for the life of her fill it. She would drown here, in this shed, in this moment.

Cool fingers wrapped around her fists. A warm breath tickled her cheekbones as Willoughby came to stand in front of her. Her eyes were shut, but she could see him in her mind's eye. The way his brows pinched together as he studied her, the concern gathering on his face, the storm in his green eyes.

Willoughby's forehead pressed to hers, pulling her back to reality. "Stay with me, Aldridge," he said softly. "It is only a room. It is not all she was."

Air filled Clara's lungs as she parted her lips to breathe. Her skin heated from the closeness of Willoughby's body, and she struggled to form coherent sentences. Actually, Clara couldn't speak if she tried. The words didn't come, no matter how deeply she willed them to. One lid at a time, she peeled her eyes open to look at the thief. It appeared Clara knew him all too well because she was spot on with her earlier prediction. Willoughby worried for her.

Her fists loosened; she stayed rooted in one spot with her fingers lacing through his. She sucked in another quick breath. "It smells like her."

"After my father died," Willoughby said, "I spent a week wearing his clothes to feel, I don't know, closer to him, I suppose. In my delusions, I thought that if I kept the memory of him present, alive, that it would bring him back."

"Why did you decide to stop?"

Willoughby's one brow quirked. "The man wore a size eleven boot. If I were to continue the charade, I'd have broken both my ankles before the months' end."

A laugh she didn't expect fell from Clara's lips. The edges of her mouth twirled up and the heaviness in her heart lifted slightly. Standing an inch from her, Willoughby smiled, his eyes soft, saying, "There she is."

Clara was suddenly very aware of how close they stood. If she dared rise up on her toes, her lips might graze Willoughby's. Her thoughts raced to the supply closet in the mayor's office all those years ago and her skin flushed from it. In front of her, Willoughby's wide chest rose and fell, his gaze flicking to her lips as she licked them. And yet he didn't step away.

Her head spun. Clara's brain told her to let go of his hands, to walk away. Her brain was a fool. Clara wished for no such thing and so she did the exact opposite—she pulled Willoughby closer. The thief appeared surprised, but he didn't fight it, the heat of his breath against her skin fogging the small space left between.

Clara let go of one of Willoughby's hands and placed it on his chest. It followed the movement of his ribcage. Up and down. Up and down. Faster. Faster. Faster as his heart raced.

Their eyes met.

"I want to forget the pain, Will," she breathed out.

They were only words, but they were also an invitation.

Clara stared at Willoughby through hooded eyes, her lashes blinking as she waited to see what he would do. She hated him once, maybe still, but in this moment, she hated her memories more. And she had to admit, Willoughby was not the person she thought he was. Not by a mile, it seemed.

For a split second, Clara thought she had miscalculated this odd and twisted thing between them. That she made the wrong choice. It wasn't until Willoughby snaked his free hand around her neck and pulled her into him that she understood he wanted this as she did. Her body shuddered as their lips crashed together. Clara's stomach dropped into her boots. The heat between her legs rose higher as Willoughby captured her bottom lip between his teeth, giving it a light tug before he parted her lips with his tongue.

Clara's eyes closed, and she tilted her back, letting the thief run hungry kisses down her neck. Willoughby's arm moved to her back, and she arched into him until the coat hanging on her shoulders fell away. His thigh pressed between her legs, pinning her against the wall. A moan escaped Clara as Willoughby ran his teeth along the exposed skin above the edge of her corset.

This was nothing like the closet kiss.

They were not children playing at life today, and while Clara was hiding with Willoughby in a dark and stuffy room again, she had no shame about it. Whatever was happening, Clara wanted it more than she had wanted anything ever before. She wanted Willoughby. All of him.

A door slammed in the distance and echoed down the garden. Willoughby's attack on her skin stopped abruptly from the harshness of the sound. Torturously slow, he lifted his head to look up at Clara. "Are you certain no one comes here?"

"I... No... Perhaps..." Clara had forgotten how to speak.

The thief grinned treacherously. He ran his fingers up

Clara's back and took a small step away. The light from the window limned the tousled curls in his hair and for a moment, Clara couldn't find a flaw on his face. His gaze dropped to her puffy, swollen lips. "Did you forget, Aldridge?"

She didn't know if he meant the memories of her mother, how many people visit the shed, or why they came here in the first place. If she was truthful, Clara would admit that she may have forgotten her own name in the last few minutes. She pressed a hand against the wall for balance and gazed at the thief coyly.

"I had plenty of years to forget how good you are at this," she blurted out.

Willoughby's smirk dropped. "Aldridge, you should know that I was a fool."

"I'm sorry, am I hearing correctly?" Clara asked. "Willoughby Tanner admitting he was wrong, there must be some mistake. I am sure that you had very good reason for making me feel like I was not worth a speck of your time. That I was a plaything. Someone to string along."

Clara's voice had the hints of teasing but was she was serious to her very core. She meant each word. After all, she had felt them in the base of her stomach for most of her life. Every man that told her she was beautiful or asked for a moment of her time came with a warning. That they would never stay with her. That she was not good enough. That was the message Willoughby planted in her mind after he kissed her like his life depended on it in that damn closet and pretended not to remember the moment they shared the following day.

They were only thirteen, but Clara thought she aged a decade from his actions.

"It was only a kiss," Willoughby said. Then, quickly realizing his mistake when Clara frowned, added, "I shouldn't have behaved callously after. I was a dumb kid, and I didn't know how to tell you the truth."

"Which was?"

Another door banged, this one coming from the stables. Willoughby 's eyes darted to the door, the panic of someone catching them evident on his face. As much as Clara wanted to know what excuse the thief might have had, she knew he was right to be weary. They did not have time to dig up the past.

She brushed down her skirt and picked up her coat, putting it on and tying the belt in a tight knot. Her gaze landed on Willoughby. "It matters not now," she said. "As you said, it was only a kiss, the same as the one we shared now. We need not waste time discussing it."

The memory of Willoughby's teeth on her skin made Clara pause. She shoved it away, locking it in the same compartment of her brain that she put all the things that she didn't wish to think about for as long as she lived. Walking to the door, she opened it slightly and peered through the opening.

"Now," she said, turning to face the thief once more. "Why don't you tell me about the letters on the tags? Business before pleasure, and all."

CHAPTER TWENTY-SEVEN

usiness. She must have been kidding, or else Willoughby misheard. How could Clara possibly entertain the idea of any sort of business after what had occurred between them? No. No, he was wrong.

Willoughby watched the mayor's niece button up her coat all the way to the top of her throat, as if to further stake the knife into his heart. She turned her back to him, walking to the window to peer outside.

All right. She was serious.

Now what?

The ache between Willoughby's legs was yet to subside, and the woman was prancing around as though she hadn't just given him the most feverish few minutes of his entire pathetic existence. He slapped himself while she wasn't looking. What he needed was a cold bath and several hours in a pub to get his mind off the smell of her skin, the way it felt under his teeth.

Willoughby groaned.

"Something the matter?" Clara asked, her back turned. She pulled out the easel that held her mother's unfinished painting

and positioned it to stand between them. A barrier of protection from...what exactly? Him?

Fine. He deserved all of her nonchalance in this particular instance. Willoughby wasn't too daft as to not understand why she was upset, but he did try to apologize. He was a dunce when he played with her emotions in the past. After that day in the supply closet of the mayoral office, all he wanted was to spend every waking moment with her. But he couldn't allow himself to venture there. Love wasn't real, and if it was, someone always died. Watching his father become a shell of a man after his mother drowned proved it. Willoughby swore he would never let a woman break him into pieces, until Clara Aldridge. The brave, careless girl that tore down all his beliefs with one kiss. Willoughby wished he could take back how he behaved then, yet Clara wouldn't hear of it. How was he supposed to make up for what he did when she was, quite literally, erecting walls between them? And it wasn't as though she wasn't without fault in the situation. If she hadn't snubbed him after his father died, perhaps they could have gotten through this tedious patch of bad luck sooner. And gotten to...

Willoughby slapped himself again to get the image of Clara's body trembling under his touch out of his head. He looked at the woman's angular shoulders, his resolve—amongst other things—thick and hard. So be it then. If Clara wished to put an end to whatever that was before it even begun, he would not begrudge her the pleasure.

At the mere mention of pleasure, Willoughby's spine tingled. The fabric of his pants was tight and chafed every inch of him from the waist down. *Pick another word, idiot!*

He took in a slow, agonizing breath at the same time as Clara finally decided he was worthy of her attention. Facing him, she arched one perfectly manicured brow, her features twisted. "The code on the tags," she noted matter-of-factly, "you cracked it?"

"Uh, sure. Yes," was all Willoughby could muster.

"Yes or no, Will? We don't have all day to hide out in here."

Have you no mercy? Willoughby wanted to ask. Instead, he locked his jaw until his teeth felt like they might fall out and glared at the woman before him with as close to a sour expression as he could muster. "Gems," he gritted out.

"What's that?"

"The letters—they represent gems. Remember what Benjamin said in the markets? The gems they found on Soltan."

Clara's eyes widened in understanding. "A heliodor and an emerald."

"His tag read H-3, E-2," Willoughby recalled. "Heliodor 3 and emerald 2. Want to know what I believe the numbers to mean?"

"The number of times he used their magic."

Willoughby smirked. "Correct. Now why would a secret laboratory that is very obliviously studying the Cursbeasts care how many times my friend used specific gems?" It was a question he didn't require the answer to, as he had already guessed at it prior to coming here. Yet, when Clara shrugged, he took it as a chance to explain; perhaps to impress her, even. "Ever since the markets, I kept wondering what possible use Soltan might have of the gems, why those particular ones? Heliodor, sure, I kind of understand. The ability to bend light to create illusion is a valuable one for a thief, but what about an emerald? Soltan had never put himself in a situation that causes bodily harm; he had no need to for a gem that promoted fast healing."

"Unless someone was forcing him to use the gem," Clara said before he could continue. "Physically hurting him to do their bidding and healing him enough to make him do it again.

Do you think they did the same to Genevieve and your friend got caught up in it when he went searching for her?"

The rear of Willoughby's eyes burned, and his vision spotted. Of course. That must have been how Soltan vanished; the man was always a fool for love. Anger raged within him for his friend, for what he knew deep in his gut happened. "Whoever works out of that dastardly place is forcing people to use magic —affecting them until they turn. I know it, Aldridge. They are studying the affected. It's likely why the Curse Isle is emptied out. The bastards ran out of supply, so they decided to make more."

"Will, if this is true," Clara said, "it is against the law. It's in complete violation of the city's choice to protect the citizens and to control the use of gem magic. We are trying to eradicate the gems from the general population, not give them free rein of the damn stones! The gems are meant to protect the city. This... This is wrong."

"And Thomas Hawke had something to do with it," Willoughby added. He rubbed the back of his neck, shifted his weight. "Your parents as well."

Clara shook her head. "Not them. The Cookes built the laboratory. That was what I was coming to tell you earlier."

It still doesn't mean they weren't involved... Willoughby thought but kept his mouth shut. If Clara's family was involved, they'd find out sooner or later. There was no need to ruffle her feathers any more right now. He had no proof of her parent's involvement anyhow.

Dust rose around Clara as she crossed the shed, marched to a narrow table buckling under the weight of paint canisters, then walked back to the easel. Clara enjoyed pacing to clear her head it appeared. It was one thing he had noticed her do recently and it made Willoughby's eyes ache to follow her around like a moving target. Yet the exercise seemed to have relaxed her, and he was glad to see her shoulders drop away from her ears and the tension in her jaw slacken. Maybe Willoughby should consider adopting it to ease his own racing mind.

He tried it for good measure, quickly realizing that it put him directly in front of Clara. When she cast him with a gaze that asked why he felt the need to follow her, he pretended to act as casual as possible. His arm extended, and he used it to brace against the tall easel. Using all his acting skills, Willoughby attempted to appear comfortable as his hand pressed at the backboard, the wood splintering under his skin. The entire time, he refused to lower his eyes or cower before the stubborn woman. Clara wanted to pretend that the kiss didn't ruffle her feathers, but she was sorely mistaken if she thought she would get under his skin.

Two can play this game, Willoughby thought.

One side of his mouth curled into a playful smirk. He relaxed his stance, leaning further on the easel. His fingers grazed the wood paneling. A seam in the material made Willoughby stop. He peeled his gaze from Clara to look at the back of the easel where his hand lay. It couldn't be. Brushing his palm over the long line where two pieces of wood met, he narrowed his eyes and turned his head slightly toward the mayor's niece. "Why is there another secret compartment in your mother's easel?"

"What are you talking about?" Clara asked, clearly ruffled by the question. She skirted the easel and poked her nose close to the panel where Willoughby's hand lay. "I don't see anything."

Rolling his eyes, he pressed against one side and the panel split into two pieces, falling away in his hands. He caught the thin wood before it fell to the floor, placing it on the stool near his feet. Willoughby kept his attention on Clara as he reached into the hollow space carved out in the backside of the easel. His hand rummaged around briefly before he yanked it out, holding tightly onto the loot hidden inside.

He waved the thick leather-bound book in Clara's face. "What do we have here?"

"Give me that."

Clara snatched the book from his hands before he could blink. She clung to the soft, time-worn cover like a lifeline, inspecting the front and spine with precision. Grimacing, she said, "I don't think it was my mother's. She despised journaling, and this is clearly a diary of sorts. Whose?"

"Easiest way to find out is to open it," Willoughby offered. He had to admit; his curiosity had peaked to a new and monstrous level. The Aldridges had more secrets tucked away in their pompous house than he expected. When Willoughby was first granted access to the place, he assumed some might turn up, but he never considered the possibilities of items even Clara didn't know about. There was a good chance her parents were not the picture of innocence the princess thought they were. Then again, who was these days?

His vision darkened when Clara pried open the cover of the journal. He leaned in, his forehead bumping hers as they closed in on the hand-drawn symbol etched into the first page.

Clara gasped. "It's the rose insignia," she said, placing her small finger on the page to compare the drawing to the ring upon it. "An exact replica."

"May I?"

Waiting for her nod of approval, Willoughby picked up her dainty digit between his two clumsy fingers and brought the ring closer to him. His body went into overdrive, battling the urge not to place his lips to the soft skin of Clara's hand. Sweat collected between his shoulder blades from the effort. What in the gems was wrong with him? This was no time to be thinking with any part of his anatomy other than his head, which, at the moment, appeared to be about as useless as the rest of him. With much effort, he snapped out of his delusions and concentrated on the ring.

It was as Clara said—the journal bore the same symbol as her jewelry and the crate on the isle. Willoughby turned the page daintily, something telling him to handle the paper with care. As Clara predicted, it was a diary, each entry written with a precise hand, the calligraphy impeccable and flowery. He studied the swirls of the letters and the way the ink sat on the page just so. Whoever wrote the entries was educated, an upper education, if he had to guess.

Willoughby stopped himself from skipping ahead to read the name inscribed at the top of the first page. "Beatrice Rosette. Sound familiar?"

Shrugging, Clara pointed to the paper. "There's more." She neared the paper, her breath warming the ink. "Daughter of Alfred Rosette, third princess of—" she paused, her jaw gaping. Collecting herself, Clara whispered, "Hedge End."

"Pardon?"

Willoughby pulled on the diary. This couldn't possibly be what he thought it was. Could it?

Hastily, he turned to the first entry, drawing his gaze to the bottom of the page where a date was scribbled with a light hand. "It can't be," he breathed out hoarsely.

"What is it, Will? What are you seeing that I'm not?"

Willoughby turned the book to face her. "It's dated the year past the death of The Stone King," he said. "After the last of the heirs to the throne were said to have been killed by the Cursbeasts."

Silence engulfed the shed. Willoughby stared at Clara as understanding dawned on her, and the purpose of the book began to make sense. He watched her closely. Her belly filling with heavy breaths under the weight of her wool coat. The way her hair fell over her eyes piece by piece and the way she didn't bother to right it. The sharpness in her eyes as she ran scenarios through her head.

When she stayed quiet, Willoughby slammed the cover of the book closed, making dust swirl in the space between them. "Aldridge," he said, his voice cold as steel. "How did your mother get the diary of The Stone King's daughter and why did she hide it?"

CHAPTER TWENTY-EIGHT

"I am writing this for the sole purpose of record keeping, in the case that I should meet a similar fate to the remainder of my family. If you come upon this book, know that it was not written for the faint of heart. I should, as instructed by my future husband and faithful advisor, bury my true identity with the bones of the family it belongs to. And yet I can do no such thing.

History cannot be forgotten.

At the date of this entry, I, Beatrice Rosette, am ten days short of two decades. The thing I wished for most was to return from my travels to celebrate the day of my birth in my home, in the city of Hedge End with my parents and siblings. Fate, however, had alternate plans.

I will never see my family again, and the dire reality of the situation has taken its toll on my heart. Perhaps that is why this diary came into existence. To remember them as they were, not as what the city will paint them as.

My father is, was, the most honorable man I knew. I suppose he would have to be to become the king of a city, but I had seen the world beyond Hedge End and not all kings are built of the same

fiber. My father, Alfred Rosette, was special. While you may know him as The Stone King, the man who created the cursed monsters, I will only ever know him as father.

That title is enough for me. I pray by the time you finish reading this diary that it may be enough for you as well.

I do not wish to dictate what you do with the words stowed away in the journal's pages because I do not know what your future will hold. All I know is that you, my heir, have the blood of the original king flowing through you, and you deserve to know where it came from. Where you began.

As the days go by and my belly grows with the life you fill it with, I cannot help but pour my truth onto the pages. Though I will no longer be living when you read this (because of old age, I hope) remember that I love you with all my might.

I leave you with the words of our family and the legacy of the Rosettes. Through the briar truth shall bloom.

Stay sharp, my love."

Clara put the book down on the round table, taking care to avoid the sticky residue left behind by overflowing glasses of wine. Her throat was parched after reading and this was only the first entry in the diary. She reached for the water jug and poured the tepid liquid into a stained mug, downing it in one go. Across from her, Willoughby sat in complete silence. Behind him, the thick curtain closing off the private room in the Oily Spoon moved with the breeze of bodies walking past and Willoughby's hair rustled slightly from the wind blowing in. He pushed the unruly curls from his forehead, his attention remaining on the diary.

"Are you sure this is a safe place?" Clara asked.

She glanced at the curtain which continued to sway and shift, and though it never parted, it was quite obvious the establishment was filling up as the later hours of the day approached. When Willoughby suggested they leave the shed and come here, it seemed a solid plan. Clara may have felt out of place in a pub in the lowers but at least there was no chance of her uncle shooting Willoughby on sight here. Now that they arrived, she was beginning to doubt the decision. The smell alone was enough to send her running back to Aldridge House. Seriously, what was that stench? The damn port smelled better than this place.

She scrunched her nose in disgust.

"Calm down, Aldridge," Willoughby said. Finally. "The bartender owes me a favor. We won't be interrupted."

Clara did not wish to know what the thief may have done to earn the favor of someone who works in a place like this. There was much about Willoughby that continued to trouble her, particularly the way her heart jumped into her throat each time his boot made contact with hers under the table. She did not have time for the distraction. Besides, Willoughby was not to be trusted with a thing as precious as real emotion; she had known this from day one. He was a tryst. A way to forget about all the darkness that crept in on her and nothing more than a pacing fancy.

His knee brushed against hers. Clara's throat closed up. She flipped aimlessly through the pages of the diary, landing on one in no particular order. She scanned the text, only half registering the words written there.

"Anything of value?"

Clara forced herself to glance up to meet his questioning gaze. "She never returned to Hedge End," Clara replied, her voice hoarse. "Do you know what this means? The magnitude of the discovery is beyond anything the city had ever known."

"If it is true."

"How could it not be?" Clara asked. "We can have the book dated if you wish, but I am certain this is the real thing. The

Stone King had a surviving heir, Will! A living blood relative that could have taken the crown all this time."

The thief pressed a finger to his lips and reared back in his chair. His ears perked as he listened to the passing voices outside the private room curtain. A moment later, the curtain opened with a whoosh and a tall man with a thin mustache stepped through, a tray balanced on his right arm. The man approached the table and deposited a bottle of wine and two slim glasses between Willoughby and Clara.

"On the house," the man said. "Compliments of Mr. Steeles."

Willoughby grinned mischievously. "Tell Simon it will take more than the cheap stuff to make us even. But this will do for now."

With a stiff bow, the man exited, the curtain flapping closed behind him. Willoughby waited a few moments before turning back to Clara and saying, "You said your mother gave you the ring you wear?"

She looked down at her pinkie and the flash of silver around it. "Yes. Why?"

"The ring, the blueprints, the crate on the isle, and now this diary. It is no coincidence your mother had them in her possession. She was not born in Hedge End, was she?"

Clara shook her head from side to side. "My father was, as were many generations of Aldridges. Mother and he met abroad on one of his travels with Uncle Oswin. After they married, they returned to the city." Her thunderous gaze flicked to Willoughby. "What are you suggesting?"

"Isn't it obvious?" the thief asked. "Your mother was a Rosette. There is no other plausible explanation."

"There can be plenty," Clara said.

And yet, as she spoke, she sensed the lie in the statement. Why would her mother hide all these things if it were not to protect herself from her past, from her lineage? Clara wished she could speak to her now and ask her what reasons she had for the deception. Why not expose the truth for all to see? To be a descendant of The Stone King himself was an honor, wasn't it? The space between Clara's temples throbbed. Nothing fit together. Clara despised not knowing. What was her mother thinking when she hid the shards of her past throughout Aldridge House? Did she want someone to find it, Clara perhaps, or did she bury it to never see the light of day? If that were the case, why not destroy the evidence of her family line entirely?

The motives did not align.

Clara turned several pages in the diary, hoping the distraction of reading would open her eyes to new possibilities. Her knees buckled as she looked over the entry. "Oh," Clara whispered. "Oooh."

Flattening the book before her, she straightened her curved spine and read.

"The people of the city might never understand the magnitude of my father's creation, but you will, my sweet child. After his unfortunate death and the destruction of our family tree, it was easy to forget the source of the magic in the gems. My contacts in the city, ones I have not told your father about, relay the most astounding information. It appears the gems are believed to be magical in their intrinsic nature.

I am here to tell you that they are not.

Here in the north, they have a different word for what my father did—alchemy. I do not have the details of what it entails, but I do know that there was little magic involved in the creation of the stones. What there was a lot of was bloodletting. My father's blood, to be exact. The life force of our family flows through the energies of the gems. It was the glue that held the so-called magic together, the source of the gem's power.

It was what bound the Cursbeasts to our family and the foolish reason that my father let them live. Because they were a part of him through and through. He wished to garnish that control should it become of use in the future.

Sadly, it was also his blood that drew the beasts to him in the end. They could not be free until he and his were truly gone. And I suppose that is what they are now...free.

It is why we can never return to the city, not me nor you nor anyone else that follows. My brothers had already paid the price when they took the crown after our father's passing, and I am saved only by the unfair politics that deign me unfit to rule simply because of my sex. Though perhaps, in this case, I should say that I am fortunate. The beasts will not allow us to coexist, and, in some ways, they are correct to do so. Without meaning to, my father doomed them, and they deserve their peace, however dim it may be.

I have not asked anything of you, my child, but I must make one final request. Stay away from Hedge End. Stay away and you will live."

The bones left Clara's body as she sat across from the splayed book. At her back, the chair's rigid form pressed against her skin and made her spine tingle. She stared at the careful script on the aging paper. "Well, that settles it," she uttered. "My mother couldn't possibly be of royal blood or else the beasts would have targeted her the second she stepped foot inside the city."

"Possibly."

Her eyes narrowed on Willoughby. "Tell me you are not entertaining this nonsense? I am not part of some strange conspiracy to hide a legitimate heir to the royal throne. And even if I was, which I repeat, I am not, why would it matter now? There is no more crown anyhow."

"You really need to read between the lines, Aldridge," Willoughby said. "Or should I say Rosette?"

"You should not."

A leer peeled the thief's lips apart, his shiny teeth glimmering in the light cast by the dust-coated chandelier on the ceiling. "According to the diary, The Stone King didn't keep the Cursbeasts alive because of the goodness of his heart. He did it for control."

"And?"

"And," Willoughby continued, "it stands to reason that the control his daughter wrote about was established by the blood bond he used to create the magic in the gems. Rosette blood." He paused to crook a brow her way. "Did you know the king's surname was Rosette?"

Clara swallowed the lump in her throat, shaking her head. "I don't think anyone did."

"Except your mother."

Darkness coated her vision as she studied Willoughby's expression. She couldn't quite make out what the thief was thinking, but whatever it was, it was safe to assume that he held very little trust for her family. Not that Clara could blame him considering what they found. And yet, she wanted to give her mother the benefit of the doubt and no matter what the scoundrel in her company believed, Clara was not convinced her parents had anything to do with the royals that once ran the city. For all they knew, her mother could have acquired the book in her youth before she came to Hedge End and brought it with her... Clara's shoulders dropped. Why? Why did she keep it? The diary belonged in the museum, not tucked inside a dirty old easel like a discarded toy.

Nothing made sense.

What were you thinking, mom? Tears pricked at the rear of her lids, and she had to blink them away before Willoughby noticed. She wasn't fast enough, and one fell on the diary page, smearing some of the ink. A warm hand clasped hers tightly. Clara looked up, Willoughby's face coming into focus.

"I'm sure she had her reasons for hiding it," he said. "Good, honest reasons."

Clara blinked faster. "What if you're right, Will? What if I am somehow involved in all of this?"

"Would it be that terrible to be of royal blood?"

"It would be if the gem-forsaken beasts want me dead!" Clara slammed a fist on the table, her other hand holding onto Willoughby like a lifeline. "And why did she hide the land ownership papers in my father's desk? Or the blueprints?"

Clara's jaw hit the table. "Oh, sweet gems... The catacombs. It wasn't the Cookes that purchased them, was it? It was my family. Are they part of the Order too?"

"Not necessarily. We don't know anything for certain yet, Aldridge. Don't let it spin you in circles. Besides, the timeline doesn't align. The papers we found were dated thirty years ago; as far as we know, the Cookes acquired the catacombs at least several decades prior."

"My parents could have easily bought the land off the Cookes," Clara said. "They surely had the means to do so."

Not entertaining her with an answer, Willoughby reached over the table to pick up the bottle of wine delivered by the pub's staff. He kept his hand in hers, using his teeth to pop the cork and spit it off to the side. Then he poured her a tall glass, sliding it over. The smell of acidic grapes penetrated Clara's nostrils as the liquid sloshed against the sides of the glass. She crinkled her nose, taking a slow sip. To Clara's utter bewilderment, the wine wasn't half bad. Though her current state of complete chaos may have clouded her taste buds.

She took a second sip and smacked her lips together.

"Hey, look at this," Willoughby said suddenly.

Clara had been too lost in her own thoughts to notice him

flipping through the diary until that very moment. The thief's index finger tapped on another entry, but there was something amiss about the block of writing. It wasn't until Clara pressed her nose closer to the page that she realized what was wrong.

"How come this one looks different?" Willoughby asked, coming to the same conclusion.

Clara grimaced. "Because it was written by someone else." She peeled her fingers from his and clutched the sides of the journal tightly. The leather crumbled under the heat of her skin, folding beneath her vice-like hold. Clara's jaw set. "This is my mother's handwriting."

"Well, fuck," Willoughby cursed. "What does it say?"

"Oswin has lost his mind. It was terrible enough that he supported the society in their monstrous experiments on the Cursbeasts, but the new plan is beyond anything I could have imagined of my brother-in-law. He had a penchant for thinking outside the box and I do wish to believe that he is doing this to protect the city. Though perhaps I am a fool to think so.

What they are doing in the laboratory he forced Alfred to buy is no science.

I swore to my mother and she to her mother before her that we will keep the words in this book from the prying eyes of the world. Hedge End does need to be upended with the news of our bloodline surviving. Yet I have nowhere else to turn to and no one to share my terror with. Alfred will never fault his brother; he is too kind. I am less convinced.

In the spirit of this diary, I will add my own truth to the pages. If someone should ever discover the history I could not destroy, know that I will not allow Oswin to continue. He must be stopped. With such, I must make haste in noting all I know in the hopes that my writing will not be vain.

The mayor of Hedge End has been experimenting with Cursbeasts under the guise of a secret society labeled The Order of the

Stones. He had acquired the catacombs from the last remaining owner of the land and used the passages below to construct a laboratory for his so-called science. With his work, Oswin Aldridge and his companions, Stanis Hastings and Lawrence Cooke, have been finding ways to prevent the effects of gem magic on the human body. By some atrocious miracle, they have succeeded. Oswin has found a way to alter the biological characteristics of the beasts and has taken the bond from my family line, binding the Cursbeasts to his bloodline instead. In the process, he has altered the creature's biological makeup; the beasts no longer crave their creator's blood, the seal has been broken. The dreadful things are beginning to resemble each other now and it terrifies me to think that my brother-in-law is building an army of them. I am unaware of how he achieved the blasphemous task, but I fear he will not stop there.

I have convinced a man in his employ to acquire proof I could use to put a stop to this madness, but I'm not sure if we will be successful. Oswin has spies in many places and men who would do his bidding if asked. I worry I may have put another person in danger. But I am running out of choices and the man is a father himself. He understands the need to protect the city. For our children. I must stay positive. Mr. Tanner will be fruitful; we will persevere.

Oswin Aldridge will not rest until he can use the beasts as one would a rifle.

I fear for the citizens of our fine city with all my heart. The Cursbeasts were my ancestors' biggest mistake and their downfall; now, I realize there is a thing much more vicious than even the beasts themselves—a man who worships power."

Clara's mouth slacked. She rubbed at her eyelids, the loss of words making the thin skin twitch. Her expression blanched, and she moved back, away from the diary, and pressed her back into the wood of the chair. She ran her hands through her hair, her fingers catching in the pins holding her top hat in place. Her breath came out short and desperate.

What was happening? What did she read?

Her vision blurred at the edges, and she tried to make out Willoughby's face, but she couldn't bring the room into focus. It spun around her faster and faster until she was certain she would retch on the table and all over the damn book.

Clara pressed a clammy palm to her cold forehead. "I don't believe this."

A commotion outside the curtain tore her attention from the book. She slammed her hands on either side of the book, watching as Willoughby stood up slowly and took three long strides to reach the curtain. He never looked at her, not once. Using his index finger, he pried an opening in the heavy fabric and glanced out into the pub.

The color drained from his face until he bore a close resemblance to a poltergeist. "Let's go," he barked out.

Clara sat motionless, watching the diary.

"Unless you want to die here at the hands of the fucking beasts your uncle worships, you will get up and follow me."

Her body moved more by instinct than need. Registering his words, Clara gathered the diary and crammed it under her arm, then pushed from the table and rushed to Willoughby's side. They burst through the curtain to a different pub than they entered. The tables were overturned, drinks spilling over their edges and wetting the floor below. A few patrons cowered beneath the tabletops, using them to shield themselves from... What exactly? Clara's gaze met the eyes of a woman twice her age. The woman's hand moved, her finger pointing to the ceiling. Fear cut Clara's quaking spine. She grabbed Willoughby's arm to hold him back without a second thought and he skidded to a stop a foot in front of her. Her neck tensed as she tilted her chin to look over her head.

It was difficult to make out the details due to the low light in the room, but there was no mistaking what Clara saw. A Cursbeast hovered directly above them. Clara's lips shut, and she stifled a cry as warm, repulsive saliva dripped onto her shoulder. The creature used its long talons to puncture the ceiling; its long legs bent as a spider's as it skittered across the ceiling tiles. The stench of death rolled into Clara's throat when she breathed. Her stomach turned and her skin was covered in cold sweat. She blew out a breath through clenched teeth. The creature chittered, its red beady eyes searching the direction the sound came from.

A nudge at her side pulled Clara from the horrors atop her. She twisted toward Willoughby, following his eyes to the narrow door next to the bar. The thief rolled his shoulders and took one small step forward. The beast hissed, steam rising from its deformed nostrils. Sweat collected beneath Clara's breasts and drenched the boning of her corset. She took a step, mimicking Willoughby. Foot by foot, they continued to move until they were halfway through the room. Suddenly, Clara's knee knocked something over and a clatter echoed through the silent pub as a chair clamored to the floor.

Her eyes shut tightly, waiting for the inevitable.

Over her head, the sound of nails clipping metal pierced the air, followed by a fearful shriek. Not Clara's—the woman under the table. Clara turned to glance over her shoulder and her eyes widened in terror as the beast changed direction. It spun effortlessly, its body twisting unnaturally while it used its talons gripped the ceiling like pitons. In an instant, it tore from the ceiling and crashed to the ground, enveloping the woman. Clara pried her lips apart to scream, but Willoughby silenced her with his palm before she could utter a word. He yanked on her arm and pulled her toward the door, running for safety. At their backs, the sounds of flesh being torn to pieces filled the pub.

It was a sound that would haunt Clara forever.

Willoughby ripped the door open. It nearly fell off its hinges as he shoved Clara through it. Bright sunlight blinded her, and she stumbled into the alley behind the pub, her boots stomping on the cobblestone under her feet. With Willoughby right behind her, she continued to run until they were several streets away and out of danger. For now.

Breath coming out in short bursts, Clara leaned on the side of a grimy building, her elbow covered in soot as soon as it touched the brick. She rubbed her throat, wiped the tears from her cheeks, and looked down. The diary. In all her panic, she held onto it hard enough to scratch the leather.

As Willoughby approached, she started to speak, but he cut her off. His eyes burned with enough rage to set alight the city and he purposefully kept his distance from her, standing on the opposite side of the alley as though she was the Cursbeast they escaped.

"I want to make this abundantly clear, Clara Aldridge," Willoughby bit out. "This is the last time we will speak. I want nothing to do with you or your vile family. Even when the Aldridges try to do the right thing, you don't care if or who it hurts in the process."

"Will, please," she begged.

His fist met with the wall next to her head. Clara's eyes bulged, and she choked on her saliva as Willoughby slowly removed it. "Stay far, far away from me," he warned, "or gems help me, I will burn your house down with you in it."

With that, he spun on his heels and stalked away from her. Leaving Clara shivering and alone in an alley in the lowers with nothing but her guilt and her mother's words for comfort.

CHAPTER TWENTY-NINE

There was little to do in the lowers when one was not stealing or selling. Or both simultaneously, which was what Willoughby was attempting to do at this very moment. He twirled his hand like a theater performer, twisting the necklace he laid away from a previous job, so it caught the light streaming in from the cracks in the glass ceiling. The couple in front of him, a stuffy pair from the mids, oohed and aahed at the display, the woman all but seething to wear the gold choker. Shouts of other deals filled the dank street, and Willoughby fought against the frustration building within him.

"Shall I?" he asked the woman.

It was the man that nodded his approval—the prick. Willoughby stretched his false smile, his eyes sparkling as he moved swiftly to secure the necklace around the woman's slender neck. As he did, he slipped his free hand into the man's jacket, pulling out a silver pocket watch. Before the man noticed, Willoughby let the watch drop into a leather satchel, his eyes never leaving the necklace's clasp.

With the choker secured, he stepped back, admiring it. "I believe it was made for you, madam."

"We'll take it!" the woman yelped. She jabbed the man in the ribs and Willoughby waited impatiently as the nitwit muttered under his breath while pulling the coin for the purchase.

Thanking the couple, he tossed the disks into the same satchel that held the watch and blended into the hustle and bustle of the market, disappearing. The commotion of sellers and buyers formed a constant buzzing sound that filled the space between Willoughby's ears as he skulked past the busy stalls. A glimmer of orange caught his eye, and his head swung to the right, a knot growing in his stomach as he watched hands exchange gems for coin. His gaze followed the woman who purchased the stones. He cringed. It was difficult to miss the effects of the gem magic that had already taken over her body; one could hardly be remiss to spot the tail under her skirts. And yet here she was, buying more of the darn things.

On instinct, Willoughby touched his own tailbone, relief flowing through him at the lack of an extra appendage. He never should have used those gems to save Clara in the carriage. Now he was cursed to forever wonder what the stones took as payment for their magic.

I should have let her die.

The blood in his veins ran cold at the thought. Would he have made the same decision if he knew then what he did now? Or had he been too blinded by desperation, by some foolish notion that saving her was the right thing to do?

His head spun with vertigo, and he slowed his pace, skittering closer to the walls in case his legs gave out on him. His knees threatened to buckle beneath the weight of the question. The hairs on his arms rippled as his mind raced. What the actual fuck was happening? Why was he having so many doubts over an Aldridge?

He clenched his jaw. No. He couldn't think that way. He wasn't a monster. He couldn't have simply watched her die. That wasn't who he was.

And yet...wasn't it?

He knew the mayor was two stone throws off kilter on the moral scale, and not only because of what happened with his father, but this? The idea was so horrendous it was almost unbelievable. Willoughby wished they had gotten their facts wrong.

Could they have gotten it wrong?

The bottle of wine he finished an hour ago clawed back up his esophagus. Willoughby paused, his skin clammy with cold sweat. It couldn't possibly be true, could it? And yet he knew it was. The laboratory in the catacombs all but proved that what they read in the diary was nothing but the gems given truth. *That disgusting, vile son of a—*

His feet stopped in their tracks, a single thought balancing on the teetering scales of his psyche. Clara. The mayor's niece could not be trusted, not when she came from the same family that was responsible for what was happening in the city. He couldn't believe he almost fell for her lies again. Willoughby scoffed, mentally erasing any memory in which his emotions got the better of him when it came to the dreadful woman.

A shoulder bumped his and catapulted him into an abandoned stall. His arms jerked out to catch his fall, and he came an inch away from breaking his nose on the edge of the table, finding his footing in time to avoid the hit. Willoughby's heart pounded against his ribs, the market swirling around him. The world continued to spin in circles as he fought to collect his thoughts and get back to some semblance of normalcy. Somehow, Willoughby knew it would not be easy to go on with his life as though the last twenty-four hours didn't occur. How could the man tasked with keeping the city safe do this to the citizens he was meant to protect?

A blurry image of his father drifted in Willoughby's chaotic head. *Did you find information you weren't supposed to, dad? Is that why that devil had you fired?*

Another thought occurred to Willoughby then, one he hadn't entertained before. Was there a chance that his father's suicide wasn't what it appeared to be? If he came upon the laboratory under Clara's mother's guidance, if he discovered what Oswin was doing down there... Well, the mayor had the power to make any death look like a suicide, didn't he? The high position didn't come without its privileges.

Willoughby bit down on his tongue. No. Oswin Aldridge was many things perhaps but a murderer? It was too ghastly to imagine.

"Hey, watch it!"

The roar of the warning shook Willoughby back to reality. He cleared his spotty vision with a few blinks and turned to find the source of the voice. The shout came from one stall over and when he turned around, he came face to face with rows of flowers. They stood in cracked vases, each bouquet a mish-mash of colors that didn't quite pair. Willoughby scratched his head in confusion.

"Over here, handsome." A pair of beady eyes peered out from behind one tall bouquet. The ancient woman selling the flowers wiggled her brows, her toothless mouth growing wider. "Best you don't make a mess at Adrianna's stall. She will not be pleased to have to wipe your dirty paw prints off her table when she returns."

Willoughby turned to look at the wood. It was true; his hands did in fact leave prints all over the polished surfaced.

Using the edge of his sleeve, he tried his best to clean the tabletop but failed miserably.

His eyes rolled from the table to the flower seller. "Apologies. If, Adrianna, was it? If she's around, I can offer to pay for destroying the stall."

He didn't truly believe he caused much damage, but the last thing he needed was for word to spread about him in the markets. Now that he had washed his hands from Clara Aldridge and her despicable family, he needed to get his life back on track. Or back on the illegal track as truth would have it.

"You might be waiting a while," the old woman croaked out. "She's been gone for days. Left with some miserable-looking fella last I saw her. That was Adrianna for you, constantly after the gems. Not a way for a young woman to live, if you ask me."

"She was using gems?"

The woman cackled loud enough it made her cough. She wiped the edges of her mouth with a dirty rag she found on the table near a flower vase, then fixed her cloudy eyes on Willoughby. "I'd say so," she said. "The horns were a dead giveaway."

"You didn't happen to catch the name of the man with her, did you?"

"I did not," the woman replied. "But I could see why she was taken with him. He wasn't too terrible to look at, even with that nasty scar on his face."

For the briefest of moments, the market calmed. It was as if time had stopped and Willoughby was trapped in the vacuum of it, unable to move a muscle. He normally wouldn't jump to conclusions, but the pieces seemed to be finally fitting together, and he could see the puzzle take shape in his head. He had no doubt he knew who the man that provided poor

Adrianna with affected gems was. As the old woman said, the scar was a dead giveaway. If he were to show the seller a likeness of Sergei Pollen, he'd bet his life she would confirm it.

Another shoulder clipped him, but this time, Willoughby barely registered the hit. He stumbled back, his butt landing on the empty stall table behind him. Rubbing his temples, Willoughby focused his gaze like a laser on the cobblestones beneath his feet. His brain swelled with information.

More missing people last seen using affected gems. The laboratory and the mayor's foul experiments on the beasts. The deserted isle. Thomas's ledger and his untimely death. Violet. It all made sense to him now in a way nothing had ever before. Willoughby's arms drooped to his sides.

He knew what Oswin Aldridge was doing with the missing lowers people. That fucking bastard.

CHAPTER THIRTY

Family was an anchor in Clara's existence to such an extent that it defined her. Maybe it was because she had so little of it left that she clung to the remaining roots left behind to the point of suffocation. Whenever she was in doubt, she relied on her family, on her beloved uncle, to show her the way. He was, for all intents and purposes, Clara's compass after the death of her parents.

Most citizens knew Oswin Aldridge as the mayor; a symbol of strength and decent moral fiber that all should strive to live by. To Clara, he was much more. Oswin was a light in a dark tunnel, the doorway she could pass through if she were to find herself stranded without a lantern. He was the head of the Aldridge name, and the sole reason Clara got up in the mornings, when memories of her parents weighed her down.

He was half her heart, and it felt like that half had been ripped right out of her chest.

Sitting on the bottom stair of the front doors of Aldridge House, Clara felt as though the inside of her chest had been

gutted out like a turkey ready for stuffing. She was so empty that she was certain if her white-knuckled fists uncurled from the brick, she would fly away with the wind. In her lap, Beatrice Rosette's diary lay like a dead fish, its worn leather flapping in the passing breeze. Bile swirled in Clara's belly, and she fought the urge to empty the contents of her stomach with each breath. Beneath her feet, the ground shook. Her skin grew frigid, and her eyes trained on the gates at the end of the driveway opening to let a carriage in.

Clara's bones rattled. He was home.

The driver rolled the carriage to a stop and secured the horse before opening the doors for the mayor. In the darkness of the vessel, Clara noticed another pair of shining eyes and dread filled her body. Oswin did not return alone. She watched her uncle's brow furrow upon seeing her on the stoop. Behind him, Sergei trotted as an obedient dog, continually one step away from his master's heels.

The men approached Clara swiftly and with urgency. As they neared, she finally found the strength to stand up, the diary hanging on full display from her limp fingers. She waited until her uncle was close enough that she could see the glimmer of the mayoral star on his lapel to say, "We need to speak. Alone."

"Good evening to you, my darling girl," Oswin replied warmly.

The scowl on Clara's face must have been a dead giveaway because his smile vanished as instantly as it appeared. He looked her up and down, his gaze landing on the diary. "What have you got there?"

Glancing over her uncle's shoulder, Sergei attempted to get a better look, but Clara pressed the book to her chest, her arms enveloping it almost entirely.

"I need to know the truth about the beasts," Clara said. "Now."

An exchange of gleeful glances took Clara by surprise, and she watched, horrified, as her uncle wetted his parted lips. His eyes crinkled in amusement. "Very well," he said, stepping past her to the front door.

Clara bolted after him. Her breath caught in her lungs somewhere between the foyer and the sitting room, and she didn't bother clearing it from her throat. It was best to keep moving while she still had the courage to question the man she thought she knew like the back of her hand. Her eyes dropped to her hand, glimpsing a new freckle that appeared there overnight. Wonderful.

With Sergei hot on their heels, Clara climbed the stairs, following Oswin to his study. As he reached into his breast pocket to pull out a key, Clara shot the muscle man at her back with a gloomy glare. Smiling smugly, Sergei took a single step back. It was enough to make Clara's head stop spinning while she waited for her uncle to unlock the door. The mayor stepped inside and walked straight for his desk, skirting around it to sit at the tall leather chair. A knot twisted in Clara's gut. She wondered if Oswin had any idea that another man's hands have been all over his precious desk or if he was clueless to Willoughby's discovery of the secret compartment inside. By the looks of it, it was the latter.

Clara huffed out a breath. "He can't stay," she said. "I need to speak with you alone."

"As you wish, my darling girl."

With a single raise of a hand, her uncle dismissed his hound. She waited until she heard the lock click as Sergei exited the study and gave him an added few seconds before walking over to the desk. Eyes narrowed; she dropped the diary on the wide desk with a loud thump.

"What is this?" Oswin asked.

She edged the book closer to him. "You tell me."

Agony stroked Clara's spine while she waited for her uncle to skim the pages of the diary. His expression remained unchanged, up until the moment he reached the part of the book that held her mother's writing. His brow creased deeply; Clara was sure she could stuff a coin in the lines, and it would hold. Oswin's dry lips moved with each word as he read and re-read the entry. When he finally finished, he pushed the book away as though it disgusted him to be near it. "Well, well," he muttered under his breath. "I suppose you were bound to find out sooner or later."

He sighed heavily; his smile bitter.

"That's all? Are you agreeing that what my mother wrote is true?" Clara asked, revolted. Her mouth parted open, her tongue pushing its way out. Oswin leaned to rest his elbows on the table, and she found herself flinching at the movement. Her toes curled in her boots.

"It is difficult to argue with something written in stone," Oswin replied. "Though I do wish you would give me a chance to explain."

He motioned for the velvet-stretched seat opposite him, but Clara refused to sit down. She folded her arms over her chest, puffing out a cloud of air like a Cursbeast ready to charge.

Bemused, Oswin leaned back in his chair and crossed his long legs. "Suit yourself," he said. "Now where to begin?"

"How about you start by telling me what the meaning of this is? Are you truly experimenting on beasts in that nasty laboratory?"

"Ah, you have outdone yourself, my dear girl. Bravo!" He clapped, his hands falling away when he spotted Clara's frigid expression. Clearing his throat, her uncle raked his fingers through gray hair, saying, "It is not as simple, you know. To care for a city. On the day you take my place, you will understand that sometimes we must make sacrifices for the greater good. The citizens need us to lead them into the light, my dear. Even a cursed city must have hope."

Clara's hands formed into tight fists. "Stop speaking in riddles!"

"I am simply attempting to explain. If you wish to know what happened, I must start at the beginning." The lines on Oswin's skin lessened as he reclined further into the leather enveloping him. "Did you know that the stories we are told as children about the Cursbeasts are not entirely correct? The way they came to be, that is."

She scoffed. "I'm starting to realize that."

"Yes, well, it is true that The Stone King created the creatures but everything after his death became murky. For starters, what you read here is quite close to what actually occurred all those centuries ago. The king did use his own blood to forge the magic in the gems, and it did have the unfortunate effect of binding the stones to him. It also bound the gem magic to his bloodline, but I assume he did not know it until it was too late. Terrible consequence. And then everything that followed... Even worse, really."

"You mean the deaths of his children?"

Her uncle nodded solemnly. "A horrible turn of events considering that all the king wanted was to give power to Hedge End, a means by which the land could come into its own on a global scale. If only he knew what we know now about the Cursbeasts, he may have avoided the outcome."

"And what would that be, exactly?"

"That they can be controlled, darling girl," Oswin said. "I

thought that was clear. It was why The Order of the Stones came about—to find the source of the magic and to use it to the city's advantage. But the society lacked the vision for the bigger picture. They were children playing with toys they didn't understand. It wasn't until I discovered the truth of your mother's lineage that I truly saw the possibilities." He paused, his eyes twinkling. "The opportunities we had to do what The Stone King failed to achieve."

A cough ravaged her uncle's body. He bent over the desk, his body quivering until the fit passed. Wiping his lips with a handkerchief, he placed the square cloth on the side of the table and looked at Clara. "Apologies. It appears that even gem magic cannot reverse old age."

She must have misheard. Heat rose inside Clara and a fluttering in her stomach made her pause. Her chest tightened. The thought she had before froze as she swirled Oswin's words in her brain like cold lemonade on a hot summer day.

"Y-you've used the gems?" she stammered.

Oswin's chuckle broke her free of her spell, her mind racing.

"Of course I have," he said, his smile vicious and cruel. "How else would I test out the blood transfusions? Blood was the answer, Clara. Rosette blood at first, and now, Aldridge."

"No," Clara whispered as understanding dawned on her. "No, tell me it's not true. Tell me you're not pumping Cursbeast blood into your body. That's madness!"

A fist pounded on the table and Clara jumped back. "It is ingenuity!" her uncle rebutted. "We have found a way to eliminate the effects of gem magic on the human body, you foolish child! And I must say, having control of the spiteful creatures was a wonderful bonus. Do you know what that means? For the city? For our family? We can finally bring Hedge End to the forefront of the world. They will cower before us. No longer will the city stand abandoned. We will reign them with our magic and our beasts!"

Clara couldn't believe what she was hearing. This was not the same man that she trusted her whole life. It wasn't even someone she recognized. The softness her uncle showed toward the citizens, the morals he held that she adored, were all gone. Whoever it was that sat in the chair before her was a stranger. A hypocrite masquerading as a man of honor. Tears pricked at her lids, and she battled the urge to dash out of the room. Black dots swarmed her vision as she worked to regain some form of balance in her body. Her shoulders swayed; the moment heavy upon them.

Clara dared to attempt a reply, but no words came out.

"It is a lot to learn," her uncle said, filling the void in the air with more of his pompous, self-righteous propaganda. "I had hoped to introduce you to the responsibilities you will have when you are mayor, but we barely had a moment to spend together as of late." He side-glanced at the diary. "Both of us being so busy."

Clara thought back to everything she had uncovered in the last two weeks. The steps they took that led down the rabbit hole of missing people and secret laboratories. All of it had been connected to her uncle, and she never saw it. She never realized the truth. Her mother was right. There were worse things than Cursbeasts running amok in the city.

Sweet gems. The man was entirely unhinged.

"The missing people from the lowers," she said. "You're giving them gems, aren't you? Or your lackeys are. Promising them a future they will never see in exchange for them using the magic. Why?" Her eyes bulged as a thought crashed inside her head like two cymbals meeting. "I take it Thomas Hawke worked for you; it would explain the sales he ran in the markets. I knew he sold gems! What happened, Uncle? Did he cross a line?"

"Hawke was a damn greedy fool who thought he could bleed me for more money than he was worth. Not to mention the chip on his shoulder he carried over his family losing any stance in the Order. I had no choice but to take care of him," Oswin answered. "As for your other question, there are only so many beasts. In order to gain full control of the packs, I must continue the treatments."

Her heart splintered and her knees knocked together. "You're forcing people to become affected? To turn into Curs-beasts?" Tears streamed down her face. She didn't wipe them and the cold trails they left behind gave her energy to keep on. "That is why there are more beasts now than before and why all the affected are gone from the Cursed Isle."

"Oh, you brilliant creature!" Oswin exclaimed. "I didn't expect you to unearth much information. Tell me, what led you to the isle? I am beyond impressed by you, young lady. You have managed to figure out more than your pretty friend. And you didn't have to use your guiles on Sergei to do so, which I must say I deeply appreciate."

Clara's head shook. "V-Violet... It was you? You told me a beast got to her. It can't be. The way she looked..."

"I'm afraid you are not understanding, dear," her uncle purred. "When I say we can control the Cursbeasts, I mean it rather literally. Your friend was getting too close to the truth and while Sergei enjoyed toying with her, we couldn't allow her to find more out than she should. Her husband gave the final order. Lawrence knew his place. Smart chap."

"The beasts... The ones stalking the uppers—" she sucked in a breath "—The ones that attacked me and Will... That was you?"

Oswin did not reply but the slight glimmer in his eyes was all the answer she needed.

Quick, rasping breaths convulsed Clara's body. Her eyes doubled in size; she was unable to blink. She wrapped her arms over her body, but it did little to sustain the heat escaping from her skin. Clara was frozen in place. She covered her face, her muscles tense and rigid. "Did my mother try to stop you?"

"Rowena didn't see the path forward as she should have. She didn't understand what had to be done. She was too weak. They both were."

"The beast that killed my parents," Clara breathed out. "You sent it."

At least Oswin had the decency to look ashamed. Or as close to it as he could manage, considering that Clara was certain it was all performance. He didn't care. She could see it plain as day. The man had no emotion behind his gaze, save for his own well-being. How could she have been so blind all these years? Nausea rolled up her throat. Clara reached for the back of the seat beside her, holding onto it to keep the bile at bay. All this time he let her grieve her parents' death while he walked around pretending to mourn at her side. Ages of Clara looking at her feet as she passed by the paintings of her family while Oswin walked with his head held high, as though he had an invisible shield to guard against his sins.

The bastard killed his own brother, and he was single-handedly going to destroy the city unless she stopped him. Clara straightened her shoulders, her skin flushing. She rubbed the bridge of her nose until it hurt, her eyes watering. "Why Elisea? Why frame an innocent woman? She had nothing to do with any of this; has devoted her life to caring for us. Why frame her for her husband's death?"

"A domino effect, I'm afraid," Oswin said calmly. "I couldn't have the guard stomping around here asking questions, could I? There are too many things to protect, elements in play that cannot be interrupted. Elisea's imprisonment meant less work for my team to divert the public's attention. Every great discovery requires sacrifice, darling."

Clara's gaze sharpened on him. "Just not your own."

"Nor yours," Oswin argued. "Ever again if you do the smart thing and join me as you were always meant to do."

Bile swirled in her stomach. "You're evil."

"Pragmatic, I like to think," Oswin said. "You will be too when it is your turn to bear the weight of the city. Unless I was mistaken about you."

Clara seethed. Her feet planted firmly down, she reached for the diary on the table, but Oswin snatched it away before she could touch the leather. He clucked his tongue. "I see," he said.

Oswin's gaze drifted past her shoulders to the door. He gave a single nod, and someone wrapped fat fingers over both of Clara's arms, tugging her backward. It took her a moment to realize Sergei was already in the room. How long had he been standing there? Had he heard everything they said? Clara slapped herself mentally. Of course he did. She was willing to wager Sergei knew her uncle's deeds all too well. After all, someone had to kill on Oswin's behalf. Despite everything, she doubted the great Oswin Aldridge would get his hands dirty. Thomas didn't die from a beast attack, did he? She looked at Sergei's blank expression. Murderers. The whole lot of them.

Her mind quieted.

Clara locked gazes with her uncle, her bottom lip wavering. "Will's father," she said. "He figured it out, didn't he?"

"The custodian? Your mother thought she was plenty clever, hiring him to spy on me," Oswin replied. "I don't know what she paid him, but it must have been worth it for him to risk his life."

"His life? Will's father killed himself."

At her back, Sergei grunted and pulled her backward. Her back collided with his muscled chest, the breath knocking out of her. Her face paled. Will's father never committed suicide. She didn't know how he did it, but Oswin was responsible for his death, likely using Sergei to end another life. How many people died for her uncle's lust for power? How many families destroyed, and over what? For him to hold the city in the clasp of his hand. Oswin was insane; she had to stop him. Her parents may have failed, but Clara would be damned if she let him continue the tyranny.

Rearing back, she tried to free herself of the Sergei's hold, but the brute was too strong. He wrapped one arm around her waist to hold her steady and when she opened her mouth to scream, silenced her with his free hand. Clara took her chance while she had it. She crashed her teeth together, piercing Sergei's skin with her canines. He yelped, yanking his hand from her mouth while cursing her out. Clara raised her leg and used all her force to stomp the heel of her boot onto his shoe. Just as he taught her to do when she was younger. Behind her, Sergei cursed louder.

"Get her under control," Oswin instructed. He raised to stand but made no move to help contain her.

Coward.

Clara started for the door, but a hard object slammed into the back of her head. The room swam around her, her body swaying from side to side. Her legs were mushier than rotten fruit. She tried to stay upright, but the weight of her body was too heavy. Clara's eyes fluttered. They rolled to the back of her head as her body crashed to the floor. Warm liquid dripped down her cheeks and she didn't need to touch it to know it was blood. Above her, the ceiling tiles swirled and swirled and swirled.

"Throw her in the cells," Oswin said, his voice swimming. "Tell the guards she attempted to take my life."

"Should I give them any further instruction?"

There was a slight pause. Clara's foggy brain strained to listen. A second later, her uncle said, "Set the execution date for tomorrow. I will prepare a speech."

Then the room went black.

CHAPTER THIRTY-ONE

"It can't be possible," Josephine said. "The thought alone is preposterous."

She doled out a ladleful of broth and emptied it into the bowl in front of Willoughby. Though he had no desire to eat, he mixed the brown liquid with a rusty spoon, the aroma of burned onion making his stomach turn. Smiling, he left the spoon in the bowl, sipping the dregs of Josephine's homemade wine instead. The alcohol burned all the way down.

"I wouldn't believe it myself if I didn't read the Rosette diary," Willoughby noted. "Or hadn't seen that dreadful laboratory. But I am sure of it now. The mayor is turning the citizens of the lowers into beasts."

The woman's eyes glistened, but she didn't let a single tear flow. Soltan's mother had never been one to show emotion, and yet Willoughby was certain she would fall apart as soon as he departed from her doorstep. When he told her about her son's scarf and his theory for what might have happened to him, he could see part of her soul depart. There was nothing worse than a mother's broken heart, albeit

Willoughby had little to compare it to, having only spent a short time with his own mother. It didn't matter. He could feel Josephine's pain like it was his own. Then there was the matter of the soup she spent the last two hours boiling. If there was one thing he knew about the woman, it was that she always cooked when she was troubled. Once, when he was young, he got her son into more trouble than he bargained for, and the two arrived at Josephine's door in the hands of mayoral guards. They were let off with a warning, that time, but it didn't matter. Josephine spent three days in the kitchen following their little stint. Not that Willoughby could complain—hot meals were hard to come by for someone like him.

It wasn't the soup he was after now. Willoughby may have come here to break the news to Soltan's parents, or one of them since Amos was hard at work in the factory, but he had a different mission now.

His gaze settled on the hard woman before him. "We have to warn them, Josephine," he said. "If the mayor found a way to control the beasts, there is no question on his motives. He will not stop until he'd emptied the lowers for his foul means."

"What, pray tell, do you wager those are?"

"According to Clara's mother, it appears the bastard wants to use the beasts to gain control of other cities."

The color drained from Josephine's face. "He's a madman."

"He's an egomaniac," Willoughby corrected.

"He is also the head of the city, Will. I know you mean well, but we cannot possibly go against someone with that much influence. It would be suicide. We know what he's capable of. Consider what the mayor will do if you try to expose his plans." Josephine worried her hands on the table. "What about your lady friend?"

The blood rushed from Willoughby's face. "What about

her? As far as I'm concerned, Clara Aldridge is no better than the rest of her family."

A wet towel slapped him across the face before he could even blink. He sputtered, spitting out the taste of mildew and onion. Tossing the ghastly thing away, he wiped his cheek and glared at the woman who accosted him. "What in the gems, Josephine?"

"You're behaving like a brute, that's what. That poor girl was as in the dark as the rest of us. Don't you even try to imply otherwise."

"That isn't the point."

Josephine's one eyebrow arched. "And what is the point? I know you keep yourself guarded, my boy, and I don't blame you, but don't push good people away because of fear. It will not do you any favors."

"I'm not afraid," Willoughby said, his voice pitching.

"Whatever you say. Do remember that I am not easy to fool when you spew your lies, please," Josephine scolded. "A woman of her stature that would follow your filthy behind all the way to the lowers deserves the benefit of the doubt. Especially one that risked her neck to help you find Soltan and the other missing citizens."

"Only because she needed my help in freeing her housekeeper."

Josephine glowered. "How often do you hear of an upper citizen helping their staff?" she asked. "She's a good egg, that one."

The towel met his face again, this time landing in his open mouth. Josephine smirked from across the table. "Don't mess it up. People like us don't get many chances at love. Make the most of what you've given."

A fluttering in Willoughby's stomach made his pulse race. What was Josephine on about? He didn't love Clara. He couldn't. Caring for an Aldridge was entirely out of the question. Then why was his heart hammering away right now? Willoughby was suddenly all too aware of his body. His legs were liquid in the chair and there was a steady electrical jolt in his chest each time he sucked in a strangled breath. What the fuck was happening to him?

He dropped his chin into his hands, leaning his elbows on the table. There was no way in the gemmed world that he cared for Clara. He refused to believe it. What if the woman could kiss him stupid? It didn't change the fact that she was Oswin's niece; the only living relative of the actual devil. He did not love the devil's niece. No.

The door of the Dressers' apartment opened with a loud bang that made Willoughby jump a foot in the air. His neck twisted to the kitchen doorway, waiting for a Cursbeast to stalk through it. Rising from her chair, Josephine walked to the stove and readied a second bowl of broth. "Calm your britches," she said. "It is only Amos."

"I thought he was at work."

A second later, a large, box-shaped man burst into the kitchen. Amos's silver eyes flashed as he took in Willoughby slumped over the table. He walked over to Josephine, his fiery hair bouncing as he bent over to plant a kiss on her cheek. A crooked grin tugged at his thin lips. It was rare to see Amos in a good mood—the man was often skulking or complaining— and Willoughby's stomach dropped when he realized the news he would have to deliver about Soltan's disappearance.

He swallowed the boulder in his throat.

Before he could say a word, Amos slapped the kitchen counter and said, "You two will not believe what I heard!"

Willoughby exchanged a worried glance with Josephine.

"Word on the street is that the mayor had his own niece arrested," Amos continued.

Panic tore through Willoughby and he had to hold on to the arms of the chair to keep from pushing into the man's face. He pinched the skin at his throat, his eyes refusing to focus. Blinking rapidly, he tried to calm his absent mind, his attention on Amos. "What do you mean, arrested? What in the gems for?"

"Last I heard it was for treason," the man replied. "Must have been bad because he's pushing up judgment day to tomorrow. No two weeks in the cells for her. Ruthless, if you ask me, but what do I know?"

Willoughby clasped his hands together, his posture sinking as the words settled in. His stomach turned, and he bit the inside of his cheek to keep from showing just how shaken he was. If there were any way to spare Clara, he would take it— he'd give anything to stand in her place.

The air whooshed from his lungs. Willoughby's jaw slacked as he came face to face with the one thing he refused to acknowledge. Gems be damned. Perhaps he loved the infuriating woman after all.

CHAPTER THIRTY-TWO

Clara awoke to the sound of running water. Her vision swam as she opened one crusted lid after another. The back of her head felt swollen and sore, and she had to fight against the weight of her body to sit up. Her back pressed to a cold, wet surface. The same icy stones lined the floor beneath her. Her body stiffened and ached from the chill that clung to the musty air.

Groaning, she shifted her weight. As she did, her wrists pulled on rusted shackles that clanked faintly with each move. Clara's nose wrinkled to battle the scent of rot piercing her senses. She tugged at the shackles holding her and grunted in disgust. Was it truly necessary to bind her? She looked at the bars barricading the jail cell she was thrown into. Where was she going to go?

As she adjusted to the low light, she noticed the dark hallway beyond the gated doors, one that stretched into eternity. An unsettling quiet surrounded Clara. She briefly wondered if she could call for help in this forsaken place but thought better of it. Knowing her uncle, he had her locked up somewhere where she wouldn't be able to speak the truth freely. Most likely, she was the only soul on this level of the jailhouse.

Fear pulsed in her chest. How long had she been out?

There was no way to tell the time in the horrid place. Clara wasn't sure how far underground she was, but the lack of windows or natural light was enough to tell her she was deep in the belly of the building. She couldn't even hear the footsteps of the guards upstairs, though the thick layer of stone separating her from the rest of the city could have had something to do with it.

Her throat tickled and Clara bent over her knees to cough. She spit out the nasty taste coating her furry teeth, wiping her lips with the back of her sleeve. Dirt and grime spread over her skin from the filthy fabric.

To her right, she noticed a small tray tucked into a shadowy part of the cell. Upon it was a lonely silver plate that held a loaf of bread which has seen better days. Next to the plate sat a cup full of water and Clara was relieved to find it to be cold and fresh when she downed in seconds. She picked up the only other item on the tray, a letter addressed to her. Her gaze rolled over the careful penmanship, recognizing it instantly. Droplets of water fell from her lips, staining the paper and making the ink run slightly.

"I'm sorry," Clara read aloud. "You should have stayed out of it. Sergei."

Tears pricked the back of her eyelids.

The low ceiling encroached on her head and Clara slunk lower to the ground, her bones creaking with every small motion of her tired limbs. The absurdity of the situation wasn't lost on her. Her uncle, her flesh and blood, demanded her death. If she wasn't so shocked, Clara would have been angered at the turn of events. What would her parents think of the lying son of a gem? But she already knew that answer. Perhaps if she didn't waste her time admiring the man that turned out to be her downfall, she would have seen past the cracks in his self-serving facade.

Clara's mind recalled all the times she saw her uncle wince with pain. She used to think it was old age, but she knew better now. The effects of the experiments were staking their claim on his body, and she was too foolish to understand. Then there were the clothes he wore. She assumed her uncle favored the layers of fabric that covered every inch of his body as a fashion statement, a way of standing out from the rest of the citizens who had taken to bolder cuts and more showy appearances. But that wasn't it, was it? Oswin was covering up the needle marks on his skin left by the blood transfusions. Not to mention the way he seemed to charge at the beast that attacked her or the way he marched down the streets of Hedge End without a worry in the world. Clara thought her uncle was brave then. He wasn't. He wasn't afraid because he was the one who commanded the damned creatures in the first place.

Clara gasped, the air whooshing down her throat and sending her into another coughing fit. The image of Violet's destroyed body laying idle in the fountain haunting her thoughts.

"You pathetic, vile man," she seethed.

A low, painful groan in the distance made Clara stop breathing. She scurried on her hands and knees, crawling to the iron bars with the chains of the shackles clanking behind her. The screech of metal on stone echoed through the jail and down the corridor. Clara let out a heavy sigh as she clasped her hands around the bars, her face pressed into the space between them. "Hello? Who's there?"

"Clara?"

A laugh burst from Clara's lips. She wiped her eyes, tears

stinging her skin. Slouching, she forced her nose further out into the corridor. "Elisea. You're all right."

"That depends on your definition of the word, dear."

She cried out, instantly recognizing the old woman's voice despite the roughness of it. "I'm sorry. I tried, Elisea. I really did, but I'm afraid this is it. For both of us."

Somewhere beyond, locked in her own cell, the housekeeper sighed.

"Tell me you aren't here because of what my Thomas did," she said. "The last thing I wanted was for you to break the law on my behalf, my girl. Do not fret. I am certain your uncle will have you out of here in no time. Mark my words, he will."

"Oh, Elisea. I'm afraid you're wrong."

The woman barked out a laugh. "I am never wrong. You wait and see."

"There's a first time for everything."

Sucking in a slow, hoarse breath, Clara tilted her head up to look at the slick ceiling stones. She settled into a low crouch and collected her thoughts. There was much to tell Elisea, too many ugly truths to reveal, but Clara wagered she had the time. She didn't know quite where to start and the muddled fog in her brain did not help matters. So, she decided to begin at the most logical point in time—with Willoughby Tanner.

As she spoke, she took her time forming the sentences, making sure she didn't leave a detail out of place. If she were to take her last breaths, she would at least go out with a show of power. It wasn't much, but it gave Clara comfort to know she told someone about all the garish things she discovered; to divulge all her uncle's sins. She told Elisea about the diary, and the laboratory in the catacombs. She even recalled the kiss she shared with Willoughby in the shed—her skin tingling when she reached that portion of the story. When she got to the part about her parents and Willoughby's father, she had to choke down sobs. And yet she kept speaking. Each word gave her strength and resolve she didn't think she had left.

If her uncle wished to see her cower before him, he would be sorely disappointed. Clara planned to die with her head held high. Even if that head was meant to be sliced off by a Cursbeast's sharp talons. Not that she thought Oswin would go as far as to release the beasts on her. No, he wanted to make her death work in his favor, she was sure of it. He would have her die by the brutal magic of the gems at the hands of his precious guards. Then he would use those poor sods for their blood when they transformed.

She shivered. All Clara wanted was to save the city she loved. Now she would do no such thing. Instead, she would die on the order of the man who wished to destroy it.

When she finished the terrible tale, Clara slumped on the floor, defeated. She rubbed the tender skin around the shackles, gazing into the darkness. "You can see why I don't have much hope," she said to Elisea. "How could I be such a fool for all these years?"

"You are no fool, Clara Aldridge. I have had the pleasure of seeing you blossom and believe me when I say Oswin had everyone tricked. There is no shame in trusting family."

"There is when you're related to someone like him," Clara corrected. "The things he did...to my parents, to Violet...and Mr. Tanner. He ruined Will's life. He will ruin many more before he's finished with his mad ploys."

A long silence stretched between them, long enough to make Clara drift off in thought. She thought of the past two weeks and the newness of the experiences she endured. While it was true that some were mortifying, she would not trade seeing the city through Willoughby's eyes for anything. It wasn't until she reunited with the thief that she felt she could breathe again. The zest for life Willoughby possessed was infectious. It wasn't until right at this very moment that she realized how much of an effect he had on her. Clara was asleep since the death of her parents, but after the heart-jolting adventures with the thief, her eyes had snapped open, and she left the dreams behind.

It was a damn shame she would not live to have more of those days. Though perhaps with a touch less terror.

Clara wiped at her runny nose, her spine bowing. Her vacant stare landed on the darkness in the corridor and the nothingness that awaited her on the other side. Chin quivering, she pressed on her aching chest, her throat scratching. She touched the hairs standing up on her arms. "I'm sorry, this is how it ends," she whispered. "I wish there was more time."

"For gem's sake, Aldridge! Since when did you give up so easily?"

The voice jarred her. Clara's eyes bulged out of her skull. It couldn't be! Her mind must have been playing tricks on her because there was no way Willoughby could be down here. Unless, of course, her uncle had managed to imprison him as well. She rubbed the blurriness from her eyes, her neck straining to see past the bars. Beyond the cell, the corridor was as empty as before, with one small exception.

"Will!" she yelped as she saw him appear out of the blackness like an apparition.

The thief walked slowly toward her, his one side straining and his arm lagging. What did he drag with him and how did he get down here? Clara was about to ask when Willoughby grunted and swung his arm around, shoving a skinny guard into the iron bars. The man yelped as his forehead met with the metal. His skeletal arms were covered in white fur so thick it reminded Clara of a rug; the effects of the gems he used taking hold. She fought the urge to run her fingers through it.

Her gaze found Willoughby's on the opposite side of the door. "What did you do?"

He didn't reply. Bending down, he yanked on a thin chain attached to the guard's limp arm and raised it in the air. The shriek of muscle tearing as Willoughby twisted the man's arm out of its socket broke the underground silence. The man hollered, but Willoughby slammed his head into the bars again hard enough to throw him into a deep sleep. Eyes rolling back, the guard exhaled and slumped against the doors like a sack of potatoes.

Willoughby pulled on the chain, jingling the keys on the end of it. "I brought the keys," he said with a smirk.

"Will! If my uncle knows you're here, there's no telling—"

The door swung open with a loud creak; the hinges old enough to be more rust than metal. Willoughby bent to a knee before her and his breath tickled her cheekbone. In one swift move, he unshackled her wrists, pulling her up to stand. His arm snaked around her waist, his wide chest pressing against hers tightly. "Not that this isn't the highlight of my day, Aldridge," he whispered against her lips. "But we should move before someone comes down here."

"R-right," Clara mumbled. "Yes, of course. How did you make it past the guards without being seen?"

Willoughby wiggled his bushy brows. "I had a few friends cause a distraction. Let's say the guards are a little preoccupied with the fire scorching the side of the building."

"Oh, sweet gems. All right, let's move." Clara stopped at the foot of the cell. "We have to get Elisea out, too. I'm not leaving without her."

She started for the cell holding her friend, stopping when Elisea's voice boomed toward her.

"Don't you dare waste any time, child," the housekeeper said. The urgency in her voice reminded Clara of when she was little and got a talking to for bringing in stray cats. She dared not mess with Elisea when her words reached a decimal that high. "I will only slow you down. Get out of here and don't look back."

"I'm not leaving you again," Clara argued.

"You are and you will," Elisea replied. "Come back for me after you've exposed that no good uncle of yours. I mean it, Clara."

Panic twisted Clara's stomach, but she knew Elisea was right. They had to escape and warn the citizens about what her uncle was doing. She would come back for her. She had to. A hand snaked into hers and she let Willoughby pull her away from the cells and down the corridor. Every few steps, Clara turned to look over her shoulder, the guilt of leaving Elisea behind gnawing a hole in her stomach. Around them, the quiet inside the cells they passed made goosebumps break out over her skin. Knowing what she knew now, Clara had no doubt that the people who once filled those cells were long gone. Probably forced to use gems until they turned and then gobbled up by her uncle in his revolting procedures.

Her legs pumped harder and harder, wanting to get out of this terrible place and to finally bring justice to all those her uncle wronged. Fingers entwined with his, she followed Willoughby toward the winding stairs leading to the upper level.

Suddenly, the thief skidded to a complete stop. Clara's forehead smashed into his back. She tried to let go of his hand, but Willoughby only held on tighter.

Her head swirled, vision blurring at the edges.

"What is it?"

Willoughby swallowed hard, his shoulders stiff. "We're not alone," he said.

It was then that Clara realized that the silence she heard

before was interrupted—a heavy, labored breathing that seemed to shake the entire building drifted toward them. Clara bit her bottom lip, stepping around Willoughby to see who stood in their path. Her jaw hit the ground, and horror carved its way up her body.

They were definitely not alone.

CHAPTER THIRTY-THREE

As it turned out, there was a sight more terrifying than the three Cursbeasts that attacked Clara's carriage. She stifled a gasp as the creatures pushed their way down the opening at the base of the stairs, their large forms scraping against the wall. The monsters encroached on the tight space of the staircase with their scaly skin and tattered wings. Hisses and growls rose from their guttural throats and the smell they dragged in with them made Clara's stomach pitch violently. The beast leading the pack pried its black lips apart, a snake's tongue darting out of the dark abyss of its mouth. On its forehead, a twisted, gnarled horn pointed at them like the muzzle of a rifle. The Cursbeasts were so massive that the walls strained to contain them. Their shadows stretched long and deep, cast by the few torches mounted along the corridor.

Clara's breathing grew shallow, her eyes wide with fear.

The ground beneath her feet trembled beneath the beasts' paws and Clara's heart matched its shaking as their massive shapes lumbered into view. Above the hulking bodies of the

Cursbeasts, the ceiling groaned, the wings of the monsters flanking the front line tearing into the arches. Glowing red eyes cut through the gloomy surrounding. All five sets of them.

The beasts' thick, matted fur bristled as their claws scraped the stone floor, sending sparks into the air. Massive jaws opened, revealing rows of razor-sharp teeth, and deep, guttural growls rumbled from their throats. The sound shook Clara to her core.

She held onto Willoughby in pure desperation. "He knew," she whispered. "Oswin knew you'd come for me. He sent them here."

Willoughby's lips parted, but he did not utter a word.

"What do we do, Will? We cannot fight them."

She glanced around, searching for an escape, but their only options were to return to the cells and die a brutal death or march forward and do the same. The jailhouse walls seemed to close in around and the darkness here felt alive, as though it were another creature stalking them.

It was no use. The beasts were upon them.

Clara whimpered as the lead beast snarled, and its burning gaze landed on her chest. She sucked in a shaky breath through the narrow space between her teeth. Her legs shook. This was it. They were going to die.

Before the beasts could make their move, footsteps echoed down the stairs. Clara watched in bewilderment as a handful of guards rushed down the steps and flanked the grouping of Cursbeasts. There was barely any room to start with, but now with the guards here, the corridor was suffocating. Another figure joined them in the lead with zero remorse on his gruff face. Sergei.

Clara's head tilted. "They're not afraid of them," she noted quietly. "The guards aren't scared of the beasts."

"What a foolish thing to say," a deep voice rose out of the darkness.

As if on command, the guards parted way, making enough space on the stairs for her uncle to pass through. Like a king, Oswin Aldridge strolled down the stone steps with his chin pointed high and his shoulders taught. On his jacket's lapel, the mayor's ceremonial star gleamed in the light of the wall torches, a constant reminder of who was in charge down here. He reached the bottom in a flourish and when he rested a gloved hand on one beast's spiked back, Clara couldn't fight the acid rolling up her throat. She coughed into her palm, disgusted.

The new King of Stones watched her with contempt. "Why would the guards fear the weapons I created for them?" he asked. "Last chance, my darling girl. Join the city's side, my side, and I will forgive all your past indiscretions."

"You're delusional," Clara spat out.

"I am the future!" Her uncle walked around the beasts, his fingers trailing a path down their curved backs in his wake. His long coat he wore floated behind him and his hair bounced with each assured step. For all intents and purposes, he was the epitome of power. He patted one beast—a grizzly thing with three twisted horns and a tail sharpened to a point—on the head and the creature growled, steam billowing from its snout. "I do urge you to reconsider. Will you really turn your back on your family?"

Clara's shoulder bumped against Willoughby. His hand squeezed hers and she knew in that instant that whatever happened, she was not in this alone. Her eyes narrowed on the stranger standing firm before her. "I seem to recall you butchered your family," she seethed. Her chin nodded to the Cursbeasts on either side of her uncle. "Set your pets on your own flesh and blood. Tell me, dear uncle, if you're our city's future, why did you need to kill your brother and his wife to hide what you're doing? Why Violet? Or Will's father?"

Next to her, Willoughby bristled. She side glanced his way, and he nodded, letting her know the news of his father's false suicide came as no surprise. Maybe if they survived the night, she could speak to him more about what happened to Mr. Tanner. Assure him that his father died a hero.

But not until they found a way to leave the clutches of the jailhouse.

Clara looked past Oswin to Sergei and the guards. Her uncle's right-hand man was unmoving, his expression blank, but she noticed a few of the guards exchanged confused glances. The words she uttered must have struck a chord. Good. She had to keep going, push them further.

"I wonder," she said coyly, "when you *save* the city, will you finally tell the citizens how many of them had to die for you to control the beasts? Or how you've been poisoning yourself with beast blood and using the same gems that you pretend to clear off the streets?"

A few more guards shifted uncomfortably and two even lowered their rifles.

"Enough!" Oswin bellowed.

He thrust out his arm, and the beast on his right snarled in response. Four of the guards reached into their uniforms to produce whatever gems they came prepared with, while Sergei trained a rifle on Willoughby's forehead. Clara's back was slick with sweat, but she refused to let her uncle intimidate her. If she were to die, she would not do it cowering in fear. Clara may not have been with her parents in their final moments, yet she was certain they fought back tooth and nail. She would do the same.

She would make them proud.

A second flash of her uncle's hands sent the beast barreling toward them. It leaped into the air, clearing the space between them in one long stride. Its front legs crashed into the ground feet before Clara and Willoughby.

"Time to run, Aldridge!" the thief shouted.

"There's nowhere to go!"

His green eyes flashed to her, locking on her so intensely she forgot how to blink. "Do you trust me?" Willoughby asked.

Clara nodded.

"Sorry about this, then."

Her brow creased. "About what?"

Suddenly, a searing pain shot up her arm. Clara yelped, her gaze flicking to the gash that split her palm open before rolling over to the knife in Willoughby's hand. The one drenched in her blood. The red liquid dripped from her palm, and she got woozy from simply looking down at it. Her jaw locked up. "What in the gems, Will?"

The thief winked at her, actually winked, and took off running. It took her less than a second to realize he was heading straight for the beast. He looked over his shoulder, shouting, "When it comes, slap it silly!"

"What?"

Clara's question lingered unanswered as Willoughby hurled himself at the beast. In one swift motion, he flipped the same knife that had cut her and drove it into the creature's cheek. The Cursbeast's howl rattled the jailhouse walls, a piercing sound that seemed to seep into Clara's bones. Thick black liquid spilled from the wound, identical to the vials they had uncovered in the laboratory. The creature staggered, its eyes momentarily clouding before it shook its matted mane, forcing its vision back into focus.

Then it jumped for her.

As the beast lunged closer, Willoughby's words pounded in Clara's skull. Her bloodied hand stretched out, braced for the impact that would tear her apart. In an instant, memories flooded her. The beast in the rose garden, its eyes clouding as its talons ripped her skin; the skeletal creature on the road, shrieking after striking her shoulder; the vial of beast blood, fizzing and roiling as though alive in her presence.

All those moments she dismissed as nothing unusual. But they weren't. The instances were not random. The beasts had been reacting to her—to her blood.

She looked from the encroaching Cursbeast to Willoughby. *Trust him.*

Clara reared her hand back and slapped the side of the beast's cheek Willoughby cut with her injured hand. The creature crashed into her. It knocked her backward with a tremendous force. Clara thought her bones turned to dust. Her back crashed to the ground, the air whooshing from her lungs in a one quick burst. Stars swam before her. Clara cleared her spotty vision and rose on her elbows, looking around.

Hovering above her, the Cursbeast snarled. Its hooved feet kicked the ground on either side of Clara, but it didn't make a move to harm her. Head cocked to the side, it ran its glowing eyes over her body, landing on the cut in her palm. The beast sniffed the air between them. Satisfied somehow, it took a few steps back, far enough that Clara could scramble from underneath it and stutter a step away. Her shoulder blades pressed against the brick of the wall. Her eyes stayed on the monster standing before her.

At the foot of the staircase, her uncle made another gesture with his arm, but the beast did not budge.

"Kill her, you dumb animal!" he screamed.

The Cursbeast didn't register the command. It stood unmoving, gargantuan frame filling the space between Clara and the remainder of the company occupying the corridor. Her heart settled slightly. An invisible string curved one side of her dry lips. Clara craned her neck to look over the beast's body and faced her uncle head on. Next to her, the Cursbeast's forked tongue slid over ravenous teeth.

"He's not yours anymore," she said, raising her bloodied hand. "Rosette blood, Uncle. It's time for the Cursbeasts to come home, don't you think?"

CHAPTER THIRTY-FOUR

The Cursbeasts did not, in fact, come home. Or not in the way Willoughby expected them to. He gaped at the giant seething creature standing alert next to Clara, waiting for some magical show of power, but none came. The beast, while no longer trying to kill them, did little to convince the mayor that it meant business. And that was what they needed for his plan to work—Oswin had to doubt his own ego.

It didn't appear that would happen anytime soon.

The mayor's brows sat low on his forehead as he tilted his head to the side to consider the scene unfolding before him. The amusement spilling off him made Willoughby's toes curl in his shoes. The bastard really wasn't the least bit intimidated. Why should he be? Clara may have turned one beast, but he had the entire arsenal of them. Four in the cells alone and who knew how many more out there in the city? Though Willoughby doubted he brought all his loyal hounds to the jailhouse; gems forbid the citizens might raise a brow and wonder why the creatures were following their precious leader.

Ideas swirled through Willoughby's brain like hurricanes. They needed to gain control of the remaining beasts here, perhaps get the guards on their side, and then he could formulate a plan for the rest Oswin created. A glimmer of gems tugged at his focus. His gaze landed on the three guards behind the mayor that garnished the stones. In his head, he pulled at strings to come up with a quick and dirty solution.

He studied the cut on Clara's hand and the imprint of her palm on the Cursbeast's cheek. The plan dangled on the tip of his tongue, but he couldn't quite discern it. Maybe if…

Clara's scream stopped his thoughts short. Spinning, his gaze followed her terrified eyes back to Oswin and the three creatures he let loose. The mayor wasn't wasting any time. Behind him, the guards who held their gems at the ready tapped into their magic. Lightning blasted from one guard's eyes, crashing into the brick on either side of Clara's head. Stone shot out around her, and she dropped to the floor, the beast she was tethered to throwing itself above her like a shield.

Interesting.

Climbing out from under the beast's muscled chest, Clara wore a definitive scowl. She followed her uncle's gestures, commanding the creature to take on the defensive. Its skin rippled, scales like obsidian, moving with every thundering step. Clara's cheeks sucked in as she slid behind the creature and waited for the attack. The three Cursbeasts the mayor sent flew at them and Willoughby's chest squeezed with panic.

The corridor filled with snarls. Across the room, the two guards armed with gems let their magic loose. Fire tore through the space as one guard used an amber stone. The second chose a less obvious approach, and a gust of wind pummeled Clara and the beast. Their feet slid across the ground, pushing them backward. Behind them, the walls of the jailhouse blocked any escape. The bastards were forcing them into a corner.

Willoughby caught sight of Oswin's cold and calculating eyes. He surveyed the scene with disdain and cruel anticipation, his hands moving ever so slightly to direct the monsters at Clara. At his side, Sergei cocked a long-barreled rifle and aimed the damn thing at him. The scar on his face reddened, and he worked his jaw, his expression telling Willoughby he would shoot him dead without a second thought.

When Sergei's eyes flicked between him and Clara with a merciless focus, the plan finally clicked in place.

He turned over his shoulder, shouting, "Buy me two minutes, Aldridge!"

The roar of Clara's beast at his back propelled him forward. While Sergei shifted his aim to the creature, Willoughby darted for him. His elbow smashed into the side of the man's thick ribcage. Grabbing hold of Sergei's shoulders, he dug his knee into his stomach as hard as he could manage. Considering the difference in their size, there was no instance in which Willoughby could overpower the large man, but he was hoping the chaos in the cells combined with the element of surprise would be on his side. Sergei let out a raging roar. He raised the rifle, bringing the butt down on top of Willoughby's head.

"Will!" Clara shouted.

He rubbed the top of his throbbing skull, holding a hand up. "I'm good. Keep going!"

"Stay down, you cretin," Sergei growled out.

Willoughby swung his leg out and around, slicing the son of a gem across the ankles. The force of the hit made Sergei buckle back and his ass hit the ground with a thud. The rifle flew from his hands, sliding on the ground. In a flash, Willoughby dove for the weapon, saying, "You too."

With the rifle in hand, he charged at Clara. The beasts

continued to battle, the one siding with them holding its weight despite being outnumbered. Luckily, Oswin chose the biggest of the four to use first, so they had a bit of time before the other three creatures overpowered it. A giant talon sliced the air in front of Willoughby as he ran, and he had to drop down and roll out of the way to avoid being shredded. His knees scraped on the rough ground, pieces of his pants hanging loose as the fabric ripped. Blood welled on his skin. He got up. He had to keep going.

The cells pulsed with a malevolent energy as the mayor moved the beasts like a puppeteer. Saliva dripped from their mouths, their jaws snapping at one of their own. Hiding behind her Cursbeast, Clara wavered, her eyes scanning the area for an escape.

Willoughby reached her right as the abominations surged forward again. Their roars shook the stone foundation of the jailhouse, and the building continued to quake as the guards added their own magic to the mix. Fire and lighting pulsed around them. Willoughby's eyes burned as he took in the scene. They were properly blocked in.

Sliding in by Clara's side, he handed her the rifle.

"What do I do with this?" she asked in a panic. "I'm not a great shot. There is no way I can hit him from here."

"Not your uncle."

Her jaw slacked. "Who then?"

"The beasts," Willoughby instructed.

"Bullets won't hurt them."

His teeth split apart. "But they might turn them."

He could see the understanding dawn on her in that very instant. Faster than he could blink, Clara unloaded the bullets from the rifle's magazine and shoved them into her skirt pocket, all except one. She picked up the bullet, examining it before drenching it in the blood that coated her palm. In another speedy show of expertise, she loaded the bullet, cocked the rifle, and aimed it at one of the beasts.

Willoughby whistled. "The benefits of an uppers education."

"I didn't learn this from books," Clara said. She stretched her neck to glimpse at her uncle. "He was adamant I knew how to protect myself. I suppose the lessons are finally paying off."

The shot rang out, the rifle jabbing into Clara's shoulder. She yelped but stood her ground as she watched the bullet penetrate the hide of the beast's shoulder. The creature wailed for a brief moment. It stood stock still, its spine straight as an arrow. Its eyes grew foggy for a moment and the glow in them dimmed.

"Is it all right?"

"Wait for it," Clara whispered.

Neck muscles strained, she pushed out her free hand and directed it at the beast she shot. The creature, responding with a guttural roar, launched itself into the fray, tearing into the two remaining Cursbeasts commanded by Oswin with lethal brutality.

Clara winked at him. "Two down, two to go."

Her hands moved to the other bullets to repeat the maneuver and within seconds, another beast turned to follow her commands. The heat in Willoughby's chest intensified as he watched her go for the last, but before he could cheer in glee, metal tore into his shoulder. The force of the blow sent him twisting, crashing to the ground with a bone-jarring thud. Pain lanced up his spine, sharp enough to steal his breath. Another white-hot streak tore through his arm. Blinking against the haze, Willoughby's hand drifted to his shoulder, fingertips brushing the cold steel jutting from his flesh.

He looked up, his gaze flicking to Sergei's vicious sneer.

The prick threw a fucking knife at me. Above him, Clara

screamed his name. He smiled, his teeth gritting through the pain. "A little setback. Don't worry about me."

She did not appear convinced.

Hand full of tremors, Willoughby reached for the hilt of the knife, his breath rattling his lungs. He let go. *Gems help me. This is going to hurt.* He closed his eyes and yanked the weapon from his skin before he could change his mind. The pain he felt when the damn thing went in was nothing compared to this. Willoughby's body convulsed, and he smashed his head into the wall behind him. A scream shot from his lips; he bit it down fast. He would not let that bastard Sergei know he hurt him.

Shakily, he used the wall for balance and dragged himself back up to stand. A few steps ahead, Clara watched him until she was satisfied he wasn't about to drop dead, then proceeded to fire at the final beast. A cheer erupted in his chest as he watched her take control of the creatures. She spun them around with the sheer notion of a finger flick. The Cursbeasts stamped their large paws into the bricks, lining up like a wall between her and Oswin.

"What was it you said?" she asked of the man. "Oh yes. Last chance, Uncle."

"You daft, stupid girl," Oswin gritted out. He turned to the guards flanking him, yelling, "Attack!"

The few guards without gems didn't budge. For a moment, Willoughby thought this was it, that they won by some gem-forsaken miracle. It wasn't until Oswin yelled his command again that he realized that could not happen. The mayor didn't plan to allow them to leave here alive. He would see the last of his family line dead in these cells before he let his secret get out.

Oswin reached into the breast pocket of his tailored coat to produce a handful of gems. One by one, he tossed them at the guards who caught the stones with greedy grasps. They pressed the gems in their palms, their fingers obscuring the stones from view. Power jumped from stone to flesh, the guards eyes rolling backward into their skull as magic took over them. It lashed outward as they cast their new abilities, arcs of energy and fire attacking the space they stood in.

Willoughby gagged on the heat that filled the air around them. These were not novices; nearly every guard was already half-corrupted, having fed on the gems again and again. That was why the transformation hit them so brutally fast.

Their bodies contorted as the magic of the gems coursed through them. Disgust ravaged Willoughby, watching the men and women transform. Some of them remained human, but the ones who were already near the edge, the ones who had the effects of the magic too deep in their system, turned before his eyes. He wanted to look away, but it was like watching the sun rising. An otherworldly experience.

Skin shredded and bones snapped as the guards' bodies reformed. He stared in absolute horror; their human vessels distorting—becoming Cursbeasts.

Willoughby had never seen a full transformation before. The display before him was brutality at its best. The ground vibrated as one guard's magic shook the solid earth under the building. Above them, an electric field formed, the power stemming from another guard's fingers. Giant wings tore from the back of a beast mid-transformation, and it flapped so harshly that the wind made Willoughby slide back. The onslaught Oswin brought was relentless.

His eyes flashed to Clara. They couldn't hold back the barrage forever.

"How many bullets do you have left?"

Clara counted the new beasts and the guards using gems. A scowl formed on her face. "Not enough."

"Time to improvise. Give him everything you have, Aldridge!"

Following his words, Clara screamed, and her beasts charged forward. Energy crackled through the air, a storm of fury unleashed by the guards and aimed toward them. The clash of beast on beast broke out before him. Willoughby pressed his back to the wall, putting as much distance between him and the rolling, hideous limbs of the creatures. A flash of lightning in his periphery made him turn his head and his eyes widened as the energy wave grew larger, nearing him at an impossible speed. He ducked out of the way, the lightning bolt striking the place where his face was a moment ago with an angry explosion. Haze and smoke and dust filled the cells.

Amid the chaos, Willoughby saw an opportunity present itself. Oswin was alone at the base of the stairs, watching the maddening display between them but not aiding his guards. The mayor's eyes burned with a cruel satisfaction.

He thinks he's won.

Willoughby's attention ripped from the mayor, and he searched the ground for the knife that nearly did him in. A wall of fire erupted on his right and the light from it caused the metal of the blade to glimmer. He dove for the weapon. Snatching it, he checked on Clara, relieved to find her standing and unharmed, then ran to the winding stairs.

Ducking between the deformed bodies of the beasts, he skirted around the destruction, staying low and moving swiftly. A few steps from him, Oswin was too preoccupied with the battle to pay any attention to the common thief on his heels. Willoughby snaked around the mayor, his feet light. All those years of staying off the radar were finally paying off.

The mayor didn't even realize Willoughby was behind him until it was too late, and the blade of the knife was pressed against his throat.

"Make them stand down," he breathed down the mayor's neck. A drop of blood dripped down Oswin's flesh from where the knife nicked his skin. "Now."

The mayor's expression twisted with shock and rage as he struggled against Willoughby. Each move dragged the edge of the blade deeper across his throat. He growled, his arms flailing to his sides in defeat. The beasts he controlled stopped fighting, their heads shaking in confusion.

Willoughby looked at the guards left in human form. "This man lied to you, to all of us," he said. "If you care about justice for Hedge End, you will leave now. Tell everyone you see about what you heard of his ploys. Tell them change is coming."

The guards' gazes trailed the mayor's slumped figure. They looked at Clara and the Cursbeasts that stood around her, their ugly shapes obscuring the corridor and making it impossible to see further. Fear and confusion glistened in their tired eyes.

The cells fell into an uneasy silence.

Willoughby took in the scene unfurling before him, and his chest ached. So many people lost to the gems in the span of a half hour. Such an incredible waste of life.

"Look what he did to your friends," Clara said, her voice booming over the remaining guards. "To the citizens he vowed to protect. And for what? Power? Money? Greed?" She gestured to the writhing beasts. "Were their lives worth it?"

"Go," Willoughby added. "Fix his mistakes. Avenge them."

The shuffle of scurrying boots filled the cells. Willoughby stepped aside to let the guards pass, pulling the mayor with him. Surprisingly, Oswin didn't fight back, though the knife Willoughby held to his neck was surely the source of the defeat. He very much doubted the mayor suddenly came to his senses. As the last of the guards departed, there was one more thing he noticed.

Sergei was gone. The rat must have snuck out after he realized he was on the losing side. Typical.

"What do we do with him?" he asked Clara as she approached.

She didn't even glance at her uncle when she said, "Leave him with them," and pointed to the beasts. "They can guard him until we find a better solution."

"Gladly," Willoughby replied.

He lowered the knife from the mayor's throat only long enough to toss him into the center of the Cursbeasts. The mayor's body crashed down, and he crab-walked across the floor to get away from the creatures that continued to encroach on him. Realizing that he was surrounded, Oswin dropped his head in his hands, raking his fingers through his white hair. His shoulders slumped and Willoughby could swear he heard the man that was larger-than-life whimper. An elbow nudged his side.

"How did you know my blood would turn them?" Clara asked.

He shrugged. "I didn't. But we were going to die anyway, so it was worth a shot."

"You are unbelievable," Clara said.

Her breathing was labored and when she smacked his chest, he barely felt it, despite the wound on his shoulder. The woman was exhausted. They both were. Willoughby snaked an arm around her waist, ignoring the pain it sent through his body. He dragged her close, his lips brushing against her ear. "Unbelievably brilliant," he teased.

Clara's laughter bounced off the walls. In all his years, there was not a better sound he heard than that, Willoughby was certain of it. He glanced past her to the mass of Cursbeasts filling the cells. A flutter tickled his stomach. Willoughby didn't know what the future had in store for them, but one thing was clear: he would spend the rest of his days making this impossible woman laugh if she let him. Leave it to an Aldridge to get under his skin and stay there.

His expression sharpened. Sliding his fingers through Clara's hair, he nodded to the stairs. "Ready to face the city, princess?"

"Call me that again and I'll sick the Cursbeasts on you," Clara replied.

Oh, she was ready all right. Clara Aldridge was going to reap havoc on Hedge End, and he couldn't wait to see it.

CHAPTER THIRTY-FIVE
THREE WEEKS LATER

Muffled voices dragged Clara's focus away from the open city hall window. The chatter on the street below, periodically interrupted by the lively shouts of children playing, drifted off, replaced with the incessant arguments rising above the noise of the city. Clara fixed the permanent fixture of a grimace before turning her attention to the council members sitting at the table. It seemed that even without the drawl of budget meetings, she still did not enjoy these gatherings. Especially not ones as rowdy as today's.

She forced a smile, forgetting for a moment that she wished for nothing more than to be amongst the citizens below and not crammed into the rooms of the mayoral office and discussing yet another mundane issue.

"We can wait to reopen the ports until after the snow passes," she said to the needle of a man obnoxiously rapping his fingers on the table. "There is no hurry to invite other states inside our borders. We have only relocated the last of the Cursbeasts a week ago. Give the city a moment to breathe in peace."

"But Madam Mayor—"

Clara held up a finger. "Temporary Mayor," she corrected. "I am only in this seat until we take the proper measures to find a replacement. One that is appointed by the citizens based on credentials, not surname."

Anything but a surname, she thought in her head. It had taken all the council coming together and begging her to stay on until such a date as another more qualified party might take over for Clara to even agree to hold the title of mayor. After what happened with her uncle, she wished for nothing less than to be within these walls, but she felt a duty to carry on while she could. For Hedge End; considering all that her family had done to it over the decades.

Though the council did not know the extent to which Clara was entitled to the position. After much discussion with Willoughby, they decided to keep the nature of Clara's bloodline secret lest it inspire the council to forge another crown. They revealed all that Oswin did in the laboratory but left out the part about Clara being the rightful heir to the royal throne. As far as she was concerned, no one needed to know that part of her history. It wouldn't change the way things turned out. The laboratory and its gruesome machines were promptly destroyed, though there was no sign of Stanis Hastings, the deranged alchemist working alongside her uncle to power the experiments. Once a prominent student at the Hedge End College, Hastings had been cast out for pushing his studies too far. He was known for treating people like test subjects, taking risks no one else would, and leaving a string of ruined apprentices behind him. It didn't surprise Clara to know that her uncle and Hastings shared years in college together; likely the way they originally met and formed the grotesque friendship that would lead to their work together.

Willoughby suggested Sergei may have warned him and

the two escaped together on the first ship available. But Clara doubted that Hastings would stay gone for long; in her experience, men who craved power never did.

It was a plausible theory. Sergei *did* vanish without a trace and considering his background, Clara very much doubted they would unearth him anytime soon. Besides which, they had better things to take care of in the present moment; like finding Thomas Hawke's co-conspirator, whose name they did not yet possess.

And relocating the Cursbeasts, of course.

Since the incident in the jailhouse, Clara and Willoughby had made several trips to the Cursed Isle, all with a shipload of beasts in tow. When Clara first suggested moving the creatures to live their days out in peace outside the city, Willoughby argued against it. As did every council member now gathered in the room. But she convinced them in the end. The beasts weren't animals to her, as they had been to her uncle. They all had names, were all human once, and though they may never know what those names were, Clara wanted to pay her respects to the people they belonged with. Thus, the Relocation Initiative was born.

One by one Clara led the Cursbeasts from the city and to the isle. And one by one, they followed. Sometimes Clara told herself it was because they trusted her. Sometimes she chalked it up to pure luck. When it came to the beasts of Hedge End, her opinion was constantly changing. Some still made the occasional appearance in their fine city but it was nothing compared to what it once was. For all intents and purposes, Clara's connection to them held strong and kept them contained to the isle...for now.

"What of the affected gems?" one woman asked. Her top hat was so tall that it brushed the crystals of the chandelier above her, making it sway lightly and cast rainbow patterns onto the wallpaper.

Clara rubbed her chin. "The Chief of Guards recalled nearly six dozen of them," she answered. "I am convinced he will gather all the stones in time. Considering how many hands they exchanged due to my—" she paused "—the previous mayor's actions, it is harder to track them down. But the guards are doing their job, and we have not seen a gem in the markets in over a week."

The woman nodded her approval, and Clara allowed her shoulders to drop a few inches lower.

"Speaking of the previous mayor—" a man said.

Before he could finish, Clara pulled her chair out and stood up. She painted a serious expression on her face, picking up the stack of papers on the desk and tucking them under her arm. "My apologies," she said. "I do have another urgent matter to attend to. I'm afraid we will have to continue this in tomorrow's meeting."

She left the room as quickly as her legs would carry her. The gazes of the council members seared into her back, but Clara paid them no mind. She had no intention of discussing her uncle. The man was locked up in a cell and would stay there until his life's end. Clara knew the council wanted to see him pay for his crimes, but as far as she was concerned, he was doing exactly that. A swift death would not do for Oswin Aldridge. She knew that to truly punish her uncle, she had to take away the one thing he craved more than anything: his power. The natural solution was to have him rot in jail while the city he once controlled went on without him. While they all lived full and happy lives above his head.

Though perhaps Clara couldn't bring herself to condemn him to death. Both were equally real possibilities if she let herself think about it. The effects of his blood transfusions were becoming more evident. Guards reported his screams and the tremors that would take control of his body for hours on end. Willoughby suggested that once her uncle stopped the experiments, his body went into shock but to Clara, it mattered little the reasoning behind Oswin's body failing him. The punishment was still not fitting of the crime, though Clara doubted there was any punishment they could think of that would make up for her uncle's sins.

Leaving the council in the dust, she walked at a fast clip down the hallway and into the mayoral office. She couldn't wait to leave work behind and enjoy a warm meal. Clara salivated as she thought about what wonderful concoction Elisea may have created for them today and she licked her lips as she twisted the key in the door and threw it open.

Her smile downturned. "Really, Will? You're breaking into my office now?"

Glaring at her with an amused smile, Willoughby crossed his legs upon her desk, leaning back in the tall chair with his arms behind his head. "Temporary office," he said. "Unless you changed your mind."

Clara dropped the papers on the desk with more force than was necessary. She swiped across the top, knocking Willoughby's dirty boots down.

"I did not," she said. "Why are you here? I thought I was meeting you at the Oily Spoon this evening?"

The corner of the thief's mouth twitched. He jumped up from the chair, rounding the desk in a single long stride. With one arm on each side of her, he pressed in on Clara until she was forced to lean back. Her tailbone hit the side of the desk, and she raised on her toes to rest her behind onto the thick oak surface. Skirts billowing, she gulped as Willoughby leaned into her, his body pressing in between her legs.

A shudder raced down Clara's thighs.

Willoughby grazed her cheek with his lips, whispering, "Evening is too long away, Aldridge."

Clara's skin flushed, the heat rising from her pelvic bone and into her belly. She swallowed, the saliva pooling around her thickening tongue. Outside the office, feet rushed to and fro as the council members dispersed for the day. Any soul could barge right in and find them in the most precarious position. And yet...Clara's back arched, the sliver of air between them vanishing.

The way the thief watched, like he could inhale her entirely, was intoxicating. But there was something else there too, wasn't there?

Clara pressed a finger to his chest. She pushed him a touch away, her eyes narrowing. "What's the real reason you're here?"

"No fun, Aldridge." Willoughby sighed, but he didn't step out from in between her legs. "Fine. If you must be such a bore this afternoon, I have news of our friend."

The inside of Clara's body revolted against his words and the desire she felt before shriveled, if ever so slightly. Her nostrils flared. As much as she tried not to think of Sergei Pollen, he still found his way into the dark corners of her mind. For some reason, Clara could not forget the letter he left for her after her capture. Why would the man who helped her uncle do such deep damage apologize? More importantly, why did his words sound so sincere?

She closed her eyes tightly then opened them again, focusing on Willoughby. "You found Sergei?"

"Most likely."

"Where?"

Gliding his index finger along a loose curl in her long hair, Willoughby tucked the wayward strand behind her ear, his breath warming her face. "A village in the east," he said. "And that's not all. It appears the coward took something with him when he left. He has the missing gems, has been pawning them off for a ridiculous price."

Every intention Clara had for the city vanished in an instant. What good was it to clear the street of the gems and to relocate the Cursbeasts if her uncle's traitorous pawn spread the stones' vile disease to other villages? How long would it be until news of the gems' power traveled to further regions?

This was a disaster.

Her heart twisted in her chest, the gravity of the situation anchoring her in place. "He's going to get innocent people affected," she breathed out. "The same thing that happened in Hedge End will happen there. The cycle will never end."

"Not unless we stop him."

There was a strange determination in his words, a pulsing drive that could only mean...Clara tilted her chin to look down her nose at the thief. "You've already thought of a plan, didn't you?" she asked. "And surely it is deranged."

"Surely," Willoughby agreed. "How fast can you pack a bag?"

"For what?"

The thief chuckled. "I don't know about you, Aldridge, but I could do with another boat ride."

"You've roped Godrey into this mess, I take it?"

Willoughby bowed theatrically, his wicked smile lengthening. "We are to be at the port at sunset. Godrey is most excited about the possibility of another adventure, as you might suspect. I may be with him in that excitement."

Sighing, Clara shook her head, though her lips held no protest. The truth of it was somewhere along the line, she herself had grown a taste for adventure—just as wild and insatiable as Willoughby's own. Or perhaps it was there all along, hiding in the shadows of her small, well-crafted world, waiting, biding its time for release. Clara's heart, she realized, was akin to gem magic; powerful, and yet unpredictable. In many ways, it mirrored the Cursbeasts. Hungry. Reckless. Foolish at times. A creature longing to break free and fly beyond the confines of their not so cursed city. A silly thing beating inside her chest that was, yes, often too rash.

But always, always ready for another boat ride.

ABOUT THE AUTHOR

A.N. Sage is a bestselling, award-winning author of mystery and fantasy novels. She has spent most of her life waiting to meet a witch, vampire, or at least get haunted by a ghost. In between failed seances and many questionable outfit choices, she has developed a keen eye for the extra-ordinary.

A.N. spends her free time reading and binge-watching television shows in her pajamas. Currently, she resides in Toronto, Canada with her husband who is not a creature of the night and their daughter who just might be.

A.N. Sage is a Scorpio and a massive advocate of leggings for pants.

For more books and updates:
www.ansage.ca

Connect on social media:
Facebook Group:
facebook.com/groups/945090619339423/
Instagram:
instagram.com/a.n.sage/
YouTube:
youtube.com/c/ANSageWrites

OLIVERHEBERBOOKS

A small press bound by the belief that every voice matters.

Sign up for our newsletter to learn about new releases and more.
https://oliver-heberbooks.com/subscribe/

Follow us on social media:

facebook.com/oliverheberbooks

instagram.com/oliverheberbooks

amazon.com/oliverheberbooks

youtube.com/@OliverHeberBooksPublisher